KEPT FROM THE DEEP

A VENORA MATES NOVEL

OCTAVIA KORE

❀ Created with Vellum

A forgotten past, a tormented present, and a future in jeopardy.

She's been abducted from Earth, experimented on in the Grutex labs, and thrown into the path of not just one massive alien mate, but two. As a Filipina nurse living in America, she isn't a stranger to adapting to unusual situations, but nothing could have prepared her for what's to come.

He's hidden behind a mask of humor his entire life, but the fierce little female who holds Brin at gunpoint the very first time they meet, and the haunted Grutex scientist, can see right through it and into the depths of his soul where he keeps his darkest secrets. He never wanted to find them, but now that he has, Brin will do everything he can to protect them.

He was supposed to oversee their care, but he wasn't ever meant to feel anything for the human test subjects. Unlike the rest of his kind, Nuzal finds himself feeling sympathy and guilt over what's being done within the labs on the Grutex ship, but he never in his wildest dreams expected to feel love.

Will her mates ever be free of their pasts, and will they be able to escape in time to save humanity from the monsters of the universe?

DISCLAIMER

This is a work of fiction. Names, characters, places, and incidents either are the product of the author's imagination or are used fictitiously. This work of fiction is intended for adult audiences only and may be triggering for some. Strong language is used. Proceed at your own discretion. This book is an MMF romance novel. It contains adult situations, graphic sex, attempted sexual assault, and violence

DEDICATIONS:

*Thank you to our alpha readers, **Brandy**, **Amanda (Manna)**, **Jessica**, **Julie**, **Stacey**, **Kimmy**, **Annalise Alexis**, and **Dona**. You guys are awesome!*

*To **Jun**, we hope you enjoy the story!*

*And to our significant others, **Michael** and **Aaron**, thank you for supporting our dreams, giving us inspiration, and loving us no matter how weird we are. We love you.*

GLOSSARY

Adamantine (ad-ah-mahn-tINE) - A metal used by the Venium in the construction of their ships and buildings.

Allasso (ah-lah-soh) - This is the beast form spoken of in the ancient lore of Venora.

Brax (brah-ks) - A Venium curse.

Brutok (BrOO-tok) - Close friend.

Dam (dam) - Mother.

Daya (dai-ah) - A nickname (like mom) Oshen's family uses for his mother.

Feondour (FEE-ehn-dOOR) - A small duck-like creature native to Venora.

Fosalli (foh-sah-lEE) - A plant native to Venora that resembles many types of Earth coral. Mainly grows in the shade of trees within the forests on the planet.

Fushori (foo-shOOR-EE) - The glowing stripes that run along the body of the Venium.

Gleck (gleh-k) - Curse.

Grutex (groo-teks) - Alien species loosely allied with the Venium.

Gynaika (gI-nAY-kah) - Wife.

Hisar (hEE-zah) - A reptilian species allied with the Venium.

Inkei (EEn-kay) - Grutex cock

Kokoras (koh-kOOR-ahs) - Cock.

Mia Kardia (mEE-ah kAR-dEE-ah) - A Venium term of endearment "my heart."

Mikros/Mikra (mEE-kroh-s/mEE-krah) - Little one or little ones.

Mitera (mEE-tair-ah) - Nickname for mother used by Kythea.

Mouni (mOO-nEE) - Venium word for cunt. Name of Oshen's AI.

Okeanos (oh-kEE-ah-nohs) - Venium term for the ocean.

Plokami (ploh-kah-mEE) - Large aquatic creature native to the oceans of Venora.

Sanctus (saynk-tuhs) - A nearly extinct rainbow species of alien.

Sire (seye-ur) - Father.

Sol (sohl) - Day.

Solar (sohl-ur) - Year.

Syzygos (sEE-zEE-gohs) - Husband.

Tachin (tah-chin) - An insectile species working with the Grutex.

Tigeara (teye-gEER-ah) - Predator native to Venora. Feline in appearance.

Venium (veh-nEE-uhm) - Alien species native to Venora.

JUN'S LANGUAGE INDEX

Sus maryosep - "Oh my God."

Yawa - Shit.

Balikas - Damn it.

Ang Landi Talaga - "What a flirt."

Lang-Lang - (Short for palangga) Beloved.

Maliit na ari - Tiny penis.

PROLOGUE

BRIN

"*R*uvator!"

Brin's pulse immediately began to race at the sound of the voice calling him by *that* name. He froze, stopping in his tracks on the cobblestone outside the terminal.

Calm, he told himself. *Don't give yourself away.*

Sure, he could keep going, act like he hadn't heard the name, but that would do nothing but provoke her. His dam was brutal, vengeful, and petty enough to use her rank to delay the mission and make them all miserable until she felt he had learned his lesson. With a fortifying breath, Brin hardened his features and turned. He brought his closed fist to his chest in greeting and inclined his head.

"Brega."

The tall, slender female approaching him may have once been considered a great beauty, but Brin had never seen his dam as anything other than cold and unloving. Her white hair was pulled into tightly coiled braids that hung down her back and over her shoulders, jostling around her as she walked. Her deep purple gaze swept over the black uniform he wore and the military issued luggage thrown over his shoulder.

"Off again so soon?" she asked with a raised brow.

"Well, you always taught me the importance of service and keeping busy," he retorted.

The smile that tipped up the corners of her lips looked more like a sneer with the way it tugged at the scar that ran from the top right to the bottom left of her face.

"I would think, at your age, it would be time for a different sort of service to your people. You could busy yourself with the task of finally finding your mate and securing our bloodline with a new generation of warriors."

He clenched his teeth together so tight that the muscle in his jaw began to twitch.

"Ah, Brega." Brin tried his best to sound relaxed and unaffected. "How could any female measure up to you and your standards? Surely my mate would be just as much of a disappointment as I was."

His dam threw her head back and cackled. "Oh, Ruvator, I couldn't care less about the female you will eventually impregnate as long as she breeds me an heir, a fine warrior to bring back our honor and erase the shame of your weakness." Her dark eyes were calculating, seeking out any sign of a crack in his facade.

Giving into her, letting her know that her words hurt him was dangerous. This female was a predator. The moment she smelled lifeblood, she pounced and refused to let go. Showing emotions around her was like sticking your hand into the mouth of a tigeara: stupid and inadvisable.

If the goddess is merciful, she will end the line with me and not subject another pup to an upbringing like mine.

"Come now, I'll speak with your commander myself and explain the situation—"

"Brin!"

The sweet, feminine voice came from behind him and he turned to see Calypsi rushing toward him. Her light blue braids bounced around her shoulders, and her inky black eyes crinkled at the corners as she smiled. Slender white arms wrapped around his neck when she reached them, and she pressed her lips to his cheek with a giggle.

"I thought I wouldn't make it in time to see you off!"

Brin let his mouth relax into a grin as he tugged at one of her braids. "Well, lucky for you, Brega waylaid me."

"Lucky me." Calypsi turned to his dam and inclined her head respectfully. "I would have been heartbroken. It's so hard to spend time together between the missions, as I'm sure you know, General."

"You are a friend of Ruvator's." It wasn't a question. His dam might act like he didn't exist, but he knew she watched him.

"Hopefully *more* than a mere friend." Calypsi ran her hand down his arm suggestively. "Goddess willing, the cramping I've felt since seeing you again will trigger something within us both and your return will be marked by a mating."

"Goddess willing," his dam murmured with a tight-lipped grin. "Don't disappoint me further." Brega turned without a goodbye and left them both standing there looking after her.

"She's absolutely vile." Calypsi sneered as she turned to face Brin.

"And you're an amazing actress." Brin watched as her dark fushori pulsed with delight over his praise. "Better get those cramps checked out."

Calypsi laughed as she followed him through the doors of the terminal, her arm linked with his. "It's not going to keep her off of your tail for long, you know. I wouldn't be surprised if she's waiting for you on the landing pad when you return."

Brin shuddered dramatically. "How dare you say such filthy things in my presence."

Their easy banter helped to ease his mind. Calypsi and Oshen had been his only friends growing up. If he were honest with himself, the two of them were the only reason he was here today.

One of the younger warriors puffed up his chest as they walked by, trying his best to catch his friend's attention, but she looked straight ahead. He couldn't blame the male for trying; Caly was beautiful, but it was the aura of kindness and compassion that seemed to draw others to her.

During their youth, Brin and Calypsi had attempted to become pleasure mates, but the relationship hadn't lasted long. Unlike Brin, the female longed for a family of her own. She wanted to fill a home with pups and spend her days happily in love with her mate.

They had hatched with a silly plan long ago, an agreement that stated should they both reach a certain, not yet determined, age without a true mating that they would claim one another.

He knew she feared the looks and the gossip of the other females. He, Calypsi, and Oshen were considered to be in the later stages of their prime, as far as mating and starting families went, and the longer she remained unmated, the more talk there was that she would end up just like her infertile sister.

As only one of two daughters, Calypsi saw it as her duty to see to the continuation of her line since her older sister had taken off with another female. Such pairings weren't uncommon for pleasure mates, but her sister had shocked their community when she had moved away to live as a true mated pair with her female.

Brin had grown up on the outskirts of society and knew the fear of rejection better than most. If it hadn't been for Oshen's parents and their propensity to collect the unwanted, Brin wasn't sure where he and his friend would be now.

He was thankful to be leaving just as Brega was coming back.

There would be no awkward forced conversations or barbed comments he would have to deflect. Calypsi squeezed his hand when they neared the barrier that led to the outside of the underwater dome they called home. Brin stopped and looked down at her, grinning at her reluctance to release him.

"Are you trying to assert your claim, Caly?" He chuckled.

"Without a doubt." She laughed, but the smile fell away as a group of his crew members passed by. "You and Oshen be careful. We have no idea what the Grutex are planning or what they want in exchange for this information. You may not be my fated, but you're my best friend, and I don't know what I would do if something happened to you."

"You're worrying too much."

Calypsi shook her head with a sigh. "The two of you are so full of yourselves." She jerked her head, grinning at something over his shoulder. "I pity Vog. Who was the genius who put the two of you on the same mission?"

"Stop trying to slander our good names, Caly," Oshen rumbled playfully as he reached them.

"Oh, you don't need *my* help for that. You two have done more than enough damage on your own." She smiled up at his friend as he tugged on the end of her braids. "Honestly, behave up there."

"You have nothing to worry about," Oshen assured her, but she just shook her head as she stepped back.

"I'll be waiting for a call that you both made it to your destination. Until the sun meets the moons, I'll be praying for your safe travels."

They watched her go, lingering within the terminal for a moment before Oshen nudged Brin.

"We'll be late, brutok."

"Always so punctual." Brin grinned as they stepped out into the flow of traffic leaving through the hatch. "Brega was here."

Oshen's eyes cut toward him. "Did she see you?"

"She stopped me. Apparently, we needed to have a little chat about me providing *her* with an heir."

"Braxing scum. She's got one, but nothing is good enough for that female." Oshen shook his head. "I'm sorry she showed up when you were on your own."

Brin shrugged. "Caly came up on us and put on a dazzling show, played the hopeful mate very well. It seemed to work."

"For now. We both know Caly isn't for either of us, and stupidity is not one of Brega's faults. She'll figure it out and come for you even harder than before."

Brin knew what Oshen said was true. Brega never relented, and as long as she was within the dome, Brin would have no peace. He would worry about that when the time came. For now, he was free of her and all of the anxiety she heaped on him. "Brega isn't here now."

Oshen huffed as they approached the doors. "Brega might not be here, but we've still got Vog to deal with."

As if he'd heard his name, the commander's eyes landed on them, and his face immediately hardened into a scowl. "Ah, we've been spotted. Fancy seeing you here, Commander." Brin smiled as he and Oshen stuck their forearms beneath the scanner, allowing the computer to check them in.

Vog turned to the younger officer at his side. "Were you aware these two were assigned to this vessel?"

The male's eyes darted between them. "Well, yes, sir—"

"Remind me to send you out the airlock once we are far enough away from Venora."

Brin laughed at the horror on the male's face. Vog might have seemed hard and unbending, but Brin was fond of the commander's dry sense of humor. "What luck, eh?"

"Luck?" Vog's brow ridge arched. "This is nothing short of punishment." When their cabin numbers and other information had been transferred to their comms, Vog jerked his head toward the hatch. "Welcome aboard, Ambassador Oshen. Havacker, keep your tail out of trouble."

"I wouldn't dream of disappointing you, sir."

"You're going to be the one he sends out of the airlock if you don't watch it," Oshen murmured as they stepped through.

"Vog loves me. He just doesn't know how to express it properly." Brin laughed. "Besides, he needs me."

"Always so humble," Oshen said.

"I know my worth, Ambassador, and I've worked my tail off to earn those bragging rights."

Oshen held his hands up in surrender. "I never said you hadn't."

They passed the group of younger males Brin had seen earlier, and he caught part of the whispered conversation. Word of the Grutex's shocking claims had spread like wildfire among the population. The promise of a solution to the issue of their people's infertility was too good to pass up, but not everyone was willing to search for the cure outside of their species.

"What did the council have to say about everything?" Brin asked.

"I think the majority find the thought of mixing Venium lifeblood with anything alien to be revolting, but they were obviously curious enough to send us to investigate."

"How do you feel about it?"

Oshen shrugged. "If my mate is among these people, then I wish to find her."

What if his mate was on the planet the humans inhabited: Earth? He didn't want a mate, didn't want the family that he would be expected to create, but certainly the odds that these people would be compatible with them were slim. He had nothing to worry about.

CHAPTER 1

JUN

PRESENT DAY...

*W*ork in the emergency room was fast-paced much of the time, but some days her shift seemed to drag, and never more so than the shift after leaving her best friend with an alien. One who she knew nothing about, who sported long claws and sharp teeth. He was an alien who could easily mangle one of the only people in Jun's life who meant anything to her.

She had seen what claws and teeth like that could do to human flesh, and the memory of it was more than enough to fuel her imagination the entire time she was on shift. A shudder slithered up her spine at the thought of Fishboy doing anything to Amanda.

The fact that Amanda had the gun to protect her should have eased her worry, but Jun was almost certain her friend had already hidden the weapon away the moment she left. *Probably sitting in that damn junk drawer in the kitchen.* After years of friendship,

Jun knew the woman like the back of her hand. She was practically her sister at this point.

A dull ache throbbed up through the soles of her feet and made every step feel like she was trudging through the surf, sinking into the sand as the waves receded.

The constant, familiar buzz of the hospital did little to distract her from her terrible anxiety. Doctors and nurses passed in and out of rooms, phones rang, and alarms from various medical equipment sounded. Today, it all seemed to grate on her nerves more than it ever had before.

Speaking of things that got on her nerves… *Mr. Devly.* She huffed as she glanced down at the chart. The man was far too handsy with all the female staff, and she had threatened to cut his offending appendages off in her mind more than once. She swore he purposely hurt himself just so he could come in and harass them. *Murder is illegal. Murder is illegal.* Jun eased the door open, a sweet smile plastered on her face.

"Hello, Mr. Devly. Just here to check vitals and then I'll be out of your hair."

"Oh, no need to be so quick. You look like a little slice of heaven in all of this hell raging out there." A lecherous grin spread across his face. Jun managed to evade his attempt to grope her scrub-covered ass as she jotted down his stats. *Murder. Is. Illegal.* Vitals down, Jun started to back away only to feel a clammy hand grasp her wrist. "Why don't you stay and keep an old man company?"

Her lips thinned, pulling back over her teeth as she snarled at his audacity. "Contrary to what you might believe, I have an actual job to do here and it doesn't include sitting in here so you can get your jollies off."

The blaring alarm from somewhere down the hall saved her from beating him over the head with her clipboard and losing her job. She yanked her hand away and quickly left the room.

"Code G," a voice called over the handheld radio that sat at the nurses' station. *"Code G. Multiple lacerations. Heavy blood loss."*

Another attack. They were seeing more and more of these as the Grutex became bolder, showing up more often and maiming or killing those who dared to fight back. The first of the victims through the door was an older man. What was left of his clothing was shredded and drenched in the blood that continued to pour from his wounds. There was nothing left of his lower legs, Jun noticed, except for the torn tissue that still clung to the splintered bones protruding from the mangled muscle.

She said a quick prayer and rushed forward, mentally storing all of the information the EMT rattled off. Three more victims strapped to stretchers were wheeled in and soon the entire floor was thrown into chaos. Doctors barked orders as nurses rushed to meet their needs. Jun felt a cold hand slip into hers, and she looked down to see the patient she was working with watching her with wide eyes.

"They'll take us all." He breathed heavily into the oxygen mask that had been placed over his mouth and nose. "They want us. They want—" Alarms began to sound around her and Jun jumped into action when he started to convulse on the bed.

"Shit!" Kate swore as she ran into the room to assist.

The shrill ring of the heart monitor going flat sent an eerie chill through her body, and she stepped back as one of the other nurses, Javi, jumped in to start CPR. When the man's time of death was called, Jun felt her shoulders sag.

"Can't save them all," the on-call doctor mumbled.

By the time her shift was over, she felt dead on her feet. The short nap she had taken toward the end of her shift hadn't done much to refresh her. Every muscle and joint screamed in protest as she shuffled out of the parking garage elevator toward her little car.

It wasn't anything fancy, but she took great pride in the fact that she had worked hard enough to be able to afford the pre-owned vehicle all on her own. She had grown up in a small rural town in the Philippines, the oldest child of hardworking middle-class parents who put everything they had into her education. They had made sure she had all the tools needed to carve out a profitable life.

Family was a huge part of her upbringing. Not only did Jun have younger biological siblings, she also had cousins who her parents had taken into their home and raised as their own. Being alone had never been an option until she had gone away to nursing school in one of the nearby major cities.

The freedom had been unnerving in the beginning, but she found her groove, excelling in her field of study. Not long after graduation, she had been offered the opportunity to move to America on a work visa. She left her family, her home, everything familiar to her for the chance to make a better life.

The land of milk and honey hadn't been what she envisioned. The hospital she worked for was in the center of a large city, which meant the rent was astronomical, the streets were congested, and the basic human necessities were overpriced or out of stock.

It hadn't taken long for the homesickness to settle in. There was no hopping on a cheap flight back home to visit family for the weekend. No homecooked meals delivered by Mama or Lola to ease her heart when she couldn't get away from clinicals. No surprise visits from her papa to raise her spirits when the strain of putting aside her emotions wore on her.

Thank the lord for the invention of video chat. It was one of the only things that had preserved her sanity. Meeting Amanda in the emergency room after her unfortunate accident with a horse-shoe crab had given her something she hadn't imagined she needed: another little sister. There had been something about that first meeting that had drawn her.

They became fast friends, meeting up for coffee, trading recipes, and hanging out on each other's porches for hours. Teaching Amanda how to make all of the foods she had grown up eating was still something they did all these years later. Amanda had been so interested in hearing about her culture. Having someone who was so curious about her family and traditions had been wonderful and gave her a chance to really appreciate those things for herself.

She reached into her bag and pulled out her little pillbox, dumping the medications into her palm before tossing them back with a grimace. Labetalol, amlodipine, and losartan: three of the things that kept her body working like it should. Managing her high blood pressure had become the key to controlling her rheumatic heart and kidney disease. That she was already at stage four and only had one kidney didn't do anything to help the situation.

During her last checkup a few months ago, the doctors had made it very clear that if she didn't stick with the medications and change her diet, she wasn't going to be around for as long as she had planned to be.

Jun was slowly cutting out most of the salt and caffeine from her life, but damn if it wasn't hard. She had switched from three cups of coffee per day to one, and it was killing her.

Literally, she mused.

Amanda knew about her struggles with high blood pressure but didn't know the extent of her illness yet, and if Jun had her way, she wouldn't tell her until she got everything under control.

As much as she wanted to go home and crawl into bed, Jun needed to reassure herself that Amanda was all right and that the hulking gray Venium warrior she'd reluctantly left her with hadn't broken out of his bonds. She snorted as she pulled out into traffic.

If she knew her friend, and she most definitely did, then the alien had already been set free and she was probably feeding him everything in her pantry. There was no time to caffeinate, but she knew her friend would have everything she needed.

Jun pulled into Amanda's driveway, shifted into park, and then rested her head against the back of the seat. The next few days were all hers, and she had never been more grateful for surprise days off. She noticed two shadowy figures through the windows, and rolled her eyes as she shut off the ignition.

She let him out.

As quietly as she could manage, Jun shut the door and tiptoed up to the house, eyes and ears alert to any sound of distress.

Muffled conversation reached her as she approached the door. She paused for a moment to listen, but couldn't make anything out. Using the spare key Amanda had given her, Jun unlocked the door, praying that the squeaky hinges wouldn't give her away. There was no one in the entryway, but the shadows had been off to her left, in the dining area.

When she closed the door behind her, Jun turned to see Hades, Amanda's massive black and silver Maine Coon cat staring at her with wide eyes. Jun wiggled her finger at him in greeting, but that only seemed to startle him more and he bolted down the hall, retreating toward Amanda's bedroom. Take a cat back into the exam room to get neutered *one time* and they hold it against you for the rest of their lives.

"You're so dramatic." Amanda laughed from the other room.

"I am not. You just served me wet, soupy sand."

"Those are grits, *not* sand, and you're absolutely dramatic."

Jun rolled her eyes and tried to smother the grin that tugged at her lips as she listened to them banter.

"Grit: small particles of stone or sand," the AI spoke up.

"See!" Oshen exclaimed. "I am thankful for your hospitality, but I will pass on the bowl of sand."

As Jun stepped through the doorway, Amanda snorted, pulling the bowl to herself before taking a heaping bite. "Mmm, you're missing out."

"Did you leave any for me?"

Amanda flinched, the spoon dropping from her hand and splattering the contents of the bowl onto her chest. Oshen threw his head back, his laugh filling the room as Amanda glared at him from across the table. "On the stove," her friend grumbled, wiping her shirt clean.

"Coffee?" Jun asked.

"In the pot. You're lucky I love you."

She could feel her muscles ease with her first whiff of the strong brew. Jun may not have lived with Amanda, but she was here often enough that many of her favorite food and beverage items had found a permanent place on her friend's shelves. The powdered Filipino brew she was so fond of had already been mixed, and she could have wept with joy knowing she was seconds away from caffeinated bliss.

Steam rose up into the air as she poured herself a cup and turned to face the couple at the table. She took a tentative sip and winced as the coffee scorched her tongue.

"*Balikas*!" Jun cursed, blowing a stream of air across the surface of the liquid. She downed the first cup and went for seconds, knowing she really shouldn't break the rules her doctor had insisted she follow, but Jun was in for a long day with these two.

One extra cup today won't hurt.

～

She hadn't really expected to like the alien at all, but even now, only a few nights after their first encounter, she admitted to herself reluctantly that he didn't seem bad. Still, she wasn't thrilled with the idea of leaving Amanda alone with him when she eventually went back to work.

Her supervisor had been understanding when she called to explain she couldn't cover for Javi, but she had a shift tomorrow and she wasn't going to be able to play hooky. *Sorry, my best friend rescued an alien and he's living with her and I don't want to leave them alone together* just didn't seem like something she could use as an excuse.

Jun stared down into the cup of coffee in front of her, mulling over the things Amanda had told her. The thought that her friend might be mated to Oshen was something she was still trying to wrap her brain around. It sounded like the plot of one of those smutty romance novels, but Amanda was convinced Fishboy was telling the truth.

What if he was? What if the universe had decided long ago that this was meant to be? Would she lose her best friend? Would Oshen expect Amanda to leave Earth and live on his planet, Venora? And then there was the whole imaginary Grutex-looking friend who she also cared about, but didn't know if he was real… There was so much to process.

"So, what? You feel the same way about both of these aliens? Are they both made for you?" How did any of this even work? Oshen hadn't mentioned anything about this other male, and for all they knew, he didn't even exist outside of Amanda's mind.

"I don't know."

She turned to the window with a sigh, trying not to let her disbelief show. If Amanda knew she thought all of this love at first sight and mating an alien stuff sounded insane, she would shut down. A bright blue light cut past one of the windows, catching her eyes as it dipped below the edge.

"What the hell?"

She jumped from her chair and pried the blinds open. Her

eyes darted around the small section of Amanda's yard that was visible from her spot, but there was nothing there.

"What?"

"You didn't see that light?" she asked, twisting her head so that she could better see the bushes beneath the window. Where the hell had it gone?

"A light?"

"It was so blue," she muttered mostly to herself as she rushed to one of the other windows. "I swear it looked just like…" She trailed off as the realization hit her. It had looked so similar to the glowing lights on Oshen's body, but it was the most beautiful blue she had ever seen. "Must have been headlights," she said, but she knew it wasn't the truth.

Someone was out there. As she sat back down in the chair, Jun couldn't shake the nagging pull toward the window. Something inside of her needed to go out there and find the source of the light.

"Look, I don't care if you want to believe that one alien or both are meant for you. I just want you to be safe, okay? We don't know much about the Grutex, and if this guy, assuming he isn't just inside your head, has been talking to you for so long, they might have abilities we never thought were possible."

They knew there was at least one other Venium on Earth, but Oshen hadn't been in contact with Brin since the night Jun had stitched him up. No matter how many times he tried, nothing seemed to get through.

What if the blue light had something to do with this brutok Fishboy spoke of so much? If it was him, would he try to make Oshen return to their ship? If Oshen left, what would happen to Amanda? Jun wasn't ready to lose her just yet. She needed to get out there and investigate.

"I need to run home and grab some clothes if I'm going to stay longer." It wasn't just an excuse; she'd been wearing these

17

clothes longer than she cared to think about. While she stored food items here, she didn't have any clothes stashed in Amanda's drawers.

"Right now?"

"I've been wearing the same clothes for the last couple of days while I stayed with you guys. I'll just grab the essentials and be back in a little while." *I hope.*

"You're leaving?" Oshen asked as he walked in.

"You wish, Fishboy." Jun rolled her eyes as she moved into the kitchen. She almost smiled when she pulled open the junk drawer to find her gun sitting on top of rubber bands, spare buttons, and takeout menus. *Called it.* She flipped the safety on as she walked back to the dining area. "Keep this on you."

"How did you know it was in there?" Amanda frowned as Jun laid the gun down on the table in front of her. "And don't you need protection?"

"You hide everything in the junk drawer, and don't worry about me." She winked, tapping her hip where her 9mm was safely tucked inside its holster. As she walked by Oshen, Jun jabbed her finger into his chest as hard as she could. "Keep your hands and tail to yourself. Got it?"

A slow smile crept across Oshen's face as he looked down at Amanda. "I will do my very best." She didn't believe him for a moment, and from the way Amanda was blushing, she was pretty positive she'd be getting all the juicy details soon enough.

"Don't be long," Amanda told her as she walked out. "I'll be waiting."

Hades sat in the hall watching her as she took her purse from the little octopus hanger on the wall. "What's up, best friend? Are you going to forgive me now?" The big cat hissed, grumbling as he turned his back on her. "Guess not."

She stepped outside, closing the door quietly behind her before reaching for the weapon. It wasn't anything too big, but it suited her. If the Venium were anything like the Grutex, manmade bullets and blades wouldn't do much, but it might at least slow one of them down if she needed to retreat. Turning the safety off, Jun gripped the gun in both hands and kept it pointed toward the ground as she rounded the corner.

The faint blue glow was just visible behind the house, near the kitchen window where one of the taller shrubs was growing wild, obscuring her view. It grew brighter as she approached, and she adjusted her grip on the gun as she prepared to confront the threat. Amanda might have an alien bodyguard now, but in her family, they looked out for one another, and she wasn't going to take any chances.

CHAPTER 2

BRIN

A FEW DAYS BEFORE...

*T*he screen on his comm went black as he disconnected from the link with his brutok. The other male seemed a little battered and bruised, but he was alive and seemed well enough to travel the distance to the shore where they could be reunited. This okeanos was nothing like the one back home on Venora. Each time he drew the salty water across his gills, it left a distinctly polluted burning sensation within his lungs.

A small piece of the outer hull of the shuttle floated in the water next to him, and Brin groaned. He had known the look in Oshen's eyes meant that trouble was on the horizon, but he hadn't anticipated it would be quite so bad. Destroying an incredibly expensive shuttle on top of disobeying a direct order from their commander? Yeah, this wasn't going to end well.

He looked at the sky above him, scanning the star-speckled

expanse, and noticed the absence of Earth's single moon. Somewhere up there was the Venium mothership, carrying hundreds of their people and one moody commander who was going to be furious when he realized what they had done. Brin grimaced as he thought about the punishment they were in for when the distress signal reached Vog.

I hope he doesn't decide to leave us here to rot.

He should have known better than to let Oshen take the lead on anything like this. Brin grinned as he thought back on all the mischief they had gotten into as pups. None of *his* bad ideas had ever gone this awry, and he didn't plan on ever letting his brutok live it down. Assuming Vog didn't send them out the airlock.

This is going to infuriate Brega when it gets back to her.

Brin propelled himself through the water, refusing to linger too long on thoughts of how his dam would react or what he would have to put up with next time he saw her.

Tiny aquatic creatures darted out of his way as he swam. Fish, that's what the data the Grutex provided them with called the little scaly things. He marveled at some of the similarities to the life forms found on his homeworld. The depths soon gave way to a sandy bottom covered in lush seagrass. Brin ran the tips of his fingers through it, taking a moment to watch it sway in the current.

Up ahead, the shadowy outline of wooden pillars was visible. Kicking off the grassy bottom, Brin surfaced quietly, taking in his surroundings. The water lapped at the shore and the wooden dock that jutted out from the stretch of land.

The night was silent, but Brin approached with caution. There were many land-dwelling animals on his homeworld that were incredibly dangerous, even to a fully grown Venium warrior. He had only read up on a few of Earth's land species, but most of them didn't seem like they would cause too much trouble if he were to encounter one.

A pained groan caught his attention just as the wind brought him the tangy smell of lifeblood. He recognized the scent of at least one of the injured parties, and it made his pulse stutter in fear.

Oshen.

Brin moved forward, treading water as quietly as possible as he approached the pillars of the dock. With his heart racing in his chest, he gripped the edge, pulling himself up slowly to check for any signs of danger.

The moans that drifted through the dense fog that had settled in brought a frown to his face. Was this Oshen? Was his brutok lying somewhere up ahead, bleeding out? Had the Grutex found him? Had he come too late? He swallowed down the lump that formed in his throat at the thought. No, these sounds were… different. He couldn't say what, but something wasn't right about this.

Curled up on the boards of the dock a few feet away from where he had climbed up was a large mangled mass. Oshen was a large male, but this was even bigger than him. Even so, Brin felt the urge to confirm his suspicions.

Loosening the tight grip he normally kept on his emotions, he allowed the blue light of his fushori to illuminate the darkness and sighed in relief when the mauve-colored exoskeleton of a Grutex warrior was revealed.

The male's sloping head was thrown back in agony, and all six of his red eyes were glazed over. The plant-like tendrils that sprouted from his head moved along the ground around him as if they were reaching for something he couldn't see.

A few of the blunt spikes that crowned his head had been broken off, and his chest and arms were covered in deep, nasty gouges that he knew had come from the deadly claws of a Venium.

Oshen must have fought this male and been injured enough to

leave behind his scent. The Grutex's lifeblood flowed from his wounds, pooling all around him as he struggled to breathe. He was strong, Brin would give him that, but he wondered why Oshen hadn't ended the male when he had the chance.

Had he been too injured after the fight, and if so, where had he ended up? Brin readied himself to deliver the death blow, but distant voices stopped his hand. Someone or something was coming, and he couldn't afford to be caught.

A strained laugh floated up from the dying Grutex. "They won't allow you to live, Venium," he wheezed as he struggled to breathe.

Brin snarled before darting around the male, fleeing in the opposite direction of whoever was approaching the dock. If the voices were this male's recovery team, then he was correct; they wouldn't let him live if they found him anywhere near their fallen warrior. He had more important things to deal with. Finding Oshen and getting them home was his priority, and he had no idea where to even start.

He ducked behind buildings and tried to stick to the woodline, weaving his way through what seemed to be a business district. There were few humans on the streets, but he took shelter beneath a massive gnarled tree, making sure to keep out of sight.

Each call he tried to make to the mothership and Oshen only ended with cursing nearly strong enough to make his dam blush. Something or someone was blocking the signal.

Brin smirked as he began tapping in coding on his comm. There were certain advantages to being a Havacker, like knowing how to slip through the tiniest crack in the walls they had erected even without his equipment. The little dot representing Oshen's location popped up, and he pumped his fist victoriously.

Thank you, goddess!

He might not be able to reach Vog, but at least he could find his brutok and they could come up with a plan to get home together.

resent day...

*B*rin crept closer to the small human dwelling, picking his way through the small shrubs that lined the ground around the purple exterior until he could peek into the window. His fushori pulsed, lighting the way.

It had taken him far longer to reach the position than he had anticipated and he had feared for Oshen's safety. Apparently, his worry was all for naught. His brutok stood across the room, shoulders pressed into the wall as he stared down at the dark-haired female at his side.

His mouth nearly dropped open in surprise when he watched his friend run the clawed tip of his finger over the little female's jaw. The foolish smile Oshen wore plastered on his face told Brin everything he needed to know.

It was exciting and completely terrifying to see someone so close to him with that look of utter adoration in their eye. He leaned back, puzzling over the fact that they had been separated for only a few Earth days and already Oshen had found a human female.

Annoying little insects buzzed near his ears, attacking him with tiny needles that extended from their faces. How in the world did the humans put up with this? He swatted at them in an attempt to dissuade the pests from landing on his unprotected upper body.

"I am not food," he hissed.

Something hard and cold pressed against the back of his neck, and Brin went still.

"Who are you?" The sound of her hurried words caused a shiver to rush up his spine. "Only perverts hide in bushes. I've never met a pervert who put on a light show, though." Brin glanced down and noticed his fushori was indeed still glowing. He hadn't been this uncontrolled in many years. Having a warrior for a dam meant you learned quickly how to hide your emotions and the physical reaction they caused so you didn't give yourself away to the enemy. So much for that. "What are you doing here?"

"Which question would you like me to answer first?" he teased, but the increased pressure of whatever she held pressed into his skull let him know she wasn't amused.

"What are you doing creeping through the bushes and staring into windows?" she asked again.

"I'm looking for my brutok. We were supposed to meet some-where, and he disappeared before I arrived." The pressure didn't ease. "I believe the Grutex are blocking our comm signals, but I was able to trace him to this dwelling."

"*Brutok*?" He could almost hear her mind working. "Fishboy used that word earlier. Do you know Oshen?"

"Did you call him Fishboy to his face?" Brin grinned, imag-ining the utter indignation Oshen would have felt and wishing he could have been there to witness it.

"I did."

He laughed, but was silenced by the click that emanated from the weapon she held to his head. Probably not the best time for humor, but he hadn't ever been very fond of taking things seri-ously. *Why start now?*

"I wouldn't laugh, Glowworm."

Brin's chest swelled with pride. This fierce female had bestowed an endearment upon him. Never had his fushori lit with such radiance.

"I am not your enemy. If you lower the weapon, we can talk this through." He raised his hands to show her he was unarmed. "I only want to retrieve Oshen and be on my way."

"Yeah, thing is, I can't really let you do that. The woman in there with him is my best friend. Your brutok told her that he believes she is his mate and instead of thinking he's bat shit crazy she's convinced that he's telling her the truth. So, even though I'm still a little iffy on the whole thing and I'd love to strangle him with my bare hands, I'm not going to let either of us ruin this for her."

The weapon that had been pressed against him only seconds before fell away suddenly.

Brin spun around to argue, but stopped short when he got his first glimpse of the fiery female. She was tiny, barely coming to the middle of his chest, with jet black hair that was twisted into a long braid. The blue of his fushori glowed off of her smooth, tanned skin, and her expressive dark eyes narrowed on him.

She was beautiful, and she looked as dangerous as a shayfia, one of the vicious apex predators from his homeworld. They looked sweet, like the fawns from Earth's database, with four thin legs and a long, willowy tail. Instead of the large ears found on the Earth creature, the shayfia had fins and fleshy ribbons that hung from its head. Four bisected gills lined its long neck, flaring open in warning just before the beast split down the middle to better consume its prey. Her innocent allure was already working its magic on him, and he almost wanted her to unleash that carefully checked aggression he sensed.

The grin that spread across his face did nothing to placate her. In fact, it only seemed to annoy her even more. Without a second thought, Brin wrapped his tail around one of her ankles, his mind calling for him to give her comfort in some way, but an honest-to-gods growl slipped from her lips as she snarled at him.

She lifted her small foot from the dirt and, with surprising strength, slammed it down on the middle of his tail. He hissed as he uncoiled the appendage, but failed to stop the laugh that escaped him.

Vicious. I like it.

"Don't touch me." Her dark eyes flashed with anger.

"My apologies. I meant no offense." A deep purr rumbled up his chest as he placed a hand over his heart.

"Mmhmm." She eyed him as she pursed her lips.

She didn't trust him, and why should she? Who knew what sort of impression Oshen had given her of their people? His brutok might be a wonderful ambassador, but he could be unyielding and demanding when it came to something he wanted, and clearly he wanted her friend.

Oshen's mate. If he could believe what this human female was saying, then Oshen had actually found her. The Grutex hadn't lied it seemed.

"Look, I've gotta get home and change and I don't need you trying to ride in there like a knight in shining armor and I'm sure Oshen might take it badly if you were to get caught sneaking around the house by the police. You can come with me for now, *but...*" She jabbed her finger into his chest and his skin prickled with a desire he'd never felt before. "If you try anything stupid, I won't hesitate to shoot you. Understand?"

"Of course, little shayfia," Brin cooed. "I'll be on my best behavior."

A fine black brow rose. "I don't even know you, but I've got a feeling you wouldn't know good behavior if it slapped you in the face."

He knew good behavior, but all of the things filling his mind at the moment were so far from good that even he was a little shocked. "*Good* isn't always *fun*."

"Let's go, Glowworm." She jerked her head to the side as she led him around to the front of the dwelling and out to an ancient form of transportation. "Hop in. The door is unlocked."

His brow ridge rose as he pulled the door to the transport open and managed to fold himself into the small seat. He'd only just pulled his tail inside before the female slammed the door shut. She kept her eyes trained on him as she moved to the other side, sliding in behind the steering controls.

A small key was jammed into the console before she yanked on a stick that sat between them, causing the transport to reverse. Brin watched her movements.

"I've never had the opportunity to ride in such a primitive transport before."

The look the female shot his way told him that may not have been the right thing to say. "Listen, Glowworm, I worked my ass off for this car. Let's not insult it."

"You've used that endearment several times, but my translator hasn't picked up on the slang of your language. I like the name. What does it mean?"

"Endearment?" She snorted, her eyes darting over to him before she turned forward.

"Yes. A term used for someone you love or care for."

"Love?" The transport swerved to the right as she turned to gawk at him. "I hardly *know* you, and I definitely don't *love* you." Brin waved anxiously at the wheel in front of her and she righted the path of the vehicle. "It's just a nickname."

"Ah, my mistake, little Shayfia."

"My name is Junafer, but I prefer to go by Jun. I'm not Shayfia!"

"Jahn. Very pretty."

"J-oo-n! *John* is my brother's name."

Another grin tugged at his lips as he tried once more to repeat her name.

"J-oo-n. My name is Brin."

28

He liked this female very much. Beneath that prickly exterior she presented, there was something much softer and emotional. He didn't imagine very many people got to know that side of her.

If there was any Venium who knew about the differences in the mask you showed people, and the face you kept for those close to you, it was Brin. For some reason, he was determined to be let in, to be shown that side of her she kept hidden.

He hadn't ever seen himself wanting a mate, had never wanted to start his own family, but he sent up a prayer to the goddess, a plea that if he was going to be forced into a mating, then let it be with this vicious little female.

"I know you don't want me to disturb your friend as she attempts to mate with my brutok, but I should get in contact with Oshen soon."

"He really is fine. I stitched him up myself." Jun parked the transport in front of what he assumed was her dwelling.

He stepped out, watching from the corner of his eye as Jun grabbed her bag and the weapon, and when she jerked her head toward the building, he followed.

The door opened to reveal a space that would be considered small by Venium family den standards. The database hadn't given him much information on human dwellings, unfortunately, so he wasn't sure how her home compared to other humans.

There were many unfamiliar objects set around the space, and he wondered briefly if his dam felt this same awe and curiosity whenever she was offworld interacting with alien species. Perhaps her life as a warrior kept her too busy to notice the small things. *She didn't notice you.* Brin shook away the thought.

"You're a healer then?"

Jun looked at him and ran a hand over her long, dark hair. His hand twitched with the desire to do the same. He wanted to lose himself in his exploration of her, to forget all his worries for a few moments.

"I'm a nurse," she answered, shaking him from his thoughts. "That means I'm more than capable of cleaning up a few scratches."

Brin raised his brow ridge. All the healers he had ever met had a gentle nature. They certainly hadn't held a weapon to his head and threatened to shoot him where he stood. He had spent his whole life running from one fierce warrior female, and here he was, begging the goddess to grant him this one.

CHAPTER 3

NUZAL

$\mathcal{T}$he cells lining both sides of the hall Nuzal walked down were filled with humans of different shapes and sizes. Their coloring ranged from the darkest shades of brown to the palest cream, a stunning variety that never failed to amaze him. His people, the Grutex, lacked such variation, but it was not due to anything natural.

For generations, the scientists aboard this vessel had diligently worked to create the perfect species: a creature both intelligent and violent, who was more than some mindless killing machine. He and every other Grutex in existence were part of a massive genetic overhaul.

Still working out the kinks, Nuzal thought with a rueful snort.

The fact that he had only two sets of red eyes instead of the preferred three was seen as an imperfection. He might as well have been born without the set of violet eyes just beneath them. Unlike the red, violet eyes could not transition to an infrared state and were therefore useless during battle.

Nuzal had never even been considered for the warrior class, and it stung to know that he had been shunned for something he couldn't control.

Next time, he told himself. *Next time, I will be better.*

The data on his comm screen scrolled across his forearm as he followed Erusha past the cowering humans. They scurried away from the front of the cells like insects as they approached, huddling together in the corners as if this would protect them.

Nuzal had worked hard to erect his wall of indifference toward their plight. As a youngling, he had learned that empathy was a weakness, but this lesson had become increasingly difficult to remember as of late.

Their enemies had always been a match in strength and technology, but these humans? No, they were weak, with soft bodies, and they possessed no tech that could effectively repel their forces.

They were helpless to defend themselves, and there was something about that fact that repulsed Nuzal, that made him *feel* for these creatures. It was dangerous to feel, so he kept his mouth closed and all six of his eyes on his work.

Erusha was the head of their department on the ship and ran the lab where Nuzal spent most of his time. The influx of human captives kept them busy. Detailed logs and medical records of the humans were meticulously maintained in the hopes that they might discover something useful.

Like a more natural way to reproduce, perhaps?

Long ago, further back than any of them could remember now, the Grutex had been forced to resort to artificial incubation. Not only had the few females on board the ship become infertile, so too had the majority of their males. Whatever had caused this mutation remained a mystery, but the Grutex Kaia, their leader, no longer seemed focused on curing them.

They had discovered the planet the humans called Earth a few generations ago. His memory of the event was patchy, but he could remember the thrill of finding something untouched. As far as Nuzal knew, they had been the first to come upon the world and the first to take the humans.

It had started with only a handful, just enough to understand their species, but that was all he could recall. Like the others, the reproductive process had slowly begun to eat away at Nuzal's memories.

"You have the latest data from our last batch of testing?" Erusha asked.

"I do, sir." He tried his best to hide the annoyance he felt at having to defer to someone else, but Nuzal had to remind himself that he was no longer the warrior he had been in his previous lives. The power and authority he had once wielded were no longer his.

While he understood the need to test, to gain knowledge, Nuzal couldn't understand how the Grutex could hope to remain "perfect" if they were already attempting to breed with another species. Especially one that they had treated as little more than livestock for as long as they had been in contact with them.

In past generations, this would have been unheard of, and yet the superiors and scientists all acted as if this was nothing out of the ordinary.

Nuzal wished, not for the first time, that he retained more of his memories. There was no doubt in his mind these lost moments in their history would have helped to better understand the reason they had strayed from their quest for purity.

As if the other male could hear Nuzal's thoughts, he stopped and spun around to face him. "Save your musings for later, Nuzal. We are going there to report our data, nothing more. I don't need the Kaia up our tails, sticking his face into things he knows nothing of."

"Of course, sir."

They moved into the inner section of the ship, the place where all of the major decisions were made, where those motivated to lead congregated to battle for supremacy.

As much as he had wished as a youngling to be seen as worthy of participating in the warrior sect, Nuzal was grateful for the quiet of his lab anytime he found it necessary to travel here.

So much for being more than mindless killing machines, he thought to himself as a fight broke out nearby.

Warriors rushed forward, cheering on the males as they clawed at one another. Had he been like that when he was a warrior? Had he been little more than a vessel for mindless anger and violence?

Nuzal wanted to believe that he would have never started an altercation without a damn good reason. There had been rumors recently, whispers among the medical and scientific sections that the warriors were being given injections. Some theorized that this caused them to become far more brutal than he had ever remembered being, but he couldn't afford to entertain whispers.

"Brutes," Erusha sneered as they stepped around the onlookers. "Take a good look, Nuzal. This is what we are becoming. Without the humans, this is our future."

The sickening crack of an exoskeleton made Nuzal wince as he turned his head away and followed after Erusha. He knew the male didn't agree with most of the genetic modifications the Grutex had been subjected to, but he never voiced his reasons. Nuzal was sure the threat of execution and delayed rebirth was enough to keep his mouth shut.

Four armed warriors stood outside the door of the Kaia's office, their eyes narrowing on Erusha and Nuzal as they approached.

"Present for confirmation," the largest of them rumbled.

Nuzal turned his arm over and waited as the warrior passed

the scanner over his wrist before moving on to Erusha. The device chimed twice, and they were waved inside as the doors opened.

He had made trips to this sector before, but Nuzal had never been privy to any of the meetings with the Kaia himself. As the head of the military might, the Kaia ruled supreme, and not even the council could overturn his decisions. The Grutex in question was massive, with six dark red eyes that roamed over them as they stepped inside. His black xines wriggled for a moment before settling against the scarred exoskeleton.

The Kaia leaned forward in his chair, watching them from behind a long metal desk covered in souvenirs of his battles and small trinkets given as gifts from "allies." In truth, the Grutex had no friends. The Tachin, the insect-like aliens whose homeworld they were currently orbiting, were as close to friends as they would likely ever get.

In the corner of the room, pressed up against the smooth wall, a human female shivered. Her yellow hair was pulled back away from her slender face, and her dark brown eyes tracked Nuzal and Erusha as they approached the desk. The black leather collar fastened around her throat was the only thing she wore.

"Kaia," Erusha muttered as he inclined his head.

Nuzal kept his eyes on the floor, not daring to look at the male in front of them. He had an awful habit of giving his feelings away, and for the life of him, he couldn't figure out why he had been the one chosen to come along today.

If he showed even a modicum of the anger he felt over the way this little human female was being treated, he would be viewed as a challenger and subject to a brutal beating from the Kaia that no one would object to. Even though the Grutex were expected to mate these aliens, to breed them, they were in no way encouraged to actually *feel* for them.

"Erusha. You have a data report for me?"

"Of course, sir."

Nuzal heard the ping of the file he had uploaded earlier as it was sent directly to the Kaia's comm. A grunt from behind the desk had his jaw clenching with anxiety.

"There have been no successful matings?" the Kaia asked, his voice laced with a deadly chill.

"None," Erusha confirmed.

"This is unacceptable, Erusha! How many humans do we have on board this vessel and none of them are causing a reaction among the warriors?" Something heavy, most likely a fist, slammed against the metal desk, making the little female whimper.

"The warriors are not the only Grutex on the ship—" Erusha began.

"They are the only males I wish to see bred and you would do well to follow those orders." Before Erusha could speak, the chirp of a transmission sounded from the holocomm. "Stay," he barked when they moved to leave. "It will only take a moment." Nuzal glanced up to see him swipe a clawed finger across the pad, bringing the image of the younger warrior to life. "Raou. What is it?"

"The Venium have arrived on Earth. Xuvri was on his hunt when one of their males attacked him."

"Did he live?"

"He did, but his injuries are severe," Raou reported.

Nuzal remembered Xuvri from his time in the breeding program. The male had successfully bred his human female more than once, but none of the pregnancies had made it to term. He couldn't remember what had become of her, but if the warrior was participating in the hunt again, it didn't bode well.

"Have him healed and back to his hunt as soon as possible. We need every warrior ready."

"Yes, sir, and the Venium?" Raou asked.

"Find him," the Kaia growled before ending the transmission.

There was a moment of silence before things began to fly off the desk and crash into the walls and floor. "Venium scum!" The female in the corner began to cry, tugging on the chain attached to her collar. "Quiet!" he bellowed, rushing at her. With nothing more than a flick of the Kaia's wrist, the chain snapped and he yanked the female from the corner. She stumbled on wobbly legs, falling to the floor in a trembling mass. "Fix this one! She does nothing but sob and cower. Send a replacement, something sturdy."

Erusha jerked his head toward her, and Nuzal gathered up the nude female as she continued to cry. He struggled not to let his mask of indifference slip and to tamp down the snarl that threatened to rip through his chest. How could the Kaia treat any being with such disdain?

They are animals, Nuzal. He repeated the lie to himself over and over, hoping if he said it enough, he might actually believe it one day. As soon as they were dismissed, Erusha rushed him out the door, grumbling under his breath about the instability of leadership.

"Kill me, please." Nuzal's eyes jerked down to the human in his arms. "I don't want to be fixed." She cried against his chest. "Just kill me. End it."

Her soft plea tore at his heart, but he stomped down his emotions. He couldn't do what she was asking him. From the fear in her voice, Nuzal guessed that she knew what the Kaia had meant by "fix."

He wanted her modified, changed into something less human and more Grutex. Although the tests showed this did nothing to encourage the bond or increase the chances of reproduction, the Kaia had requested this many times for the females who had the misfortune of catching his eye.

"I'm sorry," he told her quietly. "I really am."

CHAPTER 4

JUN

There was an alien in her house. An attractive, half-dressed alien, but an alien all the same. *You're almost as bad as Amanda, Junafer.* What was she supposed to do with him now that she had gotten him here?

Jun narrowed her eyes at the creature who stood in her living room. His massive stature and deadly claws should have intimidated her, but Brin didn't scare Jun. He made her feel *a lot* of things when he looked at her, but fear was not one of them.

She'd spent the last couple nights at Amanda's to make sure she wasn't leaving her friend with the alien equivalent of Ted Bundy. Humans didn't have a monopoly on serial killers, right?

Jun spent most of the first night sitting up, waiting for the big alien to make his move, but he'd been nothing other than helpful and patient. While she wanted to protect her friend, Jun also realized she couldn't make all of Amanda's decisions for her. If she wanted to bring a strange alien into her home, what could she really do to stop her?

You're one to talk.

Brin moved around the space, bending down to study pictures of her family and the religious knickknacks she had brought with her when she moved from the Philippines. He ran the pads of his fingers gently over the earrings that had belonged to her lola before tracing the face of her statue of the Virgin Mary.

"What is this?" Brin asked, reaching out to touch the necklace resting in its box on the table.

"Don't touch!"

She lunged forward, grabbing his wrist. His blue eyes searched her face, and she felt her heart pound furiously within her chest as heat crept up her neck.

"I'm sorry," Jun murmured. "It's something my lolo—my grandpa—made a long time ago. He was a fisherman, and this came from one of the sharks he caught while he was out in his boat." She looked down at the necklace and smiled, remembering the man she loved so much. "This one was passed down to my papa and one day, when he is older and has proven himself, it will be my privilege to pass it to my little brother." There was no doubt in her mind she would get the chance. John took his studies seriously and worked hard for their family. "There is a belief we have back home that it's bad luck for anyone other than the owner to touch it, so even though I'm its guardian right now, I've never actually touched it."

When he did nothing but blink down at her, Jun shifted self-consciously. She knew most of these beliefs seemed ridiculous to people here and she shouldn't be surprised to find that even an alien thought their superstitions were a little crazy.

"Just silliness," she muttered before pulling her hand from his arm, but the warmth of his fingers wrapping around her wrist made her pause.

"Why is it silly?" he asked. When she only shrugged, Brin

curled a finger beneath her chin, tilting her head up until she was staring into his face.

God help her, but when he looked at her like that, Jun felt some sort of awareness spring to life within her. Scars littered the dark gray skin of his upper body, and as she took him in, the stripes on his shoulders, arms, and face that Oshen had called his fushori began to glow softly.

"Most of the people I've met here don't believe in superstitions. They think it's crazy, but it's what I've grown up with." When she tugged her hand away and pulled back, Brin let her go without complaint.

"Oshen and I once painted our ears red for days before our trials because his gia told us it would bring us luck. The stuff we used stained our skin for a month after." His soft laugh drifted over her. "Your tradition is not silly. Thank you for sharing it with me."

The lump that formed in her throat with his words made it difficult to swallow, but she smiled gratefully. He bent to inspect the necklace, keeping his hands behind his back this time.

"You said this was from a shark?"

"Yes."

"I think sharks may be one of my favorite animals from your planet. There were so many varieties in the database."

Ah, yes, she had almost forgotten about that. The fact that the Grutex had not only been collecting humans, but also information on them and everything concerning Earth, didn't sit well. To top it off, the monstrous invaders had obviously been sharing their findings with other alien species, drawing more attention than she liked to their little corner of the universe.

"I think I'd like to try swimming with them."

The statement had her brow rising, and she turned to him with a grin. "They have made so many movies about why you should *not* want to swim with sharks."

"You would never swim with them?"

"Never." She laughed. "Besides, I can't swim."

Brin's laugh died on his tongue, and his mouth slowly dropped open. "You can't swim?"

"Nope."

"You said your grandsire was a fisherman, that he went out on boats. I assume this means you lived near a body of water and yet you can't swim?"

Jun shrugged as she reached for the blanket draped across the arm of the sectional. He wasn't the first person to find this strange, and she doubted very much that he would be the last. "I've swam in pools, but you won't catch me in the ocean."

"Why not?"

"Where I'm from, we have horrible typhoons. They destroy homes, flood entire cities, kill people. We live on the beach, and I've watched the sea churn and become violent so many times. I've seen what it could do to people who were caught up in it and so I prefer to not give it the chance to take me."

"If you were to learn to swim, wouldn't it be helpful?" Brin asked, stepping closer.

"Being a strong swimmer in a situation like that won't save your life." Before she could stop herself, Jun reached up to trace the ridges of his gills. "Humans aren't as lucky as the Venium. If we're pulled under, we drown."

A soft growl rumbled up Brin's chest, and when she realized she was still touching him she jerked her hand away, retreating toward the other side of the room.

"I need to get my things together. I think it's still dark enough outside that we can get back to Amanda and Oshen before the neighbors are out and about." She waved at the dark sectional. "You can sit. I won't be long."

Without another glance to distract herself, Jun darted down the short hallway into the master bedroom. Like the rest of her house, it was small, but cozy and it served its purpose. She eyed her bed with its pile of soft pillows and blankets and wished she could climb in and shut off for just a few minutes. She was physically and mentally exhausted from the last few days.

With a groan of frustration, Jun tossed the blanket in her hands onto the bed and stomped over to her closet, pulling her overnight bag from the shelf and stuffing a few of her favorite pajama bottoms and soft T-shirts into it. A pair of her scrubs followed, in case she didn't make it back in time to change for her shift tomorrow.

When she had gotten everything together, Jun hefted the bag over her shoulder and walked back out into her living room. "Okay, I'm ready... Brin?" He wasn't where she had left him.

"Shh."

She jumped at the hiss and spun toward her front door. Brin was standing near the window that looked out into her yard, eyes narrowed as he stared at something through the slit between the blinds. "What's wrong?"

"There is someone outside," he whispered.

Her neighbors weren't normally the sorts of people who woke up at dawn to start their days. She honestly hadn't expected any of them to be out so early, but when she stepped in front of him and tilted the blinds, she grimaced at what she saw.

"Bridget." When it came to nosy neighbors, Bridget Millows was just about the worst you could find. She had appointed herself the head of the neighborhood watch, and there was hardly a thing that went on that she didn't know about. "There's no way we're getting you out of here without her seeing us." They had lost their window.

"We can leave when night falls." The rumble of Brin's voice at her back made her shiver. "It's likely the Grutex already know we're here, but we don't need to draw the attention of the human government just yet."

Brin was right; they didn't need Bridget sounding the alarm before they decided what to do, but now she was going to be spending the entire day alone with an alien male she knew very little about. What did you do with someone who you knew absolutely nothing about?

Feed them.

Her mama's voice whispered in her head and Jun grinned. "Are you hungry? I didn't have anything other than coffee at Amanda's and I'm starving."

Brin turned to her with a lopsided smile. "I haven't eaten properly since we crashed. I would be thankful for anything you shared with me." He said as he stepped away from the window. "I'd like to clean myself up a little before the meal, if it's not too much to ask."

"Oh, right." Jun lifted her chin, jerking her head toward the hallway. "Bathroom is down that way, the second door on the right side. There should be a towel on the rack for you to use." Her eyes traveled down his lean body until she reached the waistline of his black pants. "I, uh—I don't have anything for you to change into. None of the guys I've dated have been so... big." The way his eyes lit up told her that admission pleased him.

"These will do until Oshen and I get back on the ship," he told her, tugging on the material at his hips as his eyes roamed over her face.

A blush crept up her neck, and she balked at the way her pulse fluttered. *Get yourself together. Your heart can't handle all this fluttering nonsense.*

"Well, you're a smart alien. I'm sure you can figure out the shower on your own."

She left him standing there and swept into the kitchen, setting the rice cooker so that it could cook while she gathered more ingredients from the refrigerator.

The sound of the shower cutting on let her know he had

managed to figure out the controls. She cracked eggs into a bowl and whisked them together with milk and butter before dumping them into the hot pan.

The familiarity of cooking, of moving through all of the steps she had watched her lola and her mama do when she was a child, brought her comfort and a renewed sense of calm. That it also distracted her from the fact that she had a naked alien in her bathroom was a bonus.

Everything in the world may have been going crazy, but at least she had this. She set the rice, eggs, and dried herring on the table just as Brin walked in. He patted at his braided hair, wiping tiny beads off water from his face and neck.

"Sit." She shooed him toward one of the old wooden chairs she'd snagged from a thrift shop years ago and prayed to God it would hold him. The wood creaked under his bulk, but held steady. "I see you didn't have trouble working the shower. Take whatever you want," Jun told him as she rummaged through her bag for her pill box.

"It was a simple system." He shrugged. "This is very generous of you." Brin smiled as he piled food onto his plate. "You didn't need to go through so much trouble."

"It wasn't any trouble."

She swallowed her medications before sticking the box back into her bag and joining her guest at the table. Jun eyed the dried fish longingly, but she really shouldn't push her luck with the salty dishes after all of the coffee she'd been drinking the last couple days. Instead, she gave herself a scoop of rice and some of the eggs and pouted as she watched Brin devour everything in front of him.

He hummed with approval, barely chewing before swallowing and enthusiastically shoveling in more food. Was there anything she liked more than watching someone appreciate her food?

"This is amazing," he said before swallowing another mouthful of eggs. "What do you call these?"

"Scrambled eggs." They had been a favorite of Oshen's as well, but he had been so caught up in Amanda that he hadn't bothered to ask about what he was eating. Jun glanced up to find his face had turned ashen grey and he was staring at her in shock.

"You scrambled the young of an animal?" he asked incredulously.

"Not the young. They're unfertilized so they never had anything growing inside of them." She stifled a laugh as she watched him grimace down at his plate.

"Poor little creatures. They never even had a chance." Brin shook his head, a barely perceptible grin tugging at the corners of his dark lips as his eyes trailed up to her face.

"You're so dramatic. Remind me not to waste my time feeding you balut while you're here." Jun laughed as she dug into her own eggs.

"Is this another questionable food option?"

"It's a boiled egg with a duck embryo inside."

Brin narrowed his eyes on her face. "Now you are just making things up."

"I'm serious. It's delicious."

"Of all the things you could eat on this planet, you want to devour a boiled embryo? I will politely decline your offer." Brin shook his head as he folded his arms over his chest.

Jun's head tipped back as a laugh burst from her lips. "You're ridiculous."

"And you're lovely, shayfia," Brin murmured. "Especially when you smile like that."

It wasn't like she had never received a compliment before, but the words wrapped around her like a blanket and made her feel warm all over. Butterflies danced in her belly as she thanked him and finished her food.

"We still have the whole day ahead of us," she said as she brought her plate to the sink. "I'm not sure what you do for fun, but I've got an old game system out in the living room you can mess with if you want." Jun took the dishes from Brin's hands when he brought them over to her. "It's not as cool as the newer stuff, but Amanda and I have used it a few times."

The dishwasher kicked on as Jun closed the door, and she led Brin out of the kitchen and over to the TV stand, pulling the small black console off of the shelving inside.

She'd found it at one of the flea markets years ago, and Amanda had been so excited about it that she couldn't just leave it behind. There weren't many games, but she pulled out a few she thought he might like, blowing into the cartridges to clear them out.

Brin studied the controller, turning it over in his hands as Jun turned the TV on and powered up the system.

"Games go in here." She pointed to the opening in the top, he didn't need her guidance. Brin sifted through the games, plucking one from the bin and pressing it into the slot. The short cord on the controller didn't give him enough room to sit on the couch, but he made himself comfortable on her rug, grinning like a child when the dramatic 8-bit martial arts music began to play.

Jun curled up in the corner of her sectional, tucking her legs beneath her as she watched him. He might be Oshen's friend, but he was still a stranger in her home so she'd keep a close eye on him until it was time to leave.

In no time at all, Brin was taking down his opponents and the masculine chuckles that filled the room anytime the other character died a ridiculously gory death made her smile.

"Finish her!" the voice in the game demanded just before Brin's character slammed the opponent into a ceiling full of spikes.

Her eyes fluttered closed as she rested her head against the back of the couch. She hated that her medications made her tired, but she had fought the sleepiness off often enough at work and was sure she could manage it here. She just needed to keep her eyes open…

CHAPTER 5

JUN

She was burning up. Beads of sweat trickled down her neck as she struggled to kick the blanket from her body and sit up in bed. Her small, dark room had been turned into a sauna.

My room?

Jun paused as her eyes darted around her. She had been on the couch watching Brin play the game.

Oh, God, she groaned, finally shoving the thick blanket off. *I fell asleep.*

The fan above her rotated at full speed, but it did nothing to cool her heated skin. Jun flung her legs over the side of the bed and slid her bare feet into the house slippers that sat neatly on the rug.

Jun opened her bedroom and slipped out into the hallway. The thermostat on the wall informed her that it was a muggy 87 degrees in her home, and she groaned in frustration.

The unit had been on its last leg for a while, but she'd thought she would have more time to save up for repairs. The house had been dirt cheap when Jun bought it off the sweet older woman, and she soon came to see why. She had already replaced so much, and between that and sending money home to her family, Jun was finding it harder and harder to make ends meet.

Land of milk and honey, my ass, she grimaced as she smacked the plastic device.

"Is this how you repair things on Earth?"

Jun screeched, jumping away from the wall as she spun around to face her shirtless alien guest. She hadn't even heard him approach. "*Sus maryosep!*" she yelled as she covered her face. "You scared the hell out of me!"

"I'm sorry," he said, humor lacing his voice as he lifted his hands. "I didn't mean to startle you. I heard your door open and came to make sure you were all right."

"You could have announced yourself," Jun grumbled. Her hands moved to her hips, and she felt around, grimacing as she looked up at him. "Did you take my gun?"

"It's on your bedside table." He folded his arms across his chest when she glared at him. "Don't look at me like that, little Shayfia. Did you want me to lay you down with it still strapped to your hip?"

"I didn't ask you to move me."

"You slumped over onto your face." He grinned as she scoffed. "I was worried you were going to break your neck."

She would *not* find it sweet that he had moved her for her comfort; she really would not. Jun refused to let the image of him carrying her to bed in his arms with her body pressed against his bare chest, make her blush.

It's the heat, she told herself. *It's not a blush. It's obviously the beginnings of heatstroke.*

"I need a shower. Maybe you can try to get in touch with Oshen since he destroyed Amanda's phone and I have no way to let her know I'm not dead?" She spun around, not waiting for him to respond, and locked herself in the bathroom.

Cool water rained down on her from the shower head, washing away the salty sweat that had covered her body. She scrubbed her hands over her face, wishing she could rinse away the weariness just as easily.

Not telling her family and Amanda about her chronic illnesses meant she carried the burden all on her own, but the thought of telling them and seeing the fear and worry in their eyes was more than she could bear.

She turned the handle with a sigh, cutting off the stream of water, and reached for her towel. When her long hair was wrapped up and piled on top of her head, Jun stepped out and put on her robe.

She should have brought her clothes in with her, but she'd been more concerned about putting some space between her and Brin. The male wasn't where she had left him when she stepped out of the bathroom, so she darted across the hall into her bedroom and closed the door; locking it just in case.

The blackout curtains on her windows kept her room dark and a little cooler than the rest of the house. *When the AC is actually working*, she thought.

Jun shuffled toward the bed, her hands stretched out in front of her so she wouldn't bump into anything. When she found the bedside table, she ran her fingers along the lamp, searching for the tiny lever. The dim light clicked on, and Jun let out a breath when she saw the gun sitting at the base.

A low, menacing growl from somewhere behind her sent a wave of cold fear through her. Was Brin in her room? Had he snuck in while she showered? Her fingers brushed the weapon on the table as she drew in a deep breath and prepared to turn around.

"The weapon will do you no good, female," a deep voice spoke.

Not Brin. Someone—or something—shifted, causing the floor to creak. They were in the corner of her room, near one of the windows. Jun closed her eyes, listening to his breathing and collecting herself. She had one chance to get this right, and if she didn't, she was most likely going to die for what she had planned.

"Put your hands up and turn around—"

Before they could finish their sentence, Jun grabbed her gun, flipping the safety off as she spun around and fired. The blast rang through the room seconds before a sharp crack sounded and something big fell against her wall.

Standing in the corner, looking as shocked as she felt, stood a massive mauve Grutex. Her bullet had lodged into his armor, burrowing into a weak spot. Long spidery cracks emanated from the center, and the male ran his hand over the wound cautiously before all six of his red eyes jumped to her face.

Fuck. Run!

Before her brain could send the command to her legs to move, Brin broke through the door. Pieces of the cheap particle board littered the carpet, snapping under his feet as he moved forward with a snarl. His long black claws gleamed in the dim light of the lamp as his eyes swept the room.

"Venium," the Grutex spat.

CHAPTER 6

BRIN

*T*he jarring sound of a weapon discharging within the dwelling had Brin's head snapping up. *Jun!* He was on his feet within the next second, barreling down the hall. She had locked her door, but the thin wood gave way easily as he slammed his shoulder into it.

With his claws extended and his teeth bared, Brin's eyes searched the room before they fell on Jun. Her fingers were wrapped around the gun he had placed on her table earlier, her chest rising and falling rapidly as she stared at him with wide, wild eyes.

"Venium," the Grutex in the corner growled.

Jun had shot the male. If they weren't in such a predicament, he might have taken the time to marvel at the bravery she had shown. The big male pushed himself away from the wall just as Brin launched himself across the room.

They collided near the bed, slamming into one another with a force that nearly took his breath away. Sharp claws dug into his skin, but his mind could only focus on one thing: Jun. She was in danger. This intruder had threatened *his* female.

Kill him! Destroy him! some foreign part of his mind bellowed as he wrestled the Grutex to the floor.

It felt as if something were just beneath his skin, rippling and pulsing, trying to break free, but he shoved it all back, using the lessons from the harsh training he had received as a pup to regain his composure.

Stay in control, he could hear Brega hiss in his ear. *Lose control and you lose your life.*

He slammed his fist into the male's face over and over until the warmth of his lifeblood coated Brin's knuckles and splattered across the floor.

The Grutex managed to land a blow to his ribs, knocking the air from his lungs as he rolled to the side. He wasn't fast enough to escape the claws that raked down his sides and hips.

With a hiss, Brin lashed out, swiping at the spot where Jun's weapon had injured the male, but in the next moment he found himself pinned beneath the massive body. He barely felt the sting of his own claws lengthening further as hands wrapped around his throat.

A growl vibrated through the Grutex's chest, and he leaned in, crushing Brin's body beneath his bulk. Brin bucked his hips in an attempt to dislodge him, slamming his hand into the inside of one of the male's arms. He could feel his lungs seizing as black spots danced in his vision, blocking out the red eyes that stared down at him.

Do not panic! Panic will kill you, Tesol, his sire, had told him as he watched him struggle to remain conscious.

"Pathetic." The heat of the Grutex's breath washed over his face. "Do you think she will weep for you? Do you think the female will call out for you when I take her?"

There was a loud, resounding crack, and the male's eyes

widened for a moment before he slumped forward, his face slamming into the floor next to Brin's head.

Jun stood above them, a long metal club clutched in both hands. Her arms shook as she watched him shove the male away. He slid his hand along the seam of his pants, releasing the hex restrainer from the nearly invisible casing he'd sewn into the uniform.

If his parents had taught him anything, it was that you could never be too prepared. With a grunt, Brin slapped the hex onto the Grutex's hard chest, pulling back just as the forcefield encased the male within the shield, immobilizing him.

"Is he dead?" Jun asked.

Brin turned, pulling the weapon from her hand as he crouched down in front of her. "Just knocked unconscious."

"I should have hit him again," she said, grimacing at the male's crumpled form.

"You did well, Shayfia." He laughed softly. "So well..." Brin reached for her hand, tugging her closer. "Are you all right? Did he hurt you?"

"No. I'm okay."

"He won't hurt you. I won't let him near you again."

Her eyes darted back to him, roaming over his face. A frown tugged at her mouth, and her dark brows furrowed as she looked down at his torso.

"Brin..." She tsked at him softly as she bent to inspect the wounds. "Sit on the bed. I'll get my bag and clean those up."

"Don't trouble yourself. They'll heal on their own." Brin tugged at her arm.

"And what about your face?"

"What exactly is wrong with my face?" he asked, skimming his fingers along the skin of his cheeks. "It's the same as it's always been."

"Exactly. I'm not sure I've got anything in my bag that can fix that."

Brin's head fell back as he winced in mock offense, gasping dramatically as she spun away from him. The sound of her laughter made his skin tingle and he marveled at her ability to find humor in something that must have been so terrifying for her. One moment she was saving his life, and the next she was poking fun at his appearance.

With a heavy sigh, Brin lay back on her bedding and watched as Jun left the room. The cuts stung with each breath he took, but his mind felt at peace. She was safe now that the Grutex was being held by the hex.

How had the male found them though? His call to Oshen hadn't even gone through, and he had been so careful to keep his signal hidden. Maybe there was something here, in Jun's home, that had alerted the Grutex.

"All right, Glowworm, let's get a better look at those." Jun said as she swept back in. He saw her eyes dart over to the body of the other male, as if she were reassuring herself that all was still well.

His ears flattened against his head as she began to pull out a variety of instruments, some of them far sharper than he imagined she needed to close him up. "Are you sure you know what to do with those things?"

Jun gave him a droll stare. "I've been a nurse for years, Brin. I have plenty of experience."

She reached out with a small white ball soaked in something that smelled foul and he flinched, hissing at the sting it caused when it touched one of the wounds on his side. She murmured an apology, dabbing the liquid over each of the scratches.

Her hands moved methodically, cleaning and assessing each wound, tutting and fretting over things he knew would heal up before the night was over, but he didn't stop her.

Having Jun so close with her fingers brushing his skin was something he wouldn't have put a stop to even if the world were ending. He clenched his jaw as she threaded the needle through his skin, closing up the larger portions.

"Sutures aren't normally my job, but it's a skill I seem to be using a lot lately," she said with a roll of her eyes. "I think that should do for the larger ones. Oshen healed far faster than I've ever seen, so I don't imagine much of this was even necessary for you."

"No." He grinned. "I appreciate it all the same." Brin sat up on the bed, wincing at the pain the movement caused.

"You've got a cut here," Jun said, picking up one of the little white balls she'd dipped in the fluid and dabbing it at the corner of his mouth. When he sucked in a pained breath, she murmured a quiet apology, their eyes meeting as she leaned in close to blow a soft stream of air along the irritated skin.

Brin cupped the back of her head, his fingers sliding into the silky strands as he pulled her closer. The tiniest gasp escaped her as he brushed his lips over hers, testing, teasing before he dove into the kiss. The tip of his tongue swept against her bottom lip, slipping inside as she opened for him.

Mine, something inside him rumbled.

The hand he had fisted in her hair tightened, and a growl tore up through his throat when Jun's hand pressed against the heated skin of his chest.

This is where she belongs, the voice whispered.

The sound of Jun's moan coursed through his veins, hardening his kokoras within its sheath until it extruded against the fabric of his pants. An awareness zinged up his spine as the glands at the base pulsed, swelling for the first time in his entire life.

No. Goddess, please.

Jun's teeth sank into his exploring tongue, and he jerked back with a curse, his hand flying to his mouth as she shoved to her feet. Her brows were drawn together and her chest heaved as she stared at him.

"What the hell was that?" she demanded.

He couldn't stop the chuckle that tumbled from him as he watched her fume. "Do humans not kiss?"

"Of course we do!" She hissed as she stepped out of his reach. "Why did you do it?"

Brin's fingertips tingled at the thought of touching her again. *Why had he done it?* "Because I wanted to."

"You're a pervert," Jun huffed, snatching up her bag and stalking out of the room without so much as a glance in his direction.

Most Venium males waited their whole lives for the moment their glands would swell. It was a milestone to rejoice over, to be celebrated with friends and family, but all Brin felt as he watched his mate leave was gut wrenching fear. *My mate.*

"Didn't care for that, did she?" the Grutex asked from the floor.

Brin rose from the bed and moved to the male's frozen form, crouching down to place his palm against the forcefield until the barrier glowed. "Nyissa, switch the hex to transportation mode. Set hex to follow."

"Transportation mode, on. Setting hex to follow, Master." The AI on his inner wrist flashed as the hex device lifted the Grutex's body slowly off the ground until it hovered near his knee.

Stepping over the broken pieces of the door, Brin moved into the hall. He could see Jun inside her bathroom, splashing water onto the back of her neck and over her face.

Their gazes connected in the mirror, and instead of the soft, sweet look of the female who had stitched up his wounds minutes ago, he watched her sneer just before she kicked the door shut with her foot. It was safe to say she was unhappy with him.

The front room of Jun's dwelling would have to do as a makeshift interrogation room for the time being.

"Nyissa, set hex for interrogation mode," he instructed the AI when he finished sliding the couch across the floor, blocking the front door. With the middle of the room cleared, Brin turned to study the Grutex as he was moved into an upright position, his legs bending so that he kneeled on the ground. "Cancel follow command. Set hex to stationary."

"Of course, Master. Is there anything else I can do for you? Perhaps you would like me to draw you a bath or tuck you into bed?"

Brin grinned at the sarcasm in her voice. "Maybe later."

The air within the dwelling was hot and humid against his skin. Temperatures within the underwater dome on Venora and even on the ships they used to travel were regulated and kept them all comfortable.

Brin made a note to fix Jun's faulty air system as soon as he got something useful out of their guest. An involuntary rumble rattled through his chest as he locked eyes with the male. He didn't like having to keep him here so close to his mate, but Brin had no other options, especially with the sun still so high in the sky.

The laws that governed the Venium were clear when it came to interrogation. He would give the Grutex a chance to answer freely, and if he chose not to? Well, Brin had been raised on the tactics he was permitted to use.

Brin stepped in front of the Grutex, his face impassive as he stared down into the angry red eyes of his captive. If the stubbornness he saw in them was any indication, this was going to be a long and frustrating night.

Fear was not something expected from the Grutex, especially from their warriors, and this one was no different. His claws hadn't retracted and Brin felt the tips dig into his skin as he fisted his hands behind his back.

"What is your name?" he asked, but the male only smiled. "Did you track me to this location?"

The hex system kept the body immobile, but the Grutex was free to move his head and speak. Instead, the male used the freedom to spit against the forcefield, snarling as he stared straight ahead.

So be it, he thought as he leaned forward, his hand passing easily through the shielding. The tip of his claw dug into the hole Jun's weapon had made in the male's exoskeleton, finding the space between the projectile so that he could pierce the softer skin beneath it.

He jerked his hand back, listening with satisfaction to the snapping sound the shell made as a small piece broke off. A grunt was the only indication that the male had felt the pain, so he dug deeper, moving his finger from side to side as he tore through the flesh.

"Raou!" the male spit. "My name."

"How many of you came?"

"I am the only one here," he answered.

It wasn't a lie; technically he was the only Grutex here, but Brin knew they rarely traveled alone. The others might not be close by, but they would come looking for him eventually, and Brin couldn't risk being caught off guard.

He didn't want to hurt the male, didn't want to prove that he was as vile as Brega and Tesol had trained him to be, but not getting this information put Jun in danger. Whether he'd wanted to find her or not, Brin found he was more than willing to kill to ensure the safety of his female.

Raou closed all six of his eyes as Brin grasped one of the long, deadly claws, bending it and the digit it was attached to backward.

"Did you track me to this location?" he asked again, but the male stayed quiet.

Brin applied more force, pressing back until the nail began peeling away from the bed. Raou growled, his body tensing as the claw snapped at the base. It would grow back soon enough, but the pain until then wouldn't be pleasant. Brin dropped the claw at the male's feet, ignoring the lifeblood that dripped from the wound, and reached for the next one.

"Is that really necessary?" Jun asked from the hallway.

"He broke into your home, and if you hadn't been quick enough to defend yourself, he could have snatched you away before I even knew he'd be in here."

Brin could barely contain the fury he felt at the thought that he had come so close to losing her. Jun was his responsibility, whether she knew it or not. He didn't want a family, not in the traditional sense, but he could make this work, couldn't he? What if they never had pups? They could discuss it, come to an agreement. If she knew what Brega had planned for any pup he produced, surely she would see that he could never reproduce.

"I will claim her when they come for you," Raou spoke. "Pretty little breeder... Maybe they will keep you alive long enough to watch me take her."

Brin swore he could physically feel something within him snap at the words. He fisted his hand and, without even allowing himself a moment to think, spun around, throwing all of his weight into the punch. The male's head jerked back, and before he could right himself, Brin had cocked his arm back and sent his fist flying into Raou's face once more.

She is mine! Mine! his mind raged. Brin would kill him. Brax whatever knowledge he possessed. Lifeblood splattered over his hand when the tip of his claw pierced the soft tissue of one of the Grutex's upper eyes.

"That's enough!" Jun shouted, grabbing his arm in an attempt to pull him away. "He's trying to get a rise out of you, and you played right into it!"

Raou threw his head back and an eerie laugh crawled up his throat as he watched them. His five remaining eyes stayed locked on Jun as she pressed her palm against Brin's chest.

Through the haze of his anger, Brin heard the tinkling sound of music coming from the small bag Jun had brought in with her earlier. She rushed over to it, pulling out a primitive-looking comm device with a frown.

"Shit," she grumbled before swiping a finger across the screen and pressing it to her ear. "Hello?"

Brin lunged for her, ripping the comm from her hand and smashing it against the wall. The device crumbled to the ground, and he crushed it beneath his heel for good measure.

"Was this not warning enough?" he bellowed, gesturing toward Raou, who looked on with unabashed amusement.

Jun stared down at her broken comm for a moment, her lips parted slightly as she took several deep breaths.

"Is this how you fix things on Venora?" she asked in a voice dripping with sarcasm. "What the hell is up with you aliens and your obsession with destroying things that don't belong to you?"

"The signal that transmits can be tracked by anyone who knows to look for it. We have enough problems as it is without that adding more."

"First of all," Jun said with a deadly calm that sent a shiver down his spine, "you do not ever touch my property without my permission." The tip of one small finger pressed into his chest. "Second, the call you just interrupted was from the hospital, the place where I work. That job keeps a roof over my head, puts food in my belly, and supports my entire family back home." She punctuated each point with a jab of her finger. "And finally, you do *not* destroy things that do not belong to you!"

"It was not safe—"

"Then use your words, Brin!" Jun shouted. "How many languages has that little device in your head taught you? You're telling me you can't use any of them to explain why something in my home could put us in danger? I could have just told them I wasn't going to make it in, but now I have to worry that I won't even have a job to go back to once this is over with."

"You aren't leaving this dwelling," Brin informed her, crossing his arms over his chest and doing his best to stand his ground against her anger.

"Is that so?" His little female practically spit the words at him. Her body vibrated with her rage as she took a step back. "Fuck you."

"I won't have you putting yourself in danger."

"I've been in danger every single day from the moment the Grutex showed up! Today is no different—tomorrow will be no different!"

Jun spun away from him, hair flying around her shoulders as she stomped toward the door wearing nothing but a robe to cover her body.

"Stop!" he growled, but she didn't listen. *Why should she?* he asked himself. *You've done nothing but yell and make demands. You've become exactly what Brega and Tesol have taught you to be.* The thought made him flinch, and he curled his hands into fists.

"Please," he whispered. "Please don't leave."

"You can't come into my home and just start making demands. I'm a grown woman, not a child. You either speak to me like one, or you don't speak to me at all."

"You're right. I'm sorry." Brin cupped her face in his hands and leaned down, pressing his forehead to hers. "Forgive me, Shayfia. I wouldn't be able to live with myself if something were to happen to you. He is not the only one out there searching for me, and I need you to trust that I am only doing what I must to keep you from falling into their hands."

A heavy sigh fell from between her lips, and Jun reached up to wrap her hands around the braids that had fallen over his shoulders. "Was that so hard? Hmm?" She pulled back to look up into his face. "Use your words. Got it?"

Brin grinned down at his mate and nodded. "Yes, little Shayfia."

CHAPTER 7

JUN

*W*aking up in her bed covered in sweat was really getting old. Sleeping in the same room where she shot a Grutex hours ago hadn't been easy and had resulted in lots of tossing and turning.

Knowing Brin sat in her living room keeping watch while she slept clearly hadn't quelled all of her anxiety. Her gun lay tucked beneath her pillow just in case she needed to face off with another intruder.

All those lessons at the range finally paid off. The bullet might not have done much damage, but she was thankful it had shocked the Grutex long enough to allow Brin to burst in.

She looked down at the particleboard she had swept into the little trash can in the corner of the room and sighed. Losing her door was a small price to pay for her life.

Who knew what that male would have done with her if Brin hadn't heard the gun fire? The fact that gunshots ringing out through the neighborhood had become so commonplace that none of her neighbors would have thought to call the cops was something Jun never thought she would be thankful for.

Pretty little breeder...

The memory of his words made her skin crawl. She'd rather die than be taken captive by those monsters, but she wasn't going to let that brute out there get the best of her.

Jun had learned a long time ago not to let people know when you were scared. Her mama and papa had taught her that nothing stood in the way of determination, and she was more than determined to get out of this and make it back to Amanda.

There was so much to fill her friend in on, not the least of which was the kiss Brin had surprised her with. Maybe she was in the minority, but kissing someone you'd just met hours before seemed a little... rushed. The memory made her lips tingle, so she pressed them together and shook her head to dislodge the image from her mind.

She stepped through the Brin-sized hole in the door, peeking down the hallway to make sure no one was waiting for her, before creeping into the bathroom and locking the door.

The fact that this was now the only private room in her home had nearly prompted her to fill the tub with blankets and sleep in there.

It was still dark out, she noticed as she glanced through the blinds. She must not have slept very long at all. With her daily routine taken care of, Jun made her way to the kitchen, passing Brin, who sat on the edge of the sectional, watching the Grutex. He didn't look up when she entered the room, but Raou's eyes tracked her as she crossed the floor.

Don't let him intimidate you, Junafer. He already knows he can use you against Brin. Don't give him any more ammunition.

They hadn't had anything to eat since Raou had showed up and Jun's stomach grumbled, protesting the emptiness. He'd liked breakfast, so she decided to stick with what she knew.

She'd given Brin the last of her dried fish, so she pulled out some eggs and sausage. With her diet so limited now, Jun wasn't able to enjoy all of the comfort meals she had in the past.

She opened up the pantry and pulled out the hibiscus tea Amanda had bought for her after hearing that it helped to lower your blood pressure.

Gonna need all the help I can get with that, she mused. Between the smirks and fiery glances from Brin and the incident with Raou, her poor heart was working overtime. She had even found it necessary to take her emergency medicine before lying down.

When the food was finished, Jun divided it up, giving Brin a heaping helping of the eggs he had loved so much.

"Hungry?" she asked, holding the plate out to him as she stepped back into the room.

Without taking his eyes off of the Grutex, Brin reached out to take the food, but he sat it on the cushion next to him untouched.

Jun rolled her eyes, dropping down onto the couch and scooping a forkful of eggs into her mouth. Like Brin's, Raou's wounds were already almost completely healed.

She had looked over the holes Brin made in the exoskeleton, but she had no idea how to go about seeing to them. Creatures with hard shells seemed like they were more suited to Amanda's area of expertise.

"You've been up most of the night," Jun said, glancing at Brin as she finished her food. "Why don't you lie down for a little bit?"

"Yes, bottom dweller, get some rest. I'll keep the little female company," Raou sneered.

Brin's jaw clenched, and she knew he was trying to hold himself back. "I'll take a look at the air system first. This can't be comfortable for you."

"The unit's outside at the back of the house." Jun glanced

toward the window, worrying her bottom lip. She didn't like the idea of him going out alone.

"It's dark enough to provide cover. The repair shouldn't take too much time as long as we don't need to replace any components." Brin stood and traced a finger along her braid. "Don't go near him, Shayfia."

She frowned as she watched him leave. He'd been so distant since she stormed out of the bedroom after his kiss. Jun may not have known him for long at all, but something told her this was out of the ordinary. She didn't exactly hear wedding bells when she looked at him, but Jun wouldn't deny there was something about him that drew her in.

You've known him less than twenty-four hours, she reminded herself. *Brin distancing himself from you shouldn't bother you at all.*

It felt like she had known him for so long, but maybe that was due in part to all of the things that had occurred within the last few hours.

She'd always planned to marry a nice human man and have lots of babies, but now, with her health so bad and the fate of Earth unknown, Jun wasn't sure she would ever have a chance to see those dreams become a reality.

"Did you let him touch you? Did the Venium fuck you?"

Jun turned to Raou with a sneer. "Do you have to be so vile every time you speak?"

The Grutex's eyes roamed over her body, and she barely resisted the urge to cross her arms over herself.

"I was sent for the Venium, but you would be a fine trophy to bring back. I'll take you as a mate."

"I'll pass. I don't plan on being your anything."

Raou's laugh was cold and empty. "Haven't you realized that it doesn't matter what you want, little female? You all belong to the Grutex now. In the end, you will all scream the same."

A shiver of fear worked up her spine, making the hair on her body stand on end. Her stomach twisted into knots as she watched him grin.

People had already begun to assume this. Rumors of a complete takeover by the aliens had been spreading like wildfire lately, and it made her wonder if the Grutex themselves had been the ones to start them.

"What do you do with the humans you take? What's happened to the ones you've already taken?"

"Did you really think I would tell you so easily?" The male laughed. "Come over here, breeder. I'll whisper the answer in your ear if you sit on my lap."

Disgust swept through her, and she tucked herself into the corner of her couch, pulling the gun from its holster and laying it next to her on the cushion. Minutes passed in silence as he watched her and she wondered idly if she had a responsibility to feed him.

What are the rules for hospitality when you've got an alien tied up in your home? Should she offer him something to eat? Did she actually care if he was hungry? If he would have gotten a hold of her, he would have done horrible things to her. *And here you are wondering if you should feed him.*

"Is there something I can do for the wounds?" she asked. "Do I need to wash them out so they don't get infected?"

Raou scoffed. "Infected? The Grutex are not as weak as humans. These small scrapes are nothing to me, but if you really want to tend to them…" A lecherous smile tugged at his mouth. "The offer to sit on my lap still stands."

"*Panget ka,*" Jun mumbled, curling her lip as she got to her feet and marched into the kitchen.

He was ugly, not physically, although she couldn't say she found him very attractive, but everything about his personality disgusted her. Jun propped herself against the side of the refrigerator so that she could still see Raou without having to hear his nasty comments.

There was a soft hum before the blessed sound of her AC kicking on reached her, and when Brin stepped back into the living room, Jun sighed in relief.

"Did he do something?" Brin asked as he stalked toward her.

"Just ran his mouth." Jun shrugged.

"What did he say to you?" He glanced back at the Grutex and snarled.

"It was nothing. Listen," she hissed, tugging him through the doorway into the kitchen. "He said he was sent for the Venium. Either he's looking for Oshen and he's lost, or he's been tracking you."

"Brax…" Brin murmured, scrubbing his hand over his face. "It's not surprising, but we still don't know how many more Grutex will be looking for him." He jerked his head toward Raou, who watched them, a smirk on his lips. "Did he say anything else to you?"

Jun shook her head. "He said we all belonged to the Grutex now, but he wouldn't explain what that meant or what they were planning to do with us once they had us."

"Breeders," Brin said.

"Right." She felt the hairs on the back of her neck stand up. "He asked if I'd let you touch me; if we'd… if we'd had sex." Jun crossed her arms over her chest. "Look, I want lots of babies in the future, but that doesn't mean I want to be forced to *breed* with a Grutex."

Brin's face turned an ashen gray, and his long elf-like ears flattened against the sides of his head.

"I won't let them have you, Shayfia. I promise you." He moved back into the living room, taking up his previous position on the couch.

"I thought you were going to rest."

Brin let his head fall back against the furniture. "I am resting."

Jun rolled her eyes, but didn't argue. If he wanted to spend the entire day staring at Raou, then she'd let him. She kept herself busy cleaning up the mess her alien guests had made during their fight.

Her ruined door stood against the wall in the hallway. If she tossed that out on garbage day, Bridget would be at her door asking questions and just being plain nosy.

The rest of the day passed in relative silence. Brin seemed lost in thought, barely eating any of the food she brought him. The only time he moved from his spot on the couch was when he took Raou into her bathroom to allow the Grutex to relieve himself.

Jun dumped the leftover rice and chicken from dinner onto a plate and walked out into the living room, stopping in front of Raou. "I brought you something to eat."

The Grutex eyed the plate in her hands before curling his lip. "No."

Jun frowned. "Excuse me?"

"I will not degrade my body with whatever foul thing passes for nutrition on your planet."

"You can't be serious." Jun rolled her eyes.

"Let him starve if he wishes to, Shayfia." Brin growled from behind her.

Raou chuffed. "Perhaps you have something else to offer me?" He let his gaze slide down her body. "Come closer, *Shayfia*. Give me a taste."

Brin was off the couch so fast that she barely had time to gasp in surprise as she was lifted off of her feet. One of his muscular arms was wrapped around her waist, his hand splayed across her ribs. With the other, he took the plate she still held, setting it down on the couch before he marched her through the hallway and into her bedroom.

"I don't want you to speak to him anymore."

"Are we really doing this again?" Jun pinched the skin of his arm until he set her on her feet. "You can't just boss me around." Not that she really wanted to interact with Raou any more than she already had, but being told she *couldn't*? That wasn't how she worked. "Use your words, Glowworm. Tell me what the problem is."

"I don't like when he speaks to you or when he looks at you like he's already thinking of all the vile things he's going to do to you if he ever got free."

"Brin…"

"If he ever touched you, I would kill him. Do you understand?"

Jun looked up into his face. There was rage simmering in the bottomless blue depths of his eyes, and his fushori was pulsing in a way she had never seen before. It was like watching the chaser Christmas lights that her neighbors loved to use during the holidays.

"Yes," she said through clenched teeth.

This controlling, demanding attitude was something she found incredibly infuriating. Brin didn't own her. This simply wasn't how it worked. Handsome alien or not, she wasn't going to put up with this much longer.

CHAPTER 8

BRIN

She wanted babies, lots of them.

Of course she wants them, you braxing fool.

Brin wanted to give his mate everything she wished for, wanted to fulfill all of her hopes and dreams, but this one... this one he could not—would not—ever be able to grant her.

The thought of watching Brega try to mold their pup into something as awful and heartless as she was made his stomach turn. His heart ached, but he knew now that he had no choice but to back off entirely.

Unlike other Venium who searched all their lives for their mates, hoping and praying to the goddess that they would find them, Brin would live out the rest of his life knowing his other half was on another planet, creating a family of her own with someone else.

If he shut her out now, looked at her as nothing more than a female who needed his protection, then maybe he could shield his heart from the pain leaving her behind would cause.

Liar.

He ignored the whisper that slid through his mind and turned his attention to the Grutex sitting in the middle of the room. The male hadn't slept at all since he'd been captured and as a result, neither had Brin.

"Are you thinking about the little female, Venium?" Raou waited for a beat. "She is your mate, no?"

The male was trying to get a rise out of him, and if he were honest with himself, it was working. Every time he reacted to Raou's taunts, it gave him exactly what he wanted.

"They will come for me, Venium, and when we are back on the ship, I think I will request to have you present for her claiming." Raou's eyes stayed locked on his.

You can't kill him, Brin reminded himself. *Vog will want to question the male himself. Do. Not. Kill him.* He set the hex to follow and pushed himself to his feet.

"Where are we going now?"

"I'm taking you to relieve yourself."

Raou snorted. "I've already done that more times since you trapped me in here than I can ever remember going in one day."

"Well, it looks like we're aiming to break records today." Brin grumbled as he maneuvered the suspended male until he was sitting on top of the thing Jun had called the toilet.

Standing in the doorway, Brin expanded the outer boundaries of the hex to encompass the entire bathing chamber. If someone got into the room, they wouldn't be able to leave without his approval.

Brin grinned at the disgust on the Grutex's face as he realized he was being left in the chamber and quickly shut the door.

He lay back on the couch and stared up at the ceiling for a few moments before sitting up with a frustrated huff. Jun had asked him to rest, but having the male so close was wreaking havoc on the instincts he was trying so hard to ignore.

Brin turned on the viewscreen and the old gaming system like Jun had shown him and settled down onto the floor.

"*Finish her!*" the disembodied voice in the game demanded as he tapped the buttons to defeat his opponent.

It may have been simplistic and nowhere near the realism of Venium holos, but Brin found himself wrapped up in it. His gaze dropped down to roam over the wooden shelves and he laughed softly to himself.

His little female had been looking to distract him earlier, and just like a pup being given a new toy, Brin had happily let her keep him busy.

Now, with his Shayfia asleep in her bed and their Grutex captive locked away, Brin found himself alone with his thoughts, and that was *never* a good place for him to be.

Her scent clung to everything within her dwelling. It swirled around him, filling his lungs as he drew in a deep breath and let his head fall back. He swore he could still feel the softness of her lips against his, taste the sweetness of her mouth on his tongue, feel her bite.

His brow furrowed as he grimaced at the memory of her blunt teeth sinking into his tongue; of the pleasantly painful pressure. He couldn't remember who had initiated the kiss, but truth be told, he'd wanted his lips on hers more than he'd wanted his next breath.

He felt his kokoras begin to swell again and moaned into the air of the empty room as it pressed against his uniform. If he kept this up, he was going to rub himself raw, and not in any way that was even remotely pleasant.

Jun's angry eyes flashed behind his lids, sending a surge of lust through him that made his kokoras jerk painfully. The sound and feel of the unit's controller cracking in his hand brought his attention back to his surroundings, and he winced as he watched the fragile material crumble onto the floor.

"Brax!" he hissed, clutching at the pieces, trying his best to keep them together as he moved toward the shelves. "Well, there goes the entertainment."

Brin couldn't have slept even if he wanted to. Although the hex holding the male in place was powerful, it wasn't infallible, and he wouldn't risk having Raou get out and get a hold of Jun. He would never risk her.

He got to his feet and walked around the space, eyeing the shark tooth necklace she had told him about before stepping into the room where Jun had prepared their meals.

This area had the most tech, and every single piece of it was outdated. If he gave it a bit of an update, it might help keep him occupied for a while, and she might appreciate being able to use more efficient tech.

"Nyissa, start my work playlist."

"Oh, Master, not even a 'please'?" she tutted. "You know I don't care for being bossed around unless I'm naked."

Brin grinned and shook his head in amusement. He honestly impressed himself at times with the amount of personality he managed to program into the AI systems.

Oshen's had been his most recent update, and he couldn't wait to see how well that had turned out. He was quite fond of sassy females.

"As much as I enjoy opening up your programing, it will have to wait for another time." Brin spotted his first target and pulled out the small pouch that contained his tools. "Nyissa, *please* start my work playlist."

"Of course, Master. Starting *Brin is a Badass*. Would you care for a light show while you work?"

The corner of his mouth twitched, and he sighed. "Why not?"

Brin slipped a small device from one of the zipper pockets on his pants and placed it on the counter. Light shot from the top and spread around the room, changing colors and morphing into a familiar calming scene. The okeanos of his homeworld splashed against Jun's walls as creatures big and small drifted by.

The components humans used were less than ideal, but he'd make them work somehow. Aside from the room used for cooking, his female's dwelling was simple. It lacked many of the things Venium dwellings did, like holos.

When he'd taken Raou to relieve himself the first time, Brin had noticed there wasn't any sort of entertainment in the bathing chamber. Back home, holos were used to aid relaxation after long days. No wonder Jun seemed so stressed.

He kept himself busy, working his way around the room until he had finished everything that could be modified without needing additional parts. Several ure had passed by the time he started on her entertainment unit.

Brin's skin tingled and itched as if there were insects just beneath the surface, and his mind urged him to check on Jun. It seemed like the harder he fought to stay away from her, the more his body and soul ached to shorten the distance.

His initial attraction to her made more sense now that he knew she was his mate, but this constant obsession, the need to be with her and keep his eyes on her at all times? Maybe it was the lack of sleep getting to him.

You know it isn't that, his mind teased. *You know what it is that's making you feel this way.*

Brin sighed, dropping his hand into his lap as he stared at the open unit with its wires hanging from it. Mating pheromones.

They had learned about them as pups, but most Venium never truly felt the brunt of them since hardly anyone fought the pull. He took a deep breath to clear his mind, but her scent was so entrenched in everything around him that he only managed to make the swelling at the base of his kokoras worse.

The pheromones raged through him, and the longer he resisted, the more persistent they would become. The whole purpose was to bring him and his female together, but it was the last thing either of them needed. He had to fight it, didn't he? There was no other way, at least not one that he could see.

Once they were separated, it would be easier, surely. He just needed to make it off the planet and then he could work on putting her behind him. Eventually, he would forget her face, her scent, the way it felt to kiss and hold her.

Brin swallowed thickly and tamped down the denial that formed like a fist in his chest. Goddess help him forget, because he would go slowly insane if he had to live alone with only her memory for the rest of his life.

~

*J*un

*H*er night was anything but peaceful. Each time her thighs rubbed together, it sent a sharp jolt of need racing through her body.

As she tossed and turned, she tried not to remember the way Brin's lips felt against her own. She tried her best to ignore the sensual dreams that plagued her sleep, dreams of being wrapped in Brin's arms and writhing beneath him as he thrust against her.

For so long now, her job had filled up most of her waking moments. It kept her from being completely crushed by the homesickness she felt every single day.

Any spare time she had was spent with Amanda, and the two of them were more apt to spend their evenings stuffing their faces and watching movies than going out and looking for men to cuddle up to.

Now, her best friend was busy with Oshen and she was stuck with an alien of her own. One who made her blood heat, even when she was tempted to slap the smirk right off of his strangely handsome face.

Jun didn't trust aliens as a rule. She had seen far too many times what they were capable of doing to humans, but Amanda trusted Oshen so she would try her best with Brin.

She tried to go back to sleep again, but her bladder was screaming to be relieved. All the water she was being told to drink daily meant she found herself waking up more often at night to use the bathroom.

Pushing herself up from the bed, Jun crept across her floor and out the open doorway, making sure to keep the lights out so she wouldn't blind herself. She always found it so much easier to go back to sleep if she kept them off.

As quietly as she could, Jun turned the knob and slipped into the bathroom, closing the door behind her before she padded across the floor to the toilet.

She tugged her pajama bottoms down her legs and sat down, but the rumbling grunt that sounded behind her and the hard exoskeleton beneath her legs made her eyes widen.

"I thought you'd never take me up on the offer, female."

Jun shot to her feet, one hand yanking her bottoms up while the other wrapped around the nearest object. She wielded the plunger like a bat, bringing it down on top of the Grutex's head over and over as he growled and cursed at her.

What the hell was he doing in here alone with the lights turned off? Where the hell was Brin? She dropped her weapon and lunged for the door, but it wouldn't budge. The sound of her fists beating against the wood echoed in the small room.

"Brin! Get your fishy ass in here! Let me out of here, Glow-worm!" she yelled, trying with all her might to force the door open. "*Brin!*"

There was a loud thud from the other side and she stumbled backward as the door was swung open and a frazzled looking Brin burst into the room.

"Shayfia?"

"Don't Shayfia me!" Jun shouted as she shoved him. "What the hell is he doing in here on my damn toilet?!"

Brin grabbed at her flying hands, looking from her to Raou and frowned, "I didn't think he would bother anyone in here."

"I sat on him, Brin!" She swatted at him as he growled. "How am I supposed to use the bathroom with him sitting there?"

"You sat on him?" Brin froze.

"I look forward to more of that in the future, female," Raou practically purred.

"You braxing son of a—" He started forward, but Jun shoved at him again, catching him off guard.

"I wouldn't have sat on him if you hadn't put him there in the first place!" She slapped his arm, and Brin turned his angry blue gaze on her.

"Will you stop hitting me?"

"No!" Jun shouted.

With a low growl, Brin grabbed her arms and pulled her against his chest, spinning them away from the curious gaze of the Grutex.

"Enough, Shayfia! I'm sorry," he whispered as she scowled up at him. "I'm sorry."

"You should be," she grumbled, feeling her anger dissipating. She grasped at it, wanting to use it as a shield against the things she felt when he held her close or whispered to her. What the hell was wrong with her? She took a deep breath before pulling away. "Could you move him before I pee myself?"

Brin mumbled a hasty apology as he typed in a command on his wrist. She watched in fascination as the massive male was lifted into the air and moved effortlessly out the door. She was left alone to do her business and as she washed her hands Jun stared at herself in the mirror.

"Get your shit together, Junafer," she reprimanded her reflection. "You have no business feeling anything other than annoyance and frustration with that man. He won't stay, and you won't go."

That was that. She scrubbed her hands over her face and stepped out into the hall.

CHAPTER 9

BRIN

*W*hat exactly had he been thinking when he'd set the Grutex on the toilet? He hadn't even taken his mate's needs into consideration. Some time away from the barbed comments had been his only goal, and now he was paying the price for his thoughtlessness.

Brin watched as Jun exited the bathing chamber and followed her into the bedroom, a frown marring his face as he watched her tremble. Some might have mistaken the shaking for fear, but he'd grown up with a female who shook with the intensity of her rage.

"Jun—"

"No, Brin. I want to be alone right now." She dumped a small pill from one of her bottles into her hand before popping it into her mouth and swallowing.

He shifted from one foot to the other as she threw back the blankets, wanting to pull her into his arms and make it better anyway he could.

"I'm sorry, Shayfia. I'm sorry that I didn't take you into consideration."

"Didn't take me into consideration in my own home? Seriously, Brin." Jun turned to glare at him.

"I've never had a m—" Brin slammed his mouth shut and frowned. He couldn't tell her that. "I've only ever needed to worry about myself."

"Obviously," she grumbled.

"You're still shaking."

"You aliens are hell on my blood pressure," she said, slipping beneath the covers before turning her back to him. "Shouldn't you be watching Raou?"

"I wanted to make sure you were okay. He'll be fine for a moment."

"I'm fine," Jun said. "Not thrilled that I put my bare ass on a Grutex in the middle of the night, but I'll live."

The reminder that she had inadvertently exposed herself to the male made his lip twitch with the urge to sneer, but he suppressed it.

"I truly am—"

A loud crash from the main room where he had left Raou interrupted him. He spun around, racing down the short hallway.

The front door had been thrown open, and there was no sign of the massive male. Brin checked the other rooms, but he knew he'd find nothing. Raou was gone, and his female was in even more danger than she had been before.

A soft gasp from the main room drew his attention, and he stepped out of the room where they had eaten the first day to see Jun crouched down next to the fallen table that had held the necklace. She gathered the little objects that had fallen, cursing as she picked up some of the more fragile pieces.

Brin carefully lifted the table, draping the cloth back over it so she could empty her arms.

The shark tooth necklace had fallen out of its box and rested on the floor just beneath the corner of the couch. Using the top and bottom of the small black container, Brin scooped it up.

"I didn't touch it." he told her as he held the box out.

Jun ran her fingers carefully over the top and sighed. "Thank you."

His eyes roamed over the beautifully painted statues, noting that more than one of them had suffered minor damage in the fall, and grimaced.

This was his fault. He'd been careless and hadn't checked the hex after removing Raou from the bathing chamber. If Jun had touched it during their brief interaction, the device might have reset itself without him knowing. The male could have feigned paralysis until he had a chance to escape.

"A warrior leaves no room for mistakes, Ruvator. Mistakes will get you and others killed," he could hear Brega hiss.

The phantom sting of the whip against the skin on his back made him flinch, and he rubbed at his shoulder out of habit. Brega and Tesol had trained him for situations just like this and what had he done the first time he actually needed to draw on the experience? He'd failed.

Brin had endangered not only his life, but the life of his mate. He should have double— no, triple-checked the braxing device before walking away.

He couldn't blame his carelessness on his lack of sleep. How many nights had he been forced to stay awake and alert, to be on guard in case one of his parents came in to check on him?

If they had found him nodding off... Well, he had the scars to remind him to never make that mistake again.

Brin closed the front door and turned to watch Jun run a finger over the jewelry in her hands. "Is there some other place you can go where you'll be safe?" he asked.

"Is there anywhere safe anymore?" Jun swallowed hard before

she sighed. "The only person I'm close enough to who would take me in would be Amanda, and she's already got enough on her plate with this potential mating." She turned her worried gaze on him. "We can't tell her about Raou and we definitely can't lead him to her. He never told us how he found his way here, and I don't want to put her in harm's way."

The next couple ure seemed to crawl by. They checked, double checked, and triple checked the windows and doors, making sure they were as secure as possible. He hated that she lacked any sort of a security system, but he did what he could.

You should have done this the moment you realized you were going to be spending an extended amount of time here, the voice in his head chided.

Brin stepped into the room Jun called her kitchen. She was busy scrubbing the counters and cooking surface for the fourth time in a row. Her brows were drawn together, and she mumbled as she wrung water from her rag.

"Master, you have an incoming ping from Oshen," Nyissa alerted him, pulling him from his observations.

Jun's head whipped around, and she lunged at him, eyes wide with concern as she gripped his arm. "Do not say *anything* to him about this, Brin! Please."

He didn't like the idea of lying to Oshen, but there was no need to alert him to anything right this moment. Brin just needed to keep them all out of danger until they could contact Vog and bring him up to speed on Raou's capture and escape.

Taking a fortifying breath, Brin mentally tugged on his mask, praying to the goddess that it was convincing.

"Where have you been? You look awful." Oshen asked as soon as his face appeared on the display.

"Don't start with me, old man. I've been working day and night to get this braxing signal through. Fine timing, by the way."

The lie fell from his lips as easily as the smirk that tugged at his lips. He hadn't been working on the signal at all since Raou had shown up. Oshen didn't need to hear that this was most likely a ploy used by the Grutex in an attempt to find them.

If by some miracle this wasn't them, then maybe someone on the ship had finally figured out where they had gone and broken through the block. *Please be the latter.*

"I suppose I shouldn't have ever doubted your exemplary skills, Havacker. What was causing it?"

Brin looked over to see Jun watching him with narrowed eyes, daring him to tell their secret. If she were anyone else, he might have done it just to provoke her, but the memory of her fear and anxiety over telling Amanda was fresh in his mind and he'd hurt her enough already.

"What else?" he answered instead. "The Grutex obviously don't want us knowing what they have going on here. They've put up shields that scramble everything. The humans wouldn't be able to reach out for help even if they knew we were here." Something fell behind him, and he turned to see Jun crouch down quickly, picking up the pieces of a shattered plate. "What is your status?"

"My mate is in trouble. One Grutex—"

"Mate?" Brin interrupted, feigning surprise with widened eyes.

His brutok had been waiting years to share this news, and he didn't want to diminish the moment by bragging that he already knew about Amanda because he'd been staying with her best friend. Oshen would know soon enough where he had been.

"I'll explain later. I've sent our location. Brin?"

"Yes, brutok?" He glanced down at his arm as the location flashed in the corner of the screen.

"Don't get us into any trouble."

Brin gasped dramatically. "Me? I'll remind you that this little excursion was *your* idea."

"Noted. Be ready for a confrontation. I have no idea how many are out there."

"You know I'm alway—" But his words cut off as the call ended abruptly.

"Don't even think about telling me to stay here when Amanda is in danger," Jun said as she stepped up to his side. "When do we leave?"

Brin smiled down at her. "I wouldn't dream of defying you, Shayfia."

He couldn't have left her even if he'd wanted to. Raou could return at any moment, and if the male came while he was gone, he had no doubt she would be taken from him.

"We can't tell them about Raou. Nothing about him, okay?" Brin grimaced, but nodded. "From the sound of it, they've got enough on their plates without us adding to it."

Brin took a moment to admire how fierce and protective she looked as she crouched down to strap her weapon to her leg. He hadn't even noticed the holster before. His little mate was full of surprises, and he delighted in discovering each of them.

"Let's hope Bridget isn't sitting with her face pressed to the window. The last thing we need is for the cops to show up looking for you." She turned the light near her front door off before motioning for him to follow her outside. "We'll figure out what's going on there, and then we'll figure out how the hell to stop Raou."

∽

*E*ven with the craft cloaked, Brin recognized the familiar change in pressure as Oshen and Amanda departed. His tail slid up Jun's leg, wrapping comfortingly around her calf as she struggled with her emotions.

Maybe it was the pheromones causing him to imagine things

that weren't actually there, but he swore he could feel the sadness and a sense of loss.

It poured from her, washing over him in waves so strong they threatened to drown him. Brin tugged her closer, tucking her into the crook of his arm, and ran his hand over her braided hair.

He should have been putting space between them, but the instinct to protect and comfort his mate outweighed any logical thought he might have.

There had been no time to speak to Vog about Raou while he'd been on Earth, but perhaps Brin would be able to reach the commander on the ship after he'd spoken with the council.

Oshen finding his mate here was something the elders would demand to know about, and even Vog couldn't put off speaking with them for too long.

Brin and Oshen had defied the orders of their commander to warn humanity, and now that Oshen was gone, it seemed as if it were up to him to finish the job.

He looked down at Jun as she swiped at a tear on her cheek and pretended not to notice the soft sniffle that followed. She sighed as he pulled her back into the shelter of Amanda's dwelling and closed the door, blocking out the soft glow of the moon.

"I don't want to go back home, Brin," Jun said, shuffling over to the couch before plopping down onto the plush cushions.

Brin shook his head and kneeled in front of Jun. "We'll stay here for now," he told her, but he knew they wouldn't be able to hide out too long. The Grutex knew about Amanda's dwelling, but they didn't exactly have very many options at the moment. "We can figure this all out tomorrow, Shayfia. Tonight, we rest and tomorrow we seek out human authorities who can help."

Jun grimaced, and when her eyes settled on his he saw the exhaustion swirling in the deep brown depths. "Tomorrow, we sort it all out."

CHAPTER 10

JUN

Jun pressed the power button on Amanda's TV as the bacon sizzled and popped in the pan. Amanda's house was rarely this quiet and she found herself missing her friend's laughter and Hades' angry yowls as he glared at her from the doorways.

The voices of the local news anchors filled the living room as they reported the weather forecast for the rest of the week.

Rainy and hot, no surprise there.

They'd run back to her house before sunrise to grab her medicine and an overnight bag. Brin's blue gaze had roamed over every dark corner, ever vigilant. By the time they'd made it back to Amanda's, Jun was dead on her feet.

The constant worrying over her friend and everything she had been through with Raou had caught up to her. That night, for the first time since the Grutex had broken into her home, Jun slept without interruption.

No visions of terrifying monsters plagued her as she slept in her friend's bed, and even the more pleasant images of a certain dark, glowing alien warrior were absent from her dreams.

Brin hadn't been in the living room or kitchen when she woke up to use the bathroom, so when her stomach grumbled, Jun had decided to busy herself with breakfast.

Last night, she had wanted nothing more than to run after Amanda, to beg her to stay. They could find a way to keep her safe without having to send her to another planet, couldn't they?

Jun shook her head as she scooped the bacon from the pan. According to Brin, Oshen was the first Venium that they knew of to mate outside of their species. That made Amanda vulnerable, and if the Grutex got a hold of her, there was no telling what they would do.

No, Amanda wasn't safe here, and Jun was starting to feel like she wasn't either. She sighed as she cracked an egg and winced as the grease popped near her hand.

Leaving Earth couldn't be an option for her. It was hard enough having her family living half a world away. The thought of leaving them here to face whatever was to come broke her heart.

Jun didn't even want to think about her work at the hospital and the job that she likely didn't have anymore considering all the days she'd missed.

If she and Brin could take over where Oshen had left off and convince the US government to seek help from the Venium, then maybe this would all work out.

"Take over where he left off? Oshen didn't actually do anything to foster an alliance except mate a human woman," Jun grumbled under her breath.

She hissed as the constant pounding pain in her back worsened momentarily. Despite the fact that she'd been taking her medication and had cut out nearly everything her doctors told her to, Jun's only kidney was continuing to decline.

They had already warned her that dialysis and a transplant wouldn't be far off if they didn't see any improvement, but she'd foolishly hoped the changes to her diet would be enough to put that off for a few years.

Maybe it's best Amanda is gone for this.

"We go now to Trace Archilago, who is outside the District Headquarters in Tampa where Senator Telisa Moore of The One World Council is holding an informal press conference."

"Thanks, Kelly," the reporter said. "Senator Moore is approaching the podium now."

Jun peaked around the corner just as the camera panned away, focusing on the figure standing in front of the doors. She was someone Jun recognized from the local news and papers, but politics wasn't something that interested her too much. She had thick, curly black hair that framed her face and golden brown eyes that stared directly into the camera with fierce determination.

"As most of you are aware, there was alien wreckage recently found floating in the bay and other large pieces washed onto the shore of local beaches. If you know anything about this, I am asking that you report it to my office as soon as possible."

Cameras flashed and a few people in the audience murmured.

"After reviewing the recovered items and speaking with experts in the field, it is my belief that we may have discovered a new species unrelated to the Grutex." The murmurs became huffs and shouts of disbelief, and Senator Moore raised her hand for silence. "These aliens may be willing to help us."

"Or they're here to join in the destruction!" an angry voice called out.

Senator Moore grimaced, nodding slowly. "It's a possibility, but we won't know unless we reach out. Please, any person who brings information forward will remain anonymous. You will be safe."

The number of the district office scrolled along the bottom of the screen, and Jun dug through Amanda's kitchen drawer until she found a pad of sticky notes and a pen. She didn't have her cell phone anymore, but if she could get to a neighbor's or even one of the pay phones outside the gas station, maybe Senator Moore could be their chance to find help.

Brin wouldn't be happy about her going alone to make the call, but taking him with her was far riskier in her eyes. The idea of him being caught and taken captive by government officials twisted her gut and sent a jolt of panic down her spine. He could be subjected to any number of tests and torture in their hands.

No, she couldn't let him leave, but even though they had known one another for such a short amount of time, Jun knew without a doubt that Brin would never let her go alone.

It wasn't that he was controlling or overbearing—okay, maybe just a little bit—but there was something there that she couldn't put her finger on; something that told her she was safe. He wasn't a complete barbarian.

Still, she wouldn't let Brin put himself in danger. No matter how hard he fought her on it, Jun was determined to come out on top. She just needed to find a way to convince him that she could do this alone, that it was the safest route.

Meeting with Senator Moore, talking to her and getting a feel for what she was really about, was the best way to go about this. If, for some reason, the senator turned out to be untrustworthy, at least Brin wouldn't fall into their hands.

Jun couldn't handle the idea that she might be the one to deliver him to his doom.

Why do you care if they take him? You barely know him.

She frowned down at the plates in her hands as she pondered the question. Why did she care?

Because, despite her protests and her prickly attitude toward him sometimes, Jun actually liked him. He was kind, thoughtful, and protective. She even enjoyed his boyish charm and ridiculous sense of humor, but there was something beneath the personality he wore like a costume that intrigued her, and damn if she didn't want to find out what it was.

The hair on the back of her neck stood on end, and she spun around, expecting to come face to face with Raou or some other threat, but instead stared up into Brin's face, watching in fascination as his fushori pulsed that brilliant blue she liked so much.

His arm was outstretched, his fingers nearly touching her face. How long had he been standing there? Goosebumps raced up her arms as his blue gaze locked onto hers. He looked at her as if he knew exactly what she'd been thinking, and she wasn't at all sure she liked how well he read her.

Jun drew in a deep breath, taking in the morning air that drifted through the window she had cracked and a scent that was uniquely Brin.

He smelled like the beach, like waves and sand. He smelled like the salty mist that settled over the palm leaves she passed every morning on her way to the market. He smelled like home.

The sound of grease popping behind her jerked Jun from her thoughts and it was only then that she realized she had leaned into his hand so that the tips of his fingers brushed her cheek. She jerked back, wincing at the emotion in his eyes before the mask came back down and his hands dropped to his side.

"Good morning, Shayfia." Brin grinned down at her.

As odd as his face still was to her, with its lack of a human nose and glowing eyes, not to mention the fangs that peaked out at her when he smiled like that, Jun found that his features were growing on her.

They hadn't seemed to bother her at all when he appeared in her dreams, and the memory of those had her clearing her throat and praying to God that the Venium couldn't actually read minds.

"Good morning yourself, Glowworm," she mumbled, holding the breakfast plate out to him.

The sudden annoyance at his presence surprised her. A minute ago, she'd been waxing poetic over his scent, and now she couldn't get away from him fast enough.

When he'd pulled his hand away, she'd felt a twinge of... hurt? It made no sense. She had no business feeling anything for him, but here she was, getting herself all worked up.

The sooner they figured out how to bring the humans and Venium into contact with one another, the sooner she could try to get back to normal.

Well, not entirely normal, she reminded herself as she glanced around the kitchen. Amanda wasn't coming back. Her friend was off to create a life and family of her own, and Jun had been left behind to sort this all out.

You could go too, her mind whispered, but she clenched her jaw against the joy that thought brought her.

Moving on here would be hard, but Jun was no stranger to difficult situations. She'd started off alone in America once, and she could do it again.

The morning sun filtered in through the spaces between the blinds, leaving Brin's body bathed in the bright light. His dark skin practically shimmered, and her mind filled with images of her hands trailing over his chest, of what it might feel like if she stepped into him and let him wrap her in his arms.

What would it be like to have him lift her up so that they were face to face, looking directly into his eyes? Would she find the secret thing within those blue depths that had made her best friend fall so completely for her alien?

A spark of curiosity glinted in Brin's gaze, and she turned back toward the counter to dig through the silverware drawer, not wanting to give herself away.

You have responsibilities, Junafer. Your family depends on you.

"Something is bothering you, Shayfia. I can see it." The

warmth of his chest was at her back, and it made every hair on her body stand at attention.

"The only thing bothering me is you." She said with a grin as she turned around. "Sit down and eat."

Jun stabbed a fork into the eggs on Brin's plate and stepped around his massive form before taking her seat at the table. She could feel his eyes as he sat down across from her, but she did her very best to keep her gaze fixed firmly on her plate.

They ate in silence and Jun swore she felt the warmth of his demeanor slowly disappearing, turning icy and distant. He was pulling away from her, just like he had done the other night. One minute he was hot, and the next he was as cold as the snow.

Are you not the same? she questioned herself.

Jun risked a glance from beneath her lashes and frowned. Brin looked as lost in thought as she was; his face emotionless as stone. Was she doing the right thing by denying what there was between them? Could she risk it?

No. As much as she loved her best friend, Amanda had let herself be pulled in by her feelings for Oshen, and now it was up to her and Brin to propose an alliance that could change the fate of humanity.

They didn't have time to explore feelings.

This problem—this war—was far bigger than one human woman and whatever she felt for an alien man. Risking humanity for a crush was unthinkable.

And it was a crush, a silly, childish crush. Right? Her knees got weak when he turned her way, her heart sped dangerously when he smiled, and her body shook when he touched her.

And when he'd kissed her that night in her room… God, she hadn't wanted him to stop. She felt like a schoolgirl, watching and waiting for her crush to notice her.

And isn't that your problem? Brin does *notice. He sees you… sometimes,* she amended.

If she hadn't seen the way Oshen had looked at Amanda when she had been here, Jun might have thought she was imagining Brin's interest, but no matter how many times he'd pulled away from her, she still caught that same desire and longing that had been in his brutok's eyes and it gave her pause now.

There had been moments over the last few days when Jun wished she could be like Amanda and just throw herself whole-heartedly into what she was feeling, but she was the logical one. Where Amanda let her heart take the lead, Jun let her head work it all out.

This might be nothing more than admiration. He'd saved her from Raou's attempted abduction, and she'd give him credit for the bathroom rescue, even though that was entirely *his* fault.

She was familiar with Nightingale Syndrome, and had experienced it in her line of work more than once. Patients would become obsessed with the person who had saved their life or who had cared for them during their trauma. It wasn't all that uncommon, but she wouldn't let it happen to them.

"So do the Venium go around rescuing uniformed species often, or is this something new for you?" she asked in an attempt to break the heavy silence.

"We do not."

When he said nothing more, Jun shifted in her chair. "I think I might have an idea on where to start with this… situation."

"Do you?" Brin asked, shoveling a whole slice of bacon into his mouth.

"There was a senator on TV this morning who was asking people to come forward with information on the aliens who crashed. She told everyone at the press conference she thinks we might find allies among them." She raised her brows as she watched him clear his plate. "I'm going to go to her office today and talk to her, make sure she's not a threat before we reveal you—"

"You aren't going alone."

"Well, I would call and ask to speak to her so I don't have to leave, but *someone* broke my phone so that's no longer possible."

"We will go once the sun sets," Brin told her.

"You know it makes more sense for me to go without you," Jun argued, dropping her fork onto her plate and crossing her arms over her chest.

"I am capable of protecting myself should the situation escalate, despite your obvious concerns. I might not be a warrior by trade, but I've been training since the moment I was old enough to walk."

"I never said I doubted your ability to protect yourself—"

"And to protect you," Brin interrupted.

Jun rolled her eyes. "And me. I never said you weren't capable, but if we don't have to put you in a situation where you are forced to resort to fighting your way out, then I think we should at least give it a shot." Brin opened his mouth to protest, but she hurried on. "We might not have weapons that can tear apart the armor of a Grutex, but you're flesh and bone. I don't think even you have protection against bullets."

"Shayfia, it is not your job to protect me." His fushori pulsed, and she watched as the light raced along his body faster than her eyes could track. This topic was upsetting him.

"Honestly, as nice as it is to have someone looking out for my wellbeing, it isn't *your* job to protect *me*, Glowworm."

Brin's gaze narrowed on her face. "Like brax it isn't." He shoved away from the table, looming high above her. "You are *my* responsibility, Shayfia. *Mine*."

He stormed from the dining room but he didn't go far. She found him on the couch, his large frame taking up nearly half of it as he glared at the comm on his wrist. He issued quiet demands to his AI, swiping and scrolling through whatever information the device brought up.

When he excused himself to use the bathroom, Jun knew her moment for escape had come. She darted toward the front door on tiptoes, snagging her keys from the hook on the wall as she slipped her feet into her shoes.

The front door creaked softly, and she cursed under her breath as she spun away, making a mad dash for her car.

Jun turned the engine over and prayed he hadn't heard her as she backed out of the driveway and into the road. Her heart was racing, and she kicked herself for not thinking to grab her medicine bag off the counter before leaving.

Jun tapped the listen icon on the search bar at the bottom of her screen and said, "District Office for Senator Telisa Moore."

The address popped up a moment later, and she selected the first option before adjusting the GPS in the flexible grip of the mount on her dash. It wasn't far from Amanda's house.

The sensation of something smooth gliding over her arm and wrapping around her wrist made Jun jump. She yelped as her car jerked to the side before she straightened the wheel with her free hand.

Half-expecting to see some sort of snake wrapped around her, Jun glanced down and sighed in relief when she saw the dark, glowing tip of Brin's tail.

How the fuck...

"Brin?" Her eyes rose to the rearview mirror just as the alien pulled himself up from the floor of the vehicle. He didn't look the slightest bit amused. "How did you get in here before me?"

"Do you honestly think I didn't expect you to leave the moment you were out of my sight?"

Jun felt herself flounder as she struggled with what to say. Had she really been so obvious?

"It isn't safe for you out here!" she shouted. "You were supposed to be at Amanda's, safely hidden."

"There is no safe place in war, Shayfia."

There weren't many cars on the road at this point, but she grumbled at Brin to stay down as she sped down MacDill toward the office building.

The lot at the back of the small residential-style office was empty aside from a black cargo van, but the sign on the front door told her they hadn't left for the day.

"At least stay hidden in the car until I come out and let you know it's safe to come inside."

Brin rumbled low in his chest, but said, "Fine." He leaned forward, his face stopping inches from hers. His breath drifted over her skin, and she shivered at the memory of his lips on hers and the taste of his tongue, but instead of repeating the action, Brin seemed to think better of it and stuffed himself back down on the floor behind her seat. "Hurry up and be careful."

With a fortifying breath, Jun swung her door open and stepped out onto the black asphalt.

"I should have called," she grumbled when she saw the sign on the back door asking patrons to have their appointment information ready for reception, but it was a little too late for that now.

The building had definitely seen better days, as had the crumbling sidewalk. Jun cursed as the tip of her shoe caught on one of the broken segments. She stumbled forward, catching herself before she went too far.

She craned her neck to peer around the corner of the building to make sure Brin hadn't heard and busted out of her vehicle to save her from herself. She couldn't let him reveal himself too soon.

"You will be safe." That's what Senator Moore said during the press conference and Jun wanted to believe it would be true. She had to believe it would be true.

At the front of the building were two men dressed in black suits. The one to the right of the door had his arms folded over his chest, and he glowered at her as she walked up the small set of steps. She reached for the handle, but jumped back when the man on the left slammed his hand against the glass.

"Do you have an appointment?" he asked.

"Uh, no, but I have information for the senator."

The man on the right grunted as if he had heard that more than once that day. "Right. Go back to wherever you came from, call to make an appointment, and then maybe you can provide your *information*."

"Look, I get that I should have called, but this is about the press conference she held today." Jun looked between the men. "It's about that crash."

The man on the left dropped his hand to the holster on his hip and took a step toward her. "I said, make an appointment."

Jun felt heat rise in her face as she tamped down the anger and frustration bubbling within her. This was her only chance, and these idiots were going to ruin it. The loud rumble of a motor-cycle engine filled her ears, and Jun pressed her fingers into her temples to quell the sudden ache.

"I just need a moment—"

"What's going on here?"

Jun turned at the sound of the feminine voice just in time to see Telisa Moore swinging her leg over the side of the flashy sports bike parked on the side of the road. She had her helmet wedged beneath one arm and was straightening the tight curls that hung around her face and shoulders with her other hand.

"Senator Moore." The man on the right greeted her, reaching for the door as she approached.

This was her shot. "Senator!" Jun launched herself down the stairs toward the other woman. "The crashed ship wasn't from the Grutex." Shouts from the men in black went up behind her, but she ignored them. "I know who they are and they want to help!"

The senator opened her mouth, but one of the men shoved Jun

to the side. "She's crazy." He hissed. "Just like every other nut job we've had to kick out of here today."

"Marco!" Telisa reprimanded. "I specifically asked for people to come forward. I knew we would have to wade through the crazies, but you can't keep turning people away because you don't believe them."

"She's lying." Marco gripped her arm, dragging her away from Telisa, who was still arguing with the other man.

Everything after that happened so fast she could barely keep up. The hand on her arm was suddenly ripped away, and Marco went flying, landing with a thud on the grass not far from where she stood.

Brin moved in front of her, his fushori bright and angry. His body seemed even bigger than she remembered, and he growled low as he wrapped his tail around her leg.

"Do not touch her! Not ever!" he yelled.

"What the fuck!" someone said.

The front door of the office opened, and she saw two more men in black suits run out, guns raised. Large extended barrels aimed at her alien, and she gasped.

Jun wasn't stupid, she could guess what those were loaded with. There had been rumors of a new prototype ammunition that those in charge hoped would be able to repel the Grutex, but from what Jun had heard, they weren't being used to protect ordinary citizens. They were reserved for the rich or the powerful, people in government or just those who were privately wealthy.

Before she could even think about her next move, the sound of weapons discharging filled the air and Brin's massive body jerked as the anti-Grutex rounds pierced his flesh.

All aliens were deemed kill on sight. Even though Brin wasn't Grutex, the rules seemed to still apply to him. She tried to scream, but nothing came from her mouth except for a sob as she watched him drop to his knees before falling to the side.

Blue blood pooled on the ground around her, and she felt herself rush forward, her hands clutching at him as she tried frantically to make sure he was alive.

Assess the damage first, Jun heard the voice in her mind, calm and steady. She was a nurse, damn it. She was trained to work in chaos. Blood seeped from the wounds on his chest and torso.

If these had been regular bullets Jun might not have had as much to worry about, but these had been specially crafted to inflict damage to the armor of the Grutex. They were meant to shatter once inside, spilling deadly toxins into the bloodstream if the rumors of their manufacturing were to be believed.

Brin's limbs shook as he gasped and grunted. His fingers curled around her leg as she pressed her hand against one of the holes, but she knew it was pointless. The many fragments were small, and putting pressure on these wounds did nothing to stop the spread of the toxin.

"Shayfia..." Brin's voice sounded so distant and the look in his eyes sent fear racing through her.

"You didn't stay. You didn't... listen." Tears fell down her face as she clutched at his face with bloodied hands.

"You could have hit her!" someone was yelling, but Jun barely comprehended the words.

Please don't go. Please don't leave me.

Hands wrapped around her arms and waist, pulling her back, taking her away from Brin. His eyes went wide a moment before his whole body went lax. She heard screams, felt the terrible clawing pain in her throat as she fought against whoever was attempting to take her.

Everything that had stopped her from acting on her feelings, every little excuse she had come up with for not letting herself dive in heart-first like Amanda had seemed so insignificant in the face of losing him forever.

Every cell in her body screamed in agony, calling out for him to wake up, to shake off the toxin and come after her. The moment the hulking figure of a Grutex stepped into her vision, Jun's muscles froze in sheer terror. The male lifted her alien's limp body into his arms with hardly any effort and began striding toward her.

Brin was dead, and now she was in more danger than she had ever been in her life.

~

It didn't matter how hard she tugged or how much she twisted her hands, the thin glowing rope around her wrists held fast. The material was far stronger than it looked. Outside the windows of the alien transport, the world passed by in a blur. Jun wasn't sure where they were headed, but she knew it was nowhere good.

She berated herself for not anticipating Brin's response, for not paying close enough attention to her surroundings. Spotting the Grutex crafts would have been nearly impossible with their ability to cloak themselves, but if she would have handled the situation better, maybe she would still have Brin.

The last few days spent with Brin had made her complacent. There was something about him that put her at ease, made her forget that there were real monsters in this world.

She hadn't felt such a sense of safety since she had been with her family, but Brin wasn't here to calm her now. She was on her own, and she needed to be brave for herself now.

The moment they had gotten into the ship, Brin's body had been sealed within a large, cylindrical pod. She wasn't sure what they planned to do with him, but knowing he was still with her in some way was a strange comfort. She missed the comfort his small, often unconscious, touches brought her.

A particularly sharp turn of the transport had Jun landing

roughly on her side against the unforgiving metal of the floor. The air was forced from her lungs, and she gasped at the pain that shot through her.

The Grutex sitting to the right side of the cockpit glanced back, his six red eyes roamed over her as she curled into herself and he spoke quickly to the pilot in a language she didn't understand. What she wouldn't give for a translator like the one Brin had told her about.

"Ack na gru tas la vu," the pilot responded, and his shoulders lifted and dropped in a very human gesture.

The other male's eyes narrowed. "Raw ma tu la pa eskna uroesta lvonu ma." The other male's eyes narrowed on him before they cut back to her and she felt the hairs all over her body stand on end. She didn't like what she saw in his gaze. "Raiskna fumala dikun metu ara stayu."

"I can't understand you, but I'm pretty sure you already know that," she hissed in frustration, but something flitted at the back of her mind.

There was something about this male, something familiar, but with the shock still overwhelming her system, Jun couldn't think straight.

The male chuckled, or rather barked, but she imagined it was akin to a human laughing. "So pretty and full of fire." His eyes moved over her in unconcealed admiration. "I'm going to enjoy the sight of you bent over my *inkei*. Very much." The long tentacle-like protrusions around his face wriggled.

Revulsion rushed through her, threatening to bring up the contents of her stomach, but she sneered at him instead.

"And I'd enjoy cutting off your *maliit na ari*." Jun glared at him, her lip curling. "*Very much.*"

The large male threw his head back and the most sinister laugh she had ever heard filled the small space, sending an icy bolt of fear up her spine.

She stared him down as he stood, crossing the room until he was kneeling in front of her, red eyes locked onto hers.

"You are still so full of fire. I will put in a request to join the chase with you, and perhaps then you will rethink the size of my *dick*."

"Leave her," the pilot rumbled. "The female is not for you, Raou."

"Raou?" Jun stared up at the male as recognition finally dawned on her. The Grutex who had broken into her home. The male who had tried to kidnap her. She opened her mouth, but the sharp sting of something piercing her neck made her gasp in surprise.

Raou stuffed a sleek metallic device in the pouch at his waist and smiled. "Sleep well, female."

Oh, God, he'd drugged her. Jun fought against whatever was coursing through her system, but the conversation in the background began to fade as the darkness closed in.

Remain calm. She couldn't control her situation, but she could try to control her reaction to it. Darkness filled her vision, and she felt her body fall uselessly against the cold, hard floor beneath her.

CHAPTER 11

NUZAL

uzal shifted restlessly against the mattress within his sleeping quarters. Since the day he'd taken the human female from the Kaia's office, something was... off. His plating felt tight and uncomfortable, irritating the soft flesh beneath it.

He had snapped and snarled at nearly everyone who dared to come near him. No matter how much he tried to ignore the emotions the treatment of the humans stirred within him lately, he couldn't find a way to turn them off completely.

They are nothing more than humans, he'd remind himself on more than one occasion, but even as the words filled his mind, he knew he no longer believed them.

He slammed a fist into the pillow before tossing it across the small space. A growl rumbled up his throat as he dressed and made his way into the lab.

If he wasn't going to sleep, he might as well get a jump on his work for the cycle. The doors slid open as he approached, and he wasn't at all surprised to see Erusha at his desk, immersed in his work.

The male glanced up as Nuzal passed his doorway. "Another short rest cycle?"

"Yes." Nuzal opened a file on his wrist comm and swiped it onto the wall, making notes along the inner margins

"Are you feeling all right?"

Nuzal turned toward the male in surprise. Something flashed across his face as they stared at one another. Was it... concern? He supposed he wouldn't know concern even if he saw it.

"What makes you ask such a thing?" he snarled, knowing that showing any sort of weakness would be frowned upon.

Even here in the lab, among males who had never been and would never be warriors, a certain amount of violence and posturing was expected.

The strange look was gone. As if suddenly remembering himself and the position he held, Erusha sneered. "I'm making sure you are fit to handle the new batch. It would be an... inconvenience to replace you now."

"Then it will please you to know I am capable and eager to get started." The cold of the patched metal seeped into the softer underside of his feet, and Nuzal glanced down with a frown. He'd forgotten his boots. Again. No wonder Erusha had felt the need to ask after his health. His supervisor glanced down at his feet, and he shifted. "I think better this way," he mumbled.

All six of Erusha's eyes narrowed in speculation. "Is this something you've only just realized? I don't ever recall your feet needing to be free in order for you to get things done."

"Self-discovery can happen at any time, and the Kaia has been far more demanding recently."

Erusha snorted, but it seemed to have placated him. The older male went back to his work while Nuzal fought the urge to rip the plates from his body. If he didn't pull himself together soon, he was going to find himself being reborn before he was ready.

If they deemed his body unfit or compromised, they wouldn't hesitate to put him back into the rotation. *Maybe you should let them,* he thought. *Maybe next time, your dignity and honor will be restored and you can join the ranks of the warriors once more.* But something inside him balked at the idea.

Nuzal moved to the small gazer on the wall, staring out into the expanse of space. Was this how the humans felt? Trapped and restless with nowhere to run?

The sound of distant engines disengaging in the loading bay shook him from his musings and he tried to build the wall back up around his softened heart, but every time he thought he succeeded, the wall tumbled down, breaking apart, crumbling.

Instead, Nuzal tightened his jaw and tried his best to seem impartial as the doors slid open wide at the end of the corridor. A ground team shoved the floating pods past the rows of cells. Nuzal counted ten pods in all.

One of the males looked a bit banged up, but he'd seen and been in far worse shape during his time.

"I see you came in heavy," Erusha commented as his gaze roamed over the new batch of humans.

"We had a few unexpected additions," the warrior, Raou, said darkly. "More toys for the lab to play with."

Nuzal remembered him from the call in the Kaia's office. He couldn't recall ever serving with the male, but there was something about him Nuzal didn't like, something that felt suspiciously like an old rivalry.

"They were all tested for compatibility?" Erusha asked as he accepted the transfer of documents.

"We know how to do our job," the other male, a pilot, by the looks of the uniform he wore ground out.

"There is a Venium among them," Raou snarled. "A traitor

who broke the truce."

Something akin to joy and excitement flashed across Erusha's face. Nuzal imagined the older male was already thinking of all the possibilities this presented him with.

He moved toward the pod that held the Venium and placed his hand over the information pad on the top. Webs of data transmitters encased his hand, transferring all of the male's known medical data directly into his mind.

"What is this?" Erusha growled, his sharp gaze cutting toward Raou. "You have brought me a broken toy!"

"He was injured by the human males before we took him. I saw no reason to step in before they incapacitated him."

"That should have been the first thing you mentioned, you fool!" Erusha struck out at the male, his claws catching the plate at the side of his face. Three deep wounds scared the armor below one eye to his chin.

Raou stumbled back, but he made no sound nor did he move to clutch the wound. "He has bonded to one of the females," he said before Erusha could strike again. "I know he has."

"Which one?" Erusha demanded, excitement once again replacing his anger. For a moment, the other male only stared as if he was reluctant to give the information up, but he eventually stepped up to one of the other pods.

"This one."

"Nuzal, take the Venium to surgery." The older male slid the pod toward him. "All of the others aside from the bonded female will be placed in cells." Erusha's hand caressed the pod the female was locked in. All six of his eyes rolled up and into the back of his head and he smiled. "Keep her under until the male is cleared. I want to observe their interactions."

Nuzal stared at the pod, wanting nothing more in that moment than to rip his superior away from the female and break open his head against the wall, but he tamped down the madness that raged within him, suppressing the *otherness* that set him apart from his people.

The sides of his head filled with a dull, throbbing pain, but he pushed passed it, reminding himself that he had been born into this career this time and he had a duty to fulfill.

Tapping his fingers against the holo controls, Nuzal set the Venium's destination before turning toward the bonded female. He barked orders to the Grutex who ranked below him to lead the pods away as he followed his charges out of the main corridor.

He would see to these two personally.

The way Erusha had touched the female's pod made Nuzal think his superior already had something planned for the unsuspecting human, and he was going to make sure he was a part of whatever that was.

Cameras monitored the halls of this section, sending information to security concerning every move they made. The warriors broke away, heading back toward the loading bay, but already Nuzal could hear Raou venting his anger on the others in his crew over being marked.

The lights in surgery switched on as they stepped through the doors. Nuzal watched as his small team prepped the chambers and moved the Venium's body onto the flat surface before the healing gel enveloped him.

One of the younger males in his team scanned the body, identifying the six open wounds along the chest and torso. The finished scan was projected over the patient, and Nuzal studied it as he stepped forward.

After coating his arms in the liquid gloves at his side, Nuzal pressed his fingers into the gel, sliding effortlessly through the material until he reached the first wound.

When the more sensitive pads of his fingers made contact with the male's flesh, Nuzal felt a strange heat begin the creep up from his bootless feet. It climbed his legs, trailing its tendrils over the plate that covered his inkei and then higher, over his stomach and chest, until it reached his face.

It was like a soft caress, and it set every nerve ending within him on alert. Something alien and unfamiliar came to life within him, twisting and coiling like the massive storms that brewed on the planet their ship orbited.

Nuzal frowned, shaking his head before taking a deep breath and pushing it all away to focus on the task at hand. There was a decent amount of internal damage from the projectiles that had been used against the Venium.

"Whatever the humans used in the attack seems to have dissolved," he murmured.

"His lifeblood analysis is showing high levels of an unidentified toxin, sir," an assistant informed him.

"Begin the flush cycle and get me a break down of this toxin immediately." His finger swept the inside of the wound. "It seems the humans have been busy. The projectile itself is not meant to kill, but to create a path for this poison."

He knew the recording of this conversation, as with all the recordings taken from surgery, would be sent to the Kaia after inspection. He imagined their leader would be very interested in this latest development.

The more they knew about the advances humanity made, the easier it was to continue their domination of the species.

There was now a steady supply of humans, both male and female, being sent to different outposts all over the galaxy. The thought made the muscle in his jaw tick, but Nuzal resumed his work. Those humans were beyond any help he could offer.

The unexpected challenge of solving the toxin's riddle reminded him of his past lives as a warrior. In those days, there were many more unconquered planets and species, and each new world brought a new set of threats.

So many of them had come filled with poisonous or

venomous plants and animals. That work had once been exhilarating and important to him, but now, looking back, he recognized the emptiness of it all. The Grutex existed until they were no longer able to serve their purpose and then they were rebirthed. He had been made new again so many times that he no longer remembered his start, the very beginning of his story.

His entire existence had brought him to this moment, to this incarnation of who he had once been and what did he have to show for it? Nothing.

He spent his waking hours struggling to help his species mate despite the fact that they had gone generation after generation without the need for their females. There was more to it than met the eye, he knew this, but what it was exactly he might never know.

No matter how far up the ladder he climbed, no matter how far he advanced, Nuzal was still in the dark. He wanted more information on why they wanted to breed now, wanted to know why, after all this time, the incubators were not good enough.

Most importantly, he wanted to understand the new things he was feeling.

Nuzal was unhappy with what had been given to him this time around, something he had never been faced with before, but to voice that would be... unwise.

He knew the consequences of failure, of questioning the system and the orders handed down to him. The thought of losing his privilege to be rebirthed sent a chill down his spine.

Once the open wounds on the Venium's chest had been sealed, they injected the formula to counteract the human toxin and waited to see how the male's body would react.

Nuzal grinned in satisfaction when his vitals began to stabilize. With the surgery deemed a success, Nuzal removed his gloves and left the clean up to the rest of his team.

He found Erusha in his office combing over the medical

reports sent over from the monitors and scanners within the cells. "The Venium?" he asked, not bothering to look up.

"Surgery went well and was successful."

"Good."

Nuzal stepped further into the office. "The human toxin is something we have not encountered before. A counteracting formula produced during the procedure seems to have worked against it, but the male will continue to be monitored until he is stable enough to be brought out of cryosleep."

Erusha nodded. "Wonderful. Make sure the Kaia receives word of the toxin."

"Already done."

"He will want to equip the warriors with the antitoxin." His superior glanced up with a grin. "Although I personally think letting them suffer a little might do them some good."

"After meeting the warrior Raou, I would agree," Nuzal said. "What are we to do with the bonded pair?"

"Separate them for now. Let's see if we can't get the female to come into this willingly. Experiments are always less stressful on their bodies if they are cooperative." Erusha's eyes glinted with excitement. "We will begin the awakening of her DNA as soon as possible."

He'd done the procedure more times than he could count, but the idea of awakening her DNA, of preparing her body down to the very last cell to carry Grutex young, sent a thrill through him.

Nuzal wondered idly, not for the first time, if this new breeding was meant to cure the mutations within his species. Feeling bold and running off of the fumes of his successful surgery, Nuzal decided to do something he had never done before.

"What is this all for—the breeding?" Erusha looked up at him. "We have the incubators already."

"The incubators can only rebirth those of us already in existence. They cannot produce *new* offspring." Erusha sat back in his chair, his eyes locked on Nuzal's. "Perfection comes at a high price, and many of us are paying it."

Nuzal opened his mouth to ask what he meant by that, but his wrist comm flashed with a message alerting him that the bonded pair was ready for transport. Erusha's words made him uneasy. They turned his stomach and set his mind racing.

His team brought the pods the pair rested in out into the corridor, and he nodded as he stepped out of his superior's office. A cell had been cleared for the male and Nuzal instructed the team to place the bonded female into the neighboring cell with the darker human she had been brought in with.

If the bonded chose not to cooperate, she would be able to bear witness to the Venium's punishment. He watched as the male was placed into the forcefield, his arms and legs extended and spread slightly. They didn't need him fighting and putting up a struggle when he saw her.

Nuzal checked in on the female, growling at the young male who handled her. "Gentle!"

She was placed on the floor of the cell, her dark black hair spread around her head like a halo. The other female crawled out of the corner, glaring at them as she pulled the bonded one into her lap.

He stood there for a moment, his eyes roaming over the softly bronzed skin her attire allowed him to see and the smooth features of her face. What color were her eyes? Were they just as dark and enticing as the rest of her? What would he see when she opened her eyes?

Horror. Fear. The same thing you see in all of their eyes when they look at you.

Nuzal stepped back, activating the cell door so that it sealed them inside. He turned on his bare heel and made his way back to his sleeping quarters. This next cycle was important. This next cycle marked the beginning of new discoveries.

CHAPTER 12

JUN

"Place her in there with the other female," a deep voice swirled around the inside of her muddled mind, bouncing around and creating a sickening echo.

Jun was cradled by something soft and warm. She wanted to curl into it and let it pull her back under, but the sudden rush of cooler air against her skin made her shiver.

Her arms and legs refused to respond to her commands, and her eyes felt as if they had been glued shut. Where the hell was she? Was she at the hospital? Had she passed out at work?

No, that wasn't it. She hadn't been to work for days. The cold, unmistakable feel of metal pressed into her sore muscles as she was lowered onto something—a table or a floor if she had to guess. What had she been doing before the darkness? Where had she been?

An image of the office swam into her vision, of the crumbling sage green exterior and then men in black suits yelling. Visions of Brin falling...

"Brin!"

Her eyes flew open as her body jolted upright. The ache behind her eyes made even the dim lights within the unfamiliar room nearly unbearable, but she searched frantically for the male. Was he dead? What had they done with him?

There was a thin mattress at her back, and Jun crawled onto it, taking a moment to catch her breath and figure out her surroundings. On the opposite side of the small room was a similar mattress with a curled-up form. Jun recognized the bright pantsuit and the disheveled black curls.

The gentle rise and fall of the woman's sides told Jun she was still alive. She crawled across the floor, her legs still too weak to support her, before placing a hand on her shoulder and shaking her.

Normally she might feel bad for disturbing someone's rest, but this wasn't exactly a normal situation they found themselves in.

"Senator?" Jun whispered, hoping she could hear her over the steady hum that filled the air. "Senator Moore?"

The senator's body turned, and red-rimmed honey brown eyes stared back at her. She wiped a tear from her cheek before pushing herself up into a sitting position.

"It's just Telisa. I don't think my political office means anything here." She looked around the room as if she was reorienting herself. "I guess whatever they gave you finally wore off."

There were no noises from outside, no cries, no conversations, no footsteps. The only thing she could hear was the humming. She shouldn't be here. The Grutex wanted healthy, fit men and women, and Jun was as far from healthy as you could get without being dead.

Hadn't they scanned them? Didn't they know her body was slowly failing? What would happen to her when they found out?

Without her medications, Jun wasn't sure how much longer she could make it.

"Telisa." Jun placed her hand on the woman's hand to get her attention. "I'm Jun. Do you know where we are?"

The senator shivered, and she shook her head.

"The Grutex took us, came out of nowhere. There was no time to even defend ourselves." Her throat worked as she looked at Jun. "I was in here when I woke up, all alone in this cell. There were others, so many of them all around me. We have to get out of her. These monsters... they're doing things here. They're doing horrible things to people."

"What are they doing? What did you see?"

She shook her head and pressed her lips together. "You'll see..." she finally muttered.

Well, that wasn't entirely helpful, but she could see that the shock of whatever it was hadn't worn off. "Do you know how long we've been here?"

"I can't tell time in here. It couldn't have been more than a couple hours before they brought you in and laid you on the bed. I slept some, but you kept tossing and turning, talking about someone. You threw yourself onto the floor at some point, and when I got up to help you, I saw them bringing the other girl in." Fear stole her breath for a moment, and Jun watched the panic return to her eyes. "I saw her, but... I must have been dreaming. They had—" A sob burst from her lips. "It was like a nightmare..."

"What was?" Jun asked just as the sound of heavy footsteps began to echo down the hall outside the front of the cell.

Pained moans were barely distinguishable over the hum, but it sent a shiver down her spine all the same. Two Grutex stepped into view, a human woman held between them as they dragged her on the ground.

Jun frowned, scooting closer to the front. Her eyes widened when she saw the soft shimmer of scales that covered the woman's back and sides, trailing over her shoulders and the backs of her thighs. No longer completely human. The Grutex were testing on them.

This was so much worse than Raou had made it sound. They weren't just trying to breed them here; they were *changing* them.

"Have you tried to escape?" Jun asked, moving back toward Telisa as the Grutex passed.

"No," Telisa shook her head, making her tangled hair bounce around her face. "They're watching." Her chin jutted up toward the wall outside, where a small black device flashed. "I'm positive those are cameras."

Jun worried her lip between her teeth as she tried to think. They couldn't run out there half-cocked with no plan or weapons to defend themselves.

Outside their cell, Jun could see other humans, each one in a cell just like the one she and Telisa shared. She had overlooked them in her confusion.

Most of them were curled up on the thin mattresses or huddled together in corners. They looked filthy and malnourished.

"There has to be some way—" She turned to her right and the words caught in her throat as she gasped. "Brin!"

His body hung in the air, suspended within something she imagined was similar to the device he had used against Raou.

His head was lolled to the side, and the blue blood that had spilled from him after the attack still clung to his skin. Before she could think better of it, her feet were carrying her across the floor toward him.

"Wait!" Telisa gasped.

Jun stumbled, stopping as the hum in the air became louder. Something just in front of her caught her eye. In the space between them, something shimmered, a soft sheen of light that she hadn't noticed before.

With the backs on her fingers, Jun tested the forcefield

cautiously. She'd seen far too many unlucky electricians in the ER, and with the way her hair stood at attention as she approached, she was wary. The moment her hand came into contact with it, she yelped, jerking backward at the jolt it had delivered.

She hissed, rubbing at the spot and cursing herself for a fool. The last time she'd been shocked like that was when she was a child. She hadn't thought to make sure the lamp she was fixing was unplugged and stuck her finger into the socket. God, had she regretted that one.

It was obvious they didn't want her getting to Brin, and she imagined it would be the same if she tried to walk out the front.

Her heart raced in her chest, and she closed her eyes, trying to control her breathing as she willed the pounding in her ears to cease. She couldn't risk that again. Her heart was in no condition to take that.

At her clumsy touch, all of the walls around her had glowed blue. They pulsed, reminding her of Brin's fushori, before becoming transparent once more.

Well, they certainly weren't getting out that way. When the Grutex put you in a cell, they didn't leave any room for escape. A soft whimper behind her pulled her from her thoughts.

Telisa was staring wide-eyed at the walls as tears streamed down her face.

"We won't ever get out of here, will we?" Her breath hitched. "The only way we get out is when they come for us. They'll come for us the same way they came for the others!"

"Stop," Jun hissed, moving to her side and wrapping her in a tight hug. "This isn't it. We don't give up just yet. Brin will wake up, and when he does, we can figure something out. He's great with technology." She closed her eyes, smiling as she remembered the improvements to her home. "We'll find a way."

Her words were meant to soothe, but Telisa only cried harder into her chest. Honestly, if she didn't have Telisa with her, Jun probably would have broken down in tears of her own.

The senator was giving her the perfect distraction, someone to care for. God knew she wanted to let the panic and fear take over, but what good would it do for both of them to break down now?

She had once thought Florida was light years away from the Philippines, but she was so much farther from her family than she had ever thought possible. She might never see them again, might never get the chance to tell them she loved them again or that she was sorry for not telling them about her illness.

She'd been so worried they would panic and try to bring her back home, that they would tell her to forget her dreams and return so that they could care for her. Looking back on it, would that have been so awful?

Tears threatened at the corners of her eyes and Jun redirected her thoughts away from the things she couldn't change.

Her papa had been a police officer when she was growing up, and she would have sworn the man feared nothing, but he'd shared with her once that he was afraid every single night he left them at home that it might be the last time he saw them.

"Life is unpredictable. Sometimes you have no choice except to set aside the fear and take the gamble. You live whether you win or lose, so make it worth it."

He'd taught her how to handle a gun, how to hunt with a bow, and how to take a gamble. She might be one small person, but sometimes, that's all it took to start a revolution.

Jun's fingers brushed over Telisa's curls as she trembled. She looked around the barren cell, grimacing at the utter lack of anything useful.

When the other woman fell into a restless sleep, Jun stood and paced the floor. A curse dirty enough to make her papa blush flew from her mouth when her foot caught on a raised portion of the floor.

She turned back, glaring at the edge of the panel before it dawned on her that this might be useful.

The metal was thin, but strong. There were small screws of some sort in each corner of the panel, and she tried her best to use the tip of her nail to loosen one of them. If she was successful, who knew what she might find? Wiring that could disable the forcefield or maybe even some sort of maintenance shaft. Okay, maybe she had watched too many of Amanda's sci-fi movies, but she didn't have any other options.

If Brin woke up, he might be able to help her figure out what to make of her findings.

They would find a way to get through this. Life certainly was unpredictable, but that didn't mean it was against her. The Grutex had no idea how resilient humanity was.

History was full of people who had gambled with their lives, and she was willing to risk it all to see her people set free.

CHAPTER 13

BRIN

he sounds of crying and sniffling nagged at the edges of his dazed mind as he tried to fight his way to consciousness. It was like swimming through a thick black okeanos. Inky waves lapped at his limbs, threatening to pull him back, but he focused on the noise.

"Keep it up," he heard a voice whisper. "Louder. Do you think you can sound a little sadder?"

Memories of long, drawn-out arguments over him. Brega never had liked the fact that Nyissa, Oshen's dam, stood up to her.

She never backed down from the warrior's harsh words and volatile temper, but once she was back in the privacy of her home, the female often let loose what she always called "angry tears" over the way Brega treated him.

"How could any dam ever treat her pup so poorly?" he had heard her ask Calder once after a particularly bad fight. *"He deserves love, Cal. So much love."*

He hadn't known how to show Nyissa how much her love had

121

saved him. The female may not have carried and birthed him, but she had loved and protected him his whole life. She had fought fang and claw for the terrified pup he had once been. She was and would always be his Daya.

These cries though... Brin grimaced as he strained to listen. No, these weren't Nyissa's.

"I know it seems hopeless, but if you keep crying, they'll come back. We can't do anything to draw their attention." The voice was louder this time as if whoever it was *wanted* to be heard.

Shayfia?

"I want to go home!" another voice demanded.

Brin willed his eyes to open even as the darkness tried to overtake him. His need to see Jun, to know she was alright, was stronger.

He managed to lift the heavy lids and peered around. Nothing from his neck down responded to his commands. Brin knew this tech; it was similar to the hex he kept on him, the one he'd used to immobilize Raou.

It was like being caught in the vise-like grip of the plokami, a large creature from his homeworld who lived within the okeanos and restrained its prey with its powerful tentacles.

The room he found himself in was small, but open on all sides. The last thing he remembered was being shot by the human males and then watching helplessly as the Grutex carried his mate away.

"Jun?" Her name was barely recognizable to his own ears. He swallowed hard and tried again. "Jun!"

There was another cell in front of him, and a pair of dirty, underfed humans turned toward him with wide, curious eyes.

The floors and what walls he could see were made of a black metal similar to adamantine, the metal the Venium favored for all of their crafts and off-world structures.

A well-built forcefield separated the cells, and from the hum he could hear, Brin knew touching it would deliver a nasty little shock.

He had come across the types of cells during his travels, but had never seen them used on the ships of their allies. If he were honest, the Grutex had always been more foe than friend.

A prickle of panic slid across the back of his neck as he imagined all of the terrible things they could inflict upon her. Raou's words taunted him, making his heart race.

"Brin?" Jun stepped into his field of vision, off to his left, and relief swept through him. "I'm right here."

The tightness that had clutched at his chest moments ago released, and he wished, not for the first time since meeting her, that he could wrap her up in his arms and hold her to him. He would have given anything at that moment to be free, not just physically, but mentally. He wanted to tell her she was his mate, the most important being in his world.

Brin wanted to be free to give her everything she wanted: the children, the home, the family she deserved. But even if they escaped this, Brin would never be free to offer the things she dreamed of.

"Are you okay? Have they hurt you?" He fought to clench his fist, to pull free, but it was no use.

Jun shook her head, her eyes roaming his chest. "I'm fine. No one has hurt us." Her tongue swept over her lips as she narrowed her gaze, distracting him for a moment. "You can't even tell."

"Can't tell what?" he asked.

Jun thrust her chin toward him. "That you were shot six times. They're gone. Completely healed."

He remembered the pain of his flesh tearing as the human projectiles burrowed into him, and the gut-wrenching fear of his mind slowly slipping into the darkness as his mate screamed for him.

"The Venium are quick healers, remember?" he reminded her, but something told him he had some outside help this time.

"God, I wish we could bottle that," she murmured. "Are you okay?"

"I can't move anything below my neck, but I think I'll live. Do you know where we were taken?"

Jun shrugged, stepping close enough to the forcefield to give him anxiety. "Telisa said we're on one of the Grutex's ships, but neither of us has any idea where exactly that is."

She glanced behind her to a spot he couldn't see, but the soft weeping resumed.

"How long have I been unconscious?"

"I have no idea." She sucked her bottom lip between her teeth as her shoulders rose and fell. "I woke up not too long ago, and Telisa thinks she was only here a couple hours before they brought us in."

Her arms wrapped around her midsection as if she were trying to hold herself together, and he caught a glimpse of her red, swollen fingers.

The sharp, tangy scent of her lifeblood reached him as he inhaled desperately, tasting it on the air. His whole body tensed involuntarily.

Mine. My mate.

"Who hurt you? They touched you!" he growled.

"No one touched me, Brin," Jun said, looking down at her fingers. "I managed to do this to myself."

He needed to find a way to get her out of here before they realized what they had. If the Grutex put their hands on her, if they harmed her in any way, Brin wasn't sure what he would do.

His muscles ached from the lack of movement, but his brain blocked it out. Brega put him through far worse as a pup during her training sessions. All he needed was a way out...

A Havacker being held captive by tech. The irony of the situation was not lost on him.

Brin cursed his immobilization and the fact that he didn't have any of his tools on him. Despite the way they looked, most of the Grutex weren't stupid.

The tools in his clothing would have been the first things to go after his capture. A thought occurred to him, and he sent up a prayer to the goddess that they hadn't considered it.

"Nyissa?" he whispered.

There was a short pause, but the sound of her voice made him smile. "Yes, Master?" she whispered back.

They obviously hadn't thought to disable his AI. "Can you sweep my bindings for any weakness and run a check on security?"

"Security on the ship is... formidable. Getting through will take time."

"And the bonds?" Brin asked.

"I won't be able to touch those until I can bypass security."

He'd figured as much. While they waited on Nyissa to work her magic, Brin watched Jun pace in her cell, stopping only to check on Telisa, the senator she'd snuck out of her dwelling to speak to. The crying had stopped, but Brin caught a sniffle every now and then.

Jun stepped up to the forcefield that separated them and held her hand up like she was going to touch it. "Don't," he warned her. "It's—"

"Electrified? Yeah, I figured that out already, Glowworm." She grimaced, rubbing a spot on the back of her fingers.

The nickname brought a smile to his lips. When she settled on the floor, Brin craned his neck as far as he could to get a look. One of the panels in their cell was lifted a fraction, and she worked her nails between the edges, trying her best to pry it up.

"What are you doing?" he whispered.

"Mostly just hoping whatever I find under here is worth the scrapes and broken nails," she muttered. "I figured, if I'm lucky, there might be some sort of wiring I can get access to. You're Mr. Tech, so I was thinking you might be able to use it to get us out of here."

His mate was something else. She didn't cower in a corner, waiting to be rescued. No, his shayfia took her fate into her own hands and worked with what she was given.

Out of every female in the galaxy, the gods had selected him for her, and he couldn't have been more humbled by their decision.

Hours seemed to pass in silence, with nothing but Telisa's sniffles and the rustling sounds of the other captives to break it up. By that point, it was getting progressively harder to ignore the burn in his limbs, and his mind was demanding he move already, even just the tiniest bit. Heavy footsteps echoed down the hall.

"Shayfia!" he hissed, hoping she heard them as well and covered her work.

She scurried back to the mattress at the opposite end of the cell and he heard the crying begin again, this time a little louder for show. If the Grutex thought the females were fearful, perhaps it would keep them from noticing the panel.

"You're awake," a deep, familiar voice spoke from the front of the cell, and Brin turned to see Raou. His armor was still chipped on his chest, and he seemed to have acquired three more scars across his face in the time they had been apart.

He'd suspected the male would have been eager to capture him after his time in the hex, but he was surprised to find him still on the ship.

From the intel the Venium had on the Grutex, they kept a very rigid system, and warriors were most often kept on the ground or stationed nearby with their teams, ready to deploy at a moment's notice.

This ship didn't seem like any of the ones they kept in rotation, but he hadn't been inside enough of them to be able to tell for sure.

"Get kicked off the ground team? I suppose being captured didn't look very good on your record," Brin said coolly.

Raou grinned, and his eyes strayed into the other cell, roaming over Jun's huddled form.

"Actually, I requested to stay. A lovely opportunity may be opening up for me soon."

The thinly veiled threat was clear. Raou wanted Jun. He'd said as much doing his time in her dwelling, but Brin would die before he'd let the male get close enough to make good on it.

At his earliest opportunity, Brin was going to pluck each of his six eyes from their sockets and force them down his throat until he choked on them.

Jun was *his* mate and he was the only one who would ever touch her.

Raou didn't deserve to look at her like she was something to savor. He didn't deserve to touch her, or even breathe the same air as her.

Make him suffer.

Raou's gaze slid back to his, and he chuckled darkly before raising his arm and sliding his palm along the outside of the cell.

Whatever was there triggered the bonds to release him, and he fell onto the hard metal of the floor. His knees took the brunt of his weight and he groaned as pain sliced through his hips and up his back. Every joint ached, and the prickle in his muscles from the lifeblood rushing back into his limbs stung.

His head swam as he tried to right himself, falling forward onto his hands. Everything doubled as he looked up, watching the male pull a tray from the hovering cart at his back.

He pushed the food through the barrier, and Brin lurched toward him, swiping at both of the hands as his brain tried to figure out which was the solid one, but Raou must have been expecting it. He dropped the tray onto the ground, jerking his limb back through the forcefield.

"A valiant attempt, Venium, but you're in my territory this time." Raou continued on down the corridor, stopping at Jun's cell to slide two trays along the floor.

Brin stared at the meager meal: a nutrition brick and a water pod. It wasn't the worst thing he'd ever had, but his mouth felt dry just from looking at it.

With little thought, he shoved the brick into his mouth, softening it with sips of the water. If they were going to break themselves out, they would need to fuel their bodies. Sooner or later, Brin was going to be free, and Raou would pay with his life.

CHAPTER 14

NUZAL

*N*uzal grunted, his muscles shaking as he pushed through his morning workout. It was a habit left over from his days as a warrior, a routine so ingrained within him during a past life that even now he continued it.

When he'd physically exhausted himself, Nuzal stepped off of the track and jogged into the cleansing room, inhaling the hot, steamy air. He let the water run down his plating, groaning as it heated the sore muscles beneath.

It was something he did every day cycle, and yet something felt off. It had felt that way ever since the bonded pair had been brought into the lab.

Although he had felt sympathy for the humans in his care from time to time, he had never been so consumed by one of them. Not even the little light-haired female he had removed from the Kaia's office had stayed in his mind for this long.

He closed his eyes and let himself imagine the bonded female there with him, water trickling down over her golden brown skin and her hair as black as the endless void of space. What would it be like to reach out and touch her?

She would be soft, like the others, but Nuzal knew there would be… something different. The thought made him shudder, but he wasn't entirely sure whether it was in disgust or need.

There was something about this female that had drawn his interest, and like a beast sighting his prey, Nuzal couldn't shake the urge to hunt; to know everything he could about her and this male she had bound herself to.

It's a new project, he told himself. *Some obsession is to be expected.* After all, this was the first Venium-human bonding they had ever seen. The information they gathered from them could be useful.

With his morning routine completed, Nuzal dressed and headed toward the lab, giving his feet a quick glance to make sure he was, in fact, wearing his boots this time. He didn't need Erusha's lectures or questioning gaze falling on him today.

There was a quickness to his step that surprised even him. While Nuzal was good at what he did, top of his class, in fact, he hadn't ever felt *excitement* over starting his day. He made sure his speed was the only indication of his interest in the day's work. Unlike Erusha and many of the other males he worked with, Nuzal never revealed his feelings.

Until recently…

Although he'd intended to go to the lab, Nuzal found himself at the entrance of the holding cells. Raou was standing in the night guard's nook, his red eyes watching as the doors slid open to allow Nuzal entry.

The scratches on his cheek from Erusha's outburst had already healed, leaving behind a pink scar. This was nothing new. Most of the warriors carried these as proof of their bravery in battle, but only a few would know this was a mark of shame and failure.

Unless the younger males who had witnessed his punishment

wanted to challenge the male, they would keep their mouths shut and go along with whatever lie he made up about it.

Nuzal might have questioned why Raou was still aboard the ship were it not for the obsession he too seemed to have with the bonded human. He'd seen the way he watched her; it made his lifeblood heat and muscles tense with the anticipation of a fight.

That instinctual urge to dispose of a competitor was wasted on him, anyway. Nuzal would never be considered a suitable mate; not in this lifetime.

"Will you be working with the bonded human today?" Raou asked.

Nuzal nodded, moving past the male as he continued down the corridor.

"She is compatible with the Venium male, yes?"

"If she is *bonded* to him, then I would assume so," Nuzal ground out, already annoyed at the intrusion into his work.

"It's unheard of," Raou continued. "A mating between a Venium and any other species has never occurred."

Nuzal shrugged. "As far as we know, but I'm sure there are things they do not share with us; things they do not wish us to know about them."

"Yes, but what is it about this female that makes her so... unique?"

"Perhaps she isn't unique. Perhaps she is only the first of many to respond to the species, but we won't know that until we begin our testing." Nuzal rounded the corner with the warrior hot on his heels. "Her DNA will tell us if she is descended from the first experiments."

Raou's eyes widened with interest, and Nuzal wished he had kept his mouth shut.

"Outside DNA? You think she may be compatible because she isn't completely human?"

"It may be a possibility. I wasn't in the lab during those experiments, but I've read the reports. They used a wide variety of DNA samples."

Nuzal had poured over them after leaving the female last night cycle. Pages of notes, files filled with documentation of just how many species they had attempted to recreate. The scale of their efforts had shocked him. The Kaia at that time had ordered them to capture human women already carrying offspring so that they could insert foreign DNA into the already developing fetus.

The goal hadn't been to change them completely, but to alter them just enough that they could pass down desired qualities from their donors. *Trial and error.*

The humans taken in those early tests had gone back to tell their abduction stories, but they had been ridiculed. For generations, the Grutex brought males and females on board, altering their genetics, changing the very essence of what made humans human. The fact that their families, friends, and even their governments decided to ignore them had worked in the Grutex's favor.

Every birth was recorded, and included photos and exact locations of where the successful experiments had been released back into the human population. One could fault the Grutex for a lot of things, but they were meticulous recordkeepers.

The majority of the offspring modified during the experiments were born with the desired human physical traits, but for those born with the traits of their donors—tails, horns, claws, fur, extra limbs—they were disposed of.

Something akin to sadness had come over him as he read the files of those "failures." They couldn't allow them to return to Earth and risk others in the galaxy finding out exactly what they were doing to this primitive species. Especially the Venium.

Their fragile alliance rested on a razor-thin edge, and the exploitation of the humans would have surely pushed it over. The current Kaia no longer saw fit to cover up their deeds. The Grutex, he believed, didn't need allies.

"Do you believe she will be able to breed successfully?" Raou asked as they neared her cell.

Nuzal didn't even register the movement of his body until he was staring into the other male's eyes, his clawed hand wrapped around his throat as he slammed him into one of the stark white walls between the cells.

A grunt of surprise left Raou's mouth, and his hands instinctively clutched at Nuzal's as he increased the pressure. The shock of the attack lasted only a moment before the warrior began to struggle, fighting against his hold. Raou slammed his forearm down onto Nuzal's inner elbow, loosening his grip just enough for the warrior to drop down and slip free.

Nuzal's body, though noticeably out of practice, instinctively blocked each blow from the younger male, and he even managed to land a few sloppy jabs of his own.

The loud clearing of a throat brought them both to a halt, and Nuzal turned to see an amused Erusha standing next to a decidedly less than amused Kaia. He righted himself immediately, straightening his clothing and stepping away from Raou.

"What kind of warrior allows himself to be overtaken by an imperfect specimen?" The Kaia's voice was low and cold as he fixed his gaze on Raou. "Perhaps I should have you sent back to training to refresh your skills?" The cruel smile that tugged at his mouth caused the plates that covered his cheeks to creak eerily.

"There is no need for that, sir. I was merely refraining from injuring the scientist. I would hate to delay any of our advancements by taking one of these... *genetic failures* out of the rotation."

The verbal swipe hit its mark, and Nuzal balled his fists and gritted his teeth against the urge to crack the male's skull open against the wall. He knew Raou was pushing him, trying his best to get under his plates.

The male was deferring, trying to hide his own shame at being bested in front of their leader. Nuzal had spent countless lifetimes as a warrior, and this little scuffle had shown him that this body could respond just as easily as every other form he had taken.

"It is a shame this rebirth cycle saw you unfit for warrior training," the Kaia said as he glanced toward Nuzal. "We lost a great male, a decorated and honored warrior. You could have taught this embarrassment a thing or two about a *true* warrior's character."

Raou bristled beside him, but Erusha, perhaps sensing the rising tension, spoke up. "If I might, Kaia." He gestured toward the cell where the dark females sat huddled together in the back corner. "This one, with the long hair, is the human female I spoke of earlier."

"The one bonded to the Venium?"

Erusha nodded. "Yes, sir. We will be drawing a lifeblood sample from her so we can start the process of isolating the gene that has allowed the bond to form."

One of the lab assistants, a young male still in training, stepped forward with a tray. The Venium took one look at the instruments and threw himself against the forcefield, growling and snarling. His body shuddered as the electricity pulsed through him, and he stumbled backward, only to throw himself against it once more.

Had the injuries he received from the human weapons caused him to lose his mind? The shock wasn't enough to kill him, but repeated exposure to it would eventually cause damage.

Like the Grutex, the Venium were equipped with translators as very young offspring, so while the male knew what they planned to do to his bonded female, the cell assured that he was helpless to stop them.

"Will this help us to breed them?" The Kaia's eyes lit up in fascination as his gaze bounced between the angry male and the little human female.

"That is our hope," Erusha told him. "At the very least, we should be able to isolate the breeding hormone. We've noted in the past that the Venium who have delayed their bonding have become irrational and restless. If we can pinpoint it, we may be able to weaponize it—increase it in those who have yet to mate and watch as their forces fall into unrest."

"Seems like there will be no downside to this project then. I'm pleased, Erusha."

Nuzal watched the male carefully, noting the strange way his eyes narrowed before he grinned.

"Yes, we are very eager to start." He swept his hand out toward the long row of cells. "In the meantime, I'm sure you'd like to find a replacement for the human female we collected from you."

The Kaia grunted as he turned his back on them.

"I looked forward to the report." His voice boomed through the hall. "And I expect it to be on time... unlike the delivery of the female I've been waiting for. I don't want to have to come down here again. And Erusha?" He looked back at them over his broad shoulders. "Don't be afraid to use a little force if his female needs a little coaxing. Humans are weak creatures, easily manipulated by the suffering of others."

"Of course, sir." Erusha dipped his head as their leader turned his attention toward the cells.

Nuzal watched as the Venium stood from where he'd fallen, his legs and arms shaking from the current he was subjecting himself to. He didn't want to have to injure the male, but he knew without a doubt that Erusha wouldn't hesitate if the female put up a fight.

It seemed unfair to him. She had no idea what they wanted from her, and yet she was still expected to cooperate completely.

"Retrieve the female," Erusha told Raou, waving his hand toward the cell as he motioned for the assistant to bring the tray.

"Gently," Nuzal growled, hating the idea of the warrior being given permission to touch her. "We don't want her damaged."

He watched as the male input the code so he could pass through the forcefield.

"Against the back wall," Raou hissed in the humans' native tongue. "Don't cause any trouble and you may come out of this alive."

With a look Nuzal could only describe as pure and utter hatred, the females stayed where they were, their arms folded over their chests in defiance. The bonded human stepped in front of her companion, narrowing her dark eyes on the much larger warrior.

"Fuck off," she spat. "We aren't going anywhere with you."

The Venium in the other cell threw his head back and laughed, finding his mate's refusal amusing. If it weren't for his concern over Raou's reaction, Nuzal might have laughed as well. He made note of the interaction in his log as he stepped forward, hoping to calm her.

"Test Subject Z2062, we only need you for a moment."

She spun toward him, dark brows drawing together as she sneered. For something so small, she was fierce.

Nuzal was rarely surprised by the things he experienced, but this little female intrigued him. So many of the humans they received were terrified, quivering messes, and for good reason. The Grutex as a whole were not a soft race.

This human, however, refused to cower or let herself be intimidated. She looked their warrior in the eye and defied him. She was brave... and incredibly stupid.

"My name is Jun, *not* Test Subject Z blah, blah, blah."

He couldn't help the way his eyes lingered on her long dark hair, and he found himself wondering what it might feel like sliding between his fingers. It would be soft, he decided as he watched it fall over her shoulder. Not only did the humans come with a variety of skin colors, they also had different hair colors and textures.

He knew from previous experiments that the alterations they made could change these features. In a few of the subjects, the human hair had fallen out, replacing the strands with xine-like tendrils.

The thought that she might be changed in such a way repulsed him. Rage curled in his belly, lashing at his insides as he tried to beat back his reaction.

You can't let them! They will change her! the voice inside his mind shouted. *Not her. Not Jun.* Her name echoed through his head. It was so soft. Nothing like the brutal, hard names they had been given.

"Jun," he amended. "We just need samples of your lifeblood. If you cooperate, this can be over quickly."

She looked at him for a moment, her eyes boring into his. "Wow." She sighed softly. "I must look so stupid to you. Do you think I haven't seen what the other humans who come from that lab of yours look like? I know a simple blood test isn't all you have planned for me."

Raou snarled, his hand shooting out to grasp her chin as he jerked her forward. "You," he whispered, nuzzling his face against her cheek, "are going to be my greatest conquest." His black tongue slipped out to caress her skin, and she shuddered, visibly repulsed. "Our offspring will be the embodiment of perfection."

Before Nuzal had a chance to react to the ridiculousness of the statement, Jun had reared back and brought her leg up, connecting with the plating between the male's legs.

Unlike human males, the Grutex didn't walk around with their genitals hanging out and vulnerable. The blow she delivered hadn't hurt him, but the fact that she had dared to try seemed to anger Raou.

With little warning, the male lashed out. The back of his hand connected with her cheek, and the force of the blow sent her backward. She was sprawled on the floor at the feet of the other female, red lifeblood dripping from her mouth onto the metal beneath her.

Nuzal leaped forward, intending to shield the female, but to his utter amazement, Jun jumped up and launched herself at the warrior's face with what could only be described as a battle cry.

Her fingers plucked at his eyes as the other female rushed to assist, grabbing the warrior's arm and dropping to the floor to throw him off balance. At his back, the Venium was throwing himself against the barrier and roaring.

"I will not be your toy! I will *die* before I let you touch me!" she screamed, jabbing a finger into the lower right eye socket.

Guards rushed into the cell, tearing the females away and freeing Raou. The males, all trained warriors, eyed the two small humans warily as they retreated. Jun seemed proud of herself as she stood, breathing heavily as she looked them all up and down.

Her whole demeanor changed when the Kaia appeared in front of her cell. There was no missing the cruel intentions that swirled with his eyes as he stared her down.

"Whip the male," he said in her tongue.

"If I could just be allowed to speak with her for a moment, I could get her to agree—" Nuzal began.

"I will see to it, sir," Raou said, wiping the lifeblood from his injured eye as he stepped forward. "Let a *warrior* see to his punishment."

The Kaia watched Nuzal's face, and he prayed to every god in existence that his features didn't give his anger away. While

Nuzal could barely recall most of his earlier lives, many of the details of his warrior past seemed to haunt his dreams. He told himself he only imagined the red haze of rage and the uncontrollable urge to conquer... everything.

Had he really been like this once? Had he also been this eager and willing to inflict pain and suffering on others simply because he could? Nuzal wondered, as he watched the glee in Raou's eyes, if the loss of so many memories was intentional. What more had he done that he couldn't remember?

Perhaps this realization was something their leaders feared. Warriors who questioned leadership, who looked at the things they were told to do and decided it was wrong, were a danger to their authority. Was this the driving force behind the sudden interest in breeding new Grutex? What role did these rumored injections for the warriors play in it?

Raou pulled an electric whip from his belt as the guards reactivated the bindings and removed the forcefield. Nuzal wanted to turn away, but the Venium caught his gaze and held it, and something strange passed between them in that moment.

The first strike of the whip broke the dark skin on the male's back, and Nuzal steeled himself as Raou readied for another blow. This was only one punishment that awaited him should the Kaia learn of his weakness toward the humans.

"Again!" the Kaia growled.

Jun gasped, stumbling forward as the whip lashed against the open wound. She slapped her hand over her mouth, muffling the scream.

"Brin! Brin..."

The tail of the whip tore the smooth skin, and tears fell down her cheeks as she reached out to him.

Brin. Was this the male's name? No sound escaped him as Raou took his anger out on his body. He spoke cruel things, words meant to incite anger in the Venium, but Nuzal felt himself bristle with rage at them instead.

"I will take her from you, Venium. I will bind her in body and in mind." The whip landed against him again and again. "I will breed her while you watch. I will break her until all she can do is beg for more."

The red haze he experienced in his dreams slid down over his eyes, and he knew without the shadow of a doubt that he could kill this warrior. His hands itched to tear him limb from limb, to make him suffer as he watched the fear swim in his eyes as he faced his death.

The sight of Jun's tears broke his heart, and her sobs echoed in his mind so strongly he wasn't sure they would ever go away. Something moved within him, a force he'd never experienced before.

Nuzal would risk his life, and every life after this one, to protect her.

CHAPTER 15

BRIN

*C*rack!

The sting of the electric whip cutting through his flesh made his stomach fly into his throat. The sounds and pain brought back those long-buried memories, and he swallowed down the bile and the guttural noises that threatened to spill from his mouth.

The only outward sign of the agony he was feeling was the flashing of his fushori as he struggled to remain in control. How many times had his father done this to him? How many times had he strapped his own pup down and whipped him until his lifeblood was dripping down his back so that he would be able to withstand the torture?

"You won't be like him," his father had whispered as he poured water over the wounds. "You'll be better."

The sound of Jun calling his name over and over reached him through the haze of his agony and he turned to see her on her knees, reaching for him, but stopping before the barrier of the forcefield.

He wanted to tell her everything was all right, that he would take this lashing and so many more if it meant they left her alone, but his jaw was clenched so tight he wasn't sure he would ever be able to open it again. He didn't want her to give in for him.

"Stop!" she cried, pounding her fists on the floor. "Enough!"

"No!" he ground out. "Don't."

The whip dug into his back and shoulders again, stealing his breath. Tiny pulses of electricity raced up his spine, making his muscles tense.

"I'll do it! Leave him alone! I'll give you the blood samples!"

No, no, no!

Darkness was creeping into his vision, blurring the edges. He fought against it, not wanting to lose sight of his mate; afraid of what they would do to her.

"Just let me help him, please. I'm a nurse. I'll do whatever you need me to if I can just make sure he's okay."

Don't trust them, Shayfia! You can't trust them! He tried to tell her, but his tongue felt as if it were stuck to the top of his mouth, and his jaw was locked tight. His entire body throbbed with each labored breath he took, and his heart pounded within his chest as he listened to the heavy footsteps enter her cell.

He wished he had told her she was his mate before Oshen and Amanda left Earth. He wished to the goddess that he had begged her to leave with her friend, to come to Venora with him so that he could protect her from everyone who would want to destroy her.

Instead, he'd let his past poison his future, and now he was going to lose the only being in this galaxy that meant more to him than life itself.

Goddess, forgive my failure. Protect her.

JUN

Open wounds crisscrossed Brin's back and shoulders. Jun struggled to draw air into her lungs as she watched him collapse against the hard, cold floor when they released his binds.

She wanted to break through the barrier and wrap him in her arms, to soothe his pain and let him know she wasn't going to let him suffer alone, but the logical part of her knew these monsters would not allow that.

A hard, clawed hand grabbed her upper arm, yanking her to her feet and pulling her from the cell. She tripped, wincing as the hand tightened around her to keep her from falling.

"Wait! I said I'd go if I could help him!" she protested, trying and failing to dig her heels in. She was like a doll in this alien's grasp.

"He will live. You may see to him after the tests," someone told her, but she couldn't twist herself around to see who was speaking.

Had she really expected them to let her go in right away? No, but that didn't make the ache in her chest hurt any less. Everything inside of her called for him, screamed with the need to put her hands on him so that she knew he was all right. She caught a glimpse of him as she was pulled away, and the soft glow of his fushori eased some of her worry.

If she just cooperated and let them get their samples, she could return to Brin. The sooner, the better.

Jun tried to run alongside the Grutex who held her, but she simply couldn't keep up with the long strides, and ended up being half-dragged, half-carried down the hall.

Everything here looked the same, and she doubted she would

be able to remember the route in the event they actually succeeded in escaping from the cells.

They passed through a set of doors into a brightly lit room. There was a metal table against the far wall, and in the middle was a white recliner, similar to the chairs you sat in at the doctor's office during a blood draw.

Guess some things are oddly universal.

Jun's heart was hammering in her chest, like the frantic fluttering of a caged bird as it struggles to break free. She tried her best to push back her anxiety, but the moment she was placed in the chair and felt the pressure of the invisible bonds clamp down on her wrists, Jun began to panic.

All she had to go off of was their word that this was all they wanted from her. She was helpless to stop them from doing anything they pleased, but Brin's life depended on her continued cooperation.

There were machines against every wall, and it made her wonder exactly how far behind the Grutex the humans were when it came to their technology.

"Out," the Grutex who had attempted to speak calmly to her demanded. "I don't need the assistance of five males to draw lifeblood from the female." When Raou lingered in the doorway, the male growled low in his chest. "That includes you, *warrior*."

Jun watched the exchange, waiting for one of them to act on the unchecked hatred, but Raou eventually snarled before shoving the doors open and stomping off.

"Jun?" The way her name slipped from his mouth to dance over her skin made her shiver. The same warmth she felt in her chest when Brin teased her spread into her arms and tickled the tips of her fingers.

There is something wrong with you, Junafer. The sensation was both wonderful and terrifying. *Is this what shock feels like? I can't be getting butterflies over the way a Grutex says my name.*

"My name is Nuzal," he told her as he readied the tray one of the other males had set out for him. "I will be drawing samples of your lifeblood for analysis in the lab. Do you understand?"

Jun fought the urge to roll her eyes. "Yes. I'm a nurse. I've done things like this before."

"Good." Nuzal looked down, staring at his hand as it hovered over her arm. "Is it okay if I touch you, female?"

"Do I actually have a choice in the matter?"

Nuzal frowned at her before shaking his head.

"No. You have no choice." Although his words seemed harsh, his eyes were conflicted, as if he couldn't figure out why he'd even asked her that ridiculous question in the first place.

The pain in her back took her by surprise, and she felt herself tense at the realization that she hadn't taken her medication since before she left to meet with Telisa. How long had she been without them?

The tingling sensation started in her toes and crept up her right side, a reminder that her body was weakening. This was the last place in the galaxy that she could afford to be weak, and yet she was helpless to do anything to remedy that. If the Grutex didn't kill her soon, her own body surely would.

A deafening rhythm began to pound in her head, her own rapid pulse as loud as crashing ocean waves during a storm. An excruciating jolt of pain shot from the base of her skull down to the small of her back and she hissed, drawing the Grutex's attention.

How long was she going to make it before her heart and kidney gave out? She distracted herself by watching Nuzal prep the needle before he turned toward her. The seat she was strapped to began to rise, bringing her closer to him, allowing him easier access. He reached above her, drawing down a slim metal instrument that cast a light onto her arm, displaying the network of her veins beneath her skin.

145

They had these on Earth too, but this one was like nothing she had ever gotten to work with before. It was as if someone had peeled away the flesh, leaving her veins exposed, and damn if the nurse in her wasn't impressed and just the tiniest bit jealous.

This would have been useful so many times over the years.

Nuzal leaned down to examine the pathways, his hand moving her arm gently as he looked for the best option. Where their bodies met, Jun noticed a faint glow, a fascinating, beautiful shimmer of iridescent color.

It spread over the back of his hand, dancing up his wrist and forearm in the same way the aurora borealis danced across the sky. She couldn't recall ever seeing a Grutex glow, but aside from what she saw on the news channels, Jun admitted she didn't know very much about them. Maybe Nuzal was a subspecies, or a hybrid.

The light it cast onto her skin was warm and soothing, like being kissed by the first rays of the sun. Her chair shook as Nuzal released her arm and stumbled backward. He stared at his limb as if it was alien to him, turning it this way and that as the lights receded.

The fleshy tendrils around his face wriggled over his shoulders, thrashing against the plates of his upper chest. Two of his eyes, the lower violet ones, focused on her, and she saw the shiver run through him as he rubbed his fingers together, smoothing away the last of the pretty light.

If she had to guess, she might say he looked just as surprised by the glow as she was. He watched her for a long moment and something about the way he looked at her made her feel, for the very first time, like they were on equal ground.

He wasn't the huge Grutex looming over her, but a male, just as confused and bewildered as she was. His entire body shuddered as he took a hesitant step forward, his eyes darting to his hand as he drew closer. Nuzal reached out, plucking something from the tray as he stared down at her.

This wasn't the empty syringe he'd had before. A thick pink liquid filled the tube, and before she could warn him about her conditions and the fact that whatever was in there could have a negative effect on her, Nuzal had pierced her skin and pressed down on the plunger, sending the mysterious contents into her body.

God, please let me live through this. Let me get back to Brin.

Almost immediately, the pain in Jun's head and body faded, and black smoke began to curl around the outside of her vision. If she hadn't been so concerned about possibly dying, she might have thanked him for taking away her pain.

"This is just a fast-acting sedative," he told her, as if he sensed her panic. "The lifeblood draw seems to put undue stress on many of your species. I don't wish to upset you."

"What? Wh—" She tried to speak, to ask him what was so stressful about it that he needed to put her under, but her tongue was so heavy and refused to do as she demanded.

He was speaking to her again, but his voice was distorted, like a toy with dying batteries. She stared at him, watching as his mouth moved, before her gaze dropped to the needle he held poised above her arm.

The vein finder flashed, and she watched in absolute horror as the syringe in his hand morphed into some sort of needle-nosed creature as it pierced her skin, burrowing into her like one of the terrifying man-eating scarabs from that mummy movie Amanda had made her watch once.

Her last conscious thought before the darkness closed in was that she was going to give Amanda hell for giving her this nightmare fuel if she ever got to see her again.

CHAPTER 16

JUN

$\mathcal{T}$he first sensation she was aware of as she struggled to clear her mind was the warmth of something firm pressed against her cheek. Was she on the floor of her cell again? No, something was holding her, cradling her. She was being carried, Jun finally decided as she felt herself sway.

Pushing through the fog of the lingering sedative, she forced her eyes to open and stared at the multi-colored glow as it danced over mauve plating. Jun pulled back and was actually relieved to see Nuzal, the scientist who had drawn her labs.

While it was true that the Grutex looked incredibly similar, being this close to them had shown her that there were indeed small differences that allowed her to tell some of them apart.

Those lower violet eyes were trained on her face, but when he realized he'd been caught staring, he quickly averted them. If the Grutex could blush, she was sure he'd be doing so.

"I'm returning you to your bonded," he spoke in hushed tones as if someone was listening. "I couldn't risk letting one of the warriors do this."

Couldn't risk it? Was this male, a member of the most feared race of aliens she'd ever met, really protecting her from his own people? What would move him to do something so... kind? There was no reason to help her, and surely doing so would only put him at risk.

What if this is a ploy? What if he was trying to gain her trust so that he could use it against her? Jun thought of Brin, and her resolve hardened. She wouldn't risk it.

Give an inch and the Grutex would take her life, or the lives of those she had come to care for. And even though she was curious about the glowing plates beneath her touch, Jun turned her head away. She wouldn't give him any indication she was interested in his kindness.

Nuzal's steps slowed as they approached another line of cells, and she anxiously peered inside. Brin was on the floor, still curled up where they had left him after his whipping.

The Grutex keyed in the code and stepped into the cell, gently placing Jun on her feet. There was an acute absence at the loss of his touch, but she erected her wall and dropped to her knees beside Brin, letting the warmth of his skin soothe whatever ache her body thought it was feeling. She wouldn't allow herself to make it more than it actually was.

The Grutex held out a tube filled with a pale paste, waiting for her to take it from him. "What is that?"

"A healing balm."

Jun reached up, careful not to let their fingers touch as she slid it from his hand and inspected it carefully. "I'll need something to clean out the wounds with. He'll get an infection if it's not properly cared for."

Nuzal shook his head, sending the tendrils dancing. "The gel will be enough. You have my word."

Jun wanted to laugh at him. What good was the word of a monster? Instead, she nodded and turned toward Brin. "Thank you."

"Jun?" She froze at the sound of her name. "Use it sparingly. A small amount is sufficient for the wounds he received. Using too much of the balm has been known to cause adverse reactions."

She removed the lid, bringing it close to her nose, testing its scent. It was... pleasant, almost minty, like Mama's efficascent oil. She dipped the tip of her finger into it and frowned at the cool sensation that spread into the palm of her hand. Jun looked back up at Nuzal, who was standing just inside the cell, his eyes trained on her and his body rigid as if he wasn't exactly sure what to do with himself.

Guess that makes two of us.

He reached out, the tips of his claws almost skimming her hair, but she shrank away from him, pressing against Brin's big body. The hand jerked away, and she watched as the male struggled for a moment.

"I am truly sorry for this... for all of it." He frowned as he ran his hand over his chest where the glowing lights originated from when she woke up in his arms. "I wish there was something I could do."

"You could let us go," she challenged, but she knew that wasn't an option.

Nuzal said nothing, only stared at her for a moment longer before his gaze fell on Brin. His jaw clenched like he wanted to say something, but he spun on his heels instead, stepping through the forcefield before reactivating it and disappearing down the hall.

"Jun?" Telisa's whisper startled her, and she turned to see the woman watch her through the barrier.

"I'm all right." She told her, forcing a small smile.

Are you though? she asked herself. Jun looked down at her arm, the one she'd seen the needle-bug burrow into, and shivered. There was nothing there, not any kind of indication a needle, let alone a bug, had pierced her skin. Maybe the sedative had caused her to hallucinate.

"Where did they take you? What did they do to you in there?"

"They gave me a sedative to calm me, and then took my blood."

"That's it? How do you know they didn't do more?" Telisa questioned, inching as close as she could without getting herself shocked.

Jun shrugged. "I don't think they did anything other than what they said they would."

"You don't look any different…"

"I don't *feel* any different," she responded.

"Do you think I should keep up the crying, or have they caught onto us?" Telisa asked.

"I honestly don't think the crying is going to help. They've already got plans for each and every one of us and tears aren't going to sway or distract them."

Jun grunted as she tugged at Brin's arm, rearranging him so that he was sprawled on his stomach. Telisa gasped as his back was revealed, and she did her best to swallow her own emotions at the sight of his torn and burned flesh. She had witnessed so much during her years in the ER, but she had never had to tend to someone she cared for with such serious wounds.

The edges of the fresh wounds were charred, and the smell choked her as she dabbed the gel into the mangled skin. Woven between the marks from the electric whip Raou had used were old, faded scars. How had she not noticed these before? They crisscrossed over his back from the very bottom to the tops of his shoulders.

Her hands were bloody and torn from her attempts to pry up

the panel, but she figured it probably didn't matter much at this point. She applied what she felt was a sufficient amount, while keeping Nuzal's warning in mind. Brin groaned, his body tensing as she tended to one of the worst ones.

"I'm sorry, Brin. I'm almost finished," she assured him.

The balm was already beginning to work wonders. The marks looked less angry, the swelling and redness having gone down significantly. Even the cuts and tears on the tips of her fingers were looking better. What she wouldn't give to get this in the hands of hospitals back on Earth.

Paired with Brin's natural healing abilities, Jun was sure his wounds could be closed within a day or so. He would most likely still scar, but judging from the ones already there, it was something he already lived with. She touched the thick, faded lines and wondered what had caused them.

By the time she'd finished and recapped the tube, Brin was stirring, tail and limbs twitching as he slowly came back to consciousness. Jun brushed her fingers over his brow and tucked a few strands of his pitch black hair behind his pointed ear. Her heart clenched in her chest when he opened his eyes and stared up at her.

"Shayfia," he rasped. "Did they hurt you?"

"I'm okay, Glowworm," she whispered as she bent down to press her lips against his, not caring that they were being watched by the Grutex and every other human in the cells, or that they were both filthy and covered in blood. The feel of his mouth moving against hers, the reassurance that he was still alive and here with her, was so overwhelming that she nearly burst into tears.

All of those reservations she'd had on Earth, all of those reasons she'd come up with for not doing what her heart wanted her to seemed so silly now. She should have just taken a page from Amanda's book and jumped head first into... whatever this feeling was he stirred within her.

She didn't care what anyone else might think about her decision. They could call it rash, spontaneous, stupid, and sure, maybe it was all of those things and more, but Jun *wanted* Brin more than anything she had ever wanted in her entire life. Nothing was going to keep her from holding onto whatever moments they had left.

She'd dive right into the sea of emotions. She'd learn how to swim in those waters just to have him.

A shaky hand brushed against the side of her head as Brin's claw-tipped fingers tunneled into her hair, fisting the locks as he pulled her closer. His kiss was urgent, but gentle, and even though neither of them spoke, Jun felt *something*, some kind of silent understanding, pass between them.

Jun belonged with Brin as surely as Amanda belonged with Oshen. His tongue pressed against her lips, seeking entrance, and she shuddered when it slipped inside to dance over her own.

She forgot where they were and what they were facing as she allowed herself to become swallowed up in the sensation of this alien—of *her* alien. Need curled in her belly, spreading through her like wildfire.

It wasn't until he pulled away with a groan that she felt the cold hard floor beneath her sore knees again, and heard the humming of the forcefield. Brin pressed a sweet kiss to her forehead as he caught his breath, his eyes roaming over her face as he wiped away the crusted blood on her cheek.

Jun felt the beginnings of panic well up within her chest. She didn't want to die here. She wanted to go to Venora and create a life with this male. She wanted to see her family again, to hug her papa and mama again and tell them she loved them. It couldn't end like this.

Brin sat up, wincing as he twisted and tugged at the healing wounds. She knew from the cuts on her fingertips that the balm didn't numb the pain, but she hoped it had at least taken the worst of it away from him.

"What happened to your back?" she asked as she tucked the tube into her pants pocket.

Even with his back torn open, mischief sparkled in his blue eyes.

"I was whipped."

A grin tugged at the corners of his mouth and Jun rolled her eyes.

"Yes, I was there. I meant the other ones."

The lightheartedness from only seconds ago faded immediately, and Brin's jaw tightened.

"The scars?"

Jun nodded. "Who gave those to you?"

"My—" He looked around, likely expecting to see Telisa peering through the barrier, but she seemed to have taken the hint during the kiss and made herself scarce. "Tesol—my sire—gave them to me."

"Your father?" Horror washed over her as she stared at him. "Why would he do that?"

There was no trace of the confident, wise-cracking Brin she'd known. His face was dark, eyes swirling with pain. She wanted to tell him he didn't have to tell her, that they could forget she'd brought it up, but something told her this was what he needed.

Brin reached for her hands, pulling her into his lap and wrapping his tail around her waist. He ran the pad of his finger over her cheeks and across the nose she had always thought too wide. She stared at her reflection in his eyes and tried to see herself from his perspective.

"It's a long story."

"I've got time." She smirked, trying to brighten his mood.

He grinned back at her, but it never reached his eyes. "Brin isn't the name I was given at birth," he began. "I was born Ruvator Machit. It's a name I share with my older brother."

Jun scrunched her face. "I bet he hates that. Having a brother named John was similar enough to annoy me half the time."

"He died long before I was ever born."

Open mouth, insert foot. Jun wished a hole would open up and swallow her right at that moment.

"Ruvator was the perfect son for my parents. He was a warrior, excelled in all of his training, rose through the ranks as he was expected to do." Brin frowned. "My brother was everything my dam wished I'd been. My sire and brother were deployed together, and while they were out scouting, they were taken captive."

His face twisted as if he were in pain, and Jun stroked his tense features.

"They were tortured, treated cruelly, had pieces of their bodies removed from them. After watching our sire suffer the loss of his eye and being starved for days, Ruvator gave in. He gave them the information they sought, thinking it would end their misery, that they would be free. Instead, they killed my brother and left Tesol for dead."

"You don't have to tell me anymore today, Brin," she assured him, not wanting him to have to experience more pain than he already had.

Brin shook his head and continued. "My dam, Brega, was the one who found them tied up in the building the aliens had abandoned. Tesol had spent days alone with the corpse of his only son. I'm sure you can imagine the toll it took on him."

Jun's lip quivered and she shook her head. "That's unimaginable."

"My dam was devastated at Ruvator's loss, and my sire... he could hardly function. They were barely given time to recover before they were called before the council.

"At first, the elders *politely* asked them to produce another pup to replace the one who had been lost. The Venium need numbers. Losing even one pup, especially their only one, was disastrous for Brega and Tesol, but losing a warrior in his prime... the elders eventually demanded Brega produce another and so I was brought into being.

"Conceived in hatred and disappointment, created only so that she and Tesol would not face any more punishment. Brega blamed my sire for his failure, and for Ruvator's weakness. She had lost them both in her mind. My sire was no longer fit for service after the loss of his eye, and that shamed her a great deal.

"The council had demanded she replace Ruvator, so when I was born, she did just that. I was given his name and all of the shame that came with it. I'd failed in her eyes before I'd even drawn my first breath."

Brin's fingers combed absently through her hair.

"She nursed me for as long as she was forced to, then gave me over to someone else, telling them she couldn't bear to look at me a moment longer. Her place, she told them, was on the field where she could exact her revenge, and regain the honor she felt had been taken from her."

Jun opened her mouth to speak, but Brin silenced her with a finger to her lips.

"When I was old enough to walk, Tesol began my training. I needed to be stronger, both mentally and physically, than my brother had been. I wouldn't fail, wouldn't give in. If it came down to the loss of my life or the loss of my honor, I would choose death. Crying, flinching, any movement to defend myself resulted in lashings.

When my sire became angry over the fact that he was left behind to raise me on his own, we would train even harder. Every day, every moment I was with him was literal torture until one day I stopped feeling, stopped reacting, just... stopped. I was their perfect warrior. I think Brega might have even been proud of me then."

Brin's grip in her hair tightened and she tugged at his arm until he released her. Jun interlaced her fingers with his and squeezed. He'd been through so much.

"I was supposed to continue my military training, but I had no intentions of ever following in their footsteps. I enlisted as a Havacker the moment I walked into the building and shattered all of their hopes and dreams."

"How old were you when the whipping started?" Jun couldn't help asking.

"I'd seen eight birthdays pass the first time he used it on me."

"Why didn't someone intervene on your behalf? Why didn't the council do anything to stop them?"

Brin laughed darkly. "The council found my parent's training methods to be 'quite successful' in turning me from a rebellious pup into a model warrior. The fact that I was so young didn't seem to bother them at all.

"That doesn't mean I didn't have anyone in my corner, though. Nyissa, Oshen's dam, heard about the truth of what was being done to me after her mate told her my story. Nyissa and Calder took me in when things became too much, fought tooth and claw for me.

"His parents kept the training guidelines the elders sought to pass from being written into law, and when I was old enough to leave Brega and Tesol's home, I was given a place among their family. I had love and support for the first time in my life. They are my *real* family."

A small sweet smile tugged at his lips.

"Nyissa gave me my name the day I came to stay with them. It was the first, and most wonderful gift anyone had given me."

"Hold on," Jun frowned, swiping at her tears. "*Nyissa*? Did you seriously name your AI after Oshen's *mom*?"

Brin had the decency to at least look abashed, rubbing the back of his neck. "It started out as a joke to get under Oshen's skin."

Despite the seriousness of what they were dealing with, Jun felt a giggle bubble up from her chest. She sniffled, shaking her head in disbelief as she looked up at him. Getting under Fishboy's skin was something she'd enjoyed immensely during her time with him.

"Does he know you did it?"

Brin chuckled. "Not yet. I was biding my time, waiting for the perfect moment."

She glanced around their cell, the humor fading as she realized that perfect moment might never come now. Jun tried to hold on to the spark of laughter he'd given her, but she couldn't seem to stop the sadness from encroaching. Her hand smoothed over his tail as it tightened around her waist.

"Brin..." Jun whispered through her gathering tears. "I'm so sorry. I'm sorry for everything they put you through."

"Don't be sorry," he told her. "It all led me to a backwater planet, where one of the most beautiful inhabitants held a gun to my head, kidnapped me, and then fed me the scrambled young of a domesticated bird."

Jun fought the grin and failed. "Wow, what an awful person." She brought his hand to her lips and pressed tiny kisses to his knuckles. "Still, I'm sorry for the pain they caused you."

"They are the reason I've made certain decisions about my future." Blue eyes searched her face as if he were trying to read her, waiting for her reaction. "I won't ever have biological pups. I won't pass *their* lifeblood to another generation. Their legacy, their hatred, will die with me." Brin stared down at their joined hands. "I won't let her use them the way she used me, Jun. Never."

She'd dreamed of a huge family her entire life. While it was true she wanted her own babies and the chance to experience pregnancy and birth, Jun knew better than most that you could love children not born of your body just as much. She'd watched her mama and papa love and raise her cousins as their own.

Something Nuzal said on their way back to the cells nagged at her. He'd called Brin her bonded, but she wasn't exactly up to speed on her alien terms. Was being someone's bonded the same as being their mate, and if so, how did the Grutex know? Brin hadn't mentioned it on Earth, and there hadn't been an opportunity here.

"It's why I tried to ignore the pull," he was saying. "I couldn't take that from you, not after you told me you wanted your own children." He cupped her chin so that she was forced to look at him. "I don't want to lose you, Shayfia, but I would understand if you chose not to accept my condition. You're my…"

She wanted to hear the words, *needed* to hear the words. "Your what, Brin?"

"You're my mate, Shayfia," he whispered against her lips, pulling her face to his. "My end and my beginning. The sun, the moons, the air in my lungs."

Jun wrapped her arms around his neck as she pressed closer. "When did you know?"

"The night you kissed me in your bedroom as you tended to my wounds."

"*I* kissed *you*?" Jun sputtered as Brin grinned. "I recall it happening the other way around."

Brin shrugged. "You kissed me, I kissed you. Either way, I felt the swelling and knew that night."

"You've known all this time and didn't think to mention it to me?"

"I can't give you what you want. I won't, so I saw no point in sharing that knowledge."

Ah, there he was, the Brin who thought he knew best—the irritating male who tried to make her decisions for her.

"Do you think Oshen's mother loves you any less just because she didn't give birth to you?" The muscle in his jaw ticked, and he swallowed thickly as he shook his head. "Don't keep things from me just to spare my feelings. If you had told me, I would have told you that sometimes children aren't born into families, they're brought in. A child doesn't have to share your blood to be loved, Brin."

The look he gave her made her stomach drop and she gasped in surprise when he ducked his head, stealing her lips in a desperate, hungry kiss that took her breath away. God help her, she wanted him. His tail tightened around her waist and Jun hummed, wriggling in his lap.

"Goddess, help me, Shayfia, you're going to kill me," he rasped when he was finally able to pull away. Brin scooted closer to the solid wall at the back of the cell and propped his shoulder up, resting the side of his head on the cold metal. "Come here." He tucked her into the crook of his arm, shielding her with his body as he got comfortable. "My Shayfia," he murmured against her hair. "Sleep."

"My bossy alien." She chuckled, even as she felt her lids begin to close. "I should check your back again."

"You should let me hold you. My back will heal. Thank you for seeing to me."

Jun closed her eyes and listened to the rhythmic beating of Brin's heart. *Don't keep things from me*, she had told him, but she was a hypocrite. As she lay there in his arms, her body was slowly shutting down. Without an exam, Jun had no way of knowing how much longer she could fight. How was she going to tell him he would have to say goodbye?

CHAPTER 17

NUZAL

*N*uzal pored over the journals he'd kept in his past lives, but there was nothing in them that would explain the strange glowing he'd experienced last day cycle with the bonded female. *Jun.* What did it mean, and why had it only happened when she touched him?

Nuzal had left her in the cell with the Venium and moved to the next corridor. The cells here were larger and held a wide variety of humans. He'd stormed up to the first one on his right, tapped in the code, and then grabbed the first female he saw.

Nothing.

No lights danced over his skin; no warmth spread through him from their contact. He repeated it with every female in the cell before frowning at their quivering forms as the last female jerked out of his grip.

Jun was the only human who had ever elicited this type of response from him.

Nuzal was no closer to finding out the answer than he had

been when he returned to his room to search for any clues. Had anyone seen him as he carried her back to the cell? Had they reported him to Erusha or even the Kaia?

Surely, if they had, he wouldn't be here at his desk, swiping furiously through page after page of these glecking journals that contained nothing but the ramblings of an overconfident warrior.

The results of Jun's lifeblood analysis had been delivered to his comm sometime after he'd returned, but he hadn't opened them. He needed to check them. If Erusha caught him slacking on something so important, he was sure the male wouldn't hesitate to remove him from the project. The thought of another male in the lab touching her, of Raou touching her if he wasn't there to protect her, filled him with rage.

Nuzal tapped on the flashing icon that indicated there was an unopened report waiting for him. He checked her subject number against her file and scanned the results of her lifeblood tests.

There were DNA matches for four different species in their data banks: human, Gri'ku, Ihod, and Venium.

Three of the four were aquatic species that the Grutex had been in communication with for as long as he could remember. It wasn't surprising to see that more than one species had been used in her ancestor's line.

The idea at the time had been to overwhelm the human DNA with that of the other species. It would lay dormant for generations, passing on the traits silently until they were awoken within the descendant.

A sudden anxiety jolted through him. The awakening process was hard on humans. It changed them, reformed them. Recovery took days for some, weeks and months for others. Would the little female survive it?

Nuzal had kept himself locked away long enough. He needed to see Jun, to calm his fears over her safety so that he could best figure out how to protect her.

Nuzal's first instinct was to go straight to the cells. He wanted to see her, to look at her with his own eyes and know she was all right, but he never went in so early. Working under such scrutiny meant he needed to keep to his routine, especially after his out of character behavior from the last day cycle.

If he'd wanted to be on the Kaia's good side, Nuzal was almost certain he'd failed. After his morning workout, Nuzal headed for the common room. It was a multi-purpose area, used mostly as a dining hall during meal times.

It was early enough in the cycle that many of the males in this section of the ship were either still on duty, or they were just waking up. That meant Nuzal wouldn't have to deal with a packed meal line or crowded tables.

The doors parted as he approached, and he squinted against the intensity of the lights. Since the majority of the males in this sector were scientists and other intellectuals, they remained on board most of their lives.

The lighting in this room, and in most areas of the ship, was intended to provide them with certain vitamins in the same way Earth's sun did. Nuzal passed through the meal line, taking his tray of nutrient packed food and scanning his wrist so that the system could track him.

In one of the corners of the room, tucked into the egg-shaped chairs, sat Erusha. He took a distracted bite out of his protein bar as his eyes scanned something on the holoscreen of his wrist comm. The male looked up when Nuzal took the seat across from him, nodding in greeting.

"Nuzal, getting an early start?"

He nodded as he broke the dense bar in half.

"I thought it best to get a jump on the cycle." The food was bland at best, and Nuzal chewed quickly, drawing from his water packet to help wash it down. "The Kaia seemed to take a keen interest."

Erusha grunted. "Dipping his hand into things he has no understanding of. I'll be happy when he moves on to something else so we can be left in peace."

Nuzal glanced up in surprise. He knew the male didn't care for the Kaia, but to voice his dislike in a common area where any number of warriors could overhear him was dangerous. His superior looked up at him then, narrowing his eyes on his face as if he were trying to find something.

"Vodk mentioned that you looked unwell after the lifeblood draw on the bonded female last cycle." Nuzal froze, his body going cold and rigid. "Are you well?"

There was something in the way the male spoke that made Nuzal uneasy, like he knew whatever came out of his mouth was going to be a lie. He needed to be more careful.

"If Vodk would have come to me with his concern, I would have assured him I was fine."

A pregnant silence stretched between them, eyes locked as Nuzal tried his best to hide the anxiety clawing at him. Erusha finally inclined his head, stuffing the last of his bar into his mouth.

"Good. We have a long cycle ahead of us. I assume you've received the female's results?"

"I have."

"And?"

"Although predominantly human, her results show the presence of three separate aquatic species."

"A descendant of the original test, perhaps," he mused. "I don't recall much from that life cycle, but I do remember combining the handful of aquatic DNA we had in our possession. For whatever reason, they weren't as compatible as we'd hoped. Very few of those offspring were satisfactory."

"Her Venium markers were high enough to make me think it's what has allowed the bond to form between her and the male."

"Was the hormone present in samples?"

Nuzal shook his head. "It doesn't seem like it was a trait she inherited. From what I could tell, she is not bound to him in the same way he is to her. Our answers regarding the hormone will most likely be found within the Venium."

The male's comm flashed against the inside of his wrist, and he frowned down at the screen as his eyes darted back and forth. A hum filled the air between them, a sound his superior often made in the lab as he worked. It told him he was mulling something over in his mind.

"What did you make of the rest of her results?"

Nuzal shifted in his seat. He'd been so worried about keeping up appearances that he hadn't even looked over the last few pages of the report.

"I only skimmed the first page before deciding to come in."

"Bring it up."

The look on the other male's face made his stomach clench and he activated the holoscreen, selecting her file and scrolling past the DNA results. Their knowledge of human anatomy at this point was excellent. They had generations of test subjects to compare her to, and the findings were shocking. The little female was incredibly sick.

"Her kidney function is far below normal. It's dangerously low."

"Even lower now," Erusha corrected. "That was at the time of the lifeblood draw."

Her kidneys and heart were in terrible condition. Why hadn't they given her a proper evaluation before sending her to a cell? The excitement of their arrival and the critical condition of the Venium male had thrown them out of their normal routine. Had they followed protocol, they would have caught this much sooner.

"Gleck," Nuzal mumbled as he swiped a hand over his face.

"How long has she been this way? Why didn't the cryo pods alert us?"

Erusha shook his head as he gathered his tray and got to his feet.

"The cryo pod likely kept her body stabilized until she was transferred into the cell. You'll go to her immediately. The last thing we need is for the female to die before we can even pinpoint the hormone."

His appetite having disappeared, Nuzal stood and dumped his half-eaten meal into the disposal. When he'd left her in the cell with the Venium, Jun had seemed fine, but he knew from his lifetimes as a warrior that some beings were better at hiding their pain.

With a hasty farewell to his superior, Nuzal took off down the hall toward the cells. The guard frowned when he barreled through the doors, but made no attempt to stop him.

Row after row of prior test subjects filled the cells on either side of him, some of them covered in scales or feathers, while others brushed their shaky hands through the soft fur that now grew on their backs and arms.

Those who had gained other attributes like telekinesis, psychometry, and telepathy were located farther down the corridor, kept under strict guard. They had been the most interesting cases of his career, but when he looked at all of these subjects, these *humans*, he wondered how much of them was still human.

As he neared her cell, Nuzal's heart began to race. Pained noises and hushed words reached his ears, and he propelled himself forward, coming to a stumbling halt in front of the forcefield.

Brin sat on the cold metal floor, his hands running the length of Jun's back as she gasped and writhed in his lap. Her knees were pulled up into her chest, and she clutched at the Venium's arm, burying her face into his thigh.

"What did you give her?" the male growled as his eyes darted up to Nuzal's face. "She can't stand, can barely move she's in so much pain."

"It'll stop," Jun hissed, swatting at Brin's chest. "I just need my medicine. Please…"

When she turned her head, Nuzal felt his entire body tighten in fear, something he hadn't experienced since his first lifetimes as a warrior. The terror of his first battle was something he didn't think even the rebirth process would be able to erase. If her obvious pain hadn't given it away, the ashen color of her skin and the exhaustion on her face told him something was wrong.

"I only gave her a mild sedative," Nuzal said, frowning down at the male. "It shouldn't have caused this reaction."

"*Shouldn't* have? You're not even sure?"

"It's been extensively tested on humans—" Jun moaned again, her nails digging into the Venium's dark skin as she wriggled. "I need to take her with me. I cannot help her here, Venium," Nuzal said.

The male's lip curled, and a long glistening fang peaked out as he growled. "Why should I trust you?"

"Is there any other option?" he countered. "I'm going to open this cell and you're going to hand her to me." He watched as the male's eyes darted toward the corridor and he growled. "Do not even think about it, Venium. Even if you were to get past me, where would you go? There are guards at each exit, and several of them roam throughout the cells. Will you be able to fight all of them off and look after your injured mate? Would you risk her life?"

The male's blue gaze bore into his as he considered, before he finally shook his head. "I wouldn't risk her. It's all right, Shayfia," he whispered to the female when she whimpered.

Nuzal disabled the forcefield as the Venium stood slowly. The moment Jun was placed in his arms, color splashed against his plating, casting its brilliance on her pale skin. The brush of the Venium's hand against his arm sent a tingle of awareness through him, but there was no time to explore what any of this meant. He tucked it away in mind, saving it for a more appropriate time.

"I'll return as soon as there's news." He stepped back, watching as the shield fell back into place, before turning on his heel. Nuzal went as fast as he could, trying his best to keep from jarring her body as he sprinted down the corridor toward surgery.

"My medicine," Jun mumbled against his chest. "I need my bag."

"There was no bag with you," Nuzal told her. The doors to surgery slid open, and he turned to the left, heading toward the room he'd used to operate on Brin the first cycle they were on the ship. "You know what's making you sick?"

Jun nodded weakly. "Kidney disease." She sucked in a breath as he shifted her in his arms. "Heart disease and—shit!"

"I'm sorry," Nuzal grunted as he clipped the corner of the wall with his shoulder, jolting her sharply. The air in his lungs was forced up through his crest, creating a low rattle. It was a sound he couldn't ever recall making, but it seemed to settle her pained movements.

He slipped between the double doors as they opened for him, mulling over the information she'd given him. With murmured apologies, Nuzal laid her out on the table, gently moving her onto her back.

Large brown eyes stared up at him as he brushed the long dark strands of hair from her face. He let his fingers linger on her cheeks, reluctant to break their physical connection, but the shimmer of the lights as they receded from his palms reminded him that he needed to be careful. This was unknown territory and the feeling this contract stirred within him was addictive.

Concentrate, Nuzal, he chided himself, pulling his hand away. *Your female is unwell.*

His female? Gods help him, he was losing his mind. Perhaps it was time to have a conversation with Erusha. He'd never been this way with any of the other test subjects, so what was it about this female and her mate that made him feel this way?

"I'm going to put you under—"

"No!" Jun tried to push herself up, but the pain forced her back down onto the table. "Please, just get me my medicine."

The small panel on the side of the operating table lit up under his hand, and he tapped the icon in the right corner, praying she wouldn't put up a fight.

"I will fix this, female. Let me help you." The forcefield activated, creating a small chamber around her, sealing her inside as a sedative was released.

He saw the panic in her eyes as she realized what was happening, and it took everything in him not to reach inside to comfort her. When she'd finally drifted off to sleep, Nuzal hit the alert icon on the screen, sending out a request for assistance.

Her vitals began to scroll across the holo projection above the table, making Nuzal frown. The numbers were concerning.

The first assistant to answer his call was Qrien, one of their youngest males. Like Nuzal, he'd once been a warrior, but with only two sets of eyes, Qrien had been designated to an intellectual position.

"Where do you need me, sir?" he asked, all business.

Nuzal appreciated the fact that he didn't waste any time.

"She's already under. Prepare a full tray. We'll start with the transcorp, but I have a feeling we'll need to go in."

Two more males rushed into the room and Nuzal called out instructions as he slid open one of the sleek wall panels, revealing an equipment storage space. The transcorp, a small wand-shaped instrument, sat nestled within its slot. Nuzal grabbed it, pressing his thumb into the little scanner on the side so that it could read his print. A green light flashed, indicating that it was ready for use.

The healing gel had replaced the forcefield, encasing Jun within its warmth as it worked to maintain her body's necessary functions. Nuzal placed the transcorp on the tray and dipped his hands into the liquid gloves Qrien held out for him.

"Monitor her vitals," Nuzal said as he picked the wand up. He slid his hands into the gel, scanning Jun from her head down to the very tips of her toes. It only took a moment for the black and white image to load, and when it did, Nuzal was surprised by what he saw.

"She's... incomplete?" Qrien asked, clearly perplexed.

Nuzal shook his head. "She's missing a kidney."

"This isn't normal, is it? Could this be some sort of mutation?"

"From everything I've read, humans can be born with only one, but see this?" Nuzal pointed to a set of thick white lines. "This looks to me like scar tissue." He lifted the hem of her shirt, tugging it up to reveal the telltale marks on her side. "It's been removed."

Her only remaining kidney was failing, and doing so at a far greater rate than he had ever seen before. Perhaps Brin was right and the sedative Nuzal had given her during the lifeblood draw was causing this acceleration. Fear tried to take hold of him, but he beat it back, focusing on the task at hand.

"Qrien, send Erusha a request for permission to acquire bionics."

The male frowned. "Bionics? You would waste resources on this human?"

Nuzal struggled to contain the angry growl that clawed at his throat.

"This human is vital to our research. Perhaps you would like to volunteer to be the male who has to explain to the Kaia why the only bonded female we have in custody died on my operating table, because I certainly don't want to."

"Of course not, sir," Qrien mumbled as he pulled up his comms holoscreen.

They weren't kept waiting long. Approval for the transplants was sent directly to Nuzal's comm, and he wasted no time making sure Jun was prepped and ready for the procedure.

When the bionics arrived, Nuzal uploaded the scan and a sample of her lifeblood into the case. While they began their work on Jun, the bionic parts began the short process of altering their form, reshaping and modeling theirselves to better suit the female's needs.

Even with the healing gel working to correct her other ailments, the surgery took up most of the day cycle. Nuzal stepped back, head tilting as he watched the bionics integrate into her system.

By the time the gel had finished closing her wounds, Jun's vitals were already looking much better. Her lifeblood pressure had leveled out, and all of her stats indicated the surgery had been a success, but Nuzal knew better than to assume she was out of danger. Although the rejection rate for the bionics was incredibly low, he didn't want to take any chances.

Jun was kept inside the gel and transferred to a private room where Nuzal could monitor her progress, giving only himself, Erusha, and Qrien access to her.

"You should rest," Qrien told him as he rubbed his lower set of eyes.

"Keep an eye on her, and do not bring anyone else into this room." He waited for the male to nod before leaving, refusing to look back at her tiny form on the much larger bed.

Nuzal stopped outside the doors to the cells, struggling with his desire to let the Venium know his mate was out of surgery.

It was too soon, he finally decided, guilt gnawing at him as he turned instead toward Erusha's office. He would wait until Jun was fully recovered before going to see Brin.

The lab was quiet when he stepped through the doors, but that wasn't unusual. Many of the males started their cycles early so they could leave before the mealtime rush.

Vodk, one of the males Nuzal had gone through training with, sat at his desk with rows of vials and physical files scattered about.

"Looking for Erusha?" the male asked, leaning back in his chair.

"I'd hoped to speak with him."

"He left in a hurry and hasn't returned."

Nuzal looked toward the male's office and sighed. "It can wait then," he said as he turned to leave.

"The transplant went well, I assume?"

Nuzal froze. Operations on cases as important as Jun's were not discussed outside of those assigned to them. The males who had assisted him would not say a word about what had gone on in the room, and Erusha would never have mentioned the request to anyone except Nuzal himself.

He would not play into Vodk's hand. "If Erusha returns, you will let him know I was looking for him?"

"Of course." The male nodded.

Vodk's words played over and over in his mind as he retreated to the section of the living quarters where his room was located. He was exhausted, and his entire body ached from the lengthy surgery, but he knew he would do it all over again to ensure the little female's survival. His door slid shut behind him as he stepped inside, but his steps faltered when he noticed the bound book resting on his pillow. It wasn't something he recalled owning.

Pinned to the soft animal hide cover was a note, written in an unfamiliar hand.

Keep her close. Do not let them find out what she is to you.

What in the name of the gods was that supposed to mean? Nuzal grimaced, picking up the book and turning to the first page. It was a journal, written in the same hand as the note. There was no doubt in his mind this was old, citing events that he was sure none of the Grutex could remember anymore.

Nuzal sat down on the edge of his bed, flipping through the pages until a phrase caught his eye and sent his pulse racing.

"The lights appeared today. I fear what this may mean for us."

He spent nearly an entire day cycle reading through the bulk of the journal, but something was making him uneasy. The memory of his contact with Jun in the halls made him freeze. It was on the surveillance footage, and he needed to destroy the evidence before someone else discovered it and his secret. All of the things they would put her through if they knew ran through his mind, and Nuzal growled. He couldn't let any of that happen.

Frame by frame, Nuzal deleted the proof of what she was to him, feeling his chest tighten with the knowledge that she could never be his. When he came upon the footage of her and the Venium within the cell, he lingered for a moment, watching them as his female accepted the male's kiss. His eyes took in the way she moved against him, and he felt... something.

What was this?

His fingers brushed over the image of the bonded pair as they touched, and longing, so strong and swift, filled his body. His breath huffed out of his lungs, and when he felt himself begin to harden, Nuzal deleted the entire file, wanting to give them privacy.

The little female enticed him, and if he was being honest with himself, it wasn't just her he craved to possess. There was some-thing about these two, something that made him *hunger* and *want* things he had no right wanting.

CHAPTER 18

BRIN

*T*oo *long,* his mind screamed. *They've been gone too long.*

His muscles tensed, rippling beneath his skin as he paced the tiny cell. If Jun's absence didn't drive him completely insane, the constant hum of the forcefield would do the trick.

He wanted to throw himself against it, to beat on it until his fists were soaked in lifeblood. Jun was in the hands of the Grutex, and here he was, stuck inside of a cell.

Useless.

He was going to tear every Grutex on this ship limb from limb when he was free. His lifeblood sang at the idea, claws extending in anticipation of the fight. There would be no mercy afforded to them.

"Nyissa, update." His voice was low and clipped.

"I am still unable to infiltrate the system," she responded.

"Work. Faster!"

"Of course, Master. Give me a moment to sprout legs and

walk down to the server room. I'm sure the Grutex will simply hand over control at that point."

Brin glared down at his wrist, cursing the AI and her smart mouth response. The longer he was separated from Jun, the more he felt himself slipping into madness.

The last image of her in pain, curled up against the Grutex's chest, haunted him. How long had it been since their capture? Did Oshen or his other crew mates even know he was missing yet? Would they be able to find him?

"You're going to wear a path into the floor if you keep up that pacing," a voice from the cell next to him said.

Brin looked over to see the female Jun had called Telisa on her hands and knees. She hissed, jerking her hand away before placing the tip of her finger in her mouth. Red lifeblood gathered at the tip as she frowned down at it. "Damn it!"

"What made you do it?" Brin asked, his curious gaze tracking her movements.

Telisa grimaced. "I saw Jun do it—"

"Not that." Brin shook his head. "Jun told me about what you said during the press conference. You thought the Venium might be willing to help. What made you think that?"

The female sighed, sitting back on her heels as she stared at the floor. "I was hoping against hope, I guess. I was willing to take a chance."

"Why?"

"Because someone once took a chance on me. I was the underdog, someone many people didn't want to trust, but they gave me the opportunity to prove myself."

Brin moved closer to the barrier that separated them. "What was it that made you so hard to trust?"

Telisa held out her arms and grinned humorlessly. "My skin. People who look like me don't always have the same opportunities as some of our fellow humans. It took a lot of hard work to be able to run for a senate seat, and without the support of some key people, I'm not sure I could have won."

"The color of your skin on Earth allows you certain privileges?" Brin asked, more confused now than when the conversation started.

"It's complicated, and I doubt I can explain hundreds of years of human history without confusing you even further." Telisa scooted closer, her eyes darting toward the front of the cell as if she expected a guard to show up at any moment. "I was willing to take a chance on you all. The Grutex are winning. They're taking people daily. If I was wrong and your species was there to help them, then we were screwed anyway? It's no secret that we were failing, but if we could find help, if we could acquire an ally who was their equal, maybe the Grutex would give up." Telisa shrugged, shoulders drooping as she shook her head. "Would your people have helped?"

"It was, as you said, complicated." Brin thought back to the last meeting on board the ship when Oshen had pleaded his case with Vog. "The Venium follow galactic law, and the protocol for aid is clear in most cases. A species must request assistance before we are able to intervene on their behalf. I came down with one of our ambassadors with the intention to inform your people, but the Grutex shot us down. We were separated, and in that time, Oshen, the ambassador, was taken in by a human female who he identified as his mate."

"So what you're saying is he got distracted." A grin tugged at the corners of her mouth, and she chuckled. "Men are the same all over the galaxy, aren't they?"

"I don't follow."

"Once you all get a little taste..." Telisa's brows wiggled suggestively.

Brin bit back a laugh and shook his head. "I suppose you aren't wrong."

"My mom used to say men will stay around for three things: fighting, fucking, and food. I don't imagine Earth food kept you around, and there isn't much fighting going on when you're hiding out, so..."

He wouldn't deny that he'd stayed on Earth for Jun, and if she'd given him any indication she wanted to fuck him, he wasn't sure he would have hesitated.

"Oshen is a very good friend of mine. He left Earth with his female to protect her from the Grutex who were hunting her. I stayed to find a way to warn humanity."

"What were you all doing there in the first place?"

Brin opened his mouth to respond, but clamped it shut when the heavy footsteps began to echo down the corridor.

"Press the panel back down! Don't let them see it."

The humans in the cells across from them scurried into the corners, huddling together as if it did something to hide them. Two Grutex appeared, coming to a stop in front of Telisa's cell. One of them he recognized from the day they'd come for Jun. The Kaia had called him Erusha.

He was smaller than most of the Grutex Brin had met, but even so, he towered over the humans. The other male, a warrior by the look of him, deactivated the force field and stepped inside. He reached down, snagging Telisa by her upper arm and yanking to her feet.

"Let go of me, you asshole!" Telisa yelled, kicking out at the male's body as she twisted away.

The warrior turned toward Erusha as if asking what he should do about the wild display of defiance. "Pick her up," he ground out. "That's enough out of you, female."

With hardly any effort at all, the larger male hoisted Telisa up and over his shoulder as if she were nothing more than a doll. She continued to fight, pounding on the warrior's exoskeleton and screaming for him to release her.

Brin stepped up to the forcefield, his hands fisting in frustration as he watched the scene, knowing he could do nothing to help her. Erusha moved past them, not even sparing her a glance as he swiped through something on his wrist comm.

Brin listened to her shouts and threats all the way down the hall, until they eventually faded away. He lowered himself to the floor, closing his eyes as he let his head fall back.

He wouldn't call himself religious, not after everything that he'd gone through in his life, but Brin had spoken with the goddess on more than one occasion since his crash landing on Earth and now, more than ever, he hoped she could hear his prayers for Jun's safety.

It was nearly impossible to tell how much time passed as he waited for his mate to return. Humans, both male and female, were brought in and out of the cells, their eyes wide and fearful. Was Jun feeling the same things they were? Was she afraid? Was she being tortured?

Brin toyed with the panels, digging his claws between them and picking at the screws like Jun and Telisa had done. When he finally managed to lift one side, Brin was not surprised to find nothing but welded metal plates beneath it. No useful wiring like Jun had hoped for.

Watch over her, he pleaded to the goddess and her mates one more time as he stared up at the ceiling. *Keep her safe. Protect her.*

CHAPTER 19

NUZAL

*J*un stayed safe within the healing gel for two day cycles as her body adjusted to the bionics. While he hadn't ever personally known them to fail, Nuzal refused to take any chances where she was concerned.

More than once he'd stood at the entrance of the corridor that led down to Brin's cell, struggling with his desire to reassure the male that she was safe and well cared for, but each time he forced himself to turn away. If he was caught comforting the Venium, he might come under fire.

Nuzal hadn't spoken with Erusha since they'd shared a meal in the common area, but he hadn't found much time to seek him out.

If he wasn't checking on Jun's progress, he was poring over the mysterious journal. The pages contained valuable and shocking information that Nuzal wasn't completely sure what to do with.

He looked down at his comm as he closed the book and

sighed wearily. He'd been putting off the start of Brin's testing for far too long, and if he didn't send out samples soon, he feared Erusha, or even the Kaia himself, might become suspicious and investigate.

Pushing back from his desk where he'd sat reading, Nuzal passed his wrist over a spot on the inside of the wide leg, revealing a hidden compartment. He slipped the journal inside before pressing it closed, listening for the sound of the lock moving into place.

It was well into the day cycle by the time Nuzal stepped out of his room. He made his way through the busy halls, avoiding any and all conversations, but most of the males seemed to sense his irritation and stayed away.

The thought of having to bring the Venium into the lab for testing had him in a foul mood, and the fact that it was even bothering him to begin with did nothing to ease it.

A persistent voice inside of him told Nuzal this was wrong, that he should refuse, but what good would that do? He would be punished and removed from the project, and depending on how much it annoyed the Kaia, he risked having this life ended and a delayed rebirth. Who would be there to protect them if he was gone?

These strange emotions were foreign to him. Anger, indifference, contempt, those he understood, but these softer things? They made him uncomfortable, and he felt exposed, as if anyone who looked hard enough could see what was happening inside of his mind.

At the last minute, Nuzal banked to the left, deciding to check on Jun one more time. The least he could do before taking Brin into the lab was to give him an accurate update on her recovery. He'd worried over her throughout the entire night cycle. Humans were fragile beings, and even the healthiest among them had expired unexpectedly.

Nuzal input the code into the pad on the wall and stepped through the door into her private room. A glance at the log where her vitals were recorded told him that it was safe for her to be removed from the gel. He keyed in the command and waited patiently as the substance retreated, leaving Jun's nude body exposed to the cool air of the room.

The small incisions on her side from her previous surgery had faded considerably, and the ones he'd created during the transplant only a few day cycles before were healed and had faded to a pinkish brown.

Although the gel had kept her body clean and free of harmful bacteria during her recovery, Nuzal doubted she would enjoy waking up to the slimy film that clung to her skin.

A quick tap of his fingers on the bed's display screen brought the forcefield up. Warm cleansing fluid swirled around her, tangling her long hair as it began to cover her limbs and torso. He filled a small basin with warm water and took one of the cloths from the cabinets beneath the counter. As the cycle ended and the fluid receded, Nuzal disabled the force field and began to gently clean her face with the soft cloth, running the material over her brows and the bridge of her nose. Within his chest, his heart raced, pounding like the old drums of battle he'd once marched to.

He brushed a bare knuckle over her cheek, marveling at the colors that flowed over the smaller plates on his fingers. No matter how many times he witnessed it, the display never failed to amaze him.

"My mate touches my body, leaving a trail of shimmering color in her wake. It is beautiful and terrifying to know she is mine."

The words from the journal echoed in his mind as he pressed his palm to her skin, watching the color flow like water. "Beautiful and terrifying," he murmured.

This tiny, fragile being was his mate, and since Brin was bound to her, they too were bound. The shock of reading the journal entry, of realizing what he was experiencing with Jun was something ancient and most likely lost to them, hadn't worn off just yet.

He knew now that this was something he should cherish, a gift from the gods, but the joy was overshadowed by fear that the Kaia would discover it, and the shame over what he had done in this lifetime. His mates would never accept him, and as he thought back on all of the things he'd had a hand in, Nuzal couldn't say he would blame them.

The fact that Jun was his mate mattered little, he tried to convince himself as he slid his claws through her hair, gently tugging at the knots that had formed during the cleansing process. Nuzal was imperfect, flawed in more ways than one. He would not be permitted to pass these genes on to a new generation of Grutex. The idea of having offspring had never interested him, but now, as he looked down at his female, at his *mate*, Nuzal wondered what having one might be like.

Behind the plating covering his groin, Nuzal felt his inkei grow hard, twitching and pulsing with desire. Like Nuzal, most of the Grutex had not engaged in sexual intercourse for lifetimes, possibly ever. His body wanted her just as much as his mind did. He closed his eyes, taking a moment to slow his breathing and bring himself under control. Nuzal had seen the warriors violate the humans while they slept, and had been instructed to turn a blind eye to their activities, but he could not imagine harming his mate in such a way.

When his claws were able to pass through her hair without catching, Nuzal wrung the excess water from the strands before twisting them into a damp knot at the top of her head. He patted her skin dry with a towel he'd found, careful to avoid scratching her with his claws as he moved from her head, down her chest, and over her belly. Nuzal spread her legs, running the cloth lightly over the dark thatch of curls at their juncture and the insides of her thighs.

"Brin…" she groaned softly.

He jerked his hand away as his gaze swung toward her face, relief rushing through him when her eyes remained closed and her breathing evened out. *Still asleep.* The touch, even as innocent as it had been, reminded him that she had someone waiting for her; someone who must be worried about what was happening to his female.

Nuzal dried her legs and feet before turning her on her side to make sure her back received the same treatment. A clean dressing gown, the same ones they used for all of the humans after the awakening procedures, was hung on the wall. He brought it to her bed, slipping her arms through the holes of the garment. As carefully as he could, Nuzal lifted Jun into his arms, pressing her body against his upper body as he tried to figure out how to clasp the binding at the back.

"Wha…" Jun hummed, her breath huffing out against the side of his face. "What the hell?"

The pounding of her pulse could be felt against his plating, and Nuzal rumbled softly in his chest, hoping it would calm instead of frighten her further. "Be still. I'm trying to dress you."

"I had clothes on before you took me!" she hissed, shoving weakly at his shoulder. "Didn't I? God, I can't even remember."

"You were taken for surgery three day cycles ago," he told her, struggling to find the binding as she twisted in his arms.

"I was naked." She narrowed her dark eyes on him, the accusation in her voice clear. "Why?"

"Did you want me to make the incisions through your clothing?"

"What exactly was this surgery for?"

Nuzal grunted as she pressed her elbow into his xines. "To

save your life." With a frustrated growl, Nuzal set Jun on her feet, dropping to one knee as he spun her around. "I fixed you."

"Fixed me? How?" Jun twisted, grabbing at his hands as they moved over her back.

"Stop that," He grumbled, swatting gently at her hands as he began to fasten the bindings. "I replaced your damaged organs."

"You—you replaced my kidneys?"

"Yes. The only remaining one was damaged beyond repair. Your heart is also functioning much better now that the gel has had time to work through your body." Nuzal fastened the last of them and turned her around. With him crouched as he was, they were nearly face to face. Her lips were parted slightly and her eyes were wide as she stared at him.

"Why would you do that?" she asked him. "I'm human. I thought we were disposable to the Grutex."

"You are not disposable to me." The way her brows furrowed had him biting his tongue. He was going to say more than he wanted to if he wasn't careful. "I wanted to save you, and I did."

The inside of his wrist lit up, a reminder that he still needed to get Brin into the lab before the end of the cycle. It was something he was sure his mate would not soon forgive him for.

"Thank you."

The soft words halted his movement. Tears formed in her eyes, and she caught her bottom lip between her teeth as she fidgeted with the material of the gown. Had anyone ever thanked him before?

"Are you in pain, female?" he asked, gently wiping away the tears as they fell from her eyes. "Is it from the incision?"

Panic... That was the feeling that made his chest tighten uncomfortably.

Jun shook her head. "They're just tears. Haven't you ever seen a human cry?"

More times than he cared to admit, but he ignored the question. "Is it from pain?"

"No." She shook her head, stepping away from him. "I just... I never thought I'd be healed, not completely."

"The valves of your heart still show small signs of the damage, but it is my hope you notice a considerable difference."

A selfish, delusional part of him wanted to keep her tucked away in this room, hidden from the others, but he thought of Brin, of the fear and uncertainty he must be feeling, and he scooped Jun up into his arms.

"Hey!" she squeaked, clutching his xines as he spun toward the door. "What are you doing?"

"Taking you back to Brin."

As soon as the door opened, Nuzal stuck his head out, making sure none of the other males were standing around. The lights shimmered as her hands moved over his chest and he gritted his teeth against the pleasure it brought him. It was dangerous to be out in the halls with her.

"Is he okay?"

"I haven't seen him since your surgery. Your health was my priority."

He swiped through his comms features, bringing up the ships grid. Thousands of small dots appeared within the ship, but he narrowed its focus on the path he planned to take back to the cells. Most of the males were in rooms with patients or gathered in the common areas.

"Oh." She frowned down at his screen. "What is that?" Jun asked as they approached the corridor where Brin was being kept.

He heard it too, loud shouts and growls as someone struggled in the hall. Nuzal took off, running to see what was happening as dread sank like a weight within his stomach. Something inside of him whispered that this wasn't good. One of the guards, a male he recognized, stumbled out of the cell with his arms wrapped around Brin's legs. The Venium was struggling, lashing out at the male who was attempting to restrain his arms.

"Hold him!" the guard at his feet was growling.

Brin hissed as one of their barbed tails dug into his side. His lifeblood trickled from the open wound as he twisted free, but the male who had dropped him recovered, raising his foot and slamming it down onto Brin's chest as hard as he could.

Nuzal felt something within him snap at the sight. Jun slid down his body, her feet barely touching the floor before he lunged at the male who had injured the Venium. His body responded as if it knew instinctively what to do, and Nuzal supposed that after so many lifetimes as a warrior, it actually might.

His fist slammed into the guard's face, cracking the plating above his middle set of eyes. He snaked his arm around his neck, cutting off his air supply as Brin twisted in the other guard's grasp, bringing him down to the floor before wrapping his legs around the male's head.

Both Grutex guards clawed and flailed, but as they began to lose consciousness, their struggle faded. When the one in Nuzal's arms went limp, he carefully laid him down within the cell before pulling the other one from Brin's grasp.

They were unconscious, but alive.

"What is going on here?"

Nuzal turned to see Vodk and Raou storming down the corridor toward them. "I requested the male be brought in for his tests!" Vodk growled. "You are interfering!"

"They were damaging him." He pressed his hand to the Venium's side, trying to stem the flow of lifeblood.

Jun rushed toward him, and he didn't miss the way Raou's eyes tracked her movements. "Brin!" she gasped, pushing Nuzal's hand away so she could inspect the damage.

"You're alive," Brin whispered, his fingers brushing her face.

"You doubted me," Nuzal murmured, leaning in close so the others wouldn't hear.

"Of course I did," Brin spat. "It's nothing but a scratch, Shayfia. Leave it. Are you all right? Did they hurt you?"

Jun turned her face up to stare at Nuzal for a moment before shaking her head. "I'm okay."

The look she gave him nearly stopped his heart. She was the most gorgeous, perfect being he'd ever laid eyes on.

"You injured two of our guards in defense of the Venium?" Vodk demanded. "Have your flaws blinded you so completely that you would allow them even the smallest opportunity to escape?"

Nuzal sneered up at the male, but he couldn't afford to be questioned like this. Careful to touch only the areas where Jun was clothed, Nuzal nudged her to her feet.

"Into the cell. I will be with him. Do as I say."

Jun opened her mouth, but whatever she had planned to say died on her tongue as more guards, drawn in by the noise, began to arrive. He deactivated the forcefield on the neighboring cell containing the female she'd been in with before, waiting as she stepped inside and turned to watch him bring it back up. Guards hauled Brin to his feet before securing cuffs around his wrists and ankles. Nuzal moved to follow them, but the hand around his arm stopped him.

Raou's red eyes stared into his, and the grin that tugged at the male's mouth made Nuzal wish he could bash his face into the flooring. "The Kaia has requested a meeting with you. Immediately."

He knows, the voice in his mind whispered. *They know.*

CHAPTER 20

BRIN

*J*un was alive.

His body had filled with relief at the sight of her face. Her skin had a healthy glow to it, and her eyes had been bright and clear. No sign of the pain that had crippled her in his cell remained. Nuzal had done that.

The guards on either side of him growled, shoving him forward when his steps faltered. He could feel Raou's eyes on his back, burning into his scarred flesh. If he was here, then Jun was safe from him. For now.

The male who had arrived with him, a scientist, Brin assumed by the way he scrolled through the files on his comm, walked ahead of them, barking orders as they passed through a set of doors into a large room. A single reclining chair sat in the middle of it, surrounded by high-tech machines Brin was unfamiliar with. These looked nothing like the medbays on the Grutex ships he had been on. They were keeping secrets.

The lights in the room flickered for only a second, making Brin wonder if it was Nyissa attempting to hack into the system. She needed all the time he could give her. He'd hoped she would be able to find something, anything, but so far, she hadn't even been able to tell him how long they had been on the ship, or even how much time had passed since their abduction from Earth.

Nyissa rested when he did, so she would have been completely unaware of what was happening during his time in the cryochamber. Perhaps his cooperation would bring her closer to a more helpful source. His AI was resourceful and good at what he'd programmed her to do. He had faith in her.

A rough hand pressed into the middle of his back, knocking him forward. Brin turned his head to see Raou glaring at him, a grin pulling at the newer scars on the side of his face. The male caught him around the throat, and he stumbled backward, trying to stay on his feet as he advanced.

"This time," Raou growled as Brin's legs bumped into the lower section of the chair. "This time, *I* will torture *you*."

Brin hit the seat so hard he felt the air leave his lungs. He managed a smile as the guards removed the cuffs before placing the chair's bonds around his wrists and ankles. A thick strap was secured over his chest and hips as Raou stepped away. Brin watched him converse with the other male, the scientist who didn't seem to like Nuzal. Their heads were bowed close together, and they spoke in hushed tones as they looked over whatever was on the other male's comm.

Taking a deep, calming breath, Brin closed his eyes and thought of his little mate. She was alive and waiting for him in that cell and he would do anything to get back to her. Being away from her, not knowing if she was okay, had been the hardest thing he'd ever been through. Brin had been separated from people he loved before, many times, but having a mate was something entirely different. How had he ever presumed he could live without her? All those plans to leave her on Earth, to go on with his life like she had never existed, were laughable now.

His heart would have never allowed it.

"Your heart will get you killed, Ruvator," Brega had once sneered at him.

Brin peered down his body at the bindings and resisted the urge to laugh. *Perhaps she was right about that after all.*

Raou looked up from the holoscreen as Brin chuckled, the lid over his missing eye caving into the empty socket as he frowned. "Come, Vodk. Let's begin."

"Yes, Vodk, I was wondering when the torture was going to start. It's rude to keep me waiting." Brin grinned at the obvious irritation it caused in the warrior. "Do the Grutex regenerate missing parts, or will you always be this ugly?"

Raou rushed him, jumping onto the chair as his tail dug into the outside of his thigh. "I should have just killed you that night. I should have bathed in your lifeblood and taken your female."

"That's enough, Raou. You'll tear him apart before I can even find the information the Kaia seeks." Vodk nudged the warrior's shoulder until he climbed down, yanking his tail from Brin's flesh so hard that his leg jumped on the table. "There are other ways to exact revenge, warrior."

"What do you have in mind?" Raou asked.

Vodk tapped on the pad to the right of the chair, stepping back as it began to rise and straighten out into something resembling more of a table than a chair.

"What is the one thing the Venium value above all else?"

"Their mates?" Raou frowned. "We already have the female."

"Besides that." Vodk huffed in annoyance. "Their offspring. We take away his ability to sire offspring."

Brin couldn't have stopped the laugh that burst from his chest even if he'd wanted to. The one thing most Venium hoped for was the one thing he feared. Nothing these males did to him today could be worse than what the people who had brought him into existence had done. They had stripped away the joy he should feel at the idea of having pups with Jun. Taking that ability from him would be a blessing.

"But the Kaia needs the bonding hormone. Is that not the reason I was denied the female?" Raou asked in a hush voice as a forcefield was activated over Brin's body.

The sweet smell of the sedative filled the chamber, and Brin struggled to stay conscious, not wanting to miss anything important. If they survived this, he wanted to have something to bring back to the council. He closed his eyes, pretending to sleep.

"If we are the only ones with the answers to his questions, who do you think will win the Kaia's favor? I've worked too hard to let Erusha and Nuzal take this away from me. By the end of this, I will hold the power here and the true research can begin."

∽

NUZAL

He must have slipped up. Somehow, no matter how careful he had been, someone must have noticed the lights, or maybe it had been his increasingly odd behavior. Had it been Erusha? The male knew him better than anyone. If he was acting strange, he'd have been the first to notice.

Nuzal stepped out of the lift and into the chaotic inner section of the ship. Just like the last time he'd found himself up here, Nuzal was struck by how much he appreciated the quiet atmosphere of the lab. His mind raced as he made his way through the rings of warriors. What was Vodk doing to Brin? Would the male go after Jun next?

What would Nuzal do if something happened to them? And if

he didn't return, what would become of them then? He wondered if he would ever see them again.

"Present for confirmation," one of the warriors said.

Nuzal moved his arm beneath the scanner, trying his best to steady his nerves before walking into the Kaia's office. Any show of fear would be taken as weakness, and the Kaia wouldn't tolerate that.

Calm, he told himself. *Be calm. Show nothing. Remember your days as a warrior. Remember your strength.*

The doors slid open, and he was gestured inside. The Kaia sat behind his desk, and he waved Nuzal forward.

"Someone finally relayed my message, I see," he growled, his voice laced with obvious agitation.

"My apologies, sir. I came as soon as I was informed."

The doors behind him opened once more, and he glanced sideways to see Erusha step up beside him.

"Erusha." The Kaia grinned humorlessly.

"My Kaia." The male inclined his head. "We're quite busy in the lab at the moment. Is there a problem regarding the new human female you selected?"

The human in question sat at the Kaia's feet, her bright blue eyes watching them carefully as she pressed her cheek against their leader's leg. She had long red hair and skin as pale as the medical chairs they used in the labs. This female was a recent acquisition, one Nuzal remembered checking on after the warriors had brought her on board.

"No, no, I find this one quite satisfactory." He ran his fingers through the female's locks, an almost tender look crossing his face as she tipped her face up. "My problem," he growled, turning back to Erusha, "lies with the questionable loyalty of one of your scientists."

Nuzal's xines writhed as the Kaia's eyes fell on him, but he stayed silent. To speak out of turn would do him no favors.

"You speak of Nuzal?" Erusha asked with a confused tilt of his head. "He is one of my hardest workers and does what is asked of him without question or complaint."

"If that is so, then should I assume *you* were the one who approved the bionics he used on the human?"

Erusha's jaw ticked, and his superior's upper set of eyes turned on him, his head canting toward Nuzal. The genuine confusion on his face gave Nuzal pause. Did he truly have no idea? If he hadn't signed off on the bionics, then who had?

Vodk's words from cycles ago replayed in his mind. *The transplant went well, I assume?* He'd wondered at the time how the male had known, but now he suspected he was somehow behind this.

"Yes," Erusha answered. "I gave Nuzal permission to use the bionics on the human."

The Kaia opened his mouth, but Nuzal stepped forward, shielding the male with his body before a word left his mouth.

"The human who received the bionics wasn't just anyone. The bonded female's body was failing. If we allowed her to die before we found the hormone, we couldn't be sure what would happen. It's very possible that the hormones we need for our research would have disappeared, along with any resulting pheromones."

The larger male was silent for a moment, his hand running over the female's head as he stared Nuzal down.

"Be that as it may, something so important should have been brought to my attention."

"The female's decline was swift, sir. Time was of the essence," Erusha answered.

"I see." The Kaia's eyes remained on Nuzal. "And this fight I was alerted to before you arrived at my office, Nuzal? I was told you were the aggressor."

"I returned to the cells to find two young warriors assaulting the Venium male. They had already injured him. His role in this research, as you know, is vital," Nuzal answered.

"I value your knowledge, and I respect your honorable past, Nuzal, but if I am given another reason to question your loyalty, I will personally end this life. Am I clear?"

Nuzal inclined his head. "Yes, sir."

"And Nuzal, you will begin the female's awakening. She's been here far too long without it already. You're both dismissed." He waved his hand at them before tugging at the chain connected to the human's collar. She scurried up as the band tightened around her neck, crawling into the Kaia's lap.

Nuzal turned away quickly, Erusha on his heels. Neither one of them spoke a word as they made their way back to the lab. It was eerily quiet, and Erusha jerked his head toward his office in a silent command for Nuzal to follow. There were no cameras or recording devices here, but even so, they lowered their voices.

"Who gave you permission to acquire the bionics?" the male asked.

Nuzal shook his head. "The approval came from you."

"Show me." A quick search through his messages brought up the interaction. Erusha frowned, his eyes darting over the words before he turned to the holoscreen on his desk. "Who assisted you?"

"Qrien." Nuzal glanced out into the main space where the younger males worked. "I came in here after to speak with you. Vodk was at his desk and told me you had left, but something he said didn't seem right. He asked me how the transplant had gone, but there was no way he would have known about it."

"It seems that someone is trying to sow seeds of dissent within us." Erusha shook his head. "Who took the male?"

"Vodk. He was with the warrior, Raou."

"Found out what he's done. Review the footage from the

surgery. I want you personally on this, no one else. Do not speak a word of this, and come back here with whatever you find. They cannot know we suspect them."

"Yes, sir."

Nuzal rushed next door to the office he rarely used, running his arm beneath the scanner so it could read his comm. Files and documents containing all of the information from past and present cases appeared on the holoscreen, but he didn't need those. He moved through the icons until he found the security files.

Everything that happened in the lab and the surgery rooms was sent here. It took a moment to identify the room Vodk had used, but when he pressed play on the footage, Nuzal felt his anger begin to bubble beneath his plates.

Vodk was nothing more than a greedy, overly ambitious fool. After Brin was put under, the male took his samples, handing the vials off to Raou instead of the trained assistants who would normally be present. His hands fisted on the desk as he watched Vodk complete the sterilization procedure. Raou laughed before patting Vodk on the back, as if what they had done was something to celebrate.

Brin would never be able to reproduce.

Nuzal looked through the logs, noting there were no results requested, nor was there any information input concerning the surgery and what had been found. He suspected there would be no trace of the hormone if they were to check now.

He stared at the footage of Raou and Vodk as they worked, and he felt a growl work its way up his chest. Something within him fell into place at that moment, a piece of him that he'd been denying.

He knew three things. The first was that Jun and Brin were his mates, whether they accepted him or not. The second was that he was going to do everything in his power to free them. It wouldn't right his wrongs, but he couldn't let them stay here any longer. The third, and most satisfying, was the silent promise that he was going to kill both of these males for daring to lay their hands on what was his.

CHAPTER 21

JUN

Every time she twisted, Jun felt the incision on her stomach pull uncomfortably. It wasn't painful at all, but it reminded her that she'd been open and at the mercy of the Grutex—of Nuzal.

The guards had brought Brin back what must have been days ago, but she had no way of knowing for certain. He'd been barely conscious, wrapped in one of the plain gowns like the rest of them, and if she had to guess, she would have said he'd come straight from surgery. Unlike her, they'd allowed Brin no recovery time. She'd tried to fuss over him, checking on his incision, but he assured her he was fine and her worry was misplaced.

He remained quiet for the most part, whispering only to his AI. Jun couldn't hear what they were saying, but there was something different about Brin. Whatever they had done to him that day had only seemed to spur on his resolve to see them set free.

In the time since they had returned him, Vodk had come for both Jun and Telisa. They'd been put through more testing and scans, and Jun's arm was still sore from the tissue sample they had taken earlier. The IV they placed in her arm the last time she was in there had transferred a thick purple liquid into her body, and while she wanted to fight, to rip the needle from her skin and tell them all where they could shove it, Jun knew resistance would not be tolerated.

Nuzal had been notably absent during all of it, and she wondered where he had gone. She shouldn't care what he was doing, but something within her worried over it, telling her things weren't right. Wherever he was, Jun doubted very much she'd ever see him again.

From what little Brin had relayed to them, Nyissa was making some headway. She had successfully set the cameras on a loop for the last hour while she worked her way in the cell security grid. Brin now has maps of the entire ship at his disposal.

"Master," the AI spoke, a hint of excitement in her voice, "the cells have been disarmed."

A second later, the force fields that had kept them inside flickered before the annoying hum of the electricity stopped completely. Jun and Telisa jumped up as Brin sprang forward.

"Now, Shayfia! Come!"

Jun grabbed Telisa's hand, tugging her to the front of the cell. "Let's go! We're getting the hell out of here."

Even knowing there was nothing keeping them in, Jun still stuck her hand out cautiously, feeling for any resistance.

Brin reached inside, grabbing her wrist. "Now! We don't have much time."

"What about the others?" Jun asked, twisting to look at the stunned faces of the humans in the cells across from them.

"So many of us running through the halls is bound to draw attention."

"We can't leave them behind!" Telisa hissed, eyes narrowing on Brin. "Who will rescue them?"

Brin hesitated a second before swiping a finger over his inner arm, disarming the forcefields along the entire length of the corridor.

"We need to arm ourselves," she reminded Brin as the other humans began pouring out of the cells. "Stay close and as quiet as possible." She told those around her. They nodded, passing the message to those nearest to them.

Brin and Jun moved to the head of the group and as one, they made their way down the hall, their bare feet making hardly any noise. They reached the armory, and Jun was surprised to find it unguarded. Brin passed them through the door to her, and she began handing them out, instructing the others to pass them to anyone who was capable of wielding one.

"Don't hold back," he told the group. "They would sooner kill you than capture you. They showed you no mercy, afford them the same treatment." He handed Jun one of the weapons, smiling when she rubbed her hand over the barrel in appreciation. "I'm not sure if that look terrifies or excites me," he told her as his fushori pulsed softly.

Jun shook her head, pressing her lips to his chest since she couldn't reach his mouth. "Be careful, Glowworm. You keep this up and I might accidentally fall in love with you."

Brin frowned as he stared down at her, stepping backward toward a set of doors Nyissa had indicated would lead them toward the exit for this section. "You say that as if you weren't already."

Without warning, the doors burst open and mauve arms snaked around Brin's neck, long claws digging into the skin on his chest. The people behind her scurried back in fear, already forgetting the weapons they held in their hands as weeks and months of abuse came rushing back. Jun raised her gun, but Brin fought his attacker, preventing her from getting a clear shot.

His tail wrapped around the other male's leg, knocking him

off balance and loosening his hold on Brin's throat. She swore under her breath as she staggered back, trying to keep out of the way of their big bodies as they struggled against one another. As they turned to the side, the male's face came into view, and Jun froze.

Raou.

She knew that scarred, evil face. He landed a blow against Brin's jaw, knocking him back, and Jun leveled the weapon at him, training it on his head as he sneered at her.

"What do you think you will do with that, fem—"

His words were cut off by the sound of the weapon discharging as Jun squeezed the trigger. Where his bottom and middle left eyes had once been, there was now a gaping, bloody hole. His body swayed for a moment before going slack. He crumpled to the floor, his remaining eyes staring up at the ceiling lifelessly.

It wasn't how she had imagined his death. There was no suffering or calls for Mercy, no payment for all of the horrible things he had done to them and the terrifying promises he made that had given her nightmares, and would probably continue to haunt her even once they had escaped. It was too good for him, but it was done and Brin was okay.

Raou would never touch them again.

"He might have called for backup," Telisa said, her voice calm and collected as if she watched women murder giant aliens on a daily basis. "It's all right," she told the people huddled behind. "He's dead. It's okay."

Brin stared up at her from where he'd sunk down to the floor, rubbing at a spot on his jaw.

"Shayfia indeed."

Jun laughed in spite of the situation.

"You can't even take near death seriously."

He got back to his feet and motioned for their group to follow him. Nyissa called out directions, leading them up and down two corridors before they reached one of the intersections just before the doors. Brin came to a stop, throwing his arms out to catch Jun and Telisa as they slammed into his back.

Nuzal stood in the middle of the hall. Jun felt her stomach drop as their eyes met across the space. She should kill him too, but her hand shook at the thought of even aiming her weapon at him. The only kindness she had known here had come from him.

"You're missing the humans in solitary," he said, looking at Brin. "This way." Nuzal didn't wait for them to respond. He turned on his heel, running down the hall.

"Are we really going to trust him?" Telisa asked in disbelief.

Brin looked down at Jun and she saw something in his eyes that she wasn't ready to explore.

"He saved your life, Shayfia, but don't let your guard down."

They took off after him, weapons raised as they kept an eye out for any of the roaming guards Nuzal had once warned them about. When they reached the doors at the end of the hall, Brin insisted on going fist. As they slid open, the body of one of the guards fell at Brin's feet, his neck clearly broken as he stared up at them from the floor.

Nuzal was already moving toward the two rows of cells, each one containing more frightened humans. He looked back at them before tapping in the code on the keypad of the first cell, then the second, and third. Telisa was there to greet them, encouraging them to join the others out in the hall.

Jun stepped over the body of the guard as Nuzal reached the last cell of the first row, entering the code before captives rushed past him. She laid her hand over his where it rested on the wall, watching as the lights shimmered beneath her fingers and warmth spread up her arm.

"Why are you helping us?"

"I was coming for you," he said, his eyes following the colors. "I was going to get you out."

"Why, though?"

"This," he told her, turning his hand so that her palm rested in his. The warmth of the breath he released rushed over her, and she shivered.

"The glow?" He nodded as she tilted her head. "What is it?"

His eyes darted to her face before he looked away almost sheepishly, as if whatever it was made him self conscious.

"It means that you are my mate." Before she could think of a response, he rushed ahead. "I don't expect either of you to accept the claim. I just want you to be safe." He glanced sideways at Brin. "Both of you."

If Nuzal hadn't already fixed her heart, Jun might have feared it would give out right then and there. It pounded fiercely within her chest as she stared up at him, struggling to make sense of the admission. Was it possible to be mated to two aliens? She hadn't ever imagined she'd even have *one* mate, and here she was, being told she now had *two* of them.

"Shayfia," Brin said, his hand slipping into her free one. "There's no time for this now. We need to get the rest of your people out before we're caught."

Nuzal moved to the second row, and Jun and Brin followed behind him, helping the ones who seemed too shocked to move on their own. Brin pulled up his comm and frowned.

"Nyissa isn't able to access the star map from here. We need to get someplace where we can find out exactly where we are."

Nuzal nodded, hurrying toward the doors. "I know a place. Follow me."

The humans scrambled out of his way. Jun looked at Brin as she ran after him, hoping the group could keep up. Many of them were mentally and physically exhausted, and all of this sneaking around was fraying the last of their control.

"The records room," Nuzal told her when she caught up. "It's the only place I know of that keeps updated star maps for this region. "Stay here. I'll clear the way."

They watched him slip inside, listening at the door for any sign of trouble. Brin raised his brow at the silence, gripping the weapons as he prepared himself for a fight, but when the door slid open once more, Nuzal stood in front of them, his exoskeleton covered in blood. "It's clear now."

That's one way to do it, she thought as she and Telisa ushered their growing group into the room. Brin took a seat at the massive holoscreen, wasting no time. Jun had never seen anything like it in her life. He ran his fingers over the pad in front of him as he moved through different files, swiping away the ones he didn't need.

"Someone has been in here," Nuzal murmured, his eyes narrowing on the files that had been on the screen. "Wait!" He leaned forward, his head tilting as he read one of the filenames. "First mating. Pull it up."

CHAPTER 22

NUZAL

"There's no time for this," Brin growled.

"We will make time! This is the only chance we might ever have to access these files." When Brin huffed in irritation, Nuzal shook his head. "There will be maps on board the ship. We can figure out our location there."

"We'll be caught if we stay here too long," Brin argued, his fushori pulsing and racing angrily over his body as he looked back at the humans huddled in the corners.

"We won't be caught. I've made sure of it."

Most of the males, warriors and intellectuals alike, were far too concerned about the massive hole that had been blown into one of the docking stations on the other side of the ship. He'd rigged one of the visiting Tachin vessels with a small bomb Vodk had once designed, hoping to impress the Kaia. It had been far more powerful than expected, taking out not just the Tachin ship but also ten of their own crafts.

Someone had been in here before them. These files required a clearance Nuzal didn't have, and likely never would have, even if he hadn't planned on leaving. Brin tapped on the file, opening the document on the large holoscreen.

"What does it say?" Jun asked, stepping up beside him.

"Test Subject A0001: the female has shown no notable progress this cycle. The effect (illumination) she has on the scientist, Erusha's, plating remains the only indication that there is something different about her genetics. Erusha reports no discomfort from the lights. We await the results of their testing."

Jun blinked up at him before looking down at her hands as if she were discovering some mystical power.

Nuzal frowned at the screen as he stared at the words. Erusha had experienced this before? He thought back to the journal he'd found in his room, and an uneasy feeling settled in his stomach. Was it possible?

Brin swiped, bringing up the next entry. "Test Subject A0001: the female successfully endured her awakening and has made a full recovery," Nuzal continued. "Erusha was instructed to engage in the hunt, and a breeding followed. We do not expect to find proof of fertilization for many cycles, but past observations of human pregnancies and the memories that remain of Grutex pregnancies tell us that any fetus should be fast forming. Breeding will continue each day cycle in the hopes of a successful pregnancy."

"The hunt," Jun shook her head. "What does that mean exactly?"

He hated the shame that rushed through him over the acts of violence his people had committed.

"The hunt is a breeding tradition from our past. It stopped for many generations ago, sometime after we began to forego the reproduction process, but it seems that it was resurrected after this."

"Forego the reproduction process? How are the Grutex born if you aren't reproducing?"

Nuzal looked down at his mate, trying to decide how best to tell her he was far older than she could ever imagine.

"Every Grutex in existence now was born for the *first* time many, many generations ago."

"The first time?" Brin asked, turning in his seat with a frown.

"Each of us goes through a lifetime, and when this body is ready to expire, we are simply reborn into another vessel containing our modified DNA. We leave the tube and are raised in groups of offspring by females from previous birth cycles."

Jun's mouth was hanging open, and she gaped at him for a moment before turning to Brin who shook his head. "So you're... immortal?"

"I wouldn't say that, but we carry on the memories of our past lives, most of the memories, that is. I suppose, in some ways, that makes us immortal." Nuzal lifted his shoulder and dropped it.

"You don't have biological parents then?" Jun asked.

The word sparked something small in his memories, the oldest in his mind, and the hardest to recall.

"I can't remember what those are."

"A mother and a father? People who created you?"

"We do, in a way. The scientists who recreate us and care for us as we grow, and the females who look after us before our training begins are our parents, yes?"

"That's not really what I meant—"

"Shayfia," Brin interrupted. "We don't have time to discuss family dynamics right now."

Nuzal wanted to ask her what she meant, wanted to understand her question, but Brin was right.

"Are there other files?"

"Just this one here," Brin answered, opening the document.

"Test Subject A0001: the breeding has been deemed a failure. None of the offspring from the breedings have been viable. Each of the four separate pregnancies has resulted in loss prior to birth.

The Kaia has ordered her to be terminated, citing her poor mental and physical health. Erusha is visibly upset over the ruling and has been confined to his quarters until he regains his composure. The assistant assigned to him has expressed concern over his condition. Final log."

"Concern over his condition?" Nuzal growled, frustrated over how little was actually mentioned within the files.

"I died with her that night."

Nuzal spun toward his superior's voice as the male stepped from the shadows where he must have hidden himself when Nuzal disposed of the guard. The humans in the room pressed back against the walls, their eyes going wide with fear. Many of them knew this male. Jun's weapon was trained on him, but Nuzal placed his hand on the barrel, lowering it to the floor.

"They brought the female in with a small group of others, and she was assigned to me for testing. The moment she touched me, the moment I saw those lights on my body, I knew it was something special. I tried my best to keep them from hurting her, but I'm afraid I caused the worst of it." Erusha approached them, reaching over to select something from within the code of the file.

A photo of a human female appeared on the screen. Her dark brown eyes wide and fearful, set inside a softly rounded face framed by short, brown curls. The pale skin on her face was sprinkled with golden freckles. Erusha reached out to touch the image, his hand balling into a fist when he passed through the holo.

"I was told to breed her, to force her, and I did because I knew if I didn't, they would punish us both. We found comfort with each other eventually, understanding, even love. She conceived like they wanted, but the pregnancies and their constant testing were too hard on her body. I was made to watch her deteriorate with each failed pregnancy. She grieved the loss of each one of our young." Erusha faced Nuzal. "After the last, I refused to force her to go through it ever again. The Kaia ordered her death, calling our breeding a failure. I don't think he expected me to die with her, but we had sealed our bond already. You were part of my revenge."

Nuzal frowned at the male in confusion. "How so?"

"The samples they took from me, the ones they needed to recreate the bond? I stole them and placed them into as many of the waiting tubes as I could get to. You were the first, I recognized your name—the honored warrior, Nuzal, one of the strongest among us. I could not have foreseen the effect the artificial placement would cause." He gestured at Nuzal's eyes.

Nuzal felt as if someone had knocked the breath from his lungs. "Why?" he asked, his xines writhing as his anger grew. "Why would you burden me with imperfection?"

"For her!" Erusha growled, making a sweeping gesture toward Jun. "I remembered after the bond. It was as if someone had unlocked all my forgotten memories. The Grutex have lost their way, Nuzal. We are nothing like the males and females who set out from Venora."

"Venora?" Brin interjected. "What do you mean set out from Venora?"

"The memories returned to me," Erusha told them, his eyes wide, almost craving. "We left Venora, our home, to find the females that had been taken from us. This Kaia, and all of the others, have lost their way! They've become so obsessed with these side ventures and apparent immortality that they have grown complacent."

"And this is why you corrupted those tubes?"

"Corruption," Erusha spat, stepping closer to Nuzal. "I gave you a gift! You have the chance to *live*, to *love*, to bring new life into this world! Turning back to our origins, to the way the goddess meant for us to be, is the only way to fix the mistakes we have made."

Nuzal couldn't stop the snort of disbelief that escaped his mouth as he turned away from the male. He'd lost his mind.

"The Venium have them," Erusha continued. "Our females, their females, they have found them, but they don't even know it. The gene that allows you to light up beneath your mate's touch is a recessive gene passed down from them."

"The lights," Brin said. "The lost females are the Sanctus?"

"I saw it, Nuzal. We have our answers within our grasp." Erusha grabbed his arm, spinning him around. "We can heal ourselves."

"Wait, if you knew all of this, then why keep testing on us?" Jun spoke up from behind him.

"I'm the only one who has this information. If they knew…" He shook his head. "They cannot find out. I just needed time to find a way to bring her back." Erusha's eyes darted back to the picture of his lost mate on the holoscreen. "Without knowledge of the human body, of their minds, I wouldn't be able to recreate her, to give her the rebirth I promised."

"Humans can't do whatever it is you promised her. You've been chasing a ghost all of this time, and all you've done is hurt countless innocent human beings in the process," his mate sneered.

The other male was silent as he looked first at Jun, and then at the rest of the humans in the room. "It no longer matters. You should go before they come looking. We'll go to the docking stations in sector five."

Erusha gave them no time to respond, dashing out the doors as they all glanced curiously at one another.

"We're going to trust him?" one of the human females asked as Jun and Brin moved to follow the male. Nuzal recognized her as the one who had shared Jun's cell.

His mate turned to him, her gaze unsure as she searched his face.

There was a question in her eyes, as if she were asking *him* if it was okay to trust Erusha. Nuzal wasn't sure how he felt about everything he'd heard since reading the files, but he couldn't imagine Erusha would go through all of the trouble of ensuring his DNA was passed on and placing the journal in his room just to turn them over to the Kaia. He nodded before joining Brin in the hall, just outside the doors.

"This is our only chance, Telisa." Jun held out her hand.

Telisa frowned, but she slipped her hand into Jun's with a sigh as she moved forward, gesturing for those behind her to follow. Erusha stood at the end of the hall, focused on his comm and the small dots on the display.

"Our way is clear for the moment," he told them. "Stay close together and move quickly."

They met no resistance as they exited the lab, and when they reached the small alcove just outside of it Nuzal saw that the guard who had been on shift lay dead on the floor in a pool of his own lifeblood.

"He gave me a hard time." Erusha shrugged, not stopping to explain himself further. He brought them to one of the loading tunnels, tapping in the code and releasing the lock on the door. "Inside, all of you."

Telisa ushered the frightened humans inside, murmuring encouraging words to some of the ones who seemed to struggle the most. When the last of the rescued humans was inside, Telisa turned to Erusha, her mouth opening as if she were going to speak, but said nothing. She shut her mouth, pressing her lips together before stomping off after the others. Erusha watched her go, his head bowed and fists clenched.

Nuzal moved to follow Jun and Brin, but when he looked back, expecting to see Erusha on his heels, he was surprised to see him preparing to seal the doors. "You aren't coming with us?"

"I have made grave mistakes, Nuzal. I can see that now. I only ask that I be allowed to make amends for some of those." Erusha stepped into the loading tunnel, a grim smile tugging at his lips. "I hope that one day you will forgive me."

He felt the male's hand at the back of his head, drawing his face close, and he froze. Erusha's forehead rested against his own, and the male's xines wrapped tightly around Nuzal's.

"I remember this," Erusha spoke quietly. "It was both a greeting and a farewell, something shared with one's offspring in the time before we lost our way. You are the closest thing I've had to offspring since... for a long time. My pride in you goes beyond words." The male's voice broke as he pulled away. "Your time here is over. Protect our future." He watched as Erusha stepped back out into the corridor, sealing the door just as a commotion broke out somewhere beyond him.

"Nuzal?"

He turned to see Jun watching him, her dark eyes reading him as she waited.

"I'm coming."

Nuzal stepped into the ship, closing and sealing the hatch behind him as he struggled to process everything.

On one hand, Erusha had been the only friend he could remember ever having. He had encouraged his studies, had spoken up for him when Nuzal felt he had no voice. Was this what a parent was?

On the other hand, Erusha had been the cause of all of his misery. He'd altered him, made him into someone he was never meant to be. And hadn't he had a hand in altering countless humans, in changing them into versions of themselves that were unnatural? He was no better.

The floor began to vibrate beneath his feet, and he reached out to catch Jun as it lurched to one side, sending her stumbling toward the wall.

"Damn it, Brin," she grumbled, pushing out of his arms and heading into the main body. "Who taught you how to fly?"

"I'm a Havacker, Shayfia, not a pilot," Brin told her, tapping the icons on the holo display as he maneuvered the ship away from the dock.

"I'm just gonna say, it would really suck to die after escaping, so try to keep us alive if you don't mind?" Telisa yelled from the rear of the ship.

"Is this a bad time to confess that the last time I flew a vessel it ended in a crash landing?" Brin asked as he pulled up the star map.

"Let's not talk about that." Jun squinted at the display as planets within the sector began to appear. "Are any of those Venora?"

"No," Brin grunted, tugging at the controls as the ship shuddered all around them. "Sit!" He barked at Jun, jerking his head toward one of the seats against the wall. She grimaced at the back of his head, but made no attempt to argue, throwing herself into the padded chair before tugging the straps down and across her chest. "Strap in!" he yelled.

Nuzal heard Telisa echoing the command, and imagined she was frantically ushering the humans into the rows of seats meant to hold warriors for transport. He dropped down into the co-pilot's chair, buckling himself in before engaging the ship's shields and activating its defenses. Another shudder wracked them, this one forceful enough to make his teeth rattle in his head.

"Damage taken," the ship's AI informed them. "Main engine failing."

Nuzal returned fire, spraying the side of the docking station as Brin tried to pull away. He managed to disable one of the smaller crafts that had followed them, knocking out one of their thrusters and damaging the hull.

"Activate cloaking system. Nyissa, get inside and see what we're working with. Disable any tracking devices."

"Cloaking system is activated. Disabling tracking, Master."

"Set a course for the nearest planet and pray they don't follow us there." Brin growled.

To Nuzal's surprise, no other ships were dispatched to follow them, and he counted that as good fortune seeing as they barely made it into the atmosphere of the dark planet. The ship's alarms were blaring in his ears, and the humans in the rear screamed, their panic filling the interior as the vessel dropped through the air, hitting the ground with a loud and resounding thud.

CHAPTER 23

JUN

*a*larms blared all around, and the lights above her flickered as the ship came to an abrupt stop. Falling out of the sky had nearly brought up the meager ration she had eaten earlier.

Jun hadn't ever been a thrill seeker, preferring to keep her feet planted firmly on the ground, but she'd let Amanda talk her into riding one of the roller coasters at the local amusement park back on Earth, and she had thoroughly regretted it. It had been one of those coasters where the floor drops out from beneath you, leaving your legs swinging as it flips and spins you around.

Like that first roller coaster ride, the flight to the planet had sent her heart into her throat. Her head spun as she hit the release on the straps that crisscrossed her chest, and her stomach churned when she dropped to the floor, landing on her hands and knees. She took deep, full breaths as she tried to stave off the urge to vomit.

Hold it in! Hold it in!

Each breath she took sent sharp pains through her chest, and she winced as she pushed herself up to rest on her heels. Jun could hear the others in the back of the ship, their cries and shouts for help spurring her on as she climbed to her feet.

Nuzal was up and out of his seat, all six of his eyes locked on her as he dropped to his knees at her feet. His thumb swept over her cheek, and she hissed at the sting it caused, jerking away from his as she reached up to touch the spot. A streak of blood stained the tips of her fingers, and she grimaced.

"You're injured."

"I'm fine," Jun said, trying to move past him, but Brin's body blocked her path.

"Shayfia," Brin crouched down, his hands going to her injured cheek, "let me clean it for you." He took her hands, pulling her into his arms.

"It's a tiny cut, Brin. I need to get to the back to check on the others." She turned to Nuzal as he stood. "Do you know if there's a supply of the healing balm you gave me on this ship? I lost the rest of the vial with my clothes."

"The medbays on these ships are small, but it should be something standard. I'll check." He stepped around her and disappeared down the hall.

"What are you doing about him?" Brin asked.

Jun frowned up at him, swatting at the tail trying to sneak up her leg. "Nuzal? He helped us escape... he saved my life. I thought we trusted him."

Brin shook his head, reaching out to take her hand in his. His thumb ran over her knuckles, warming her skin as the lights of his fushori cast a blue tint onto her body. "That's not what I'm talking about."

The awkward, uncomfortable look on his face told her he was referring to the fact that they had learned of Nuzal's mating claim less than an hour ago. The news was still sinking in and she was going to need time to process it all. Right now, she had people to care for.

"I don't know," she told him honestly. "Let's just get through this and then we can decide what's best." Jun gripped Brin's hand tightly before shaking free and slipping past him.

Although the others in the back had strapped in, many of them had small cuts, bruises, and bumps from the rough landing. It took Jun and Telisa an hour or more to get through everyone. Calming their frayed nerves and assuring them that they were safe with these aliens had been just as important as healing their physical wounds.

Jun sighed as she crouched on the floor staring under a small table at the blonde woman who had plastered herself against the cold metal wall. "Want to join us out here?" she asked.

The woman curled herself into a ball and shook her head violently. "No!"

"All right, that's okay. Can you tell me your name then?"

"Esme," she said, her voice suddenly small and terrified.

"My name is Jun," she told her. "I'm a nurse and I just want to make sure you're not badly hurt. Why won't you come out?"

Esme looked up, and with a shaking hand, pointed at Nuzal where he sat on the floor, cleaning the wounds on one of the older women.

"Nuzal?" Esme nodded. "He won't hurt you. He helped us escape, remember?"

"We can't trust them. He's one of them, one of the scientists," she whispered, panic lacing her words.

"I don't want to hurt you, female," Nuzal said, turning away from the woman in front of him. "I was the one who took you from the Kaia's office that day."

"And I told you to end my suffering that day! I begged you to end it, and do you remember what you said to me?!" Tears streamed down her face as she glared at him. "You told me you were sorry. Well, fuck your apology! Instead of the relief of death, you sent me back to my cell and they *fixed* me. I will never forgive you. *Never!*"

Something flashed across Nuzal's face, sympathy or pain, but he turned away from them, his head lowering as if he were actually ashamed of what had happened to Esme.

"I think we've got the rest of them handled," Jun told him, moving closer to rest a hand on his arm. "Would you mind checking on Brin for me? Maybe see if he needs a hand with anything?"

He looked down, his eyes following the lights before nodding. "Let me know if you need assistance."

Jun waited for him to leave before she turned back to Esme. "There now, he's all gone; it's just us humans. Can you come out now and let me help you?"

"You're mated to that," Esme sneered, practically spitting the words at her.

The defensiveness she felt at the venom in Esme's voice surprised her. She'd hardly had any time at all to even begin to wrap her mind around what any of this meant, and here she was, feeling like she needed to defend Nuzal against this stranger. Jun didn't understand anything about alien matings, and yet she'd found out she was mated to two very different aliens within the same week, or so she figured. The timeline was still very foggy for her.

Polyamorous relationships existed on Earth, but this was nothing like any of the ones she was familiar with. The idea of her belonging to both of them had seemed to make Brin uncomfortable, and it made her wonder if the Venium engaged in these kinds of relationships at all.

There was something about Nuzal, something she'd been able to feel despite the danger she had been in. The way he'd cared for her, the way he'd protected Brin even against his own people.

She'd made a promise to allow herself to feel, to experience life and love, and it seemed as if the universe called her bluff.

"I can't help that, Esme, but I can tell you that I'm still struggling with the idea of it too. I don't know what any of this means, but right now, all that matters is making sure we're all safe and cared for." She held her hand out. "I just want to help you."

Esme stared at her hand, the battle within her mind raging behind her eyes as she considered. Finally, after several minutes, Esme reached out, clasping Jun's hand as she slid out from under the table. "Do we have to use their medicine?"

"It's the only medicine we have, and it works wonders on these small cuts and scrapes." Jun dabbed a bit onto the cut on her forehead, blowing a stream of air across it when she hissed.

The next few days on the ship did nothing to cool Esme's hatred of Nuzal, and Jun noticed she wasn't exactly fond of Brin either. She caught her telling the others more than once to watch their backs around him, that Nuzal would turn on them sooner than later. Her days were spent trying to reassure everyone Nuzal and Brin were on their side, that the males wanted to be free of the Grutex as much as they did.

By the third day, Nuzal's willingness to help and his calm and patient demeanor had begun to win over a few of the humans. One of them, Clara, the woman he'd been helping the day they crashed, sat across from him on the floor. Her legs were tucked beneath her, and she smiled up at him, not saying a word.

"Psychic abilities," Telisa whispered, handing her a water pod.

She took it, sipping slowly as she watched Nuzal grin. "Clara?"

"That's what some of the others have said. Telepathy and psychometry, or something like that. Whatever it is, she's a big part of why so many of them are willing to trust Nuzal. She says he's a good alien, and they trust whatever power she has." Telisa shrugged, turning her back on the scene. "How are you doing?"

Jun pulled her eyes away from the pair, trying to hide the smile that tugged at her lips. "I'm all right. Doing a lot of thinking."

"About the Grutex? They haven't shown up yet, but I'm afraid of staying here too long."

Jun blushed, shaking her head. "Not exactly."

"Ahh," Telisa pursed her lips, "the mate dilemma. Some of the others are calling it 'Mate Gate.' It has a fun ring to it." She laughed when Jun groaned. "I can't imagine one alien mate, let alone two of them. And a Grutex?" She shuddered. "No offense, but mark me down as not interested. What are you gonna do?"

Jun sighed, rubbing her free hand over her face. "Would it be unreasonable to hope the ground opens up and just swallows me whole the next time I walk outside?"

"No," Telisa laughed. "That sounds like a reasonable enough request to me." She placed her hand on Jun's arm. "We've all been through so much and to have all of this piled on top of what we just went through? I don't know what the right choice is, but you're the only one who can make it."

Jun found her gaze traveling back to Nuzal, and she sighed. "I know he did things that must have been horrible, but he's trying, and he saved me, saved Brin..." She knew it sounded pathetic, but she couldn't explain exactly what it was that told her this was the way it should be.

God, if she ever saw Amanda again, she knew she wouldn't hear the end of it. Hadn't she just been on her friend's case about her love for her not-imaginary friend *and* Fishboy? By the time they were reunited, Jun wouldn't have any solid ground to stand on in an argument.

"Do you think we can trust the Venium?" Telisa asked. "After what we heard from that asshole in the records room about how the Grutex came from Venora, I'm wondering if I should rethink my request for their assistance."

Jun frowned, thinking back on what Erusha said. *"We are nothing like the males and females who set out from Venora,"* she repeated his words. "How many generations do you think have passed since then?" Clara patted Nuzal's hand where it rested on his knee, and Jun couldn't help but smile at the startled expression on his face.

What do you actually know about your Grutex mate? she asked herself. He'd told her he was old, far older than she could imagine, and that he'd been "rebirthed" multiple times. From their time on board the Grutex ship, Jun knew he was a scientist of some sort, and that he knew how to perform medical procedures, but she didn't know *Nuzal*.

"Brin mentioned a council on Venora once. I wonder if they know about the history, if they know the Grutex originated from the same planet."

Telisa shrugged and finished off her water pod. "Who knows? If it's anything like the governments back home, it's likely a well-kept secret."

Jun wasn't a stranger to secrets—hell, she'd kept her illness from Amanda for months—but the idea that Brin's leaders might be hiding something didn't sit well with her.

First things first, Juna, she chided herself. *We need to get off of this planet before the Grutex find us or before the creatures in the area get brave enough to investigate the ship.*

CHAPTER 24

JUN

$\mathcal{J}$un peered into the first room off of the hallway she'd turned down, glancing around at the spartan conditions. Aside from the shelves lining the farthest wall, a massive, curved bed, and a small desk off to the side, the room was bare. It felt sterile. According to Nuzal, all of the rooms here would have been assigned to the crew members in charge of caring for the warriors while they were in cryosleep.

"I haven't seen any pods though," Jun said as she stepped inside, gawking at the size of the bed.

"It's been a long time since I was on one of these vessels. It's possible this one is used for something other than long distance troop movement. If that's the case, they may have found it more efficient to remove the pods and use the space for something else."

Throw in some medical equipment and this would pass for any of the hospitals she'd worked at. *Might even be nicer than a couple of them.*

"It's so… empty."

"I'd say this was a pretty standard room," Brin commented, inspecting the small desk before heading toward an indented section of the wall that turned out to be a door into an adjoining room. His fushori flashed, and when she stepped up behind him to see what he'd found, he turned to her with a playful grin. "Found the bathing chamber."

"You're ridiculous," she murmured, but she didn't bother trying to suppress her amused smile. She was sure the others would be thrilled to know there were bathrooms on board.

Nuzal was still standing just inside the room, his big body filling the entire doorway. When their eyes met, he turned away, as if embarrassed that he'd been caught staring. Although he seemed to have appointed himself as her personal security, never straying too far, the big guy had hardly said more than a handful of words to her since the standoff with Esme less than a full day ago.

"Are they all like this?" She gestured vaguely around the space.

"Mostly. It's more practical than it is comfortable." He jerked his chin toward another indent in the wall to her left. "Storage." Nuzal placed his massive palm on the wall and she watched as it slid open to reveal a closet.

An empty closet. "It was probably stupid of me to hope the rooms were stocked with something other than these gowns." She grimaced, sweeping her hand down her body.

The lab clothes weren't necessarily uncomfortable, but Jun and the rest of the humans on board weren't exactly thrilled to be stuck in them for longer than they needed.

"Most of the crew are not assigned to a specific ship, or at least not long term. Most bring only enough for the mission. I wouldn't be surprised if these have been empty for a long time."

The rumbling of his voice at her back sent a shiver of awareness down Jun's spine, and she turned her head, peering up at his as he looked down at her. At a mere four foot eleven inches, being the short one in the room was a common enough occurrence, but these guys were giants.

Not so long ago, she'd stared up at Brin and Oshen and marveled at their height, but if she had to guess, she'd say Nuzal had a solid foot on Oshen, coming in close to eight feet tall. No wonder the bed in here was so big.

It was so large in fact, that she was almost positive all three of them could climb in and sleep comfortably. The thought made her cheeks flush, and she mentally berated herself for acting like some blushing virgin from one of lola's old romance novels. Clearing her throat, Jun slipped around Nuzal, only to run head first into Brin's chest.

"It's always a pleasure running into you, Shayfia." Brin leaned to the side to peer into the empty space. "Most ships this size have one or two molecular synthesizers on board."

The dark tentacles on Nuzal's neck swayed when he nodded. "Likely in the common area."

"A what now?"

Brin grinned, tapping her chin playfully with the tip of his finger. "A replicator, usually for food or clothing."

"I knew that," Jun mumbled, swatting his hand away as she squeezed between their bodies.

Nuzal led them down the hall, past the other open doors leading to nearly identical rooms as the one they had ventured into. The hall came to a stop at a set of double doors that slid open to reveal a large, open room, big enough to fit all of the rescued humans and then some.

There were a few tables with wide chairs set around them, and a long counter top to her right with trays and small storage boxes stacked on top of one another. Some sort of tech was set into the wall on their right. Lights flickered on and off as characters scrolled across the screens in front of them.

"The last Grutex vessel I was on was *not* this well-endowed," Brin murmured as he moved to take a closer look, running his fingers over the edges of consoles. "The Venium don't even have these upgrades yet. Imagine the things Nyissa and I could do—"

"No improvements, Glowworm. We need these things to be fully functional."

Brin turned slowly, placing his hand on his chest in mock offense. "Are you insinuating that I wouldn't leave them in proper working order? They'd be even better than before."

"You're full of yourself."

She was going to strain her eyes with the amount of rolling they'd done in the time they had known one another, but he looked genuinely excited for the first time since their capture. The sight of the light sparking in his eyes again made her chest tighten and she looked away, not wanting him to see how close she was to tears.

Instead, she focused her attention on Nuzal, watching him as he stepped up to one of the other displays. Jun still wasn't sure how they were going to move forward, or if she was even making the right choice by entertaining the notion of having two mates, but something about these two alien males made her *want* to see it through.

As if Nuzal could sense her eyes on him, he glanced over his wide shoulders and cleared his throat before gesturing for her to join him. His long, armored tail curled around his leg as she approached his side. Whether it was a shy, self-conscious gesture or one meant to keep her away from the barbs at the end, she wasn't sure.

"If it's clothing you're looking for, this is as close to it as you'll get on this vessel," Nuzal told her as she stared at the machine, her eyes following the alien characters as they moved across the screen. "A molecular synthesizer, or a replicator, is simply a matter-energy converter, which means it converts energy into—"

"I'll take your word for it, Nuzal." Jun laughed. "How does it work and will it make clothing sufficient enough for the group to move around comfortably?"

While Jun was used to patients complaining about their hospital gowns and how uncomfortable their accommodations were, she'd found herself frustrated and overwhelmed by the number of times she heard her fellow humans gripe that the gowns bothered them, that the lights on the ship were too bright, or that the floors where they had chosen to rest were not soft enough.

Aside from Jun, the group had remained in the large space where they'd sheltered during the trip and subsequent crash landing. They hadn't wanted to venture any further to find more accommodating spaces, but she figured the promise of clothing, bathrooms, and even beds might lure them down here.

"Jun? Are you guys in there?" The doors slid open, and Telisa peered in cautiously, her eyes darting around the room until they landed on Jun. Her shoulders sagged with relief, and she turned back into the hall, gesturing toward the common area. "Come on, nothing to be afraid of. Jun's already inside."

The first one through the door was Roman, a beast of a man who had been in a cell close to her and Telisa back on the ship. Onyx-colored tentacles, just like the ones Nuzal had, ran up his neck and into the braids at the base of his skull, just behind his ears. Roman's skin, once as dark as Jun's, now had a mauve tint to it that was even more pronounced under the bright lights in the common area. His blue eyes lit up when they landed on the replicator in front of Nuzal.

"Holy shit," he breathed, his mouth dropping open as he

gaped in fascination. "Is this an honest to God replicator? Like, a real life produces-food-and-textiles replicator?"

"I was just about to show Jun what it's currently capable of producing."

Oh, God, another tech junkie. "Nuzal said this one should be able to help with the clothing situation."

"This is the strangest way one of my dreams has come true," Roman said with the shake of his head. "But I'm not going to pass up the opportunity to see one in action."

"You don't even know if it's safe," a tall, slender man with short brown hair cautioned. The gills on his neck flared, and he lifted claw-tipped fingers up to brush over them.

"Listen, if it can get me out of this getup," he waved at his gown, "then I'm willing to take the chance. Let's get started, big guy."

Nuzal narrowed his eyes at Roman, but directed him to stand on a circular plate a few steps away. "Stand still. It only takes one rotation."

They all watched as Nuzal brought up a different screen and a voice began to speak in a language she recognized as one the Grutex used during the start of the conflict on Earth.

"That sounds reassuring," the one with gills deadpanned.

Xavier, that was his name. Jun side-eyed him, but remained quiet. It was understandable that many, if not all of them, were weary of the Grutex and their tech, but that didn't mean this wouldn't wear on her nerves.

"Will we be given translators?" Telisa asked as a few more curious people stepped into the common room behind her.

"What for?" one of the women asked. "I don't plan on staying on some alien planet long enough to need one. I'm going back home as soon as I can." There were a few murmurs of agreement from the gathering crowd.

"I'm sure when we reach Venora, those of you who wish to receive them will have the chance to," Brin answered.

Nuzal looked over at Roman, his finger hovering over the screen. "Are you ready?"

Roman chuckled, practically trembling with excitement. "Fire her up!"

The replicator beeped once as Nuzal backed away, and twice more after that like a countdown. A thin line of light shot out, stopping on Roman's torso and extending from his feet all the way up to his head. The plate he stood on lit up, and a moment later it spun him slowly as the light moved over his form. It stopped after the rotation, and a three-dimensional image popped up on the hologram display. It gave what she assumed were Roman's measurements at his shoulders, chest, and waist just before chimes sounded and a drawer just beneath the replicator slid open.

"Take it out," Nuzal instructed him. "See how it fits."

The group watched with bated breath as Roman reached inside and began to pull out something black.

"Whoa!" Roman exclaimed as the material began to encase his wrists and forearms, running up to his shoulders and spreading downward. Gasps and cries of distress filled the room, but when the material finally stopped, Roman looked up with a grin before tearing his lab gown away.

Beneath the soiled and ragged article, a sleek black suit clung to Roman's body. It looked as if it had come straight out of the superhero movies that were popular on Earth before the invasion occurred. Roman twisted and turned, giving them all a good look and showcasing the fact that these things, just like the superhero suits, left little to the imagination. The black material stopped at his neck and wrists, but encased his feet.

"How do you get it off?" Jun asked, as Roman ran his hands over the collar.

"These are a relatively recent invention, but from what I can recall, the suits are actually a living organism. In exchange for the protection it offers, the organism feeds off of the dead cells from plating, or in your case, skin." A small smile crept over Nuzal's face as Jun scrunched her nose at the description. "Once the suit is on, you can remove it by saying, *suit down*. It will shrink itself down, but it remains on your body in the form of a small circle somewhere on the foot. To bring it back up, you say *suit up*."

"It knows English?" Telisa asked, reaching out to touch Roman's arm.

"It can comprehend English commands, yes, as well as any other language in the Grutex database. That includes many other human languages."

"A symbiont," Roman breathed as he looked down at himself. "Never in my wildest dreams did I think I'd be wearing something like this."

"The engineers who created them were hoping to come up with a more sustainable clothing option, but they are not being widely distributed yet. The organism takes time to cultivate, so very few warriors have been given the chance to actually use these." Nuzal held his hand out to Jun. "Do you want to go next?"

She was as eager to shuck this gown as any of the others, but having some organism attach itself to her body to feed off of her dead skin cells was so... alien. Jun cast a glance toward Brin, seeking silent reassurance.

He gave her a very human shrug and grinned. "If you don't take your turn, I will. I've had it with these rags."

With a huff of amusement, Jun placed her hand in Nuzal's, allowing him to guide her through the same process as Roman. The plate in the floor spun her as the replicator scanned her body.

"These suits—the organism—it's not sentient, right?" The thought sent a shiver down her spine.

"Of course not." Nuzal frowned.

Jun waited for the plate to stop rotating and for the chimes to sound before she stepped up to the drawer.

Nothing to it, she told herself. *Just stick your hands into the dark drawer and wait for the living suit to swallow you.*

Even though she knew it was coming, Jun still jumped when the suit crawled up her arm and began to spread. It was smooth and cool, gliding across her skin as it moved beneath her clothing. It took only moments for the suit to travel down her legs and fully encompass her feet. It was light and flexible, moving with her as she bent to check out her wiggling toes.

Clara, the woman Nuzal had helped after the crash, and Telisa went next. Soon, all of the humans, including Esme and Xavier, who seemed to be the most suspicious of Nuzal and everything related to the Grutex, had received the new suits.

"Excuse me." A dark-haired woman raised her hand in the air. "The new clothes are nice and all, but I've been holding my bladder since the crash and I'm pretty sure my eyes are going to start floating if I don't get to a bathroom."

Brin laughed behind Jun, but Nuzal looked as if he was wondering how they'd missed floating eyeballs in their observations of human specimens.

"I'll show you to the bathrooms."

There were moans and sighs of relief as people broke off into pairs and small groups, ducking into each room for a little bit of privacy; something they hadn't been afforded for too long.

Jun looked back down the hall into the room where the two males who claimed to be her mates stood and let loose a deep sigh. She wasn't sure she was ready for everything the future had in store, but at least she was wearing pants again.

CHAPTER 25

BRIN

*B*rin cursed under his breath as he fought the urge to throw the tool into the heap of useless metal the Grutex called an engine. He'd fooled around with more than a few engines in his time, but he wouldn't call himself a mechanic, not by a long shot. Even with the blueprints Nyissa had managed to dig up, this wasn't going to be an easy fix.

It was looking more and more like they weren't going to be leaving this planet unless someone came down and got them, and at this point, Brin almost hoped it would happen. With a frustrated sigh, Brin adjusted one of the intake valves before stepping back to look at the readings on the small holoscreen.

No change. *Brax it all!*

This engine was almost as frustrating as dealing with Telisa. The female hounded him every single day since their escape, questioning him about his knowledge of the Grutex's origins, and asking him if he was sure the Venium hadn't come to Earth in support of their allies after all. Nothing he said seemed to reassure her.

As if the mere thought of her had somehow summoned her, Telisa stepped through the open doors of the engine bay. Brin barely contained a groan as her eyes locked onto him.

"There you are! I've been looking for you."

"I've been in the exact same place since the day we crashed," he growled, moving around to the other side of the engine to recheck the electrical components for the tenth time.

Despite his annoyance at not being able to fix the engine, Brin found the work more agreeable than the constant ache from his kokoras pressing against his slit anytime he was around Jun and Nuzal. The sexual tension between the three of them did nothing to ease the building frustration.

If what they had learned in the records room was true, the male was Jun's mate, and they had yet to discuss what this meant for all of them. Triads weren't completely unheard of in their culture. One of the first stories Brin remembered hearing from Oshen's gia was the tale of the goddess and her mates, the original triad, but there hadn't been such a mating in many generations, and most believed them to be a myth.

Brin should be elated, but here he was, a male who hadn't wanted even one mate, with two. His mind was at war with itself, struggling to understand what he felt about Nuzal. He'd saved Jun when Brin was certain he was going to lose her, had stopped the attack on him, putting himself at great personal risk, but he had also been one of the scientists tasked with experimenting on the humans they had rescued from the lab.

Ah, and you are the embodiment of innocence?

Brin wasn't naïve. He knew he'd done things in his past that he wasn't proud of, that he would take back if he could. Perhaps Nuzal was feeling the same way now after spending time with the people whose lives he had helped turn upside-down. Aiding in their escape wouldn't make up for everything he may have done, but his calm and patient manner since the crash seemed to have gone a long way with some of the humans already.

Telisa stepped over the tools that lay scattered on the ground as she made her way to where he worked. The nearness of the female made his skin prickle, and he sneered involuntarily, not liking the invasion of his space. After his sterilization, Brin had expected the sexual urges and irritation to diminish, but it seemed to have had the opposite effect.

He'd done his best to distract himself in the cell afterward, throwing all of his energy into planning their escape, but nothing so far had helped. Distancing himself had almost made it worse. The need to find her, to touch her and draw in her scent, burned through his veins like liquid fire.

If having his ability to reproduce removed hadn't dowsed the flames, what would? Many Venium reported that their urge cooled after their mates became pregnant, or their heat cycles faded, but humans didn't have heats as far as he knew, and he would never be able to reproduce with her. What did this all mean for him?

"Listen," Telisa said, propping herself up against the railing that circled the engine, "I've been thinking, and I really want to discuss this with you."

"What haven't we discussed at this point?" Brin grumbled.

"I'm not sure who we can trust anymore, but out of all the aliens we know, the Venium seem to be the best bet for an alliance. If we make it to Venora and get an audience with your council, what do you think they might ask for in return?"

Brin shook his head as reached down into the engine to run his hands over two of the small hoses. "You're asking the wrong Venium. Oshen's the ambassador, not me."

"Yeah, well, Oshen isn't here, so you're my only option,"

Telisa quipped, crossing her arms over her chest. "Give me an idea of what we're working with."

"You have no resources we need, or have any use for. Your planet is polluted, your waters would be no good to us. The only thing you might have going for you is that two of our people have found mates among your kind."

"You think they would ask for us to—to mate with their people?" She seemed taken aback.

"The Venium have traveled space for many generations and have never come across another species who was compatible enough with us to actually form the mating bond with. Our numbers are declining. If there is anything that will convince the elders to aid humanity, it will be the promise of compatible fertile males and females."

"That sounds like the plot of a bad sci-fi movie. 'You need women? Save us and we will sacrifice our women to you, oh, great and powerful reptilian overlords!'" Telisa rolled her eyes.

Brin actually chuckled as he pulled his arm back. "The Venium aren't reptilian, but mates would be useful. The fact is, we're going to die out eventually, and no one on Venora seems to have an answer. If we can believe what Erusha said, maybe it was the capture of the females that started it."

"So in exchange for help, humanity will have to sell people into slavery? That sounds like what's already happening with the Grutex, but with more steps."

Being compared to the Grutex raised his hackles, but Brin reminded himself she had no idea what his people were like.

"Mating isn't anything like what the Grutex are doing. There is no choosing when it comes to a mate for the Venium. We can't just select a partner and reproduce. If it was that simple, we might not have to worry about our numbers."

"So then how does it work?" she asked.

"When mates meet, it triggers their reproductive systems.

Before this happens, all Venium are infertile. The recognition doesn't always happen right away, but when it does, it's impossible for one to miss." He remembered the moment he'd felt the swelling happen in Jun's bedroom, right after Raou's attack, and just like every other Venium male who had come before him, Brin's body had filled with the urge to reproduce with his mate.

That would never happen now, and instead of being devastated at the loss of the pups they would never have, Brin found that he'd been filled with a sense of *relief*, as if a weight had been lifted from his shoulders. He could be with his mate without the constant fear of her becoming pregnant. Brega would have to face the fact that her bloodline had come to an end, that there would be no pups for her to train.

The only thing holding him back now was their uncertain future, and where Nuzal fit into everything. They needed to talk about it, to get it out once and for all so that they knew where they stood. Brin wouldn't deny that the fact she was human caused him a great deal of worry. While Brin was mated to her for the rest of his life, Jun could realistically decide she wanted nothing to do with either of her alien mates.

"If that's the case, how would we know which people to send to Venora?" Telisa questioned.

Brin sighed, mentally and physically exhausted. "I honestly have no idea how they'd decide to go about something like that. Maybe they could ask for volunteers and have them brought up to the ships to see if they react to any of the crewmembers? This isn't my area of expertise."

Telisa eyed the crippled engine and grinned. "I'm guessing neither is engineering. Come on, I'll buy you lunch. I haven't seen you eat at all today, and if you die, I'll have to deal with Jun."

"Well, if you're paying…" Brin shoved the tools to one side of the walkway before following Telisa out of the room. Maybe getting a meal into him and taking a break would help him look at the engine with new eyes.

The doors to the small common area slid open, and Brin groaned. Half of the rescued humans were gathered around the lone food replicator, and the sound of their raised voices filled the room.

"How the hell did you manage this?" someone grumbled.

"Who let the klutz touch the machine?" another shouted from somewhere off to the left.

"I'm sorry," a small voice came from the center of the group. "I was hungry. I only pressed the button we were shown."

"What's going on?" Telisa asked.

The crowd turned as one, parting to let a small female through. Her head was bowed, causing her dark hair to curtain half of her face, but Brin could see the tears welling in her eyes. He crouched down, kneeling in front of her when she stopped.

"Was the replicator giving you problems?" he asked.

The female nodded. "I swear, I only pressed the button you told us to and it just shut off."

"She's got the touch of death," one of the human males grumbled.

"Okay, that's enough. Lay off of her." Telisa's stern tone left no room for argument, and the male lowered his gaze before shuffling away.

"I'll take a look. I'm sure it's something simple," Brin told her, but as he approached the machine, the touch screen that normally displayed the menu items sparked and crackled, sending up a small plume of smoke that made the humans gasp and fall back. "I'll have to take it apart," he told Telisa with a sigh when she came up beside him.

"Well, shit." She waved her hand in front of her face.

"Someone get Nuzal. We're going to need to venture out for water and something to eat while I try to repair this."

"You heard Brin," Telisa said. "Time to make stone soup."

"He was in the medbay last time I saw him," one of the females spoke up. "I'll go get him."

Brin slanted a look at Telisa, thinking, not for the first, that humans said the strangest things. "Yes," he said slowly. "The hunger will sit in our stomachs like... a stone."

Telisa threw her head back and laughed before placing her palm over her face. "Bless your heart, Brin."

CHAPTER 26

NUZAL

𝒲ith every day that passed, Nuzal felt himself falling further into his feelings for his little human mate. The gentle, patient way she handled the other humans, even those who didn't seem to like her or want to cooperate with anything she said, made him hopeful that he might find acceptance with her. He tried to be respectful of the fact that she hadn't initiated anything between them and she might never see fit to do so. He'd even given Brin as much space as he could manage given the small area they had to work with.

Instead of focusing on the things he couldn't control, Nuzal turned back to the storage unit in the medbay, and wondered if sorting and cataloguing the contents within it for the sixth time was too much.

"Nuzal!"

One of the human females, Harper, appeared in the doorway, her face flushed and her eyes wide as she looked up at him. He was making an effort to commit their names to memory, but so far, he could recognize a few of them. "The replicator broke and Brin asked us to find you."

"I know nothing about the replicators," he told her, closing the doors to the storage unit before securing them.

With a final sweep of the bay to make sure nothing had been left out, Nuzal stepped through the doors, grimacing when Harper scurried out of his way. She recovered quickly, a considerable improvement just from the day before.

"He said something about going out to find water and food," she said, running alongside him as he moved down the hall toward the common area.

Outside the ship? They knew nothing about the surface aside from what they could see through the windows, and that wasn't very much if he were being honest. Sensors indicated the atmosphere was suitable for them, but Nuzal was hesitant to allow anyone off of the vessel unless it was dire.

The smell of smoke reached him a few paces out from the room, and Nuzal felt panic well up inside of him. If they lost the ship, there was no way they were ever going to be able to leave this planet. What if there was a fire on board? What would he do if Jun or Brin were injured? He sprinted through the door, his heart pounding in his chest as his eyes darted around the room, searching for the danger.

His dramatic entrance startled some of the humans closest to the entrance, but he didn't stop to apologize. Brin stood in front of the smoking replicator, his shoulders and the muscles of his back bunched as he yanked on the frame of the machine. Nuzal felt arousal course through him, and a rattle danced up his chest before he could stifle it. Brin turned his head, his glowing blue eyes drifting over Nuzal as his fushori flashed for a split second.

"You sent for me?"

"The replicator is…" He looked down at the smoking interior

and frowned. "Currently nonoperational. I'll have to take time away from repairing the engine to fix this, but we can't go too long without provisions. I need you and a handful of volunteers to go out and gather water and anything edible you can find."

"You want *me* to find volunteers?" Nuzal questioned. "I'm sure they'll be lining up to go with the Grutex." His words dripped with sarcasm.

"Why can't you go out with us?" One of the males asked, giving Nuzal a wide berth as he skirted around the wall.

"If Brin goes, that means one of *us* has to fix this thing, and I don't know about any of you, but I have absolutely no idea how a replicator works," Telisa spoke up.

"I'll go with you," Roman said.

"I wanna go too," Layla stepped up next to Roman. "I broke the replicator, so I want to help, and I'll be useful if we happen to run into any natives." A descendant of a rare, nearly extinct race known to the Grutex as Leq'anis, Layla had the ability to understand and learn language at a far faster rate than even their best translators.

"If it's okay with you all, I'd like to come along." Clara's voice slipped into his mind, and from the looks on the faces of the others, they could hear her as well. Her telepathy and her ability to gain impressions through touch, something passed down to her from her ancestors who originated from a planet very close to Venora, had made her one of his earliest allies among the humans.

"Xavier," Brin said, turning to a younger male standing at the back of the common area. "Do you mind going? They could use another set of claws."

Xavier's gaze fell on Nuzal, and he could almost feel the distrust radiating from him. Along with the claws, the male sported a set of gills, marking him as one of the Venium descendants.

"Sure thing." He nodded.

"Great!" Telisa clapped her hands. "We'll call you the Fellowship of the Forage. Let's arm you and get you out there."

A few of the humans laughed at Telisa's words, but the meaning was lost to him, and after a quick glance at Brin, Nuzal knew he wasn't alone in his confusion. Those who had agreed to go with him followed Telisa out the doors, while the rest of the humans in the common room chatted quietly. Some watched him with suspicious eyes as he approached the Venium. He curled his tail around his own leg, not knowing what to do with it or even how to act around the male.

"Is your comm still working?" Brin asked without looking away from the interior of the replicator.

"It is."

"Are you able to scan any of the vegetation you find out there? We need them fed, but we can't risk poisoning the humans, or ourselves, for that matter."

"It's no longer connected to the Kaia's network, but I should still have access to the comm's internal database. We're close enough to the Tachin's planet that they should have catalogued whatever we find out there." Nuzal took a moment to glance around the room for her, but he'd known the moment he stepped inside that his mate wasn't here. "Where is Jun?"

"Most likely with Esme, trying to talk her out of murdering you in your sleep." Brin twisted the head of one of the bolts, frowning when it didn't move. "Do me a favor? Don't tell her until you're all back on the ship. I don't want her sneaking out. I can't risk her."

Nuzal didn't want to risk her either, but something told him Jun was going to be less than pleased when she found out about this.

"These might help."

"Goddess above, Clara!" Brin growled, his hand slipping from the bolt as he jumped. The female held out a bag of tools, a small smile tugging at her lips, no doubt amused by whatever it was she could hear in Brin's mind. "Thank you."

Clara nodded, but the mischievous sparkle in her eye made Nuzal frown. Aside from his mate, Clara was his favorite human. She was kind and patient, forgiving even when it wasn't in her best interest. That look, though, it told him she was up to something. She turned on her heel before he could question her, darting through the doors and back out into the hall.

Brin's hiss drew his attention and he turned back to see him sucking on the side of one finger. When he pulled it away, dark lifeblood welled along a jagged cut. Nuzal was no stranger to lifeblood; he'd even been covered in Brin's during the surgery to remove the human toxin from his body, but the sight of the injury, even as small as it was, set his heart racing.

He pulled a small vial from the pouch that hung at his hip and grabbed Brin's hand, inspecting the cut. With the flick of his thumb, the top popped off and he carefully dribbled a small amount onto the wound. Brin tried to tug his hand away, but Nuzal's loud rattle seemed to startle him into compliance.

"You're worse than Jun," the Venium grumbled, but he settled down and let Nuzal finish his work. "It would have healed just fine on its own."

"Now it will heal even faster," He told him, brushing his thumb over the top of the finger. The spark of awareness, of something he now associated with the attraction he felt for his female and her Venium mate, moved through him. "I should get the packs for water collection." Nuzal said, feeling far more awkward in that moment than he could ever remember feeling in any of his lives.

He dropped Brin's hand, turning away and passing through the doors, not wanting to make a fool of himself. Roman and

Xavier stood near the airlock, checking the Grutex weapons Brin had given them when they escaped the Kaia's ship.

In the storage to the left of the door, Nuzal pulled out five packs. They were lined with waterproof material, meant to be used as emergency containers in the event of... well, something like this, he supposed. When warriors were out on missions, they couldn't rely on the water pods the replicators produced, so they carried the packs instead.

Nuzal passed two to each of the males, and also to Clara and Layla when they reached them. He took four packs for himself and a few of the empty tool pouches, thinking they might use them to hold whatever food they managed to collect.

"Are you ready?" Roman asked, stepping up beside Nuzal as he pressed the release on the door.

"Let's get this over with," Xavier grumbled.

Clara and Layla stepped past Nuzal, gawking at the world around them as they took their first steps through the open door. It was one thing to see the surface through the windows of the vessel, but it was something else entirely to be out in it.

Nuzal hit the button to close the door and stepped out onto the soil, enjoying the feel of the grass beneath his feet. It was something he hadn't experienced since his last life, and he hadn't realized until then just how much he'd actually missed it. There was a soft grunt behind him just before something fell against his back. He wasn't sure what he expected to find when he spun around, but it certainly wasn't Jun.

"Were you trying to leave without me, big guy?" she asked with a smile.

Her voice drifted over him, caressing his exoskeleton as if it were a physical touch. It swirled up his sides, settling over his chest before nestling somewhere deep inside of him. With gentle hands, Nuzal lifted Jun from his back, scanning the immediate area for any sign of a threat.

"What are you doing out here?" he asked her, frowning when he saw Roman and Xavier moving toward the tree line.

Calls and whistles from what he assumed was the native wildlife rang out from the depths of the forest that surrounded them. Now that he was outside the ship, Nuzal realized he recognized some of the trees. The rippled white bark of the icia tree made them look like pillars of milky ice topped with dark foliage. Their branches hung low, some even sweeping the forest floor as they stirred in the light breeze.

Silvery clouds spun gently around the snow-capped mountains that towered over the landscape. The peaks were so tall and imposing that their shadows nearly reached the landing site. Nuzal could just make out the trickling sound of running water in the distance, most likely runoff from the melting snow and ice. They would head there first, before the planet's sun slipped behind the mountains.

"Sort of reminds me of Earth," Jun whispered, staring up at the blue sky as she gripped his forearms, ignoring his question entirely.

"You shouldn't be out here."

Jun's brows drew together as he set her on her feet, waiting for her to get her balance before he released her. "Why not? Clara said you were going out to gather some supplies and I figured I'd come along."

Nuzal turned to Clara, whose normally pale cheeks had turned a bright red. Her eyes narrowed on Jun's face and she frowned, shaking her head. It still fascinated him that humans could change color in this way.

"Oops," Jun pressed her lips together as if she were trying not to laugh. "I guess I wasn't supposed to say that." His little mate tugged at one of the packs on his shoulder until he gave in and handed it over. She slung it across her chest. "Too late now. I'm outside, so we might as well get going before we lose the light. Wait for us!" she shouted, running after the other humans.

Brin wasn't going to be pleased about this, but if there was one thing Nuzal had learned in his short time with their mate, it was that Jun was stubborn and she didn't take orders very well. He followed after her, his long strides eating up the space between them.

CHAPTER 27

NUZAL

"This way," he called, snagging Roman and Xavier's attention before jerking his head toward the sound of the stream. "There should be a water source nearby where we can fill the packs before we start our search for something safe to eat."

Nuzal led their group into the shade of the forest, taking in lungfuls of the fresh, clean air. Every fiber of his being seemed to rejoice at the cool breeze that danced across his face and the soft grass beneath his feet.

Jun and the others looked as if they enjoyed it just as much as he did. He watched his mate reach out to touch one of the icias, only to pull her hand back at the last minute, as if she expected the bark to bite.

"They're safe to touch," he told her, placing his palm on one of the rippled trunks. It was smooth against his fingers, and he trailed the tips up and down one of the sides. "The Grutex call them icia trees."

Jun followed his lead, pressing her hand to the bark. "Have you been here before?"

"Not here. Not that I remember, at least. These trees are hardy and can survive in many different environments. The Grutex and other species capable of space travel have planted them on many different worlds. I haven't left the ship since my last lifetime, but these trees are something I remember vividly."

"You spent your entire life on that ship?" she asked as they began to walk again.

"In this lifetime, yes. I was rebirthed on the Kaia's ship, and because I was imperfect, that's where I stayed for my training."

"Maybe it's the language barrier causing things not to translate right, but I'm not understanding what you mean when you say you're imperfect. I heard you mention it in the records room to Erusha, but it didn't make sense to me."

Nuzal pointed to his violet eyes. "These disqualified me from becoming a warrior in this lifecycle. They are an imperfection, something undesirable, so I was selected for lab training instead."

"And that's where you met Erusha?" She squinted at him before reaching up to touch the vine-like features around his face. "Real quick question: what are these called?"

"They're xines, and the answer to the first question is yes." Nuzal was still unsure of how he felt about what the male had done, but he'd already decided to forgive him.

Jun stepped over rocks and fallen tree branches, keeping her eyes on the ground as she went. "So you weren't always a scientist?"

Nuzal shook his head. "I've been a warrior as far back as I can remember."

"Did you like being a warrior?"

"I enjoyed certain aspects of it," he answered.

"So you didn't choose to be a scientist, but was it your choice to be a warrior?"

"I suppose at some point, in some lifetime, it might have been, but as far back as I can remember it has been something that was chosen for me. I was selected for service and training."

"I don't understand what your eye color has to do with you being a warrior or a scientist, but I like your eyes, all of them."

Nuzal didn't realize he had stopped, his feet frozen to the ground, until Jun stopped to look back at him quizzically. No one had ever complimented his eyes before. When he was a warrior, his leaders had complimented his skills, his build, his strength, but his eyes? Never. This little human, who was so very different from him, looked at his features and found something to appreciate.

What would it be like to close the space between them, to run his fingers through her hair the way he had wanted to the first time he saw her? He'd done it in recovery, untangling the strands, but it had been practical, not for pleasure, not the way he'd seen Brin do it in the cell back on the Kaia's ship when he kissed Jun. How would it feel to be allowed to touch her in a way that brought her pleasure and joy, to know that it was *his* touch that brought that flush to her cheeks?

His whole existence was centered around what he could do in service to the Kaia, to his species. Every single thing he had ever done had been to better them, and thinking back on it all, had it really been worth it? It had brought Jun and Brin into his life, but it had also caused him lifetimes of loneliness and, at some points, absolute misery. He'd been given many lives, but how many of those had he actually been allowed to live?

Both his mate and bondmate had years of experience when it came to love and affection, but Nuzal had been a stranger to those until they came into the lab in their cryopods. Being near them now, working so close, and having the ability to speak to them freely was making him see just how much his cold, sterile upbringing may have damaged him.

The Grutex were not solving their problems with rebirth; they were creating long-lasting problems. Even now, he couldn't bring himself to touch his female, to open up to Jun and Brin in a way that would help them see *Nuzal*, and *not* a Grutex scientist.

He'd tried his best to accept the likelihood that his mate and bondmate would never be able to overlook his past, and it might have worked for a short time, but now? Nuzal didn't want to be alone anymore. The realization struck him like a punch in the gut, and he swayed on his feet as he struggled to focus his vision on Jun's face.

"Nuzal," she moved closer, reaching out to touch his forearm, "are you okay?"

An eerie growl echoed around them, bouncing off of the trees that surrounded them. The humans up ahead stopped, their faces paling as their eyes darted between the white trunks. Something was watching them.

Clara turned, her features pinched in frustration as she looked back and forth between Nuzal and Jun. *"What is it? I can feel the vibration, but I still can't hear the way you all do."*

He held a finger to his mouth, not daring to speak even through his mind to her in case the animal was sensitive to it. With a crook of his finger, Nuzal beckoned for them to move closer. Xavier and Roman were the farthest away, with Clara and Layla a short distance behind.

A thick mist he hadn't noticed before crept toward them from the direction they had come. The edges of it curled over stones and roots like smokey talons clawing their way across the forest floor.

"I can smell the stream," he told the group. "We stay close to each other. Do not walk off."

"I don't like this, Nuzal," Jun said, watching the trees as they continued on.

Neither did he. The swinging branches of the icia trees made it hard to tell if there was any movement in the distance. This wasn't the situation he wanted to be stuck in with a group of humans. The fact that one of them was his mate made it all the more stressful.

Roman and Xavier kept their weapons up, ready to fire, but when they reached the stream without incident, the males lowered the guns, rushing forward, twisting the caps from their packs as they stepped into the water.

"Wait!" Nuzal growled. "You have no idea if this is safe. Keep watch while I scan it, and don't let the females out of your sight."

"Something is watching us, Nuzal," Clara spoke. *"I feel it out there, just outside my reach."*

Nuzal crouched, dipping his fingers into the water, as tiny chunks of ice floated downstream, breaking apart against the smooth rocks that jutted out from the shore. He shook off his fingers before turning his arm over, allowing his comm to scan the surface of the stream. It took only a moment for it to finish, but Xavier was already becoming restless.

"Is it safe?" he asked impatiently.

The scanner icon flashed green before a chemical listing appeared, stating the water was safe for consumption.

"Yes." He uncapped his first pack, holding it beneath the surface so that the water flowed inside. "Fill your packs with as much as you're able to carry."

The air around them, much like the water in the stream, was frigid. The humans dipped their packs in, shivering as the water rushed over their skin. Jun took a second pack from Nuzal, and despite the fact that his instincts urged him to pluck them from her hands and shoulder the burden, pride welled up inside of him at the sight of her. He was becoming oddly sentimental on this trip.

Clara and Layla finished up their work, securing the caps so that none of the water leaked out. The pebbles shifted beneath

Jun's feet as she joined their group, giving him an encouraging smile.

"Now what?" Layla asked as the others looked to Nuzal for direction.

In the past, Nuzal led battalions of warriors into battle, and even in the lab he was second only to Erusha, so why was the idea of leading this group so daunting?

"Now we look for something to eat."

Layla slung both packs over her shoulder and sighed as her eyes roamed over the rocks and loose soil beneath their feet. "Think they have pizza on this planet?"

Laughter spilled from his mate's lips as she started up the small incline, her packs swaying from side to side as she steadied herself. "God, I could go for some rice and shrimp. I'd settle for an entire plate of bacon."

Clara moaned, her hand moving to her stomach as she hunched over, falling dramatically against the trunk of the nearest tree. *"Where are all the space food trucks?"*

"Zero out of ten, would not recommend this uninhabited planet to friends." Roman's tone was serious, but the way the females laughed told him this must be part of the joke.

Nuzal pulled the tool bags from his pouch before distributing them. "Try not to touch anything you find with your bare hands. If you see something that looks edible, let me know so it can be scanned. Let's be sure to stay together so no one gets lost."

He extended the last one to Xavier as the others began to inspect the plant life in their immediate vicinity. "You think this makes what you did okay?" the male asked, his gills flaring and his voice low as if he didn't want the rest to hear what he had to say. "I've seen what you monsters do, so don't think I'm not watching you out here."

Nuzal's xines writhed around his shoulders, his eyes following the male as he trailed after Roman. Xavier, like Esme, seemed to hold much more animosity toward him than any of the others, and while he didn't expect them to forget everything that had gone on in the lab, Nuzal couldn't help the frustration he felt.

What could he do to prove to them he was trying his best to unlearn everything he'd been taught over his lifetimes? *Trust takes time,* Nuzal reminded himself.

"Nuzal?"

Clara's lilting words brushed against his mind, and he turned, his eyes scanning the group until he found her attempting to climb up a small tree with gray bark. Hanging from some of the highest branches were large, pink fruits, their skin covered in smooth bumps.

"I can't reach them." Clara huffed as she stretched up onto the very tips of her toes.

Leaves and branches crunched and snapped beneath his feet as he stepped up to the tree, reaching his arm out to allow his comm to scan the outside. His comm flashed green a moment later and Clara clapped in celebration. Nuzal plucked the only one he could reach, handing it off to Clara.

"Just the one?" Jun asked, leaning in to inspect the fruit in Clara's hands.

"I'd have to climb the tree in order to get the others, but I'm not sure it would be able to bear my weight. We can look for other trees—" Nuzal's words died on his tongue when Jun began scurrying up the side of the tree. She was nearly over his head by the time his body reacted. "What are you doing?" Nuzal reached out, wrapping his hand around her slender ankle.

"I'm climbing the tree," Jun said, her eyes dancing with humor as she glanced down at him. "You're going to make me slip if you keep pulling on me."

"It's dangerous," he grumbled, reluctantly releasing her so she could climb higher.

"I've been climbing trees since I was a little girl. In fact..."

She grunted, her arms straining as she pulled herself up before swinging her leg over so that she straddled one of the thicker branches. "My lola's cooking was so good that when I took it to school for lunch, I'd have to eat it in a tree just to avoid being bothered by the other kids. This little guy," she said, patting the tree, "is nothing compared to the ones back home."

Nuzal's jaw clenched and his tail flicked from side to side as he positioned himself beneath her, prepared to catch her in the event she lost her balance, but Jun moved with ease, pulling the fruit from the highest branches and dropping them into his hands.

"That's enough," Nuzal called up to her when they had filled his and Clara's pouches. "Let's see what else we find."

He shifted nervously as he watched her descend, clenching his hands to keep himself from reaching out and plucking her from the tree. She landed with a quiet thump on the soft ground, clutching at Nuzal's arm, causing light to flare beneath it as she steadied herself.

The group made their way back toward the ship, stopping to scan anything they thought might be edible, making sure to keep their guard up. Both Roman and Layla found root vegetables growing beneath the long branches of the icia trees, so they stopped to investigate further.

"They look like potatoes," Roman commented.

Judging by the excitement on the faces of the others, Nuzal assumed this was some sort of Earth delicacy. Whatever it was, he was looking forward to eating something that hadn't come from the replicator. It had been lifetimes since he last had that luxury.

Jun and Clara filled two of the pouches he'd brought, wiping their dirty hands on the pants they wore as Nuzal cinched the ties. Up ahead, Xavier spoke hurriedly to Roman, his face pinched in frustration as the larger male attempted to shake him off.

"He doesn't like you," Clara spoke. *"Xavier thinks that all*

Grutex are bad, that there's no redemption, but he isn't able to see what I see. Roman, though, I think he'll come around."

The sharp snap of twigs or branches behind them put Nuzal on high alert. Small rocks crunched beneath his feet as he moved closer to Jun, pulling her into his side as he scanned the trees. He motioned for Clara to join them, but her face drew down into a frown as she stared at the spot the females had dug up.

"Where's Layla?" his mate asked, pushing against his hip as she struggled in his grasp. "Nuzal—"

"She probably wandered off," Xavier grumbled as he plucked a dark leaf from one of the icia branches, completely oblivious to the dread he and the females seemed to be feeling. "Her damn head is always in the clouds."

"Don't be such an ass," Clara narrowed her eyes on the male.

The rustling of branches overhead was the only warning they were given before a creature dropped from the tree above Clara, pinning her beneath its massive black body. Her surprised scream was cut off as its jaws closed around her throat, its long, sharp teeth sinking into the soft flesh. The shock of seeing the little female die, of watching her blood spray through the air as her eyes locked on his, rooted Nuzal to the ground. His pulse hammered in his ears, drowning out all the commotion around him.

Before he knew what he was doing, Nuzal was in motion, charging the beast as it tried to escape into the trees with Clara's limp body. From the corner of his eye, Nuzal caught the dark flash of another creature, but he wasn't fast enough to dodge the attack.

They went down with a thud, limbs tangling as they rolled across the uneven ground, both of them attempting to gain the upper hand. How Nuzal ended up on his back with the creature's jaws snapping shut a mere breath away from his face, he didn't know, and he wasn't going to stay there long.

With a grunt, Nuzal threw his legs up and around the large body, trying his best to flip the beast, but he was far heavier than expected. Jun shouted his name from somewhere in the distance, and the terror in her voice spurred him on. With one hand on the beast's throat to keep him from tearing his face off, Nuzal slammed his other fist into its face, trying his best to aim for the two sets of eyes.

There was a terrible shriek a moment before a massive, club-like tail buried itself into the soft ground to the left of his head. When it was pulled back, Nuzal got a good look at the deadly, dripping stinger that tipped it. This thing was armed to the teeth, but Nuzal wasn't some soft-skinned human; he was Grutex, and he wasn't going to go down so easily.

With his teeth bared in a snarl, Nuzal swung his arm once more, this time using his claws instead of his fist to stab at the eyes and the sensitive flesh surrounding them. Hot, acrid liquid dripped onto his face and neck as the creature twisted away. He gasped for breath, clawing at the large paw that pressed down on his chest as the predator struggled. The loud crack and the pain in his chest that followed told Nuzal that his exoskeleton wasn't going to hold to that weight much longer.

Bright blue light, originating from somewhere to the right, flashed a second before the beast jerked violently, its eyes going wide just as two more pulses of light flew over them. With an ear-piercing shriek, the wounded creature bolted, kicking up soil and pebbles in its haste.

Jun stood among the trees, her arms held out in front of her with one of the plasma guns clutched in her hands. She stared wide-eyed at the retreating form, her chest rising and falling rapidly as she began to tremble.

"Layla!" one of the males was shouting. "Layla!"

With all of the strength he could muster, Nuzal pushed himself onto his hands and knees, crawling over the exposed roots and rocks toward his mate. A low rattle worked its way through his chest as he reached up to pry the weapon from her hands before pulling her against his body and wrapping her tightly in his arms.

Almost as soon as the attack had begun, it was over. The fact that he couldn't see Clara's body anywhere in the immediate area told Nuzal that the first creature had likely made off with her. Not far from where the first one had appeared, Roman stood, gun raised as he frantically swept the trees.

Thick black lifeblood, the same that was splattered across his face and neck, dripped from leaves and branches, looking to Nuzal like liquid adamantine as it glistened in the fading sunlight. The forest around them had gone silent, as if even the trees and wildlife were holding their breath, hoping not to draw the creatures back.

Nuzal pulled back, cradling Jun's face in his hands as he leaned down to press his forehead against hers. *She's alive. She's still here,* he told himself, breathing past the pain that radiated through his chest. His xines reached out, tracing her features and tangling in her hair as they sat in silence.

"They're gone," Xavier whispered. "That thing... it fucking killed her."

"Where's Layla?" Jun's voice shook as she turned her face away to glance around. "I thought I heard her... I thought she screamed."

Nuzal closed his eyes, and the image of Clara's shocked face surfaced in his mind.

"Clara?" he tried tentatively. *"Are you out there?"* No answer.

"What the hell?" Roman breathed. "You all saw it, right? You saw the blood?"

The dark red lifeblood that had been splattered across the white bark of the trees and pooled on the forest floor was gone, and no sign of Clara's mangled body existed. Her footprints in the soft soil near the exposed roots were the only indication that she had even been there with them. Where there was once carnage, there was now only the rocks, soil, and blue-green grass dancing in the breeze.

"We saw it," Nuzal murmured, stepping closer to inspect the black lifeblood on the leaves. *Why would everything except for this disappear?*

"How the hell does that much blood just *disappear*? There were pieces—" Jun's voice cracked, and she shook her head as if that would erase the memory. "I saw the animal—I saw what it did to Clara."

"We should go back to the ship," Xavier said quietly as he stood from his spot on the ground. "We need to go."

"We can't just go back. What about Layla? She might still be alive," Jun protested.

"Did you see what that thing did to Clara? Layla doesn't stand a chance. She's fucking dead, and I'm not going to waste my time chasing a corpse!" Xavier's pale face was flushed a bright red and his eyes were wide with fear.

Something in the brush not far from where the humans dug up the root vegetables caught Nuzal's eye. He got to his feet, bile rising up and gathering in the back of his throat when he realized it was one of the packs they had used to collect water. Strands of Layla's dark hair still clung to the fibers, and worst of all, there was a smattering of fresh red lifeblood across the shoulder strap.

Nuzal turned to Jun, offering her the pack. "I don't think we'd find her alive."

"This doesn't prove she's dead."

"You said it yourself." A nasty sneer pulled at Xavier's mouth. "You heard her scream."

Roman stepped up between them, pressing a hand firmly into Xavier's chest when he tried to move closer. "Jun, they're gone.

There's nothing we can do for them now. We need to get back to the ship and let the others know what happened."

His little mate's face fell as she stared down at the pack. Taking it from his outstretched hand, Jun brushed her fingers over the fabric before slipping the strap over her shoulder. "Fine. Let's go."

They made their way back through the forest, each one of them far more alert than they had been before. The crunch of fallen leaves or the snap of branches beneath their own feet set Nuzal's heart racing. It wasn't hard to keep Jun close; she'd pressed herself against his hip and didn't let him get more than a breath away.

The rushing of her lifeblood and the pounding of her heart were so loud in his head that he had almost mistaken it for his own. Nuzal worried that her heart, the one organ he couldn't completely repair during the surgery, was going to beat right out of her chest if she didn't rest soon.

Jun looked up at him as he lifted her over a large intertwining root system, and he wished more than anything that he could make the pain he saw in her eyes vanish. She was fierce, but even someone as strong as she was could suffer from the shock of what they'd been through.

Gloom seemed to chase them, creeping over the rocks and slithering through the trees like some giant serpent. The animals stayed hidden, but he imagined the whispers he heard were warnings being passed on, telling the others of the horrors they'd experienced there. Where Nuzal had found pleasure among the icia trees at the start of their search, he now found only a sense of wariness as his eyes scanned the open spaces between them.

"I can carry you—" Nuzal tried to offer when Jun's legs wobbled, but she thrust her hand out toward his face, shaking her head.

"I'm fine. I can make it."

He didn't understand her resistance, but Nuzal didn't push it any further. Perhaps she didn't want the males to think she was weak, that she couldn't push through and get back to the vessel on her own. They once had warrior females like her, or so the legends said. Courageous and fierce, just like his human mate.

"Finally," Xavier sighed when the vessel appeared in the middle of the clearing just up ahead.

The humans must have posted a lookout, he thought as the large ramp leading into the cargo bay lowered at their approach.

"Hurry up," Jun urged, glancing behind her as if she was worried the beasts had followed them. "Get inside!"

Their hasty steps rang along the metal of the ramp as they took shelter within.

"Close it! Close the damn door!" Xavier gasped, hunching over to rest his hands on his knees.

"Wait, where are the others? Where are Clara and Layla?" Esme asked as she pushed her way through the gathering crowd of onlookers.

"They're gone," Jun told her.

"What does that mean?"

"It means they are gone," Roman said. "They didn't make it back."

"We were attacked by something in the forest while we were gathering food. Whatever it was, it took them." Jun pressed her lips together, but it didn't stop the trembling of her chin. "We couldn't save them."

Esme turned to Roman and Xavier, her eyes narrowing as they nodded in agreement. "I knew this would happen."

Jun frowned. "What?"

"I knew you would come back without people. I knew it would be Clara, but I hadn't guessed you'd take poor Layla too." Esme turned toward the small group of humans at her back, her arms spread wide. "Didn't I tell you? I knew we couldn't trust him!"

"What the hell are you talking about?" Roman asked.

"Clara could read his mind—she knew what sick things he was planning, so he killed her!"

The humans murmured, a couple of them gasping as they backed away from him. He hadn't hurt Clara or Layla, and he certainly wasn't going to hurt them, but Esme's words fed the fear in their hearts.

"Esme," Jun reached out to place her palm on the blonde female's arm. "We all saw what happened to Clara."

Esme recoiled, jerking her arm away from Jun's touch. "How can we trust you to tell the truth? You're his *mate*." The word flew from her mouth like a curse. "Maybe he's got some sort of mind control and you're all just little puppets in this game he's playing. If they can give humans the abilities we all have, then who knows what they've done to themselves?"

"We were all there," Nuzal took a step forward, sending all of the humans except Esme into a panic. "We all saw the same thing. I fought one of the creatures off." He gestured to the healing crack on his chest.

"There was nothing left." They all turned toward Xavier. The male stared at Nuzal, shaking his head as he moved closer to the group. "There was nothing left. No blood, no pieces... there was *nothing*."

How could they all have experienced the same thing and still not be unified? Was it the shock of the events? Had it somehow muddled this male's mind? No, Xavier, unlike many of the humans, had never trusted or liked him. It wasn't something he held against him, but to blame him for the deaths of the females, to sow doubt when he knew the truth? It caused anger to rise up within Nuzal.

"Nothing you do will ever make up for all of the shit you and your friends did to us. We'll never trust you." Esme turned her hate-filled gaze on Jun. "And *you* shouldn't either."

Back in the forest, Nuzal had wondered what he could do to prove he was trying to unlearn the things he'd been taught, but it was clear to him now, that no amount of proof was going to convince many, if not all, of the humans. He spared a glance down at Jun and felt icy fingers tighten around his heart. Would it be the same with her? How long would it be before she looked at him with such venom and disgust?

They will never trust you. Not the humans. Not Jun. Not even Brin.

A growl rumbled up his chest, spreading the pain of his injury and his heartache. He stalked passed the group, leaving the cargo hold. He heard Jun call him, but he wouldn't go back. Slipping out through the door they'd left through the first time, Nuzal turned toward the forest. He checked the charge on the weapon he'd taken from Jun and looked toward the trees.

Nuzal would find the bodies of the females. He'd prove to them all that he could be trusted.

CHAPTER 28

JUN

"Oh, let him go!" Esme hissed at Jun as she moved to follow Nuzal.

"You weren't there! If you were so worried about Clara, then why didn't you volunteer to come with us? Clara defended Nuzal, she stood up for him, so why the hell would he want her dead?"

"Because he's a monster! They are *all* monsters!"

"He would never have hurt Clara. If anyone had a reason to want her dead, it was you."

"So what, you get yourself some alien dick and you're on their side? You won't even stand up for your own people?" Xavier's tone grated against her nerves, and she itched to introduce his face to her fist.

"I heard things in the Kaia's office," Esme stepped closer to Jun, her voice lowering as she leaned in. "The Venium are working with the Grutex. Did you know they were allies?" When Jun said nothing, Esme's lips turned up into an almost triumphant grin. "You did know. Are you even human at this point, or did they manage to *fix* you too?"

She'd been angry before with Xavier, but the feeling that crashed into her now with the force of a hurricane was pure rage. Her nails dug into the skin of her palm as she clenched her fists even tighter.

Nurses don't give people black eyes. Nurses do not *give people black eyes,* she chanted.

"You're so fucking ridiculous! I'm sorry for what you went through with the Kaia, but your paranoia is out of control, Esme. Nuzal is *not* the Kaia! Stop blaming him for whatever happened to you!"

Esme didn't respond, but the look on her face told Jun that her outburst was exactly what Esme had wanted from her.

"What the brax is going on?" Brin's voice rang through the bay, making the group of people in front of her jump. "What happened to you, Shayfia?" He asked, reaching out to brush the back of his finger over her cheek.

As happy as she was to see him and to know she finally had some back up, Jun knew she was going to get hell for sneaking out. Her nails still had dirt beneath them from digging up the vegetables, and she was sure she looked a mess after their hasty hike back to the ship.

"I went out with the others to gather food." She lifted her hand to silence him the moment his mouth dropped open. "You can yell at me later. We were attacked by something in the forest. Clara and Layla didn't make it."

"By something? It was Nuzal, and she's trying to cover it up for him!"

"That's enough!" Telisa shoved herself between them just in time to catch Esme by the shoulders. "I understand where your hatred is coming from, and I know you're afraid because we all are, but Nuzal helped us escape and has done nothing but care for each and every one of us since the crash. You cannot accuse him of murder without proof. I'm putting my foot down."

Esme's shoulders slumped as she stared up at Telisa before backing away, melting back into the crowd. Sympathy welled up inside of Jun. She hadn't gone through the same things as Esme, but she wasn't going to let the woman accuse Nuzal of something she knew he hadn't done. Those beasts, those nightmares, were the ones responsible for Clara and Layla's deaths.

She felt Brin's hand brush over her hair and turned to look up at him. "Where's Nuzal?"

"He got upset when Esme blamed him and he left."

Brin slid the packs from her shoulders and gathered the pouches filled with the roots they had collected, handing them off to Roman, who gave her a half-hearted grin. "It'll be all right, Jun."

Realizing the show was over, the humans began to trickle back out into the more comfortable areas of the ship, leaving the two of them alone in the cargo hold. Jun took a deep breath, moving toward the outer walls so that she could sag against them. She felt Brin's fingers slide over her cheek and the tingle it caused made her close her eyes in pleasure. He kneeled in front of her, lifting her face to his so that he could look at her properly.

She ran the tips of her fingers over his jaw, brushing the faded scars that marred his dark skin as her stomach tied itself in knots.

"Are you okay, Shayfia?"

"Physically? I'll be fine. I'm worried about him, Brin. I know Nuzal didn't do it. I was there—I saw it attack him, and I fired the shot that injured it before it could kill him."

Brin tugged her closer, pulling her into his arms. "Tell me what happened."

In this position, with Brin kneeling as he was, Jun's head was able to rest against his shoulder. She told him everything, about the growling in the beginning, the water, the fruit, the roots, and how Layla had disappeared just before the attack on Clara.

"I've never seen anything like them. They looked like wolves, but there was no fur and their legs were so long and slender. They had these yellow and blue rows on their heads, and their tails... they were hooked with a long barb at the end and the one that attacked Nuzal used it like a scorpion's." She didn't ask if he knew what a scorpion was, just shook her head and ran her hands over her face. "He almost died. He was almost gone like Layla and Clara.

"There was blood, *so* much blood, but when the creatures disappeared it was like they took all the evidence of the attack with them. I wanted to look, but Xavier didn't want to stay, and Roman and Nuzal agreed that there was nothing we could do, so we came back here and Esme practically met us at the door."

"It wasn't safe for you to go out there."

Here we go, she thought. "Nuzal is out there now. It's not safe for him either." Brin's mouth flattened and she knew from experience that he was trying to dig in his heels. "He went back out because of what Esme said, I know it. I saw the look on his face, Brin. She's convinced him that none of us will ever trust him, but *I* do. I know what I saw, and I know he's innocent and my gut is telling me that we need to find him."

"I'll find him. You go check on your people."

"Fuck that," Jun growled. She shoved away from him, grabbing one of the weapons someone had discarded on a work table against the wall. "I'm going. I don't want to lose either of you, Glowworm." He opened his mouth and she just knew he was going to argue. "Look, I don't have military training, but my papa taught me how to handle a gun as a kid, and I've been going to ranges and classes back on Earth for years. I want to help find Nuzal."

Silence hung between them for a moment, and she knew Brin

must be struggling with the urge to scoop her up and lock her in one of the rooms, but after a moment he relented. "I'm not sure how I'm ever going to be able to tell you *no*." His tail whipped back and forth as he reached out to take one of the other weapons for himself.

"Don't waste your time. Much easier to just agree with me."

"So I'm learning."

Once they were outside the ship, Jun looked around, hoping Nuzal would be nearby and that he hadn't actually gone off into the forest alone.

"Over here." Brin was crouched near the tree line where a set of fresh footprints had been left in the soil. The size and shape made it pretty obvious who they belonged to.

"So he's gone into the forest," Jun grimaced, staring into the trees. "How the hell are we going to find him?"

"Smell."

"I know we're all still trying to work out a schedule for sharing the showers, but I didn't think he smelled bad enough for you to be able to track him on scent alone."

If anything, the way Nuzal and Brin smelled had been affecting her in ways she had never noticed before. There had been times over the last few days when she was in close quarters with one of them that the scent made her desire nearly unbearable and she'd had to make up excuses to avoid the both of them.

"It's not like that. I can smell Nuzal in the same way I can smell you. I'd know your scent anywhere." The smile on his lips didn't quite reach his eyes.

Jun knew he was still on the fence about this mating, but there had been moments where she'd caught them working together and it had filled her with such a sense of happiness that she knew she'd done the right thing by following her gut instinct.

They headed in the direction of Nuzal's scent, stopping every few feet so that Brin could check the air and make adjustments.

The whispers of the animals from earlier had stopped, but she wasn't sure if it was due to the setting sun, or if it was a bad omen. Jun stuck to Brin's side, not letting him get far, but she knew she didn't have to worry about losing him with how tightly he had his tail wrapped around her waist. Even through the suit she wore, Jun could feel the heat of his skin, and it made her entire body tingle.

"Do you think we're getting clos—" Jun's words were cut off by the shriek of one of the Grutex weapons discharging somewhere close by.

"This way!"

"Brin, go! I'll catch up." She could tell by the racing of his fushori and the irritated flare of his gills that he wanted to sprint forward.

The forest floor in this part was littered with exposed roots and larger rocks than on the outer edge, and she struggled to keep her balance and hold her weapon as he pulled her along.

"I'm not leaving you here on your own!" Without even bothering to ask her permission, Brin scooped her up against his chest, holding her with one arm and bringing his weapon up with the other.

He'll be all right, Jun told herself, clutching at Brin's shoulders as he burst through the hanging branches. *He's a Grutex, for God's sake. Nothing gets rid of those guys.* A strange warmth unfurled within the pit of her stomach, spreading up her chest and shoulders before racing down her arms to pool in her palms.

The growling and snarling grew closer, and the scene that unfolded before them as Brin came to a stumbling halt would have torn a scream from her lungs if they hadn't seized at the sight of Nuzal's bloody body pinned beneath one of the beasts from earlier. Brin fired his weapon, startling the creature. It raced away, crashing through the underbrush as Brin took aim and fired again.

She twisted out of his arms, hitting the ground and racing over to Nuzal's body, not even stopping to see whether or not the shots hit their mark. With a ragged gasp, Jun dropped to her knees beside him, hands shaking as she tried to pull herself together enough to assess the damage. It was extensive. The plates covering his abdomen had been shattered, and some of the larger shards had turned in, piercing the softer flesh it was meant to protect beneath it.

Dark blood ran from the wounds the creature had inflicted, spilling over his sides and onto the ground she kneeled on. There was blood at the corners of his lips, and all six of his eyes turned to focus on her. He tried to speak, but nothing more than a terrifying gurgle reached her ears.

No, no, no!

"Stay with me," she pleaded, brushing her hands over his chest. "Please stay with us, Nuzal." His hand shifted across the ground to grasp her leg, and she turned back to inspect his body, placing her palms on the broken plate.

She hadn't thought to bring the gel from the medbay, but even if she had, Jun doubted it would do anything for wounds this severe. Although the shards had done a lot of damage, it was the creature's claws that had torn him open. The punctures were deep, and she lacked even the basic knowledge of Grutex anatomy that might enable her to figure out what internal damage these had caused.

There had been times over the years when they'd lost patients where Jun felt helpless, but this time, it broke her heart in a way that she knew she would never recover from. Tears spilled from her eyes as she watched him struggle to breathe, and all of those buried memories of watching her papa lying in the hospital bed, weak, and in pain came rushing back. She'd felt just as useless then as she did at that moment.

He was her mate. He couldn't die.

"I won't let you go," she whispered as the heat in her palms intensified.

It felt as if it were being pulled through her from somewhere deep within, like a well being sucked dry. Her muscles tensed, and Jun's head fell back as her mouth dropped open. The broken pieces of Nuzal's exoskeleton began to move beneath her outstretched fingers, shifting and sliding as warm fluid flowed over her hands and beneath her palms.

Nuzal gasped just as a coolness, starting at her fingertips, began to spread through her body, numbing her limbs. *What's happening?* She wondered as her body began to list to the side. *What's wrong with me?* Strong arms caught her before she hit the ground, and the most beautiful blue light filled her vision. *Brin.*

"What did you do, Shayfia?"

She'd never heard such fear in his voice. It made her want to reach out and touch his face, to reassure him that everything was going to be okay, but she couldn't seem to move her arms. Heavy lids closed over her eyes, and she struggled to open them.

"She healed me," came Nuzal's stunned response.

CHAPTER 29

BRIN

"Healed you?" Jun's voice was barely above a whisper. Darkness had settled beneath her eyes, and she didn't even seem to notice when Nuzal slid her head into his lap, brushing his fingers over her hair. Brin didn't bother trying to suppress his emotions as his fushori pulsed with his fear and anxiety.

"How did she do that?"

"They must have started the awakening process." Nuzal's mouth turned down as he frowned. "I didn't think they would have attempted it so soon after her surgery."

"Is that what happened with the others?" Brin asked.

"Roman and Xavier are examples of completed awakenings. They both have physical characteristics, but it takes time. If we were to rush the process, the humans would die. Erusha has almost perfected it, starting off by injecting a serum to trigger the dormant DNA."

"What dormant DNA are we talking about?"

"The recent conflict on Earth isn't the first time the Grutex have been to the planet. Generations ago, our scientist experimented with the idea of placing alien DNA into human test subjects. The original purpose seems muddled now, but from what I can recall, there was an interest in seeing how the DNA would mutate in future offspring, if it would stay within the line, or be bred out." Nuzal glanced down at Jun before focusing on Brin. "All of the humans who were in the cells, including Jun, are hybrids."

"So the DNA lays dormant until this awakening, which Jun apparently went through, but there are no physical features to indicate she's anything other than human." She looked the same to him as she had on the day they'd met.

"They couldn't have finished. The process is often difficult on the human body and requires medical care. Like I said, they start with a serum—"

"The purple stuff," Jun murmured, burrowing her face into Nuzal's hard thigh. "In my IV."

"How many times?" Nuzal slid a finger beneath her chin, turning her face so that he could see her. "Can you remember how many times was it given to you?"

Her face scrunched as she thought. "Twice, I think?"

"Vodk was trying to move into the Kaia's good graces. It doesn't surprise me that he would attempt to speed up the process. We hadn't reached the level of speed and ease the Kaia wanted. I don't know what he has planned, but if they perfect this process, if they somehow find a way to streamline it so that they don't have to do it manually, I imagine Earth's inhabitants are going to be in for a shock."

How many human-hybrids were there on Earth? Assuming this dormant DNA had been passed down successfully through each generation, Brin imagined it could mean a decent amount of the population were not as human as they believed. "That's what the lifeblood draw was for?"

Nuzal nodded. "I viewed her results just before finding her in pain inside your cell." He frowned as if the memory of that day had left its mark. Brin knew he still thought about her cries and the terror he'd felt as Nuzal carried her down the hall. "When the original experiments took place, the scientists didn't use just one species per subject. They injected a combination of species with similar traits and hoped something would take. In Jun's case, we found the markers for three different aquatic species in her DNA: Gri'ku, Ihod, and Venium."

"She's Venium?"

"According to the tests."

Was this why they were compatible enough to mate? The Venium had never mated outside of their species, yet he and Oshen had both found their mates on Earth. If Amanda was also tested, would they find traces of Venium DNA within her lifeblood as well?

"The Ihod," Brin said, taking her cold hand in his and running his thumb over her delicate fingers. "A few of the clans there are known for their healers. Whoever the Grutex took the DNA from must have been one of their members."

"It's possible."

"If they hadn't finished the process, then how is it that she was able to use this ability to heal you?"

"In the lab, physical pain was found to trigger many of the transformations."

Jun hadn't been in physical pain, though, at least not that he'd noticed. "She was worried about you." Her eyes were closed, and her breathing had evened out. She looked more peaceful and at rest now than she had in weeks. "She heard the weapon discharge and tried to convince me to leave her so I could get to you faster."

Nuzal said nothing as he stared down at their mate, the fingers on one hand trailing over the shell of her ear while his other hand ran over the network of scars that now marred his torso.

"We should take her back to the vessel where she can rest more comfortably," the male said, looking up at the darkening sky.

"The two of you need to rest." Nuzal gazed up at Brin as he stood, repositioning Jun so that she was curled up in the male's lap, her hands tucked beneath her cheek as she sighed in her sleep. "The sun has already fallen, and I don't want to risk moving either one of you after what just happened."

"I'll be fine..." Nuzal began to argue, but Brin shot him a look that he hoped conveyed how serious he was.

"You'll rest. That's the end of it. We can head back as soon as the sun begins to rise."

He knew Nuzal wanted to challenge the decision, but an intense silence, he simply slid himself and Jun across the ground, propping himself up against one of the trees. With the way his mind and body were buzzing, Brin was grateful for the quiet and stillness of the night. The pheromones Nuzal gave off and Jun's scent swirled around him, creating a tempting concoction that invaded his senses and made it difficult to think clearly. His body was being sent into overdrive, producing its own heady mix of pheromones he worried might affect their Grutex mate.

Their Grutex mate.

Brin had spent his entire time on this planet working to avoid being caught alone with the two of them. Not since the day they'd explored the ship together had he allowed that to happen again for this exact reason. He knew they needed to rest, to recover after the trauma they'd been through, but all he could think of was crawling across the ground to them, of sliding his hands over his little Shayfia's legs and parting them so that he could bury his face between her thighs.

He could have lost them today; more than once. They'd been

through the attack during the foraging, and just now, they'd come so close to losing Nuzal that it made his chest clench with the lingering anxiety. And Jun, he could have lost her to her ability. She wasn't Ihod and didn't know how to use the gifts that had been passed down to her, didn't know that she could hurt herself while trying to save someone else.

Leaves and small rocks rustled beneath his suit-covered feet as he moved around one of the trees, listening for any sign that the creature might return to finish what it had started. He stood guard over his mates, and while he attempted to keep his distance, Brin found himself moving closer to their sleeping forms, drawing in their scent.

His kokoras throbbed painfully within its sheath, trying its best to breach the seam. With a pained moan, Brin let himself fall back against the trunk of a tree, keeping his mates in his line of sight for peace of mind. His hand snaked down to cup the pulsing bulge, and he groaned as his hips jerked up in response to the stimuli. He was at the end of his rope.

Beads of perspiration slid down his neck as his eyes moved over Nuzal's face and chest. After he and Caly had faced the fact that they weren't suited, Brin had found that taking other males on as pleasure mates caused him far less anxiety. There was no fear that *this* one might be *the* one, that she might want a family and to have pups of her own. Those males on Venora had been safe, but Nuzal? *This* male was anything but safe.

Never in his wildest dreams would he have thought he'd find himself in such a situation. He found himself praying to the goddess, begging her for mercy. The thought of seeking relief, of pleasuring himself while they slept made him feel dirty. The guilt ate at him until he finally stood, legs trembling as he turned away. He needed to put distance between them before he drove himself crazy.

~

J un

H eat.

There was so much heat. There was fire in her veins, rushing through her body, burning everything it touched. Flames licked at her flesh, making her moan as they swept over her most sensitive areas. This wasn't the heat from before, not the heat she'd felt when she healed Nuzal. It was so different.

Instead of pooling in her palms, this flowed down from her belly, wrapping around her hips, and caressing her thighs. She felt it brush against her clit and smooth over her folds as if it were a physical touch and she writhed beneath it.

A soft, rumbling growl reached her ears and she forced her eyes to open. It wasn't quite daylight, but the sky was turning a gorgeous mauve color with oranges and pinks woven into the edges. Her mind struggled to piece together what was going on.

This looked like Earth, even smelled like it could be, but the trees were strange in color and in form. Whatever she was lying on shifted and she shot up, startled to find herself in Nuzal's lap, wrapped in his arms.

We're in the forest, she remembered now. *I healed him.* Jun looked down, tracing the scars with unsteady hands. *We almost lost him.*

We. Where was Brin?

"You're awake, Shayfia."

Her head whipped around, following Brin's voice to a spot just beyond a small gathering of young trees. If it weren't for the soft glow of his fushori, Jun might not have seen him at all.

"Brin?"

The glow of his eyes was far more intense than she had remembered, and it spoke to the fire within her, making her ache.

A soothing rattle brushed across her senses, and she looked up into the face of her other mate. It was a sound she associated with Nuzal, something comforting that never failed to put her at ease, but even his rattle couldn't douse the flames.

"Thank you."

Jun closed her eyes as Nuzal's voice rolled over her. "For what?"

"For saving my life." He placed his large hand over hers where it still rested on his scars, his throat working as he closed his eyes. "In all of my lives, no one has ever cared to save me. All of the other times I've laid there dying on a battlefield they've simply waited for my rebirth, but this time—this time, there would have been no rebirth, no more lives, no more chances."

The fact that he'd given up his immortality to come with them hadn't occurred to her before then. When she'd seen him lying there, his body broken and the life fading from his eyes, Jun had realized that she couldn't imagine a world in which she had to live without him, just like she could no longer imagine living without Brin.

Make them yours. Show them.

It was as if something was taking over her body, instructing her to stand so that she was looking directly into Nuzal's eyes. Well, one set. She couldn't look into them all at the same time, so she took her pick and stuck with the lowest, the purple ones he'd referred to as his *imperfections*.

"The things they said about me, about the Grutex..." Nuzal shook his head. "Esme is right. Nothing I do will ever be enough. *I* will never be enough. You should have let me go."

The words broke her heart. "I know they might not all be able to forgive you, but I do." She stepped into him, running her hands

275

over the tentacle-like vines and up to his jaw. Her fingers played along the harsh edge, tracing the angles as she dipped her head. "I accept you just as you are."

Jun's pulse raced as his palm skimmed up her side, and she glanced sideways, catching Brin's eyes as he stepped out of the shadows. The look he gave her sent a shiver down her spine. Nuzal's xines curled around her wrists, and she turned back to him, smiling as she pressed her lips against his.

The adrenaline from the attack had long worn off, but her heart hammered in her chest the same way it had when she heard the weapon fire. They did this to her, Brin and Nuzal. They made feel crazy with need, made her want to lose herself in them and forget that they had very real problems. Back on the ship, she'd made the decision to dive into her feelings, to allow them to take over, and she did the same now with Nuzal, letting the tide of emotions carry her away.

The three of them had taken too many chances with fate over the last few days, and she wasn't going to let another day pass before taking what she wanted, what she knew to be hers.

Nuzal's lips were surprisingly soft and pliant, not at all hard like the plating that surrounded them. Jun wasn't sure if it was shock that kept him from responding, or if he just didn't know what to do, but she brushed her mouth over his again before letting her tongue trace the seam of his lips. A moan slipped from her mouth as his xines began to thrash around, and she wriggled as slick began to coat her thighs inside the suit.

Her entire body pulsed with need, and the ache between her legs threatened to send her over the edge of reason. She gasped as another set over large hands gripped her jaw, pulling her lips from Nuzal's. Brin kneeled behind her, his knees pressed into the ground on either side of Nuzal's long legs. With a low growl, he crushed his lips to hers, his arms wrapping around her torso as he pressed himself against her back.

Jun felt the warmth of his tail around her leg, twirling up the inside of her thigh. She gasped against Brin's lips, clutching the xine she held in her hand tightly when she felt the tip of his tail slid between her legs. It pressed into her sensitive flesh and she circled her hips, chasing the pleasure, seeking more. There was nothing and no one out here to stop her from taking what she wanted, what she craved more than anything.

They belonged together, the three of them. Being there with them felt like the most natural thing imaginable, and she grinned, looking up into Brin's face as she stroked Nuzal's jaw. This was her place.

Run!

The heat within her exploded at the sound of Nuzal's rumbling growl. Every single hair on her body stood on end, and before she knew what she was doing, she had jumped out of Brin's arms.

Go!

Nuzal made a grab for her, but she danced out of reach of those long arms. Brin frowned at the behavior, but the way Nuzal's eyes widened before narrowing on her told her he knew exactly what she was about to do.

Hurry!

Before Nuzal could get to his feet, Jun snatched the weapon from the ground and turned, fleeing into the trees. She knew she wouldn't get far, not with that measly head start she'd given herself, but it was the thrill of the chase and the knowledge that she could give this to Nuzal, could show him in this way that she accepted him as her mate.

Faster!

Her blood called out to her, but it wasn't fear she felt when she heard the heavy footsteps and snarls closing in behind her. It was excitement, and she welcomed the rush of adrenaline that shot through her. She wanted them to catch her, to show her she was theirs, but she didn't want to make it too easy.

Jun veered to the right, leaping over rocks and other small debris in her path, thankful again for the suit that protected her feet. She swore she could feel their breath on the back of her neck as she ducked beneath a twisted branch, bursting into the small clearing. *Run! Go! Hurry! Faster!* The words were a chant, echoing in her mind over and over. Just when she thought she might be winning her little game, a massive arm slipped around her waist, scooping her up. Her feet dangled above the ground as she struggled to free herself.

"*Yield.*"

That one word, spoken in that deep, husky voice, was nearly enough to make Jun come as she hung there, pressed up against Nuzal's body. His chest rose and fell rapidly behind her, and she closed her eyes, listening to the thundering of his heart.

When she opened them, Brin was standing a few paces away, eyes locked on her face. "Yield, Shayfia."

"Make me," she whispered.

Nuzal's claws pressed into her ribs as his grip on her tightened. Okay, maybe it wasn't in her best interest to taunt them, but she couldn't seem to stop herself, and when Brin began to close in on her as Nuzal lifted her higher, she couldn't say she regretted it. *Not one bit*, she thought, moaning when one of Nuzal's hands slid up the front of her throat.

Off to her left were a couple of large icia trees. They looked like they'd been uprooted and had fallen across one side of the small clearing, catching on the bigger boulders on the outside edge. Nuzal swung around, testing the stability of the trunks before placing her face-down across them. Jun glanced back over her shoulder, watching Nuzal as his gaze moved over her. Brin moved around to stand in front of her, taking the weapon from her hand as he crouched down face to face with her.

"Lower the suit," Brin told her.

She shook her head, gasping when Nuzal spread her legs wide and pressed his hips against her covered sex. God help her. *Right there,* she thought, writhing against him, trying to ease some of the pressure.

"Remove the suit," Nuzal purred, grinding against her.

Oh, fuck. "Suit down!" The cool bark pressed into her abdomen, and the way her nipples brushed against the second trunk made her moan. "Please."

"Now *yield*," he whispered, bowing over her body so that the warmth of his breath fluttered against her shoulder.

She felt something shift against her thigh a moment before the pulsing length of his cock slid against her wet heat.

"Please, Nuzal. I yield! I yield."

"I can't control this," Nuzal hissed, resting the tip of his cock at her entrance.

"I'm not asking you to control it." Jun licked her lips as she glanced over her shoulder at him. "I don't want control or for you to hold yourself back."

He shook his head, digging his claws into her hips and drawing a moan of anticipation from her. "Not like this…"

"Stop," she whispered. "I want this. I want you to be exactly who you are, not who you think I want you to be."

There was no foreplay, no teasing or preparation for his entry. He reared back and pushed into her, a ragged, broken growl climbing up his throat as she cried out in surprise and pleasure. Brin was kissing her a moment later, reaching up to run his fingers over her nipples as Nuzal moved within her, helping to ease the sting of his intrusion.

She should be afraid, shouldn't she? The way he held her, the way he thrust into her, was rough and brutal, but she found that it only excited her more. There was a certain amount of danger in this, in being out here in the forest where they'd already lost people that should put her off, but it didn't. All she wanted right then was for her mates to relieve the pressure that had built inside of her, and to know that they were just as desperate for her as she was for them.

"*Mine,*" Nuzal growled as he drove his hips forward.

"*Ours,*" Brin corrected, smiling as he pulled back to watch her face contort in pleasure. "So beautiful, Shayfia."

He took a step back before commanding his suit down, and she took in every inch of him that was revealed as the organism retreated. The first time they met, Brin hadn't been wearing his top, but she'd never had the pleasure of seeing him completely naked before now, and God, was she glad to be looking. Lean, well-defined muscle rippled beneath his dark skin as he shifted. She caught just a glimpse of his cock as it slipped free of his body before he took it in his hand.

When Nuzal lifted her hips, Brin slid his hand between her body and the tree, rubbing the pad of his finger over her throbbing clit and sending jolts of pleasure spiraling through her. She felt herself contract around Nuzal, taking a moment to let his groan wash over her when his rhythm faltered. Brin's other hand caressed her breast, pinching and tweaking the sensitive peak as he pressed his lips to the side of her neck, letting his teeth scrape over her skin.

"Please," she whimpered when Nuzal grabbed her braid and wrapped it around his hand. "*More.* I need more." Jun squirmed as much as she was able, pushing herself back onto Nuzal's cock.

A quick jerk of her hair was the only warning she got before Nuzal lifted her body, urging her to her knees on the trunks. He moved one hand to her hips as the other gripped her throat so he could thrust up into her body. Brin's fingers continued their assault and she pinched her eyes shut, keening loudly when she felt his mouth close over one of her breasts. His tongue rolled around her nipple, flicking it back and forth to the rhythm Nuzal was setting. It was like he recognized Nuzal had lost all control, and he took it upon himself to help her body adjust to their mate.

The combination of Nuzal's thrusts and Brin's fingers coaxed a moan from somewhere deep inside of her. "More, Nuzal. *More.*"

CHAPTER 30

*M*ore.

The sound of their female moaning as his bondmate pleasured her with his hands and mouth destroyed what little control he'd been holding onto. All the times he had tried to imagine what it would be like to take her, to feel his inkei surrounded by the heat of her body paled in comparison. The desire he had to take her slow, to touch her the way he saw Brin touch her, was being overruled by the instinct to mate, to claim them.

The smell of Brin's pheromones in the night had slowly driven him mad as he'd laid there with Jun curled in his lap. Her scent and the warmth of her pressed against him had done little to keep his mind clear. He could have made it back to the ship, into one of the rooms even, before taking her, but when Jun had taken off into the forest, Nuzal had known they were out of time, that the chance for gentleness had been thrown out.

This wasn't just about the need to mate Jun; this was about

domination, about reminding both of his mates that they belonged to him.

Nuzal's jaw clenched almost painfully as he surged forward again and again. His need was so demanding, so violent, that he feared he would hurt her, but every time she asked for more, pleaded with him in that breathless manner, it fed something dark within him. The tips of his claws dug into the soft flesh on her hips, and he watched with disturbing satisfaction as her lifeblood made tiny rivulets down her body. She would bear his marks, would remember him when she saw them, and it sent a thrill through him.

A sweet, throaty moan of pure pleasure fell from her lips as her body began to shake; her core contracted around him, pulsing as she gasped and circled her hips. He watched Jun's hand reach out and wrap around Brin's length as she continued to throb around him. Nuzal leaned forward to grasp the dark braid that hung down Brin's back, pulling the male close and sinking his teeth into the side of his neck.

My bondmate. My male.

Lifeblood rushed over his tongue, and a groan of satisfaction moved through him when Brin's hand came up to cup his head, pressing his lips closer as if it brought him just as much pleasure to receive Nuzal's claim as it gave Nuzal to make it.

"Tell us what you want, Shayfia."

The husky rumble of Brin's voice washed over him, sliding over his chest as if it were a physical caress. He released his hold on his bondmate's neck, laving the wound he'd left with his tongue before he pulled back to watch their mate's hand move over Brin. His inkei jerked within her, and Jun gasped, letting her head fall back against his chest as she undulated.

"What do you want?" Brin questioned her again, sliding his hand up her throat.

"I want to *feel*," she whined, reaching up to grasp one of his xines. "I want to be taken. I want everyone to know I belong to my mates."

"Do you, Shayfia? Do you belong to us?" Brin thrust into her hand as Nuzal pressed into the slick heat of her body.

"Yes," came her breathy response.

"Louder, Shayfia. Do you belong to us?"

"Yes! I'm yours." Her declaration echoed through the forest around them.

Nuzal's breath stuttered out of his lungs when she looked up at him with wide, glassy eyes. She watched him, touched him, like the fact that he was a Grutex didn't repulse her, like she accepted him even though he'd done horrible things to her people.

"Nuzal..."

Her breathy whisper barely penetrated the fog encroaching on his mind as he struggled to process everything happening around him. *Too much*, some insecure part of him screamed. He released Brin's hair to adjust Jun, bending her body forward so she couldn't watch his descent into madness. In a move that startled both males, Jun thrust backward, impaling herself on Nuzal as she took Brin into her mouth, humming and circling her hips.

"Brax!" Brin groaned, burying his fingers in her dark hair and making shallow thrusts between her lips. "Sweet little shayfia," he purred as he slid his hand over Nuzal's xines, dragging his claws over the plating on his chest as he watched their mate. "I wish you could see how beautiful you look with Nuzal's cock filling your cunt and mine filling your mouth."

Nuzal's body begged for release, begged for him to spill himself inside his mate, but he gritted his teeth and forced himself to take a breath. He wanted to see them, to experience their pleasure with them. What was it Brin had called his inkei? A cock. He liked the way it sounded coming from his bondmate's lips. It repeated within his mind, over and over as he moved, each thrust stretching her a little more than the last, until he was almost fully seated within her. The stem just above his cock quivered as it brushed against her, skimming over her small puckered hole.

Whatever this was that had taken him over wanted—needed—to claim every part of her, and he meant to see that through. Nuzal pulled back, allowing himself to slip free of her body so that he could run the wet length of his cock over the hole. Even though both his stem and his cock created their own natural lubricant, he had the presence of mind to assure she was prepared for his entrance into this part of her body. When he thrust back into her this time, Nuzal bottomed out. His stem sank into her, pushing through the ring of muscle as it clenched around him.

Jun bucked, humming around Brin's cock as one of her hands flew back to circle his wrist. "Relax," he hissed, grinding himself against her as he adjusted his grip on her hips. "Yield, little one. Let me in." Curling his fingers into his palm to protect her from his claws, Nuzal tucked his fist beneath her pelvis, pressing his knuckle against the nub that sat just above where they were joined.

The tension in her body receded slowly, and Nuzal groaned as the base of his stem disappeared. Jun's head bobbed up and down on their bondmate, fast and hard one moment before switching to slow and drawn out the next. When Nuzal turned his attention to Brin's face, he was surprised to find his blue gaze locked on him, a grin playing over his lips as the tip of his tail slid beneath their mate. Nuzal grunted as it brushed past his knuckle, squeezing up against his cock so that it moved in and out of Jun with his thrusts.

"Fuck!" Jun cried, pulling away from Brin and twisting around to see what they were doing. "God—like that!"

Brin pushed in further, stretching Jun as the thicker part of the appendage wrapped around his cock, squeezing him in time to the pulse of Jun's cunt. He wouldn't make it much longer if they kept this up, and the madness within him had plans for these two.

When he found himself on the edge, Nuzal lifted her from the fallen trees, one hand pressed against her belly to hold her in place, while the other stayed between her legs, spreading the outer folds of her sex for Brin.

"Here," he growled, jerking his head down toward the ground at his feet. "Lie down."

Brin did as he was told, his tail gliding over Nuzal's length and rubbing against Jun's walls. She hissed his name like a curse, but her focus stayed on their bondmate as he rounded the uprooted tree and positioned himself beneath them on the forest floor. He wasn't sure if Brin followed his instructions because he wanted to, or if it was because he sensed how close Nuzal was to losing his mind, but he was grateful either way.

He lifted her off of himself, taking satisfaction in the way she moaned as her body clutched at him. With a knee pressed into the soil on either side of Brin's outer thighs, Nuzal lowered Jun onto the other male's cock, growling as they sighed in unison. He slid his hand over her spine, nudging her down until she was bent over Brin with her breasts crushed against the lower half of his chest.

The sight of his mates, exposed as they were, made him snarl, and he curled his hips under, angling his cock so he could work the tip of it inside Jun's already full cunt.

"Oh, God! Nuzal—" Her words ended on a strangled cry and she went still, panting as he slowly worked his way back into her tight sheath. Brin's cock jerked against his as Jun's inner walls clenched tight around their combined girth. She was so small in comparison, but she opened for them.

"Shayfia," Brin groaned as he bucked his hips. "You were made for us—take all of us."

Jun clawed at Brin's body as Nuzal finally seated himself, her cries muffled against Brin's chest as she sank her teeth into his flesh. *So beautiful. So strong.* The way she met their thrusts, taking his stem back into her ass as it began to vibrate, stole his breath.

Brin's swollen glands rubbed along the base of his cock as they moved against one another and Nuzal knew he must also be trying his best to hold back.

"Who do you belong to?" Nuzal's voice was barely recognizable to his own ears. Jun gasped, unable to respond as the pleasure began to take her over. He wrapped her disheveled braid around his hand, pulling her head back. "Tell me who you belong to."

"My mates!" she cried. "You! Brin! Oh, God, I can't—please, Nuzal!"

A moment later, Jun's entire body went stiff, and she let out a long cry as her cunt fisted around them. Without a second thought, Nuzal sank his claws into the soft flesh of her back; marking her, showing the world that she belonged to him.

"Come, Nuzal," Brin panted, his eyes shining with excitement as Nuzal placed his bloodied palm on his bondmate's chest, gauging the dark flesh. The male covered his hand, pressing his claws deeper as he hissed. "Come for us, Nuzal."

He felt the pressure at the base of his spine shoot through his core and into his limbs a moment before his body stiffened with pleasure so intense that his vision darkened. He spilled within their female, coating her walls and Brin's cock as he jerked and pulsed violently.

Mine.

My female.

My male.

The buzzing in his ears began to recede as his vision cleared, and he stared down at them in utter amazement. The smell of her arousal mixed with his and Brin's made him want to bury his face between her thighs. His cock was still inside her, still spilling the last of his seed, but he pulled out, stumbling back on unsteady legs as he watched Brin pump up into her over and over until his jaw clenched and the back of his head pressed into the ground as pleasure washed over his features.

Nuzal blinked his eyes and shook his head as he felt reason and clarity return to him. What had he done? He stared at Jun's back, horror washing over him as her lifeblood dripped down toward her hips. He had done this. He had scarred her.

For all his talk about how far the Grutex had come since their days of the chase, Nuzal had acted little more than a beast, and his mate would bear the proof of that on her body for the rest of her life. And Brin? He'd done nothing but add more scars to his bondmate's already marred flesh. Never had he thought himself capable of reverting back to his most basic and primal form, but he stared down at the evidence of that on his hands.

Jun slumped down onto Brin, both of them gasping and panting. His bondmate soothed a hand over her hair and shoulders, murmuring something he couldn't quite hear as his lifeblood began to pound in his ears and his mind replayed the things he'd done.

He wanted to be with them, wanted to lie down beside them on the floor of the forest and gaze at them, fascinated by the fact that he'd been given this gift, but how could he? Nuzal stood, trying to put distance between them. He needed to think, to silence his mind.

"Nuzal? Wait!"

Brin called after him, but he couldn't turn back. His body felt cold, numb to everything around him.

Take a good look, Nuzal. This is what we are becoming, Erusha had once said in regards to the increased violence of the warriors.

Look what you've become.

CHAPTER 31

BRIN

*B*rin frowned after Nuzal's retreating form, watching as he disappeared behind a grouping of trees. One moment he'd been lost in their mating, dragging the head of his cock up and down Brin's length as they took Jun, and the next the male had looked at him with something akin to horror. There had been shame and shock in his eyes as he stumbled away.

Jun hummed against his chest, her breath warm on his skin as she slowly drifted down from her release. "Jesus." She mumbled as Brin's cock jerked within her, drawing a soft flutter from her cunt.

"Who's Jesus?"

Laughter burst from her mouth, and they both groaned as she tightened around his swollen glands. "Jesus is…" She shook her head. "I'm not going to talk to you about religion right now."

Fine by him. He wasn't interested in anything aside from what had just happened between the three of them. The feel of her nails trailing over his abdomen sent a tingle down his spine, and he shuddered.

"What's that?" Jun asked a moment before she gasped, pushing herself up as her hands pressed into the lifeblood on his skin. "God, Brin, you're bleeding!"

"So are you," he murmured with a satisfied grin, brushing his finger over the marks Nuzal had left on her body.

Heat emanated from her palms as she pressed them against his chest, but he grabbed her wrists, tugging her hands up so he could brush his lips across her fingertips. "These are scars I wish to keep, Shayfia. You left the proof of our mating on my heart, but Nuzal left it on my body." His tail wrapped around her hips, minding her fresh wounds. The sight of them did little to relieve the nearly painful swelling.

"Nuzal?" Jun shifted on top of him as she turned to look for their mate. "Where is he? Nuzal!" She leaned over to his side, grabbing the plasma weapon from the ground where it must have fallen during their mating and attempted to stand.

"Brax!" Brin grunted, grabbing Jun's waist as she gasped, and he held her still to keep from doing either of them any damage. "Don't," he panted, gritting his teeth as pleasure and pain tore through him.

"What was that?"

"Do you remember when I told you I knew you were my mate when my glands swelled for you?" Jun nodded, adjusting herself on his pelvis. "They swell just before I release and tie us together."

"So... we're stuck here?"

"Just for a moment longer," he growled when she wiggled her hips. "You aren't helping, Shayfia."

"Sorry. Did you see where Nuzal went?" Her brows furrowed as she scanned the trees. "He just got up and left after *that*."

She was hurt by the male's behavior, but Brin suspected he

understood a little bit of what Nuzal was feeling. They'd been rough with her, and perhaps that's where the shame in his eyes had come from, but like Brin, Nuzal had been raised in an environment where love and physical affection were not the norm.

After Nyissa and Calder took him in, Brin had struggled to associate physical touch with kindness. It had overwhelmed him and made him feel uncomfortable to the point that he'd tried to distance himself from his new family. Lucky for him, they were a patient lot.

"Give him some time. Learning to process so much physical contact is hard enough, but he's Grutex. Most of them are raised for the battlefield from the moment they take their first breath, and Nuzal's never known love and acceptance the way you or I have." Brin gripped her jaw, turning her head until her focus was back on him. "Patience is a wonderful gift to give someone, Shayfia."

Her small hands ran up and down his arms, and he sighed in relief when his glands began to deflate, allowing the combination of their seed to spill onto his pelvis as his kokoras slipped back into his sheath. "I'm sure the pheromones didn't do anything to help him." Brin said, reaching down to run a claw through the fluids. "I struggled with them while the two of you rested."

"The pheromones?" She grimaced. "What do they do exactly?"

"The Venium produce them during mating to encourage the bond between mates. If we fight it… Well, it usually ends like this." He swept his hands over their bodies.

"So waiting too long sends you into overdrive?"

"Essentially. It makes it hard to think clearly, drives you mad with need—" The look on her face told him he'd said the wrong thing. "I'm sure the fact that I could have lost the both of you twice in one day didn't help."

"The fact that you're producing these pheromones to

encourage bonding didn't seem like something you should mention?"

Abort mission! This won't end well, his mind warned. How had he managed to brax this part of the mating up already? "It didn't occur to me that it might be something we needed to talk about."

"Really, Brin? Is Nuzal's body doing this too?" She laughed humorlessly when he nodded. "So the two of you are just pumping out these pheromones, driving all of us crazy, and you didn't think that either of you should have mentioned it at least once?"

"Shayf—"

"No! Don't you use that on me right now." She glanced down at the proof of their mating as it slid from her body onto his and shook her head. "Was any of this real?"

Brin frowned as she jerked her hand out of his. "Of course it is."

"When did this start, Brin? Back on Earth, in my house? Or was it on the ship? Have all of the things I felt for the two of you been *my* feelings, or were they the influence of the pheromones?"

It had never before crossed Brin's mind that something his people produced naturally could actually change the mind of another being. This was normal for the Venium, the *only* way for them, but it was obvious to him now that this wasn't the case for Jun's people.

"I would hope that everything you have felt has been real, Jun."

"You would hope? God, Brin. All these things—" Her eyes brimmed with tears as she pushed away from him. "Everything I feel for you... for Nuzal..."

Jun tried to stand, to move away from him, and something inside Brin snapped at the thought that he might lose her over this. His hand shot out, closing around her throat just beneath her jaw as he snarled, fear making his entire body shake. "You are ours! You belong with us."

"Let me go." When he made no move to follow her command, Brin felt the cool metal of the plasma weapon press into his chest. "Let. Me. Go." His hand dropped away, and she sprang to her feet, moving out of reach. "Suit, up." She waited for the Grutex suit to completely envelope her body before turning in the direction Nuzal had gone and taking off into the trees.

Brax! He stood, giving his suit the up command and took off after her.

Nice communication, Brin. Your first argument as a mated male and you managed to upset her enough to have a weapon drawn on you.

For someone with such short legs, she was surprisingly quick. By the time he caught up to her, they were approaching Nuzal. He turned to watch them, his head lowered and his eyes not quite meeting their gazes. Brin could understand Nuzal's distancing, but what he couldn't wrap his mind around was the depth of Jun's anger over.

"I'm sorry." Nuzal dropped his chin to his chest. "You have every right to be upset with me."

"Nuzal, you didn't hurt me." Jun sighed. "Did you know about the pheromones too?"

The male's eyes shot to his face, and he frowned in confusion. "Yes. We knew they increased the urgency to mate for pairs that prolonged the completion of the bond. It's something the Grutex have recently thought to try and weaponize against the Venium."

Brin snarled. "Braxing traitorous scum. No offense," he added.

"So both of my mates knew I was being affected by these pheromones and neither one of them thought it was important enough that I should know about it?" She folded her arms over her chest.

Nuzal looked back and forth between them. "I don't understand. This is something that cannot be controlled, a natural part of mating."

"She's worried that everything she's felt for us so far hasn't been because *she* felt it, but because the pheromones *made* her feel it," Brin explained.

"*She* is standing right here and can speak for herself."

"I can't tell you what is real or the product of the pheromones, but I can tell you that they didn't become overpowering until we were on this planet." Nuzal looked down at their female with kind and patient eyes.

"We can speak with the healers on Venora once we get there. They might have more answers for you." Jun didn't speak, but she nodded. "Let's get back to the ship."

"Why'd you come out here, Nuzal?" She asked as they walked.

The male was silent for a moment. "I was hoping to find the females."

"Did you?"

Nuzal shook his head. "I found no sign of them."

Jun inclined her head as if she'd been expecting the answer. "You scared the hell out of me," she murmured.

"I'm sorry." Nuzal reached out to brush a finger over her hair, but Jun shrank away.

"I think we should give ourselves some time to think this all over, to make sure it's what we want." She turned toward Brin, her mouth flattening. "I'm sorry I threatened to shoot you."

"It's not the first time, Shayfia." He grinned a little when she rolled her eyes. "I'm sorry for the way I reacted. I shouldn't have touched you like that."

They didn't speak for the remainder of the trek back to the vessel, but Brin's mind raced. He would give her time to think, but she was it for him, and he suspected it might be the same for

Nuzal. He didn't need time to ponder whether or not his feelings were real.

Two weeks later...

"*Y*ou really should have told her, you know?"

Brin sighed, shifting his focus away from his inspection of the engine. He'd been waiting for Telisa to come and give him an earful, and it seemed like the time had finally arrived. "I told myself the other day, 'Brin, the only thing this mating is missing is Telisa's opinion,' and look, here you are, ready to offer it."

The female threw her head back and laughed good-naturedly. "We've got Spicy Brin today, huh?"

Brin rolled his eyes and bent down to retrieve one of the tools at his feet. "Say what you've come to say. I've got work to do." He was moments away from washing his hands of this piece of pile of tigeara shit. Never in his life had it taken him so long to fix something.

"I'm not trying to stick my nose where it doesn't belong–not trying to be in your business," she amended when he frowned at her wording. "I'm just trying to help. You should talk to her."

"About what? About how I didn't think to explain that the Venium produce pheromones for their mates because it's something natural for us?"

"It's not natural for humans, though."

"How was I supposed to know that?"

"You talk to her."

Brin narrowed his eyes on her as she pulled one of the tools off of the engine. Jun had hardly spoken more than a handful of words to him or Nuzal since they'd made it back to the ship the day of their mating. He'd promised to give her time, and he was, but not knowing what was going on in her head was driving him mad.

"Look, relationships are hard in general, but you guys aren't even the same species. On top of having to get to know one another on a personal level, you and Nuzal have to learn the most basic things about humans, just like Jun has to learn the basics about the Venium."

"I'm not sure if you've noticed, but we haven't exactly been on a leisure trip."

"Yeah, the kidnapping and experiments sort of gave that away." He stuck his hand out toward her, and Telisa placed the wrench she'd taken into his palm. "What I'm trying to say is, talk to her."

"She doesn't want to speak to me."

"That's complete bullshit. You don't catch the way she looks at the two of you. I think she's hurt and is stubborn as hell. You guys are my favorite human-Venium-Grutex trio, and I want this to all work out." Telisa frowned, crouching down and slipping her hand between the two main parts of the machine. "What's this?"

"We're the only human-Venium-Grutex trio you know." Brin raised his brow ridges as he looked down at what she was referring to. "Did you pull that out?"

"No, it was lying back here." She gestured to a dark space beneath a row of cables. "It happened to catch my eye."

Brin nudged her out of the way before sticking his hand through, feeling around for the coupler and twisting it back onto the side of the engine. It wasn't going to be this simple; it couldn't be. He'd been working in here for days on end, had practically taken the entire thing apart at this point, and somehow he'd missed a braxing hose. His mind was still muddled from the hormones that had yet to dissipate, which was concerning, but surely he should have noticed *this*.

"Nyissa, run a system check on the engine."

"Yes, Master. Beginning system check now." The lights on the massive machine flickered on as it hummed to life, and the display screen to his right began to scroll through the operating procedures as the system booted up. "Check complete. System is functioning properly and fully operational."

"You fixed it?" Telisa asked, her eyes going wide as she bounced on her toes in excitement.

"*You* fixed it." He laughed when she punched her fist in the air and whooped loudly.

"Let's get the hell off of this planet!"

Brin bounded through the ship in search of his mates, ready to share the good news. The doors to the common area slid open at his approach, and he caught sight of Jun sitting at one of the tables cutting and preparing the root vegetables the foraging team had gathered that morning. Her hair was twisted into a long braid that hung down her back, and he was reminded briefly of what they'd been doing the last time it was wrapped around his hand.

Across the room, Nuzal sat with Roman, their heads bent close together as his bondmate pointed to something on his comm screen. They locked eyes for a moment before Telisa burst in behind him, rushing excitedly to Jun's side.

"What's got into you?" Jun asked when Telisa wrapped her arms around her shoulders and squeezed.

"Can I tell her?" Her enthusiasm made Brin grin, and he nodded as he walked over to where his female sat. "The engine is up and running! We can finally leave!"

Jun's eyes darted to his face and the smile that spread across her mouth made his heart thunder in his chest. Goddess above, she was beautiful. "You figured it out?"

"Telisa found the problem, and we were able to fix it."

"Hell yes!" She reached up to squeeze the other female's hand. "Badass senator *and* alien spaceship mechanic? What a package."

"When can we leave?" Roman asked.

"We need to figure a few things out before we actually set out, but—"

Jun made a distressed sound as she twisted out of Telisa's arms, jumping up from her chair and bolting toward the doors. Brin called after her, but she waved him off, disappearing into the hallway that led to the crew quarters.

"Her stomach was upset the other day too," Telisa said, moving into Jun's empty seat. "She thinks it might be the change in diet."

"Has she been to medbay?" He looked to Nuzal, who shook his head.

"Not recently. I'd run a scan if I thought she would let me, but it's entirely possible that it's just her system getting used to the bionic transplants or the dietary changes like she thinks."

Brin frowned at the doors, wanting to follow her to assure himself that she was all right. His mate hadn't smelled ill, though. He drew in her lingering scent and nearly groaned. It was sweeter and lighter than he remembered it being before they'd mated.

"Brin?"

He shifted his attention back to the table as Roman and Nuzal joined them. His bondmate stood close to him, letting his tail brush against Brin's leg as if trying to gauge his reaction. This was the first time Nuzal was seeking physical affection from Brin since they'd mated, and he allowed himself to find joy in the moment. He wrapped his tail around his bondmate's, smiling when he didn't pull away.

"Nyissa, can you plot a course for Venora?" Brin had avoided doing it before now, not wanting to get their hopes up before he knew they would be able to leave the planet.

"Yes, Master. Plotting course to Venora. Estimated travel time is twenty-eight soli."

Telisa frowned. "Can we get the human translation of that?"

"Similar in time to an Earth month."

Roman let out a long, low whistle. "How the hell are we going to gather and store enough food for everyone on board to last that long?"

Telisa pursed her lips and drummed her fingers on the table. "The replicator is still out of commission, so we can't rely on that."

"Why not use the cryopods? We won't have to worry about storing food for the entire trip if we do that."

Brin turned to his bondmate with a raised brow ridge. "There are cryochambers on this thing?"

"All vessels in this class are required to have them."

"Roman, can you get a group together to gather enough food for two days? We'll set the pods to wake us a day out from Venora so we have time to recover from the effects of cryosleep. And Roman?" He called after the human as he sprinted toward the door. "Everyone stays armed out there and don't go any further than you have to. Stick close to the edge."

They hadn't seen any more of the beasts since Brin chased the last one away, but he didn't want the humans to become complacent, even if this was their last day on the planet.

CHAPTER 32

JUN

"Cryosleep?" she asked, drying her face with one of the towels from the bathroom's storage cabinet. It didn't matter that she'd been in the pods before; the thought of closing herself inside one of those things again made her already sensitive stomach roil. There were so many things that could go wrong, and every single of them was going through her mind. Jun scrunched her face up as she turned to look at her mates. "Not looking forward to that."

"Using the pods eliminates the need for a month's worth of food," Brin told her as he lowered himself onto the edge of the massive bed next to Nuzal.

"I know it's necessary for the trip, but the last time I woke up from cryosleep, I felt like death warmed over. Not to mention all the things that could potentially go wrong while we're inside them."

Nuzal rattled softly when she stepped back out into the room. "You'll be safe, little one. Brin will be watching over us."

She hadn't spoken much to either one of them for two weeks now. *Two very long weeks,* she mentally groaned. Even with how awful she'd been feeling recently, Jun still found herself thinking of that day in the forest, of the way they'd touched her. Her body ached for more, but for some reason, she couldn't let go of the hurt she'd felt.

Jun wouldn't have called the Grutex ship small, but when you had mates the size of hers, it was difficult to go anywhere or do anything without at least one of them breathing down her neck. There was no doubt in her mind that she was attracted to her males, but there was something in her that balked at the idea that she might not have been in control as much as she would have liked.

"You'll be alone?" Jun didn't know why the idea of him being on his own for a month on this ship bothered her so much.

"Nuzal volunteered originally, but as you can imagine, Esme didn't care for that idea." Brin shrugged, his eyes sliding up her suit covered legs.

The heat in his eyes made her shiver, and though she tried her best to stifle the moan, it managed to slip past her lips. Nuzal's rattling began anew, and Jun was sure they'd be able to smell her arousal soon if she didn't get herself under control.

"You've been sick lately," Nuzal murmured, clearly misinterpreting her moan. "How are you feeling now?"

"I'm not sure why you care," she huffed quietly, turning to toss the damp towel into the sanitizing bin inside the bathroom. "It's none of your business." The soft rattle stuttered before stopping completely, and Jun glanced back over her shoulder to see their eyes locked on her. Brin's narrowed in a way that made her pulse jump while Nuzal simply watched her with those unnerving red and violet eyes.

"What was that, Shayfia?" Brin's tone was soft, but the look he gave told her his words were a challenge—a dare.

301

With a deep breath to steel her nerves, Jun lifted her chin and answered him. "I said it's none of your business, and I asked why you cared."

The vines around Nuzal's face began to move, slowly at first until they were thrashing around his shoulders. He was off of the bed before she could blink, and by the time she realized that she was in his path, he'd already hauled her up and against his chest. A gasp escaped her a split second before his mouth descended on hers. Long, rough fingers fisted her hair, arching her neck as she moaned against his lips.

God, yes. She kissed him back, pouring every drop of her anger and frustration into the battle their mouths were raging. A second set of hands slid down her back and over her hips before cupping her ass. Brin's mouth drifted over her neck, his sharp teeth scraping over her skin followed quickly by his tongue.

"Everything about you is our business," she heard him say against her skin as Nuzal's growl rippled through her chest. "We care how you feel because we don't like seeing you distressed or in pain. We want to make it better."

Nuzal tore his mouth away, turning her in his arms so that she was sandwiched between her mates. Her lips were free for only a moment before Brin's mouth was ravaging them, his tongue slipping inside to brush against her own as his hand moved over her ribs. Nuzal's warm breath fanned the side of her face, and her body clenched when his rough tongue swept over the shell of her ear.

"You can have the time you asked for, little one, but that doesn't change who you are to us. *Nothing* will ever change that. Do you understand me, *mate*?"

God, if she hadn't been desperate from them to touch her before, she was certainly feeling it now. Jun pressed her hips forward, wrapping her legs around Brin's torso as Nuzal slid his arms around both

KEPT FROM THE DEEP

of them. Just as she was entertaining the idea of actually letting them go further, someone cleared their throat, startling Jun. She jerked away from Brin and slammed herself into Nuzal's hard chest.

"Shit!" she hissed, looking up to see Telisa standing in the doorway, her shoulder popped against the frame and a grin on her face as she took in the scene.

"Ready to take off?" she asked, her grin growing wider as Jun's face flushed.

"We're ready," Nuzal answered.

Jun could feel the heat of their gazes on her, but she didn't dare to look up just then. Slowly, Nuzal stepped back so that Brin could slide her down his body. The loss of their heat made her want to beg them to take her back into their arms. When she'd been between them, with Nuzal rattling and Brin's mouth on her, she hadn't felt sick. It was the first time in over a week that she'd felt anything like herself, actually.

Maybe the act of dominance from them should have annoyed her or added to her anger, but she found herself more at ease, for the moment at least, than she had since discovering the pheromones. Jun smoothed a hand over her belly and took a deep breath, trying her best to regain her composure.

"Aren't we closer to Earth than we are Venora?" Jun asked as she put distance between herself and her mates.

"We are, but if we return, we risk capture not only from the humans, but also from the Grutex." Brin shook his head. "The risk is too great."

"Not to mention the One World Council would most likely hold us once they get a good look at us. Roman, Xavier, and the others with less than human features might be too tempting not to run tests on. It wouldn't be above them if they thought they could use them to their advantage."

Jun hated that Telisa was right. She missed her family so

much, and from the chatter among the humans, she knew she wasn't the only one.

"What about cloaking ourselves?" Roman had mentioned it during one of his talks with Nuzal.

"We might be able to cloak ourselves from the humans, but there is a chance we wouldn't be hidden from the Grutex ships we might encounter." Nuzal responded.

She turned to see him rubbing his vines, something she'd come to understand was a nervous habit, and felt herself soften. A few months ago, she would have never found anything a Grutex did to be soft or sweet, but she found this habit to be endearing.

"Give me some time to secure an alliance with the Venium before we risk our lives with our own people. If we bring them a readymade solution to the problem, then maybe we won't end up in Area 51." Telisa laughed, but Jun knew the threat of being experimented on again was serious, and it was something she'd like to avoid if she could.

"All right, so we go to Venora. What happens once we get there?"

"I was actually just coming to ask our brave and fearless leader that exact question." Telisa smirked at Brin, who rolled his eyes at her teasing.

Jun loved that Telisa gave Brin just as much snark as he dished out, if not more a good portion of the time. She hoped she and Amanda got along once they reached Venora.

"Once we land on the surface and exit the ship, we'll have to take pods to the main dome. The Venium live beneath the surface of the okeanos—like Earth's ocean. We should be prepared for an armed escort at the very least." Brin gestured broadly around the room. "Coming in on a Grutex troop transport vessel is going to ruffle some scales, so we need to play this right and do as we're told."

"Follow instructions. Got it." Telisa mimed checking something off of a list. "What about social etiquette? Religious beliefs that we need to respect?"

"I don't see religion being an issue, but the majority of Venora worships the goddess, Una and her mates, Ven and Nim. They play a prominent role in our society, but none of the other aliens who travel to the domes for political or business reasons are hindered by it. The thing is, even though the Venium have offworld allies and encourage trading among our people, many of the elders still dislike having outsiders within the dome."

"So we're walking into full-blown xenophobia?" Telisa arched a brow. "That's wonderful."

"It's not how everyone thinks—"

"Wait, you and Oshen told me that Amanda would be safe on Venora, and now you're telling me that I let my best friend leave Earth to go live in a place where the old people are going to treat her like crap?"

"Oshen wouldn't have taken her back if he thought she'd be at risk."

With a dramatic flourish of her hands, Jun narrowed her eyes on Brin. "Send your best friend to Venora, they said. She'll be perfectly safe there, they said."

"Shayfia, she's mated to Oshen. He would die before he let any harm come to her."

Jun huffed, but if the way Oshen treated her when she'd stayed with them was any indication, she knew Amanda would be looked after. Still, Venium heads would roll if she found out her best friend had been treated poorly.

It took them another full day to gather enough food to last Brin the entire trip and to get everyone on board with the plan. Esme didn't like the idea of Brin being the one to care for them during their cryosleep, but she disliked the idea of Nuzal filling the role even more.

At her insistence, Nuzal agreed to be the first to go into one of the pods. He reached out to touch Jun's hair, but caught himself. He curled his fingers into his palm as he moved toward the large machines that lined the wall where there had once been a row of seats.

"Nuzal." Jun's hand shot out, grabbing hold of his wrist. He looked down at the shimmering display of colors before his eyes moved to her face, waiting for her to speak. She hadn't exactly thought this one through, but she didn't want him going into the pod thinking she didn't care at all. "I'll see you when we get there," she said lamely, kicking herself when he inclined his head and stepped into the chamber.

One by one, the humans were loaded in and secured. It took many of them only moments to fall asleep, their faces were peaceful and calm behind the glass on the door. Brin held out his hand to her and Jun looked around, realizing she was the last one awake.

"Your turn, Shayfia."

She let him lead her to an empty pod next to Nuzal's, and she took a deep breath as she stepped inside. Anxiety raced through her, and for a terrifying moment, she thought she might be sick. "Brin, I can't."

"It's all right," he whispered, leaning in to drop a sweet kiss on her forehead. "I'll be right here the whole time. I won't let anything happen to you." When she nodded, Brin stepped back, closing the door to her pod before initiating the sleep sequence. "Sleep well, Shayfia," she heard as her lids dropped over her eyes. "We'll be home soon."

One month later...

. . .

*J*un felt like she was wading through sludge. Her arms and legs were heavy, and she found she barely had the strength to move them. Fog rolled through her mind as she struggled to understand what the voices she heard were saying. They sounded familiar, and the deep tones made her heart race with excitement as she began to pick out and recognize their words.

"Are you sure?" one of the voices asked.

"I'm positive. We discovered these hormones during the earliest experiments on humans," the other deeper voice said. "What should we do?"

"We tell her."

Brin and Nuzal, her mind supplied, finally catching up. Her body practically vibrated as it came to life, excitement moving through her at the recognition of her mates. God, why was she this way anytime she was around them? *Because their bodies basically drug you?* Right, there was that.

She felt a tingle in her breasts as her nipples hardened, and all she could think about was having their hands on her, running down her chest and over her belly until they reached the juncture of her thighs. Just the memory of Brin's finger circling her clit and the way Nuzal's knuckle had felt when he pressed against it had her moaning out loud.

Get it together. This is an incredibly bad time to be horny, she mentally shook herself. Was it possible for this to still be the work of the pheromones? How long would they affect her?

"She sounds like she's going to be sick," Nuzal said.

Jun felt something warm brush over her cheek, and she turned her head in an attempt to follow it. At her side, her fingers began to twitch as she fought to open her eyes.

"How do you think she'll react?" Nuzal's voice seemed to get further away, as if he'd put some distance between them.

Was that nervousness she heard in his voice? What was going on? She felt her legs and arms begin to respond slowly as she pushed further through the fog until she was blinking into a blinding white light.

"We're about to find out."

She brought her hand up to shield her sensitive eyes, groaning as she attempted to sit up. Her stomach churned as she turned on her side, threatening to empty itself. God, was it like this for everyone when they woke up from cryosleep or was she just incredibly unlucky? Jun gagged, slapping her hand over her mouth as she tried to swallow past the lump in her throat.

When she finally managed to clear her vision, Jun gazed around the room, noting that the others were still asleep within their chambers. Brin and Nuzal stood together on one side of the pod, their twin looks of concern directed at her.

"What's wrong?" she asked. "Did we make it to Venora?"

They each offered her a hand to hold as the pod began to slide up, moving her back into the upright position she'd gone to sleep in. She took deep breaths to try and control the nausea, holding onto her mates like lifelines as her head swam. *I'm never doing this shit again,* she promised herself.

"Nearly there. We'll be waking the others soon," Brin told her as they helped her from the pod and guided her to one of the seats.

Nuzal crouched down in front of her. "How do you feel, little one?"

"Like I might puke," she murmured. Jun rested her head against the back of the seat and closed her eyes, waiting until the wave passed. "What were you two talking about?" Her mates shared an uneasy look. *What the hell was going on?* Nuzal's xines wriggled restlessly, and his eyes slid down her body as he shifted to his knees.

"Nyissa, bring up vitals taken during Jun's cryosleep."

"Yes, Master. Sending you the data logs from Jun's cryochamber."

A projection appeared on Brin's wrist, but she couldn't read the language. "I don't know what this is, Brin."

Nuzal slid his finger across Brin's arm, pointing to a grouping of characters. "This here indicates higher than normal levels of human chorionic gonadotropin hormones within your body."

Jun frowned as the words began to echo in her mind. She could hear Brin speaking, saying something about how he'd woken Nuzal the moment he realized something was off with her vitals, but she couldn't stay focused long enough to hear the rest of his story.

Higher than normal levels of hCG.

For God's sake, she was a nurse. She knew exactly how babies were made and that it only took one time for it to happen, but to say Jun was shocked was an absolute understatement. She wished Mama and Papa were here with her right now. They'd be so excited to know that there was going to be a grandbaby. Her mind was flooded with a wave of emotions as she placed her hand on her belly, taking note of the slight bump that hadn't been there when she'd gone to sleep.

"How am I..." Jun frowned down at her stomach. "A month of travel and two weeks on the planet—I guess that's assuming two weeks there is about the same as two weeks on Earth—I'd only be about six weeks. I've never known anyone to show this early."

"Early? How long are human pregnancies?"

"They vary from person to person, but most people deliver around forty weeks, give or take a few in either direction."

"Forty weeks?" Brin's eyes widened.

"About nine months. Most people I've known haven't even found out they were pregnant at this point."

"A Venium pregnancy only lasts four months."

A huff of surprise burst from her mouth as she stared at him. "Four? That would mean I was almost halfway through!" She looked at Nuzal and paused. Oh, God, she hadn't *just* been with Brin that day in the forest. "What about the Grutex?"

He shook his head. "I can't recall. None of our females are fertile, and none of human pregnancies…"

"None of them were viable," Jun finished for him when Nuzal trailed off, concern passing over his face. "Is there a way to find out which one of you is the father? I can't imagine that you guys have all of this tech and no ultrasounds."

"Shayfia…" Brin's jaw clenched as he scrubbed a hand over his face and knelt on the ground in front of her. "I can't be…" His fushori pulsed, the blue lights reflecting off of the cold metal floors as bent over to rest his forehead on her thigh. "I can't be the sire."

Jun's lip quivered as her eyes filled with tears over his anguish. She'd known where he stood on the subject, but she hadn't thought about protection at all during their mating, and she'd let herself get so caught up in her hurt afterward that it hadn't even crossed her mind.

"I know this isn't what you wanted, but if the baby is Venium then—"

"What he means is that it's impossible." Jun watched as Nuzal placed his hand over Brin's where it rested on her knee. A look passed between them, as if Brin was giving Nuzal permission to speak on his behalf. "When Vodk and Raou took him that day, they performed an unauthorized sterilization."

The blood drained from her face as she stared down at their mate. "Brin—"

"They thought they were hurting me, Shayfia, but all I felt was relief." He looked up at her and she saw the truth of his words in his eyes. "I'll never have to worry about continuing the line or passing on Brega's legacy. It's over."

When she turned to Nuzal, she found him watching her carefully as if he wasn't sure what her reaction might be. *None of them were viable.* Erusha had told them about his mate and all of the babies they'd lost on the ship. Would it be the same for them?

As if he sensed her thoughts, Nuzal rattled softly. "You are not Erusha's mate, little one. I will do everything in my power to protect you. Both of you."

She rubbed her thumb over her belly and fought back the urge to cry over the uncertainty of their situation. They'd created this tiny life that day in the forest and her body had kept them safe this long, but Jun prayed Nuzal was right.

CHAPTER 33

NUZAL

$\mathcal{H}$e was going to be a sire.

The term was foreign to him, but Brin had used it before and he mulled it over in his mind now. The Grutex didn't have what Jun had referred to as parents, nor were they raised by anyone who had cared for them beyond the basics. His people were mostly brutal, violent, and at their best, unfeeling. Erusha was the only one he knew who might not fight that mold, but from the way the humans spoke of him, Nuzal wasn't so sure they considered him any better than the rest.

Being a good mate to Jun and Brin had been hard enough, but now he would have offspring to look after. How was he going to be any better at this? Jun and Brin both bore the scars of their mating with him, and the fact that this thrilled instead of repulsing him should have made him feel ashamed, shouldn't it? Nuzal closed his eyes, remembering the way Brin had pressed his claws into his chest, asking to be marked.

His fingers flexed against his thighs, claws scraping against his plates, and he opened his eyes to watch his female move through the gathered humans. She hadn't been upset like he thought she might be after finding out about the little life growing inside of her. There had been fear and trepidation in her eyes, but there had been no sign of the disgust or horror he had prepared himself for.

"So, what do we do now?" she'd asked, looking between him and Brin. "Is there a way we can check on the baby?"

"The ship is only equipped with a basic scanner, but we should be able to use it to assess the offspring's health." They'd brought some of the equipment up from the medbay before leaving the planet in the event one of the humans required care after waking, and he'd been relieved that he wouldn't have to leave her to retrieve the scanner.

Brin helped Jun up onto one of the service tables while Nuzal turned on the handheld scanner. When she was ready, he passed it over her body, from head to toe and back up again. It recorded her vitals, listing them one by one so that they scrolled over the scanner's screen.

Nuzal reset the device, this time moving it only over the small bulge of her lower abdomen. Many of the readings were off since the device wasn't normally used for things of this nature, but there was one feature they didn't use too often. He tapped an icon on the screen, and a moment later the whoosh of their offspring's heartbeat filled the room.

"Is that the baby?" Jun had asked, her eyes brimming with tears as they widened.

Nuzal couldn't speak past the lump in his throat, so he nodded his head instead.

"Should their heart beat so fast?" Brin asked, leaning over to frown at the scanner. "It might be wrong. Check again."

"It's reading the heart rate, Brin. It can't be wrong." Nuzal shook his head.

"It's perfect," he heard Jun whisper. She stared at them for a moment before pushing herself up and swinging her legs over the side of the table. "We should wake the others before we get any closer to Venora." He heard her sniffle as she swiped at the gathering tears.

Their little female had spent the remainder of the cycle waking the others from their cryopods and helping them deal with the unfortunate effects the cryosleep seemed to have on the human body. There hadn't been much time at all to figure out what this new development meant for them, but the way he caught her cupping her stomach when she thought no one was looking gave him hope.

Nuzal was standing at the gazer when Jun stepped up beside him. She peered in, pushing up onto her tiptoes for a better view.

"Is that Venora?" she asked as they neared the planet. "It's beautiful."

He nearly jumped out of his plating when he felt the warmth of her palm come to rest against his hip. She hadn't touched him with such ease in a long time, and he froze, afraid she might move away if he brought the contact to her attention.

"Very beautiful," Brin murmured, coming up behind them. "I think this is happiest I've ever been to see this place."

Nuzal watched him trail the back of his finger down the side of Jun's neck and over her shoulder. His fingers itched with the desire to touch her in the same way, but she hadn't spoken a word about her feelings toward them and, after the kiss he'd stolen before they'd left the planet, he didn't want to push her too far. Simply having her touch him was enough for now.

"Oh, God," Jun mumbled, slapping her other hand over her mouth as she squeezed her eyes shut.

Nuzal began to rattle for her, pushing air through his chest as he crouched down in front of her. He felt Jun stiffen when he clutched her thigh, and regret shot through him as he cut off the noise. Expecting to find her annoyed with his actions, Nuzal pulled back and looked up into her face. Instead, she stared down at him, her hand smoothing over her stomach as her mouth dropped open.

"Don't stop. Make the noise again."

He glanced questioningly at Brin, who only shrugged his shoulders as he kneeled next to him in front of Jun. The rattling purr he'd used to calm her when she was in pain or had been afraid had never made her react like this. Nuzal took a deep breath and forced the air through the chest as he'd done a moment ago, blinking in surprise when she gasped.

"Wait!" She grabbed each of their hands, placing them side by side on her abdomen. "Again, Nuzal."

When he did it this time, he felt something flutter against his palm. It was the smallest of movements, something he might not have even noticed if he wasn't paying attention. From the wide-eyed look on Brin's face, Nuzal assumed he'd felt it as well.

"The baby likes it." Jun reached out, brushing one hand over his cheek as the other gripped Brin's shoulder.

Nuzal closed his eyes and nuzzled against her hand, rattling for their offspring, who continued to move. Never in any of his previous lives had he experienced something as amazing as this.

"I don't mean to intrude, Master, but we'll be within range of Venora's sensors soon."

Brin cleared his throat as he pulled his hand away and stood. "Thank you, Nyissa."

"Do you think they'll give us a hard time because of the ship?" Jun asked him.

"Most likely. We might be allies with the Grutex, but that doesn't mean we wouldn't be suspicious if one of their troop transport ships showed up out of nowhere."

Nuzal's rattle trailed off, and he turned toward Brin with a grimace. "Are you sure they'll be safe there?"

"Jun and the pup will be safer there than any other place I know."

Even knowing Brin was right didn't calm the sense of foreboding he felt. They needed to be here, needed to establish an alliance between the Venium and the humans so that his mate's people would be safe, but he didn't want to trust anyone else with his offspring. Would the Venium turn on them? What if they saw this pregnancy as an opportunity? He knew his own people wouldn't have wasted anytime poking and prodding her. They would have taken Jun and destroyed her. The little life she carried now wouldn't have even had a chance.

"I don't like this, Brin." Nuzal's xines writhed. "I don't know if we can trust them."

"No one is going to touch her, Nuzal. I wouldn't let anyone hurt her, and neither would my family."

"I'll be fine, Nuzal." Jun's hand brushed over the top of his head, trailing between his upper and lower sets of eyes, and down the side of his face. "We'll be okay."

"We're receiving a communication request from Venora, Master."

"Send it through to the comm, Nyissa."

"This is Venora Air and Space Control. Identify yourself and state your business."

"My name is Havacker Ruvator Machit. I'm requesting permission to enter the atmosphere and land on the surface."

Ruvator? Nuzal had never heard either of his mates mention the name before. Brin shot him a look that said he'd fill him in later.

"One moment." There was a prolonged silence from the other end of the comm. Nuzal imagined there were hurried conversations going on within the room.

"Havacker Ruvator," came a different voice. "I'm going to

need you to provide further identification and the reason for your presence on a Grutex troop transport."

Brin responded with a series of numbers, as well as the names of his commanding officers from his last duty assignment. "The ship was taken from a Grutex space station and is currently carrying human refugees rescued from that facility."

More silence and then, "Identity confirmed, Havacker. Your request to enter the atmosphere and land has been granted, with restrictions. Please lower your shields and disable your weapons system. You will receive instructions for a guided landing, and a team will be waiting for you on the surface to escort the refugees into the dome."

Nuzal leaned forward, pressing his face against Jun's stomach and rattled softly as Brin spoke with Telisa to let her know what was about to happen. Inside his mate's womb, their offspring moved, fluttering against his face as he nuzzled closer. For this one moment, Nuzal let himself feel at peace. There was going to be chaos, and he wanted to take the memory of this with him so that he could deal with what was to come.

When the humans were secured and ready, Brin began the landing process, following the instructions given to him by his people. True to their word, a team was waiting for them on the surface. They were boarded almost immediately, and the first of the Venium team to come across Nuzal stopped short and aimed his weapon at his chest.

"You could have mentioned there was a Grutex on board," the male growled. "I'm required to take you into custody," he told Nuzal.

"Wait a minute." Jun clutched at his arm as he tried to move her behind himself. "He's with us."

The male pulled out a set of cuffs from his pockets and stepped forward. "I'm under strict orders—"

"Please, he's not with the Grutex." Her hands were pressed

against his stomach and she tried her best to push him back. Her eyes pleaded with him as she inserted herself between him and the Venium. "Nuzal…"

"Step aside." When Jun only shook her head, Nuzal stroked his hand down her hair and rattled. "Do as you're told, little one. You have someone to look after."

"Are you going to come willingly, or are we going to have trouble?"

"Brin!" Jun shouted as Nuzal allowed himself to be cuffed.

Resisting would only make things harder on him and his mates, and Nuzal knew they were already going to have a fight on their hands. The other Venium began to sort through the humans, taking those who had been unfortunate enough to develop physical characteristics during their awakening. Roman was among the ten or so who were selected, and his body seemed to vibrate with his barely checked anger.

"Who ordered this?" Brin asked, his jaw clenched tight as he glared down at Nuzal's cuffed wrists.

"General Brega has ordered the detention of all suspicious individuals. The General is waiting for you at the pod reception center."

Brin mumbled curses under his breath as they began to guide Nuzal and the awakened humans out of the ship.

"We'll figure this out, Nuzal!" he heard Jun shout as Brin continued to argue.

This was necessary, he knew it, but the beast within him, the one who had taken his mates that day in the forest snarled, hating that they were so far from him. *This is the last time,* he heard the voice growl. *This will be the last time they are taken from me.*

CHAPTER 34

JUN

*F*ucking aliens!

Jun was getting tired of them always storming in and taking things over. Her fingers twitched, and she entertained the idea of pulling the plasma weapon from her hip and shooting the Venium who kept throwing her dirty looks.

"Let's not start off with violence, okay?" Telisa murmured, as if she read Jun's mind. She watched Nuzal and a few of their people being marched out of the ship and onto the landing pad. Her arms were crossed over her chest, and her foot was tapping out an angry rhythm. "I know we'd do the same on Earth—hell, probably something even worse—but I don't like it."

"The rest of you," one of the Venium called as he stepped up to the front of them. "Exit in an orderly fashion. You will be escorted down to the dome where you will receive further instructions."

Brin moved up beside her as guards took up position on either side of the group, corralling them out onto the landing and into the bright light of Venora's sun. She turned to him with an accusatory glare. "You just let them take him?"

"We had no choice, Shayfia," he growled in frustration. "If we had fought them someone may have been injured, or worse. Your people need their help, and it would have won us no favors."

She absolutely hated that he was right about this. Nuzal had gone peacefully, proving to them that he wasn't a threat, but all of this was making her uneasy. She heard Telisa trying to calm some of the others, whispering encouraging words as they huddled closer. They were scared, and she couldn't blame them. While they knew and mostly trusted Brin, these Venium weren't as friendly and inviting as her mate.

"It's all right. You heard him, we're just going to head down into the dome. There's nothing to worry about."

"What about the others?" Jun heard someone ask from somewhere at the back of the group. "Where are they taking them?"

"We're going to sort this out, I promise. They were just taken as a precaution," Brin assured her. Once they were out of the shadow of the ship, Jun realized that there were many more Venium than the ones who had boarded the vessel. They were gathered around one side, weapons slung over their shoulders as they moved around and between the other ships on the nearby pads.

A shout went up and the guard leading them halted, instructing them to wait as the ones flanking them stood at attention. There was a ripple among the soldiers as they began to move, parting like the Red Sea. Jun felt Brin's growl rumble through him as he pulled her close to his side, glaring at the woman who stepped forward.

Deep purple eyes locked on Brin the moment she turned toward the group. The woman's long white hair was braided into rows that hung loose down her back and swung around her hips as she stalked over to them. There was an air about this woman that told Jun she wasn't to be toyed with, that she was in charge here.

She stopped in front of them, a humorless grin spreading across her dark face. "Ruvator."

Brin's hold on Jun tightened. "Brega."

Brega? Jun's eyes darted between them as the tension began to build. This was Brin's mother, the woman who had basically abandoned him to his abusive father.

"Explain this," She gestured toward the Grutex ship at their backs.

"Oh, you want to know about this?" Brin raised a brow ridge and looked over his shoulder. "It's an interesting story, but it's one that will be told before the council. After all, it's the duty of every Venium to ensure the safety of our people, isn't that right?"

Brega sneered as she stepped closer, taking in the sight of him, completely ignoring Jun who was tucked under his arm. Brin's tail twitched against her leg and his fushori pulsed as the lights raced along his body. She'd seen him agitated before, even furious when the Grutex had taken her for the blood draw, but this level of icy anger and barely restrained hatred was something new.

If Jun hadn't already hated the woman because of what she did to Brin, she would have hated her just for the air of superiority alone. Brega reached out her hand toward Brin's face to slide a finger over the fushori on his cheek before shoving his face away with a growl.

"I thought you might have grown out of your disappointing behavior, but I can see that was foolish of me. You stand before your dam with no control over yourself."

Jun felt her jaw drop and her eyes widen as she stared up at Brega in disbelief. She tried to step forward, wanted to ask her who the hell she thought she was treating her mate that way, but Brin slid her behind his body.

"You will not put your hands on me, Brega."

Her throaty laughter filled the air. "Oh, Ruvator, I'll do far worse—"

"Brin!"

Jun ducked around Brin's body just in time to watch as a woman with skin as white as a polished pearl threw herself into her mate's arms. Her tail wrapped around his upper thigh and she pressed her black lips to his cheek. Humans and Venium all around her began to murmur, but that faded into the background as she narrowed her eyes on them.

"I've missed you so much. It's wonderful to have him home, isn't it, General?" The woman cupped his cheek. "It's never easy being away from your mate."

"Oh, hell no," Telisa whispered next to her.

Brin jerked his head away as he looked down at Jun, his eyes filled with a mixture of confusion and shock. His body was stiff and filled with tension as he placed his hands on the women's hips, trying to dislodge her.

"Caly," he grunted when she tightened her grip around his neck. "This isn't necessary."

"Of course it is! I've missed you. Didn't you miss me?" She tried to press her lips to his, but Brin shook his head.

"*Ang landi talaga*," Jun muttered under her breath as she crossed her arms. What a flirt, and with *her* mate no less.

Caly's brow ridges furrowed as she glanced down at Jun. "What's a flirt?"

"That's too nice of a word for what I'm seeing," Telisa murmured.

A month or two ago, the sight of another woman wrapped around Brin might not have made her feel anything at all, but now, after everything they had been through and knowing what he was to her, Jun fought back the urge to resort to violence.

He finally managed to loosen her grasp and reached out to

Jun, pulling her into his side. He had the audacity to take the woman's hand and smile at her as his thumb brushed Jun's arm. "Jun, this is my friend, Calypsi. Caly, this is my mate, Jun."

He'd said it with such pride that she almost forgot to be annoyed with him. Almost. Jun knew Brin belonged with her and Nuzal, that they had nothing to worry about when it came to anyone else, but that didn't stop the little green monster from trying to insert itself. It also didn't mean she wanted to see some other woman, friend or not, climb her mate like a hot, glowing tree.

Brega's upper lip pulled over her teeth in a nasty sneer as her focus shifted to Jun, but she wasn't about to let this bitch intimidate her, especially not after what Brin had told her about his mother.

With her chin high in the air, Jun stared her down. She'd dealt with people giving her these looks since the moment she set foot in America. She was an immigrant, a foreigner, and many people had looked at her exactly the way Brega was: like she wasn't good enough, like she didn't belong.

"What is this foolishness, Ruvator? This *thing* isn't Venium," she huffed as her fushori began to pulse a deep purple. "It is weak and small. Shameful." She spit at their feet. "This is *not* your mate."

Jun clutched her belly. "I might be small, but I've handled some pretty *big* things lately. You don't scare me."

Caly snorted, slapping her hand over her mouth when Brega glared. "I like her, Brin."

"You would let this farce continue?" Brega demanded, turning on Caly, who positioned herself behind Brin. "You would surrender your mate so easily to this ugly little thing? Where is your honor? Have you no shame?"

This had gone on long enough. "You're one to talk about honor and shame. Aren't you the same woman who allowed her

323

child to be abused, to be scarred? You did nothing to protect him."

Brega didn't even have the decency to look ashamed. "It's obvious to me now that we stopped his training too early. He's failed himself, and now he's failed my line."

"That's enough, Brega," Brin hissed as his tail wrapped around Jun's waist, tugging her back as if he were afraid she might lunge at the woman in front of her. "You will show my mate respect or you will not speak at all."

Although there was movement all around them, something in the corner of her eye caught her attention, and she turned to see that Amanda and Oshen had arrived on the surface. Her best friend's belly was swollen, much larger than her own small bump. That hadn't taken very long.

You're one to talk Juna, she smirked at herself and tugged on Brin's arm.

"Deal with her shit later, Brin. Come on!" The guards shouted after them, but no one tried to stop them as they raced toward their friends. Finally, she might just be able to speak to people who could help. "Amanda! Hey, Fishboy! Someone who will fucking listen!"

Oshen was an ambassador. Maybe he would be able to do something about Nuzal and the others being detained.

"Fishboy, I need your help..." Her eyes moved over their familiar faces, more grateful than she could ever explain to be seeing them again, but when she came to the massive mauve figure just behind Amanda, Jun paused. He was Grutex. She'd thought Nuzal was tall, but this guy must have had him by a few inches. "The rumors are true then? Venium have teamed up with the Grutex?"

Was this why they had taken Nuzal? Were they going to turn around and return him to the Kaia?

"She called you Fishboy." Brin laughed as he reached them, his tail wrapping possessively around Jun's calf.

Amanda grinned at her. "No, they haven't. This is my mate, Zar."

At least there was that weight off of her. It seemed Amanda's imaginary friend was real. "Shut up, Glowworm." She glared at him over her shoulder before turning back to their friends. "Oshen, something is wrong."

Amanda's worried eyes searched her face, but this was something she needed Oshen for.

"Tell me what is going on."

God, she really hoped she could trust him. "Well, here's the short version: we were kidnapped. We escaped. Now we're here, and *your* people have detained some of *our* people." She hated feeling like she was pitting the people against one another, but their group of humans had been through too much already and she couldn't just let them go without knowing they and Nuzal were safe. Crossing her arms over her chest, Jun tapped her foot on the ground impatiently. "And you're going to help me get them back."

"You were missing?" Oshen turned toward the woman she hadn't noticed standing off to the side. "You knew, didn't you, Fyn?"

Jun didn't know who Fyn was, but it didn't matter to her right now. All she wanted to do was get to her mate and check on her people.

"We did not want to worry Amanda and risk her losing the pups," Fyn replied.

"Uh, Jun, someone is escaping."

Jun followed Amanda's gaze over her shoulder and mentally sighed as she saw Esme dart away from the landing pad and head of the cover of the forest. "Goddamn it! That infuriating woman! I don't have time for this." Esme was one of her people too, but Jun was trying her best to focus on the ones who had been taken from them.

"What is it?" Amanda asked.

"She doesn't trust us because my other mate is one of the Grutex scientists." She shook her head.

"A what?!" Amanda's eyes widened as she stared at Jun.

"No time to explain. He's in trouble." As much as she'd love to be able to just sit down and relax and tell Amanda what had been going on with her for the last couple months, or share the news of her baby with her best friend, Jun wanted to get this all sorted out first. The longer she and Brin and their baby were away from Nuzal, the more agitated she became.

"Don't think you're getting away without telling me, Junafer. When this is cleared up, I want the entire story," Amanda warned.

Another woman, this one not entirely Venium judging by the look of her, stepped forward. "I'll get a search party together and join in myself." As much as she hated to admit it, she was glad Esme would be someone else's problem for a little while.

"We need to speak with the council," Brin told Oshen. "The humans are in danger and something needs to be done, now."

"What about the others?" Jun wanted to know as she watched them return to the Grutex ship. Telisa raised her hand in the air, smiling as she disappeared through the large cargo doors.

"They'll be safe here for the time being. We can speak with my sire about finding them more comfortable accommodations." Oshen jerked his head toward one of the sleek buildings along the shore. "Let's go before we have to share a pod with the General."

Once they were inside, Brin guided her through the sliding doors of the pod that would take them to the domes, but Jun couldn't focus on anything outside of the windows during their descent knowing Nuzal might be in danger with the Venium. She bounced her leg and chewed her lip as Brin tried his best to calm her. Couldn't these things go any faster?

"I don't know if the council will be much help." Oshen grimaced, placing his hand on Amanda's distended belly. "They certainly weren't willing to help when Amanda was taken on the surface by the Grutex who stalked her on Earth."

"They wouldn't help?" Jun asked with a frown. "What exactly is their job?"

Oshen shrugged. "She isn't Venium. You're going to be fighting an uphill battle with these council members."

"I'm going to strangle every last one of them," she growled.

Amanda laughed, reaching out to lay a hand on Jun's arm. "It's all right. They found me just in time."

Oshen told them the story of his transformation into the mythical allasso creature and about how after he'd been fortunate enough to be able to reach through his family on his comm so that they could help them escape Zar's village and find Amanda, who had been taken by the Grutex they'd seen years ago in the streets.

Jun had questions, many of them, but she'd save them. Right now, she had an entire council to fight.

CHAPTER 35

JUN

here were guards outside the doors to the massive building Oshen brought them to, but Jun didn't give them a chance to react. She burst through the doors, not bothering to wait for Oshen or Brin. Jun stormed down the hallway and into a great open room where Venium, both male and female, were seated. The space reminded her of the floor of the Senate.

"What's going on here? Who are you?" one of the older men demanded, thumping his fists on the table in front of him. "We are in the middle of an emergency meeting!"

"I apologize for the interruption, councilman," Oshen stepped in behind her, trying to appease the man. "I'm afraid this issue is rather important and pertains to the arrival of the human refugees."

"What impeccable timing," Brega sneered as she entered the room, her gaze locked on Jun as she moved around their small group. "How lucky for you that the council was already convening."

Jun watched as Brega took a seat among the others and struggled to control the urge to roll her eyes. Brin hadn't mentioned much about what his mother did now, but she knew she was in the military, a General, actually. Maybe her rank afforded her a position here.

"When will my mate be released?" Jun demanded.

Brega grinned. "I thought my son was your mate."

"Brin and Nuzal are my mates, and I want him released. Now."

"What makes you think you can come in here and make demands of this council?" the alien man sitting at the head table asked.

"Two of your people crashed on our planet. I tended to one of them and took the other, at great personal risk, I might add. I was almost killed by the Grutex because of this, and then when I tried to help your people by going to my government officials, I was kidnapped and brought to a Grutex lab, where I spent a fucking month being tested on just to find out that I have alien DNA inside of me. It might surprise you to know that I happen to also be Venium. We escaped that lab with Nuzal's help, and when we finally make it back here where we think we'll be safe, you all take not only my mate, but also the survivors. These poor people have endured so much trauma, have been physically and mentally changed, and you're doing nothing but adding to it!"

"As... *sad* as your story is, none of that sounds like a problem for this council."

"We didn't warn Earth just to turn our backs on them now!" Jun screamed, her frustration mounting with each passing moment.

"Warn Earth? We did no such thing," the councilman sneered.

"You didn't, but I did," Brin glared at the council. "They needed to know Galactic Law, so I took over where Oshen left off."

"Ah, yes, Ambassador Oshen," the man at the head sneered as his eyes moved to Amanda's mate. "He left his station to bring back an alien female he claims is his mate and on top of that, he asks us to believe this Grutex and his lies! Havacker, your story is beginning to sound shockingly similar."

"You lied to us. There is a Sanctus female statue in the middle of Zar's village. She is Una." Jun could hear the distress in Oshen's voice.

"That is a lie! They lie!" the councilman yelled.

"We have no reason to lie," Amanda's Grutex mate growled.

Amanda grabbed Oshen's shirt and let out a pained cry. "I think the babies are coming."

Jun glanced over her shoulder as they rushed from the room, wanting to go and be with Amanda, but she knew she was safe and taken care of. Her labor might take hours, but Jun didn't plan on subjecting herself to hours of conversation with these fools.

"Perhaps now we'll see the proof of this mating," one of the women spoke up. "I will not believe these claims until I can see the proof with my eyes."

"You act like it's impossible, but you heard Jun. She's my mate." He wrapped his arms around her and placed his hand on her stomach.

Brega's eyes narrowed. "She's with pup?"

"Yes."

"A Venium pup?"

Brin stiffened. "No."

"See!" Brega stood from her chair and slammed her hand down on the table. "They are all liars! She carries the offspring of the Grutex!"

"She will never carry a Venium pup!" Brin snarled. "The Grutex in the lab made sure of that when I was sterilized."

Brega's head whipped around, and the purple lights of her fushori glittered against her black skin. "Sterilized?" Her eyes widened in shock before she spun toward the head of the council. "I demand retribution! My line... they've destroyed my line!"

"If the council had allowed Commander Vog to assist the humans, then this might have never happened! It is your inaction that caused this."

"So what, you plan to raise this creature as your own?" Brega huffed.

"Any pup born of my mate through our triad is *mine*. Calder and Nyissa proved to me long ago that a pup doesn't need to come from me to be loved by me."

Brega ignored Brin's words. She starred at Jun in a way that made her incredibly uncomfortable. "Perhaps this isn't so bad, councilmembers."

The calculating look in her eyes had Jun reaching for the plasma weapon at her hip. The Venium on the surface hadn't even thought to make sure they weren't armed.

"We can train the Grutex's offspring, raise it to become one of our warriors."

Without a conscious thought, Jun pulled the weapon up, aiming it at Brin's mother as she snarled. "You'll *never* get anywhere near my child." Brega narrowed her eyes. "I swear, I'll kill you!"

BRIN

He wasn't sure he'd ever be able to adequately describe what it did to him to see Jun face down Brega, but he knew he couldn't let her continue. Brin knew that his people looked at her and saw a small, defenseless alien, but he knew she was far stronger than she seemed. His little mate had taken on a Grutex, not just once, but twice, and she'd defended Nuzal against the beast in the forest, but she'd never been up against anyone like Brega.

The female's laugh echoed through the chamber, and she smiled as the head of the council banged his hands on the table. "That is enough!"

"She threatened my baby!" Jun yelled.

"Listen to me Shayfia." Brin crouched in front of her. "None of them are ever going to hurt this pup, do you hear? I'd give my life to make sure they're safe."

The Head of the Council sighed. "We've heard enough for one sol. We will meet again in two soli time to make a decision once we have discussed all the information you've brought forward."

"There's a senator from Earth here among the survivors. She is a representative of their people," Brin told them.

The Head nodded. "We will see that she is brought in."

"And what about Nuzal?"

"The Grutex? He is unharmed and resting in a cell." Brega waved her hand dismissively. "As for the other humans, they may stay aboard the ship. Guards will be stationed outside to ensure their safety, and food and water will be provided to them. I assume this will be satisfactory to your *human* mate?"

"It would be satisfactory if you jumped off the nearest cliff," his little mate grumbled as she took his hand and pulled him toward the hall. "Let's get out of here. I'm about to be an aunt, and I want to be there in case Amanda needs me."

"There will be no healing anyone, Shayfia." His growl echoed through the chamber. When Jun didn't answer, he narrowed his eyes and scooped her up into his arms. "I mean it, you fierce little thing. We can't risk it."

Jun pressed a hand against her belly and the other against his chest. "My first priority is our baby. I wouldn't do anything to jeopardize this little one."

CHAPTER 36

JUN

*a*manda was a mom.

Jun had watched in amazement as her best friend brought two new little lives into the world. They'd come out screaming and flailing their little arms and legs, and they were absolutely perfect.

Oshen's siblings burst into the room, faces full of excitement as they greeted the newest members of their large family. A pang of sadness moved through her chest as she thought about how much her own family would love her baby. She glanced around the room, looking for an escape as tears began to fill her eyes.

It had been a long night and an even longer morning. Amanda had struggled through a long labor, but Oshen, Zar, and Nyissa had been there to help her through it. With a quick look over her shoulder to make sure no one was going to come after her, Jun slipped out the door and made her way down the stairs to the entry of the home. There was a seating area right off of it, and she plopped down into one of the huge cushioned loungers, stretching out her legs as she scrubbed her hands over her face.

Everything that had happened within the last day or so came rushing back to her and she couldn't stop the tears as they slid down her cheeks. She was overwhelmed and while she was over the moon to see Amanda again, Jun found herself wishing her mama and papa were there for her. By now they would have known something was wrong. She'd never gone more than a day without speaking to them, and already two months, at the very least, had passed. Maybe even four if Amanda's pregnancy was anything to go by. They would be worried and thinking that the worst had happened to her, that she was dead or that she'd been abducted. Well, she had, but they would have no way of knowing.

Once they freed Nuzal, Jun swore she was going to figure out some way to get in contact with them. Even if it was just to let them know that she was alive. A door upstairs opened and closed quietly, and Jun waited to see if it was Brin coming down to seek her out.

The healer who had tended to Amanda during the birth of the twins stepped lightly down the stairs, his eyes focused on the comm projection on his forearm as he hit the entry floor and made his way to the front door of the home. This was her chance to get some of her questions answered.

"Excuse me! Sir?" Jun jumped up out of the lounger, scrambling toward the door as it began to close. "Wait!"

His head whipped around, and he stumbled to a halt, turning to stare at her as she raced toward him. "Can I help you?"

"God, I hope so," she mumbled. "I, uh, I have some questions and I thought I might be able to ask you since you're already here."

He grinned down at her and nodded. "I'll do my best to give you some answers, though I have to warn you that I'm not exactly familiar with the anatomy of your kind just yet."

"It's not about me, necessarily, but about the pheromones your males produce when they mate." God, why did this suddenly feel so awkward? She'd been a nurse for nearly fifteen years, and *this* was going to make her blush? "I guess I just wanted to know if they can make someone feel like they're in love?"

The man frowned and tilted his head as he pondered her question. "The pheromones cannot create feelings that are not already there, and many times these aren't even produced unless one party is delaying and the female begins to ovulate. It's simply meant to encourage mating so that her fertile periods are not missed."

Jun felt her breath stutter out of her chest. "So it's impossible for the pheromone to trick someone into wanting to mate?"

"For the pheromone to work, it has to play off of feelings and emotions that already exist within the other party. It's essentially a little push in the direction they were already going. The goal is mate and reproduce and it's the job of the pheromones to ensure that this happens when the female is ready." The healer smiled at her as her shoulders sagged in relief.

"Let's say the female in this case is currently pregnant. That would stop the pheromones, right?"

"For now." He nodded. "It's normal for the male to begin producing them anytime his partner is fertile. Some of our females, like Nyissa, are lucky to find themselves in a fertile period twice in one solar. As she's gotten older, they happen less and less."

"Twice a solar?" She knew that meant a year, but she wasn't at all familiar with what the equivalent would be on Earth. "Many human women ovulate at least once a month…" She frowned as she tried to remember what that was for the Venium. "Twenty-eight soli, I think?"

"Twenty-eight—" The healer blinked rapidly as if this was one of the craziest things he'd ever heard. "This is… this is wonderful news! Would you consent to let me run a couple tests?"

Jun balked at the word. "I don't think so."

"It would be a simple lifeblood draw, perhaps a scan or two? If we can gather information and show the council proof that humans and Venium are indeed compatible, then perhaps we can speed up this arduous process and get the humans the help they need."

"Brin said something while we were out there about your population declining. I just want you to know that humans aren't the cure for that, and I don't want to perpetuate the belief that using us for breeders will somehow make everything better."

"Make no mistake, I do *not* believe your species will save us. Our decline will come at the hands of those who cannot see past their own racial puritanism. Our gene pool is so muddled and lacks the diversity it once had, but none of these fools on the council want to acknowledge that." His eyes darted over her shoulders and he frowned as he took a step back. "I'll take my leave now. Please consider the offer?" The healer turned on his heel and stepped through the gate into the street.

Well, at least she'd gotten that weight off of her chest.

"Human!" Brega's voice echoed across the courtyard and grated over Jun's frayed nerves. "Come quickly!"

Jun turned to her with a frown and crossed her arms over her chest. "I'm not going anywhere with you."

"I've been searching for you!" Brega's chest heaved, her gills flaring as her fushori raced over her body. "It's your Grutex mate. He needs your healing!"

Jun frowned, narrowing her eyes on the woman's face. She hadn't told the council about her abilities yet. Had Nuzal told her? If he was injured badly enough, would he have actually told them about her healing so that they would bring her to him? She didn't trust Brega as far as she could throw her, but could Jun really risk being wrong about this? If she didn't go with Brega and Nuzal really was hurt, Jun knew she'd regret it.

"I'll get Brin and then we can go." She turned back toward the house, but Brega grabbed her arm and pulled her through the gate.

"There's no time for that. Ruvator doesn't have the ability to heal your mate. He needs *you!*"

Shit. Jun stumbled after her, trying her best to keep up with her long strides. "What's happened? How was he hurt?"

"Quickly! Run faster!" Brega released her when they reached the entrance of a tunnel that branched off of the main walkway. "This way!"

Jun was used to emergency situations, but she usually never had to go into one without knowing at least a little information. Her heart rate spiked as she realized they were alone inside of the tunnel. The blood began to pound in her ears, and she squeezed her hands into tight fists; her nails digging into her soft palms.

"Are we almost there?" she called out as she tried to catch her breath. "Where are we going?"

"The cells are separate from the family areas. Come on. Faster, human!"

There was a set of doors at the end, and Brega waved her on as she passed the woman, but they didn't slide open at her approach as she thought they would. Jun pressed her hands against the cool metal, pushing at them before turning back to Brega. "I think these are lock—"

A set of transparent doors slid closed between Jun and the Venium woman. Brega's smile sent a chill down Jun's spine, and she knew then that it had been a lie. She had done exactly what this bitch had wanted her to. Her heart was pounding so hard in her chest that Jun feared this might be the moment it actually gave out on her.

"Nuzal's not hurt, is he?"

Brega's twisted smile grew wider, pulling on the scar that ran down her face. "Not yet. He's currently safe within his cell inside the main dome."

"Brin is going to notice that I'm missing."

Brega snorted. "By the time my son realizes you aren't where you should be, you won't be a problem anymore."

"You'd do this to him?"

"Oh, little human, you don't deserve even the worst of my line."

"I wouldn't call you a good mother at all, but I didn't think you would go to this extreme. I'm his mate, Brega!"

"So he says, but Ruvator has always defied me. From the moment he took hold inside my body, he has done nothing but make me suffer! Once I'm rid of you, I'll allow him a chance to redeem himself, to provide me with an heir worthy of my lifeblood."

"He can't give you that! Were you not paying attention in the meeting when he told you that the Grutex had sterilized him? There won't be any children with your blood!"

Brega shook her head, her braids thrashing around her shoulders. "All Venium are unable to reproduce until they find their *true* mate. You, *human*, cannot be his mate." She raised her hand to the wall and tapped something into the panel on the side.

The doors behind her slid open just a fraction and cold water began to pour into the room, swirling around Jun's feet, slowly rising. Jun slammed her hands on the glass, drawing Brega's attention.

"You would do this to him? You would take away Brin's baby just because you're losing control over him? You would *kill* a baby?" Brega's face was devoid of emotion as she watched the water lap against Jun's knees. "You know what it's like to lose a child! You lost Ruvator, and you're going to force Brin to go through the same thing!"

Brega sneered as she stepped up to the glass that separated them. "You shouldn't speak of things you know nothing about."

The water reached Jun's hips, and she smiled. "If you truly are Venium like you claim, then this shouldn't end in your death. If not, then you're even weaker than that disappointment that was given my son's name."

The water was up to her chest and still rising. Jun pressed her hands over the bump where her baby moved gently and felt her anxiety rise. She knew she should control her breathing, that she shouldn't let the panic take over, but as the top of the water reached her chin, Jun felt her limbs seize. She couldn't swim.

She tried to remember what papa had told her. *Don't struggle. It's the fear, not the water that will kill you*, but that didn't seem to apply to this situation. She wasn't going to be able to float much longer. When her hands made contact with the ceiling, Jun gasped, filling her lungs with as much air as she could just before the water closed in over her face.

The sound of her heart racing seemed to amplify underwater, and she looked around, trying to center herself and think. There had to be something she could do, but she couldn't focus. She moved her limbs, struggling to get to the surface even though she knew there was nothing up there but more water. Bubbles escaped her mouth as her body began to run out of oxygen.

Her lungs burned, and it felt like she was going to be torn apart. The baby inside her belly moved as if they were feeling her panic and desperation, and her heart broke knowing that these were their last moments. She would never see Brin or Nuzal again, would never be able to tell them how much she loved them or see them hold their baby in their arms for the first time. Her baby would never get the chance to know what amazing fathers he or she had. All of this—her life and her little one's life—were going to be stolen from them, and she had no way to stop it.

Her mama and papa would never get to meet their first grand-child, but Jun hoped they never knew he or she had existed at all.

At least then they wouldn't mourn their loss. Brin and Nuzal would have one another, and she prayed they would know that in her last moments she'd been thinking of them.

Water rushed into her mouth and down her throat as her body forced her to inhale. Panic overtook her, and she clawed at her throat and chest, kicking and twisting as her lungs filled. There was a sharp pain on the sides of her neck, but she barely noticed it. She slammed her eyes closed, not wanting her last image to be that of Brega watching her drown.

She felt the water rush along the sides of her neck as her skin flared and she stilled. Was she dead? Had that been it? The skin flared again, passing more of the water into her. What the hell was happening? The burning in her lungs began to recede, and she reached up, brushing the tips of her fingers along her neck.

Gills? She gasped—well, the equivalent of a gasp. She wasn't sure how one did that when they had honest-to-God *gills*. It took her a moment to realize she could control her breathing again, that she wasn't dying. Jun tried to move forward in the water, but apparently having gills didn't mean she automatically knew how to swim. She let herself sink to the bottom so she could push off the floor, and pressed her hands against the glass.

Brega's eyes widened as she stared at Jun, and she didn't even notice when Brin shoved her out of the way. His fists pounded on the glass, as his fushori raced over the exposed areas of his body. He was yelling her name as Oshen's father ran up behind him, slamming his palm against the panel Brega had used to lock her inside.

She heard a hum and felt a vibration move through the water as it began to drain. As soon as her head and shoulders breached the surface of the water, Jun began to gag, coughing up the water that had filled her lungs and replacing it with air.

The transparent doors slid open before the water had even completely drained away, and she found herself pressed up against Brin's warm chest with his arms wrapped around her back. Jun didn't even have the strength in that moment to lift her arms and hold him. Her body was so heavy.

"Shayfia," he breathed against the side of face as he pulled her higher up his body. "Goddess help me, I thought we'd lost you."

She could hear and feel his heart thundering in his chest, and she turned her head, pressing her lips against his skin as the reality of the situation began to set in. "You came," her voice was barely above a whisper. "You found me."

"Caly saw you coming in here with Brega and rushed to find us." His hand ran over her drenched hair. "I've never been so braxing scared in my life."

Jun made a note to thank the woman for saving her life. "I'm sorry," she murmured. "I'm sorry I didn't tell you."

"What are you doing here, Calder?" Brega demanded, her tone filled with annoyance and agitation. Apparently, being interrupted during an attempted murder didn't sit well with this lunatic.

"I would ask you the same thing, but it's painfully obvious what you were doing," Oshen's father hissed.

"I was instructed by the council to have her tested, and I was in the middle of conducting said test when the two of you interrupted me."

"This was no test, Brega! You were drowning her!" Brin growled. "Is this what they asked you to do?"

"My idea of testing seemed more efficient." She shrugged. "You said she was Venium, so what better way to find out if it was the truth?"

Jun was jostled violently as Brin jumped to his feet, and she turned her head just in time to see Brega's eyes widen as Brin's hand wrapped around her throat. He slammed her back against the wall, snarling as she grasped his wrist. "You tried to *kill* her!"

Calder pushed himself between them, wrapping an arm

around Brin and Jun as he placed his hand on her mate's cheek. "Release her, son. She isn't worth the repercussions."

Brin's chin trembled as he stared at Calder. Jun could see the battle raging in his eyes, but after a long moment, he looked down at her and swallowed. Brega dropped to the ground when he released his grip on her, coughing and gasping as she glared up at them. Brin pressed his forehead against hers as his hand slid over her belly, and as if the baby recognized his presence, they moved against his palm.

How had she ever doubted her feelings for them? Brin and Nuzal had shown her in so many ways that they not only cared for her, but that they loved her. In that moment, it seemed so obvious that the only thing controlling her actions this whole time had been her love for them.

"She told me something had happened to Nuzal. I don't know if she was telling me the truth, but we need to know he's all right, Brin."

Her mate narrowed his eyes on the woman as she got to her hands and knees. "Where is he, Brega?"

"He's exactly where he should be."

"A location, Brega." Calder snapped, obviously losing his patience.

"In his cell, *Calder*. He's exactly where he's supposed to be."

"I want to see him. I want to see with my own eyes that he hasn't been harmed." Jun wriggled, trying to shimmy her way down Brin's body, but he tightened his arm around her and pressed a kiss to her temple.

"Will you just let me hold you for a moment, Shayfia?" he spoke against her skin. "I thought you were gone. I thought I'd have to tell Nuzal—" His voice wobbled, and he shook his head. "Just give me a moment, okay?" Jun put her arms around his neck and slid her fingers into his hair. "I don't trust her, Calder."

"Neither do I," the older man grumbled as he pulled up his comm. "Let me make some calls. One way or another, we're getting in to see the council *today*."

CHAPTER 37

NUZAL

*H*e'd heard the saying that time was an abstract thing, but Nuzal supposed he'd never really understood that until the Venium had placed him in the windowless cell. There was nothing to mark that passage of time here, no clocks, no night and day cycle like on the Kaia's ship.

Was this how it had been for the humans in the lab? No, he was sure it had been far worse for them.

Unlike his human counterparts, Nuzal was not afraid of what the Venium would do to him, but he did fear that his mates might be punished for his involvement in the Grutex's experiments. He wanted to see them, to know that they were safe and taken care of, but he trusted his bondmate. Brin wouldn't let anything happen to Jun and their offspring.

Still, Nuzal struggled with his frustration and the urge to break through the barrier in front of him. He tried tugging at the mental thread that tethered the three of them together, but there was only silence.

Roman sat in the corner of the cell they shared, brows arching as he grinned. "Don't like being on this side of the cell, huh?"

Nuzal knew the male was making a joke, but his attempt at humor did nothing to calm the thrashing of his xines. "I don't like being away from her. She's in a vulnerable state."

"That woman is anything but vulnerable. She's a force to be reckoned with." Roman shook his head. "I'm sure it's hard though. I can't imagine I'd want to be separated from my partner."

"*Partners*," he corrected.

Roman lifted his hands in apology. "Partners."

A sigh escaped Nuzal as he rested his head against the wall at his back. He wasn't naïve; he knew the council was in no rush to decide his fate or those of the awakened humans who had been detained alongside him, but the longer he was in here, away from his mates, the more desperate his mind became.

Rationally, he knew that there was nothing he could do from this cell to speed up the process. In fact, any rash actions would delay their decision. Nuzal closed his eyes and thought back to the moment on the ship when Jun rested her hand on him as she gazed out at Venora, and for a moment he swore he could feel the heat of her palm on his hip. She'd looked down on this planet with such hope that he had to believe this was right. It was the only thing really keeping him in this cell. He wouldn't risk ruining their chances of a better life for themselves and their offspring.

"You look a little lost in thought over there," he heard Roman comment as a door swung open and footsteps echoed down the hall. "Sounds like we've got a visitor."

Nuzal sat up on the bed, his elbows coming to rest on his thighs as a red-eyed Venium male stopped in front of their cell. "I'm going to assume you are Nuzal."

"Who wants to know?" Roman crossed his arms over his chest as he narrowed his eyes on the male.

"My name is Calder, and you're going to come with me."

Nuzal huffed. "Am I?"

"There are questions the council needs to have answered—"

"No," Nuzal growled, looking around him at the humans in the cells. How long were they supposed to suffer because of him? They'd been put through enough by his people and already had to suffer the loss of Layla and Clara.

The male's eyes narrowed. "No?"

Not long ago, he might have just left them in the cells, unconcerned about their fates, but now, after seeing what they'd gone through and getting to know them, Nuzal couldn't abandon these humans. "I won't answer any questions until the humans in here are released into the care of the others."

The male sighed as he shook his head, waving his hand behind him. "It seems you were of one mind. These two demanded the same thing."

The moment Nuzal saw his mates step around the male, he was off the bed and kneeling on the floor in front of the glass before he even realized what he was doing.

"Hey, big guy." Jun smiled at him. "We came to break you all out."

"We'll make room for all of you in my home," the Venium male was saying.

Nuzal could barely focus on the words, but the moment Jun's hand touched Calder's arm, he felt the beast inside of him clawing its way to the surface. A loud, rumbling growl filled the cell as his eyes narrowed on her hand.

Mine.

He was vaguely aware of his bondmate's laughter, and it did nothing but irritate the beast.

"Oh, stop, will you?" Jun rolled her eyes, but removed her hand. "He's basically Brin's father."

Nuzal didn't care. He hadn't touched or marked them for too long. He wanted his scent on them, wanted everyone around them to know who they belonged to. Calder reached up, deactivating the lock on the barrier. As soon as it opened, Jun launched herself into his arms, wrapping her legs as far around his torso as she could. She clung to him as he pressed his face into her hair, drawing in her scent. His xines tangled themselves in the dark strands, holding her close as he pushed air through his crest, rattling harder than he ever had.

He got to his feet, backing away on unsteady legs until he felt the bed behind him. She laughed when he dropped onto the thin mattress, bouncing her on his lap before burying his face in the crook of her neck. Her giggling ended on a gasp as he ran his tongue over her skin, using the tip to trace a path up the column of her slender throat.

Brin stepped into the cell, his blue gaze meeting Nuzal's as he gave in to the urging of the beast and sank his teeth into the tender flesh at the juncture where her neck and shoulder met. The warmth of her lifeblood flowed over his tongue, and he closed his eyes on a sigh, savoring the rich tang. The beast rumbled its pleasure, satisfied that she was adequately marked for the time being. Nuzal released her neck, sliding the flat of his tongue over the wound and smiling when she shivered in his arms.

The satisfaction lasted only a moment. Nuzal jerked his head back, staring down at the punctures he'd left on her skin. When he looked into her face, ready to beg her for forgiveness, he saw no disgust or fear over what he'd just done. Her lips were tipped up into a smile and she cupped his face with her hands before pressing her lips to his.

"Feel better now, big guy?" she asked against his mouth.

"Moderately," he grumbled, lifting her off of his lap and

setting her on her feet in front of him. He eyed the marks wearily. Once again, he'd allowed his baser instincts to take over. He knew his saliva would help to heal the wounds, but that didn't make him feel any better about making them. Calder cleared his throat, reminding him that they had an audience.

"I understand the need to uh, catch up," the male gave them a knowing grin, "but if we want the council to release Nuzal and the others into my custody, we're going to need answers."

Nuzal blinked, trying his best to chase the beast from his mind. He wasn't sure when Telisa had arrived or even when Roman and the others had left.

"We're coming," Brin told him, offering his hand to Nuzal.

Brin grinned when he took it, pulling Nuzal up from the bed and into a tight embrace. "It's nice to have you back. Let's get this over with. I've had my fill of the council."

They followed Calder out of the cells, and were escorted by armed guards into a large room. There were Venium waiting for them there, mostly elders, who tracked him and his mates with their glowing eyes. One in particular, a fierce-looking scarred female, made the beast within him uneasy. He didn't care for the way her eyes locked onto Jun as if she were prey.

"How nice of you to show up," the female said as her gaze moved to Nuzal.

"And miraculously unharmed, Brega," Jun snapped.

Nuzal frowned at the animosity between the two of them. It was obvious he had missed something during his imprisonment.

The female waved her hand dismissively. "I never told you he was injured. I merely said he needed your healing. *You* made that assumption."

"You tried to *drown* me." Jun growled.

"And yet you live."

Numbness spread through Nuzal's limbs and face as his eyes darted to the female Jun had called Brega. She'd tried to drown his mate? The darkness within him begged to be released, wanted to destroy this Venium who had dared to harm her, but he pushed it down.

Don't let her bait you into acting like the monster they think you are, Nuzal.

He turned toward his mate, and his eyes went straight to the three small slits on the side of her neck, just below her ears. *Gills.* His mate had gills? They flared angrily just above the marks he'd left on her, and he wondered how he hadn't noticed them back in the cell.

"I told you before, we needed to know if what you claimed was the truth," Brega's voice was void of emotion, like she didn't care whether or not his mate could have died.

"You risked the lives of both my mate and our unborn offspring by forcing the awakening onto her body." He tried, but failed to silence his growl of frustration.

"Yes, I've been properly reprimanded, I assure you."

His mate huffed beside him. "I sincerely doubt that."

For the first time, Nuzal was actually thankful Vodk had been ignorant enough to start Jun's awakening. The male's selfish actions had saved his mate's life.

"Why don't we begin the questioning? I have no desire to be locked in this room with you all for longer than is needed," Calder grumbled as he took a seat.

The Venium male sitting in the middle of the table puffed up as if he took offense to what Calder said. "Very well. We want information on what the Grutex have done and what they plan to do with the humans they are taking from the planet Earth."

Nuzal started from the very beginning, telling the Venium exactly what he had told his mates in the records room on the ship, along with everything they had learned from Erusha and his journal. He told them of the testing and the experiments, both past and present, about the engineering of his species, of the injections

Erusha suspected were being given to their warriors, and finally, of how they had sterilized Brin and were planning to use what they'd learned about the Venium's hormones against them.

"These humans that were with you on the ship, they are all the victims of these experiments?" one of the older females asked.

"All of them. Their physical traits are a direct result of the awakening process they were subjected to. Some of them, those with psychic abilities, were already able to use them before the serum was injected, but they were limited."

"I guess some of those TV psychics might be real after all," Telisa muttered. "Just a little alien."

"The Grutex are searching for a way to produce the perfect warrior. The answer doesn't seem to have come from cloning, so the Kaia has turned to a more natural way."

"Why would they want to produce a perfect warrior?" one of the males asked.

Brega's laugh echoed through the room. "Why wouldn't they? Isn't that what we all want? *Perfection.*" Her eyes flitted over Brin for a second before she turned back to her peers. "They want power, domination, the ability to go wherever and do whatever they want without consequence. It's foolish to believe the Venium do not want that as well."

The members of the council shifted restlessly in their seats, as if being compared to the Grutex made them uncomfortably self-aware.

"What are the drawbacks of the cloning process?" Calder asked.

"Memory loss after time, but lately," he gestured to his lower eyes, "birth defects."

The male seated in the middle pounded his fist on the table as the others began to talk amongst themselves. "In light of the recent events and the testimony of the Grutex scientist, Nuzal, we have decided to lend our support to the humans in defense of their homeworld."

Telisa jumped up from the seat she'd taken next to Calder. "Thank you—"

The male held up his hand, cutting off her words. "There is a condition, Senator. Your leaders will allow us to seek out and test humans we believe to have Venium ancestry. These individuals will be asked to travel to Venora."

Telisa grimaced. "They'll be asked or *forced*?"

"We are not the Grutex, female. What they will do here will be discussed with your leadership. It will be your job to convince them to agree to our terms."

"I can request a meeting with The One World Council," she told them. "But I can assure you that they will wish to make their own requests."

"I have no doubt." The male rubbed his temples as his eyes slid toward Brega. "If that's all on the subject of humanity, I have other matters to attend to." Brega lifted her chin in a defiant gesture as the focus of the council shifted to her. "You, General, will be going on a special assignment. Your disobedience has shamed the council. This is nonnegotiable. Stand by for your orders."

Nuzal watched the female push away from the table, her back straight as a spear as she turned without another word and marched from the room. She'd attempted to murder his mate and their offspring, and she was going to get off with nothing more than a proverbial slap on the hand. He wanted to protest, to demand her head, but he looked down at his mate where she sat curled in Brin's lap and sighed. For now, he was just grateful to be with them again.

CHAPTER 38

BRIN

"The two of you are going to tell me exactly what I missed."

They'd just stepped into his room and Nuzal was already making demands. Brin closed the door and stopped as he watched them move into his space. He'd never let anyone aside from Oshen in here, and it occurred to him now just how devoid of life it was.

Unlike Jun's dwelling, Brin's lacked any personal items. There were no family trinkets on display, no heirlooms he wished to pass down to his pups, or photos of a happy family hanging on his walls. What did she think when she looked around at the emptiness of his life? Would she be happy here without her family and the life that had been taken from her?

"What is it you want to know?"

Jun ran her hands over the soft blanket Nyissa had gifted him on the first night in this room before plopping down onto the thick mattress with a sigh. That she felt so at ease here made him smile.

"Why don't we start with you telling me who that female was who attempted to drown our mate?"

"Her name is Brega, and unfortunately, she is the female who gave birth to me."

His hands began to shake and he scrubbed them over his face as he sighed heavily. When his legs became unsteady, Brin lowered himself to the mattress, feeling it dip beneath his weight. Nuzal waited patiently for him to continue. He smiled when he felt Jun shift closer and rest her hand on his thigh in silent support.

Like he'd done in the cells on board the Grutex ship when he told Jun the story, Brin began with his birth name and the tale of his brother's death. He told him about how the council had forced Brega and Tesol to produce another pup, about his solars of abuse by Tesol and Brega's neglect. He also shared with his bondmate the stories from his many solars of happiness with his adopted family, of how he and Jun had met on Earth and that he'd been terrified of telling her who she was to him.

Jun laughed at his retelling of their first meeting, rolling her eyes at his exaggerations and complaining that he made her sound crazy. He skipped forward to all that had happened while Nuzal was in custody. When he recounted the birth of Amanda's twins and what it had been like to hold Rydel and Zenah in his arms, he didn't miss the way Nuzal gazed at Jun. Soon enough, they would have a pup of their own to dote on.

"And how did all of this lead to the near drowning?"

Brin turned to Jun with a raised brow ridge. "I've wondered the same thing, honestly. One moment I'm watching you snuggle a pup against your chest, and the next I'm trying to understand Caly's frantic shouts about how she spotted you with Brega near the airlock tunnel."

Jun groaned as she pushed herself up in the bed and tucked her legs beneath her body. "I went outside to talk to the healer and

Brega ran up to me. She was frantic, grabbing me and telling me that you needed to be healed. I hadn't told the council about my ability then, and I thought if she knew that you must have been the one to tell her."

Nuzal shook his head. "She never even came to see me. What did you speak with the healer about? Was it about our offspring?"

"Offspring sounds so... clinical." Jun's laughter washed over her, and Brin turned to brush his hand over her leg. "The baby is fine. In fact, he or she is tumbling around like they haven't got a care in the world." She patted her growing belly. "I wanted to talk with the healer because I needed to make sure that the things I was feeling for the two of you were *my* feelings and not something the pheromones made me believe."

"You shouldn't have gone with her." Nuzal frowned. "Even if I had actually been injured, I wouldn't want you to jeopardize yourself for me."

"I really did think something bad had happened to you, Nuzal." The material of Jun's suit shimmered as she moved to her knees on the bed so that she could look at them both. "It didn't matter who the messenger was, all that mattered was that I thought you needed me and I wanted to be there because I love you—both of you. I can't imagine what I would do without either of you."

The tears that had been gathering in her eyes spilled over onto her cheeks. For the first time since meeting Jun on Earth outside of Amanda's dwelling, Brin felt like he was seeing her without all of the armor she normally wore. Their mate was laying herself bare, allowing them in, and he found this glimpse of vulnerability from someone who was otherwise so guarded to be beautiful. Brin brushed his fingers over her cheeks, collecting the tears and wiping them away.

"I spent my whole life terrified of meeting you, and then you barged into my life and I couldn't help but love you. I never stood a chance against you, Shayfia." Brin lowered his head, pressing his lips to her wet cheeks. "You're the breath in my lungs, the lifeblood in my veins. I'll get down on my knees every sol and thank the goddess that she put the two of you into my path," he whispered, looking up to see Nuzal moving across the room toward them.

Jun smiled up at his bondmate, her arms opening for him as he bent to pull her against his chest. Nuzal rattled softly as he slid onto the bed next to Brin, curling his tail around his hips and urging him closer. His gaze bounced between them for a moment before he released a pent-up breath.

"This was my last beginning. I've experienced so many things over the course of all my lives, but this is the only one I've truly *lived*." He reached out to cup Brin's jaw, bringing him closer as Jun's fingers trailed over his shoulder. "There was a time before the two of you came into my life that I would have shuddered at the idea of losing the chance at rebirth, but now I look forward to seeing what we do with the time we've been given together."

His bondmate dipped his head as if to kiss him, but Brin pulled back at the last moment to press his lips to Nuzal's shoulder instead. Jun tugged on his braid, and she gave him a teary smile as he leaned in closer. "What's wrong, Shayfia?"

"Mama and Papa would love the two of you," she whispered.

Nuzal smoothed a hand over her hair, letting the loose strands slide through his fingers. "What's your family like, little one?"

"They drive me insane most of the time and they have a horrible tendency to be overbearing and nosy." She laughed and shook her head, threading her fingers between Brin's. "But I love them and I wouldn't trade them for the world." She told them about her childhood, and how she'd grown up working in the fish market, about helping her dam and sire care for her siblings, and how they'd be so proud of the day she got her nursing degree.

"They've supported me my entire life, bent over backwards to give me the opportunities they never had. They don't even know what happened to me. They don't know about the kidnapping or that I found the two of you." She sniffled as she cupped her stomach. "They don't know that they're going to be grandparents, and I have no idea *when* I'll get to see them or *if* I'll ever be able to see them again."

The look of utter despair in her eyes made Brin's chest tighten. He wanted to demand that the council send someone to retrieve her family, that they gather everyone she loved and bring them to Venora so he'd never have to see that look on her face again for as long as he lived. They owed Jun that much, surely.

"I wish things were different, Shayfia. I wish we had the power to give you everything you wanted."

Nuzal's fingers tangled in her hair and he gently tugged on the strands, tipping her face up so that she was looking into his eyes. "One day at a time," he reminded her, repeating the phrase she had spoken to them on more than one occasion.

"I'm sorry that I wasted so much time being upset with both of you. I'm sorry that I questioned not only what *I* was feeling, but what the two of you were feeling as well."

His bondmate rattled quietly. "I'm sorry for how rough I was with you the day we mated. I shouldn't have treated you like—"

"Nuzal," Jun sat up in his lap and cupped his face in her hands, "you didn't do anything that day that I didn't want to do. Do you hear me? You did *nothing* wrong. I mean, I wouldn't have said no to a little more foreplay, but…" The playful twinkle in her eyes had his blood racing. "There's plenty of time to practice."

His little Shayfia slid her palms down Nuzal's chest, setting off an explosion of color along his exoskeleton as she pressed her hips down onto his, circling slowly.

The change in Nuzal was instant. Their normally calm, patient mate snarled, gripping her waist as he twisted to press her body into the mattress.

Brin watched the display with hungry eyes, loving the way Jun smiled up at his bondmate as he struggled to maintain his control. She was taunting the beast, egging on the monster within him. He knew Nuzal loved her, that he was capable of the soft caresses and sweet kisses she wanted, but when it came to mating their female, their Grutex was rough and demanding.

The softness was left to Brin, and no one would hear him complain about that. He enjoyed being the buffer between them, the one who could take the brunt of their male's claws and teeth and still touch their female in a way that made her burn up from the inside out. He got to watch Nuzal lose that control that he held onto so tightly.

"Fore-what?" Nuzal growled into her neck. "What is that?"

Brin slid his tail over the back of Nuzal's thigh and down his calf. "She's telling you that there's more to mating than shoving your cock into her."

"How do you play it?"

Jun giggled beneath Nuzal as she wrapped her arms around his neck, tugging his face close to hers. "Well, you can kiss..." Her lips brushed over his cheek, trailing down the side of his neck and over his shoulder.

"I kissed you," he grumbled.

"You can touch..." Her fingers danced over his chest.

Nuzal frowned. "I touched you."

Jun looked so small beneath his bondmate, shielded from the world by his body. Brin got to his feet, moving along the side of the bed until he reached her face; brushing the side of her cheek with his finger and drawing her attention as he commanded his suit to drop away. His cock slipped free of his sheath the moment the suit retreated, and he took it in his hand, groaning as she watched him stroke himself.

"You can lick..." She smiled up at Brin as he leaned closer, sticking her tongue out to run the tip over the head of his cock; teasing him. "Suit down," she whispered.

Nuzal's growl vibrated through his chest and limbs. As if he'd gotten the hint, the male began to move down her body, this long white tongue snaking out to run over the dips and peaks, stopping to focus on the ones that made her gasp and squirm. He slid off the end of the bed and grasped Jun's ankles, pulling her over the blanket until she was spread open in front of him. He cupped the cheeks of her ass, lifting her up just slightly before he buried his face in the juncture between her thighs.

Jun arched off of the bed, a stunned gasp escaping her mouth as Nuzal's ridged tongue delved between her folds. The sight of their little mate's pleasure had Brin squeezing the swollen base of his cock in an attempt to stave off his release. He cupped her breast in his hand, moving his thumb back and forth over the stiff peak before catching it between his fingers and tugging gently.

Jun's fingers slid up his inner thigh as he moved closer, and his cock jerked as if it were begging for her attention. Nuzal devoured her, lapping at her cunt and nipping at her thighs as if he'd never be able to get enough of her. The smell of her arousal perfumed the air, and Brin drew it into his lungs, letting it fill him up as he watched them.

Slender fingers wrapped themselves around his shaft, sliding up to the head before slipping all the way down to the swollen base. Brin gritted his teeth as he watched her play, her movements mimicking the way he'd touched himself moments ago.

His little Shayfia groaned, trying to grab Nuzal's head. "Higher. God, Nuzal, go higher."

It might look like their little mate was being dominated, but Brin knew that they were both under her control. She had only to ask and they would have done anything for her. She chose to gift them with her submission, to allow them to wield power over her pleasure. Their mate gave them access to her body, mind, and soul, and it wasn't something they were going to take for granted.

Jun whimpered beneath Nuzal's onslaught, squeezing Brin's shaft as she writhed on top of the blankets. Nuzal slid his tongue over her thigh before lifting her into his arms, making her squeal in surprise when he fell back onto the bed. With her palms resting flat on his chest, Nuzal slid Jun back until her thighs were pressed against the sides of his head, and he renewed his efforts.

His bondmate growled when Jun clutched at his suit, mumbling the command for it to retreat against her heated flesh. Brin climbed onto the bed with them, keeping his eyes trained on Jun's face as he glided his hand up and over Nuzal's thighs.

Jun watched him with ravenous eyes, groaning softly as Brin wrapped long fingers around the base of Nuzal's shaft. His bondmate stiffened for a moment before his hips began to move, rocking his cock into Brin's hand as Jun tilted her face up to meet Brin's lips. Her moans of pleasure were swallowed as he fisted Nuzal's length, tightening his grip and twisting the palm over the wide head.

"Fuck, yes," she whimpered, trailing a wet path with her tongue over his lower lip before catching it between her teeth for a moment. She thrust her hips back, impaling herself on Nuzal's tongue and gasped.

He delved into her mouth, curling his tongue around hers, dancing back and forth within the warmth of her mouth. Nuzal's hips jerked again and again, and when Jun screamed her pleasure against his lips, Brin lost all sense of control.

With a rumbling growl, he pulled her away from Nuzal's face, laying her on the mattress beneath him as he gathered the pillows from the head of the bed. He piled them beneath her hips, raising her just enough that he could run the head of his cock through her wet folds. The sight of his length disappearing inside her body sent a thrill through him, and his breath stuttered out as he worked himself slowly into her.

Using two of his fingers, Brin carefully held her open as he pulled back and drove forward, doing his best to keep his pace slow and steady. The warmth of Nuzal's hands on his hips sent his heart racing, and he glanced over his shoulder to grin at his bondmate.

"You want to mark me?" Brin asked, moaning as Nuzal's claws flexed against his skin. "I won't break. Let me take it. Let me take the darkness."

One big hand pressed into the middle of his back, pushing him down firmly until he was bowed over Jun. The hand at his hip curled, claw-tipped fingers digging into his flesh, as the ones on his back grazed over the old scars; marking him, claiming him. Brin didn't belong to the memory of his past any longer. Something hot and slick pressed against his ass, and he swallowed thickly in anticipation of what he hoped was to come. Slender fingers clutched at his sides and Jun panted beneath them as Brin wrapped his tail under Nuzal's cock, urging him forward, guiding him to Jun's slick entrance.

As their mate finally pushed the vibrating stem inside of his body, Brin shuddered, humming with pleasure. The wide head of Nuzal's cock slid against him, spreading Jun's cunt as he pressed in beside him. Brin's tail slid around the length of him that didn't fit inside of Jun, and they moved together, finding their rhythm as they took pleasure from one another.

A feeling of completeness—of belonging—overtook Brin as their cries filled the air around him and he squeezed his eyes shut, allowing himself to merely be in this moment with the two beings he loved most in this world, in the universe.

He would relive every horrible day, every disappointment, every failure, and go through all of the pain over and over again if it meant he got to keep his mates in the end. But as Nuzal roared behind him, slamming his hips against Brin's ass as his seed pulsed into Jun, coating them both, Brin knew they would never let him go through that ever again.

When Jun cried out beneath him, Nuzal slipped free of her, running his length between their bodies and spreading his seed over the outside of her cunt. He grasped Brin's long braid, dragging him back so that he could sink his teeth into the flesh of Brin's shoulder just as the swollen glands locked him inside their mate, and he came with a thundering shout.

They would never be kept apart again.

EPILOGUE

JUN

A COUPLE WEEKS LATER...

"This isn't going to hurt me," Jun said as she tried again to slip past Nuzal to get to the treatment table. "It's just like the scanner you use, except we'll be able to see the baby."

Their Grutex mate frowned down at her, completely unconvinced. It had taken her and Brin weeks to get him to agree to let Brom perform this ultrasound. If it were up to Nuzal, he'd continue to check the baby's vitals using the scanner on the troop transport ship for the entirety of her pregnancy, but Jun hadn't had the strength to go back there since the other humans had renamed it during the memorial they held, carving Layla and Clara's names into the side in their memory.

Being inside of the ship, walking the halls and standing in the rooms where the women had been made her uncomfortable and sad. Even though they'd only known one another a short amount of time, Jun had cared for them. Now that she'd spent some time inside the dome, she didn't like going back and being reminded of their captivity.

She was ready to move on and put all of those things behind her.

"We can trust Brom, remember? He took care of Amanda for most of her pregnancy." Jun faked right, but her mate caught her around the waist.

"He's Venium."

"So am I, and so is most everyone else on this planet." Brin laughed. "That's enough protesting from you. Let Brom run his scan. The longer you stall this, the longer it will be before we get to see our pup and make sure everything is all right."

She knew he wasn't used to handing over control, not to anyone outside of their triad at least, but Jun also knew that he worried for her and the baby. He feared that what happened to Erusha and his mate might happen to them and the thought that he could lose her or their baby, or both of them, kept him up many nights.

The scan had been Brin's suggestion, an easy way to alleviate some of the fear and to check that the baby was an appropriate size. They'd all heard the story of what Zar's mother had gone through, about her horrible death, and it certainly hadn't done anything to calm Nuzal's anxiety.

"This is what you want, little one?" He asked her as he tipped her chin up.

"Yes." Jun leaned forward to press her lips against his suit-covered abdomen. "Now come on."

Nuzal sighed, turning to the side so Jun could slip past him and into Brin's waiting arms. She grinned as he lifted her up, setting her down on the treatment table on the far side of the room. Amanda, Oshen, and Zar stood on the other side of the transparent wall, and all around them, Oshen's parents and siblings were gathered. The younger pups had their faces pressed against the glass as they tried to see what was going on inside, making Jun smile as their breath fogged the areas around their lips.

Even Caly, who Jun had discovered she liked a lot, had shown up to support them. She smiled as she wrapped an arm around Fyn and gave Jun a thumbs up, something she'd learned from Amanda and was very proud of knowing.

Jun wished Telisa could be there for this, but she'd left days before to begin her duties as unofficial ambassador of Earth. If there was anyone who could make sure the human governments at least considered the Venium's terms, it would be Telisa.

Brom eyed Nuzal wearily as he approached the table. Jun tilted her head back and rolled her eyes at the way Nuzal watched the poor healer pick up the slim wand. She'd never thought of herself as someone who enjoyed a dominating man, but it turned out she really loved having two bossy alien males.

Brom tapped something on the wand and waved it over her big belly. She'd grown rapidly in the last couple weeks, and the speed of the progression had shocked her. A holographic projection appeared in the air above her, and she stared in wonder at their baby. He or she was curled up into a ball, their tail held tight in tiny hands as it suckled the tip. Jun choked back tears, pressing her hand to her mouth as she watched the xines float around the baby's head.

"Do you think you can tell if we're having a boy or a girl?" Jun wondered aloud.

Brom spun the projection, taking his measurements before turning their baby's face toward them. "Your pup is female. Congratulations."

Nuzal's hand rose, tracing their daughter's face in the air with trembling fingers as she began to wriggle inside of Jun. She looked up to see the awe in his expression. Brin leaned over the back of the table to press his lips to her head as his hand moved to cup the side of her stomach.

"She's perfect, Shayfia," he whispered into her ear.

The soft click of the door barely registered in her mind as she watched and felt her little girl stretch, her mouth opening on a yawn as her smooth tail curled around her leg. Was this the way it always felt for new moms? Did the wonder of it ever go away? Seeing the image made that protectiveness she felt even stronger, and she knew that this little girl's life would always come before anything else.

"Lang-Lang," someone behind her whispered. The voice was familiar, one that Jun would know anywhere in the universe, and one that she had missed more than she could ever put into words. That the voice had said her childhood nickname, a shortened version of beloved.

"Papa!" she gasped, nearly launching herself from the table in an attempt to get into his arms as tears streamed down her face. The feel of them closing around her, the smell of his cologne on his clothing, the way he murmured how much he'd missed her, it broke open the dam that was holding back the worst of her tears. And when mama wrapped her arms around both of them, she came completely undone.

Mama pushed at Papa's shoulder. "Enough, Junior. Give me a turn to hug her."

"How are you even here?" Jun asked in disbelief as she let her parents fuss over her, their hands moving over her belly as Mama started to cry.

"We asked Calder if it was a possibility and he pulled some strings," Brin told her, watching with a smile.

"You thought we would leave you here all alone?" Mama tsked. "We're all here for you now."

All? Jun looked up to see her siblings standing with Amanda, and she smiled when they ran into the room, wrapping her arms around them as her brother excitedly told her about the flight here and the aliens. He told her about how Mama had argued with the one in charge over how much rice she was allowed to bring, and how all of the gifts for the baby were *necessary*.

Apparently there had also been a fight over leaving the goats behind. Mama had tried to explain that they were a gift from Amanda, that they couldn't leave them, but the one in charge had drawn a line at livestock, and eventually Mama had relented, giving them to their neighbor for safe keeping.

"Did Lola not come?" Jun asked, noting her absence.

"She did." Mama rolled her eyes. "She's mad that the aliens wouldn't let her bring her TV with us so she stayed on the ship to boss them around. Here!" She grabbed a long tube from Papa and handed it to her. "I picked the best banana leaf I could find before we left."

The leaf was rolled inside the tube, and Jun smiled at the thoughtful gesture. In her province it was tradition for a woman to lie on a rolled banana leaf after giving birth to help her recover faster. Just being able to have this small piece of her culture on Venora meant so much to her.

"Come here!" Mama whispered excitedly as she wrapped her arms around Nuzal's waist. His eyes were so wide, Jun thought they might pop out of his. He patted her back awkwardly, turning to Brin for support, but their mate was busy taking count and obviously realizing that her family wasn't going to fit into their room back at Oshen's home.

Brin lifted his arm and spoke to his AI, "Nyissa, start a request for an additional dwelling."

Oshen's head swiveled around at the sound of his mother's name and the look in his eyes told Jun that Brin better be ready to run.

"Sending a request for an additional dwelling, Master." Her

mate's eyes sparkled with humor as he tried to duck behind Nuzal for protection.

"Brin!" Oshen was through the door and launching himself at him before anyone even knew what was happening. "You braxing son of a—" His words were cut off as they slammed into one another, and the sound of Brin's laughter filled the room.

She had once wished to settle down on Earth with a nice very *human* man, but looking around at the chaos of the room and the faces of her very alien mates, Jun was thankful for unfulfilled wishes.

AUTHOR NOTE

Thank you for reading our book! This is the fourth novel we've written, but the sixth work we've published as both *Ecstasy from the Deep* and *Breaths of Desire* were in Anthologies as short stories. It took us years to publish due to our own insecurities and busy schedules, but we've been writing stories since we were kids.

What made us decide to publish in 2020? Encouragement from a few friends and finding out that, even though we're cousins who live so far apart, we work well together. Being stay at home moms to lots of rambunctious children doesn't make it easy, but it's worth the effort to know our character's stories are being told.

We hope you enjoyed this story and would love it if you left a review. They help our books get seen, and in a world with many other amazing authors, every last one counts. We love to read over and hear what you think! Each and every review means the world to us. We're constantly learning and growing and appreciate all of the advice and tips.

Writing this story was tough at times and took a lot of work. We needed to show you the characters that were living rent-free in our heads. We hope you enjoyed the story of Jun, a strong independent woman who is used to doing everything herself until her mates come along. She has a hard time opening up because she has been exposed to many hardships that come with immigrating to the US.

Although Brin seems the happy prankster, he wore a mask that his childhood trauma hid behind. Understand that sometimes the happiest people are those who have been through the most unimaginable things. We know that him being sterilized may have been hard to accept, but this gives Brin the freedom to love their child without the despair of knowing his mother has another thing to hold over him. To him, it takes away that fear that he will be his parents and continue the cycle.

Nuzal falls for the very subjects he was meant to ruin. It was fun to write a male who had never known affection, someone who didn't know what it was like to have someone care about him or how to care about others. We enjoyed watching as he loses control to his baser instincts and accepts that his mates want him to dominate. To finally see him be able to love himself the way his mates freely do was touching.

As always, you may notice some unanswered threads or hints at future novels. We like to consider these easter eggs for what is to come. We hope you're able to give Esme the benefit of the doubt. Our girl is a fear biter. One of those dogs who have been abused and bite when they are scared. We can't wait to delve into her story and show you why she acted the way she did.

If you haven't had the chance, check out book one, *Ecstasy from the Deep*, on Audible produced by Podium Audio.

OTHER WORKS BY OCTAVIA KORE:

Venora Mates:

Ecstasy from the Deep (Short Story)

Ecstasy from the Deep (Extended Edition)

Dauur Mates:

Queen Of Twilight

Seyton Mates:

Breaths of Desire (Short Story)

Breaths of Desire (Extended Edition)

WORKS COMING SOON BY OCTAVIA KORE

Venora Mates:

Awoken from the Deep

Enticed from the Deep

Kidnapped from the Deep

KEEP IN TOUCH

FACEBOOK:

https://www.facebook.com/groups/MatesAmongUs/

SIGN UP FOR OUR NEWSLETTER:

https://mailchi.mp/27d09665e243/matesamongusnewsletter

INSTAGRAM:

https://www.instagram.com/octaviakore/?igshid=1bxhtr1snonz4

GOODREADS:

https://www.goodreads.com/octaviakore

BOOKBUB:

https://www.bookbub.com/profile/octavia-kore

AMAZON:

https://www.amazon.com/Octavia-Kore/e/B0845YHRVS

ABOUT THE AUTHORS

Born in the Sunshine State, Hayley Benitez and Amanda Crawford are cousins who have come together to write under the name Octavia Kore. Both women share a love for reading, a passion for writing, and the inclination toward word vomiting when meeting new people. *Ecstasy from the Deep* (*From the Depths* anthology version) was their very first published work. Hayley and Amanda are both stay-at-home moms who squeeze in time to write when they aren't being used as jungle gyms or snack dispensers. They are both inspired by their love for mythology, science fiction, and all things extraordinary. Amanda has an unhealthy obsession with house plants, and Hayley can often be found gaming in her downtime.

Printed in Great Britain
by Amazon